Praise f
bestselling

"You can't bottle v ... rts certainly knows how to put it on the page."
—*New York Times*

"Roberts' bestselling novels are some of the best in the romance genre. They are thoughtfully plotted, well-written stories featuring fascinating characters."
—*USA TODAY*

"[Nora] Roberts…is at the top of her game."
—*People* magazine

"Roberts weaves a story like no one else, and if possible, she just gets better."
—*Rocky Mountain News*

"The publishing world might be hard-pressed to find an author with a more diverse style or fertile imagination than Roberts."
—*Publishers Weekly*

"Roberts is indeed a word artist, painting her story and her characters with vitality and verve."
—*Los Angeles Daily News*

"Roberts' style has a fresh, contemporary snap."
—*Kirkus Reviews*

"Roberts has a warm feel for her characters and an eye for the evocative detail."
—*Chicago Tribune*

"Her stories have fueled the dreams of twenty-five million readers."
—*Entertainment Weekly*

Dear Reader,

Many of you may know that Nora Roberts first started writing for Silhouette Books back in the early 1980s. But did you also know that she's written books for every line Silhouette publishes? After beginning her career writing Silhouette Romance novels, she went on to write for Silhouette Special Edition, including her popular MacGregor, O'Hurley and Stanislaski family series, and one book for Silhouette Desire that was part of THE CALHOUN WOMEN. Nora also wrote for Silhouette Intimate Moments, including the two classic books we offer you in this volume: *Rules of the Game* and *The Name of the Game.*

First published in 1984, *Rules of the Game* tells the dynamic story of Brooke Gordon—beautiful, successful and totally focused on her career—a woman who has never fallen in love. That is until she meets the sinfully handsome, irritatingly self-confident Parks Jones. Then in the 1988 book *The Name of the Game,* it's instant attraction when Sam Weaver meets Johanna Patterson. But she doesn't give her trust—or her heart—easily, and Sam is a certified charmer. Can he win this game called love?

Fun Nora Fact: More than 250 million copies of Nora Roberts's books are in print. That's enough books to fill Giants Stadium more than three thousand times!

Enjoy!

The Editors
Silhouette Books

NORA ROBERTS

WINNER *takes* ALL

Silhouette® Books

Published by Silhouette Books

America's Publisher of Contemporary Romance

SILHOUETTE BOOKS

WINNER TAKES ALL

ISBN 0-373-21892-3

This edition published by arrangement with Harlequin Books S.A.

Visit Silhouette Books at www.eHarlequin.com

Printed in U.S.A.

CONTENTS

Also available from Silhouette and Harlequin Books by

NORA ROBERTS

CAPTIVATED
Book One in *The Donovan Legacy* series

WITH OPEN ARMS
Containing SONG OF THE WEST and
HER MOTHER'S KEEPER

ENTRANCED
Book Two in *The Donovan Legacy* series

THE MACKADE BROTHERS:
DEVIN AND SHANE
Containing THE HEART OF DEVIN MACKADE
and THE FALL OF SHANE MACKADE

BORN O'HURLEY
Containing THE LAST HONEST WOMAN
and DANCE TO THE PIPER

CHARMED AND ENCHANTED
Books Three and Four in *The Donovan Legacy* series

And coming soon, watch for

THE GIFT
Containing "Home for Christmas" and
"All I Want For Christmas"

and

REUNION
Containing ONCE MORE WITH FEELING
and TREASURES LOST, TREASURES FOUND

RULES OF THE GAME

Chapter 1

"A jock. Terrific." Brooke took a long swallow of strong black coffee, tipped back in her glove-soft leather chair and scowled. "I love it."

"No need to be sarcastic," Claire returned mildly. "If de Marco wants to use an athlete for promotion, why should you object?" She gazed absently at the chunky gold ring on her right hand. "After all," Claire continued in her dry voice, "you'll be making quite a bit directing the commercials."

Brooke sent Claire a characteristic look. Direct, uncompromising gray eyes bored into the soft blue of the older woman's. One of Brooke's greatest talents, and her greatest weapons, was her ability to stare down anyone from a corporate president to a temperamental actor. She'd developed the knack early as a defense against her own insecurity and had since refined it to an art. It was an art, however, that didn't impress Claire Thorton. At forty-nine, she was the head of a multimillion-dollar company that she'd started with brains and guts. For nearly a quarter of a century, she had run things her way, and she intended to keep right on doing so.

She'd known Brooke for ten years—since Brooke had been an eighteen-year-old upstart who had wheedled her way into a job with Thorton Productions. Then she'd watched Brooke work her way up from gofer to gaffer, from gaffer to assistant cameraman and from there to director. Claire had never regretted the impulse that had led her to give Brooke her first fifteen-second commercial.

Intuition had been the basis for Claire's success with Thorton Productions, and intuitively she had sensed sharp talent in Brooke Gordon. In addition, Claire knew her, understood her, as few others did. Perhaps it was because they shared two basic traits—ambition and independence.

After a moment, Brooke gave up with a sigh. "A jock," she muttered again as she gazed around her office.

It was one small room, the pale-amber walls lined with prints of stills from dozens of her commercials. There was a two-cushion sofa—reupholstered in chocolate-colored corduroy—not comfortable enough to encourage long visits. The chair with a tufted back had been picked up at a yard sale along with a coffee table that leaned slightly to the left.

Brooke sat behind an old, scarred desk that had a

drawer that wouldn't quite close. On it were piles of papers, a gooseneck lamp and assorted disposable pens and broken pencils. The pens and pencils were jammed in a Sevres vase. Behind her at the window, a dieffenbachia was slowly dying in an exquisitely worked pottery bowl.

''Damn, Claire, why can't they get an actor?'' Brooke tossed up her hands in her one theatrical gesture, then dropped her chin on them. ''Do you know what it's like to try to coax ball players and rock stars to say a line without freezing or hamming it up?'' With a disgusted mutter that gave no room for comment, she pushed the pile of papers into a semiordered heap. ''One call to a casting agent and I could have a hundred qualified actors parading through here itching for the job.''

Patiently, Claire brushed a speck of lint from the sleeve of her rose linen suit. ''You know it increases sales if a production's hyped by a recognizable name or familiar face.''

''Recognizable name?'' Brooke tossed back. ''Who's ever heard of Parks Jones? *Stupid* name,'' she muttered to herself.

''Every baseball fan in the country.'' The mild smile told Brooke it was useless to argue. Therefore, she prepared to argue further.

''We're selling clothes, not Louisville Sluggers.''

''Eight Golden Gloves,'' Claire went on. ''A lifetime batting average of three twenty-five. He's leading the league in RBIs this season. Jones has been at third base in the All-Star game for eight consecutive seasons.''

Brooke narrowed her eyes. ''How do you know so much? You don't follow baseball.''

''I do my homework.'' A cool smile touched Claire's round, pampered face. She'd never had a face-lift but was religious about her visits to Elizabeth Arden. ''That's why I'm a successful producer. Now you'd better do yours.'' She rose languidly. ''Don't make any plans, I've got tickets for the game tonight. Kings against the Valiants.''

''Who?''

''Do your homework,'' Claire advised before she closed the office door behind her.

With an exasperated oath, Brooke swiveled her chair around so that she faced her view of Los Angeles—tall buildings, glittering glass and clogged traffic. She'd had other views of L.A. during the rise in her career, but they'd been closer to street level. Now, she looked out on the city from the twentieth floor. The distance meant success, but Brooke didn't dwell on it. To do that would have encouraged thinking of the past—something Brooke meticulously avoided.

Leaning back in the oversized chair, Brooke toyed with the end of her braid. Her hair was the warm soft red shot with gold that painters attempted to immortalize. It was long and thick and unruly. Brooke was feminine enough not to want it cut to a more manageable length and practical enough to subdue it into a fat braid during working hours. It hung down the back of a thin silk blouse past the waistband of overworked blue jeans.

Her eyes as she mulled over Claire's words were thoughtful. They had misty gray irises, long lids and were surrounded by lashes in the same fragile shade as her hair. She rarely thought to darken them. Her skin was the delicate ivory-rose her hair demanded but the frailty stopped there. Her nose was small and sharp, her mouth wide, her chin aggressive. It was an unsettling face—beautiful one moment, austere the next, but always demanding. She wore a hasty dab of rose lipstick, enameled dimestore earrings and a splash of two-hundred dollar-an-ounce perfume.

She thought about the de Marco account—designer jeans, exclusive sportswear and soft Italian leather. Since they'd decided to move their advertising beyond the glossy pages of fashion magazines and into television, they had come to Thorton Productions, and so to her. It was a fat two-year contract with a budget that would give Brooke all the artistic room she could want. She told herself she deserved it. There were three Clios on the corner shelf to her right.

Not bad, she mused, for a twenty-eight-year-old woman who had walked into Thorton Productions with a high school diploma, a glib tongue and sweaty palms. And twelve dollars and fifty-three cents in her pocket, Brooke remembered; then she pushed the thought aside. If she wanted the de Marco account—and she did—she would simply have to make the ball player work. Grimly, she swung her chair back to face her desk. Picking up the phone, Brooke punched two buttons.

"Get me everything we have on Parks Jones," she ordered as she shuffled papers out of her way. "And ask Ms. Thorton what time I'm to pick her up tonight."

Less than six blocks away, Parks Jones stuck his hands in his pockets and scowled at his agent. "How did I ever let you talk me into this?"

Lee Dutton gave a smile that revealed slightly crooked teeth and a lot of charm. "You trust me."

"My first mistake." Parks studied Lee, a not quite homely, avuncular figure with a receding hairline, puckish face and unnerving black eyes. Yes, he trusted him, Parks thought, he even liked the shrewd little devil, but… "I'm not a damn model, Lee. I'm a third baseman."

"You're not modeling," Lee countered. As he folded his hands, the sun glinted on the band of his thin Swiss watch. "You're endorsing. Ball players have been doing it since the first razor blade."

Parks snorted then walked around the tidy, Oriental-designed office. "This isn't a shaving commercial, and I'm not endorsing a mitt. It's clothes, for God's sake. I'm going to feel like an idiot."

But you won't look like one, Lee thought as he drew out a fragrant, slim cigar. Lighting it, he studied Parks over the flame. The long, lanky body was perfect for de Marco's—as was the blond, unmistakably California look. Parks's tanned lean face, navy-blue eyes and tousled curling hair had already made him a favorite with the female fans, while his friendly, laid-back charm had won over the men. He was talented, easy to look at and personable. In short, Lee concluded, he was a natural. The fact that he was intelligent was at times as much a disadvantage as an advantage.

"Parks, you're hot." Lee said it with a sigh that they both knew was calculated. "You're also thirty-three. How much longer are you going to play ball?"

Parks answered with a glare. Lee knew of his vow to retire at thirty-five. "What does that have to do with it?"

"There are a lot of ball players, exceptional ball players, who slip into oblivion when they walk off the diamond for the last time. You have to think of the future."

"I *have* thought of the future," Parks reminded him. "Maui—fishing, sleeping in the sun, ogling women."

That would last about six weeks, Lee calculated, but he wisely kept silent.

"Lee." Parks flopped into a Chinese-red chair and stretched out his legs. "I don't need the money. So why am I going to be working this winter instead of lying on the beach?"

"Because it's going to be good for you," Lee began. "It's good for the game. The campaign will enhance the image of baseball. And," he added with one of his puckish smiles, "because you signed a contract."

"I'm going to get in some extra batting practice," Parks muttered as he rose. When he reached the door, he turned back with a suspiciously friendly smile. "One thing. If I make a fool of myself, I'm going to break the legs on your Tang horse."

Brooke screeched through the electronically controlled gates then swerved up the rhododendron-lined drive that led to Claire's mansion. Privately, Brooke considered it a beautiful anachronism. It was huge, white, multileveled and pillared. Brooke liked to imagine two black-helmeted guards, rifles on shoulders, flanking the carved double doors. The estate had originally belonged to a silent movie idol who had supposedly decked out the rooms in pastel silks and satins. Fifteen years before, Claire had purchased it from a perfume baron and had proceeded to redecorate it with her own passion for Oriental art.

Brooke stomped on the brake of her Datsun, screaming to a halt in front of the white marble steps. She drove at two speeds: stop and go. Stepping out of the car, she breathed in the exotic garden scents of vanilla and jasmine before striding up the stairs in the loose-limbed gait that came from a combination of long legs and preoccupation. In a crowd, her walk would cause men's heads to turn but Brooke neither noticed nor cared.

She knocked briskly on the door, then impatiently turned the handle. Finding it unlocked, she walked into the spacious mint-green hall and shouted.

"Claire! Are you ready? I'm starving." A neat little

woman in a tailored gray uniform came through a doorway to the left. ''Hello, Billings.'' Brooke smiled at her and tossed her braid over her shoulder. ''Where's Claire? I haven't the energy to search through this labyrinth for her.''

''She's dressing, Ms. Gordon.'' The housekeeper spoke in modulated British tones, responding to Brooke's smile with a nod. ''She'll be down shortly. Would you care for a drink?''

''Just some Perrier, it's muggy out.'' Brooke followed the housekeeper into the drawing room then slumped down on a divan. ''Did she tell you where we're going?''

''To a baseball game, miss?'' Billing set ice in a glass and added sparkling water. ''Some lime?''

''Just a squirt. Come on, Billings.'' Brooke's smoky contralto became conspiratorial. ''What do you think?''

Billings meticulously squeezed lime into the bubbly water. She'd been housekeeper for Lord and Lady Westbrook in Devon before being prized away by Claire Thorton. On accepting the position, she had vowed never to become Americanized. Edna Billings had her standards. But she'd never quite been able to resist responding to Brooke. A naughty young girl, she'd thought a decade before, and the opinion remained unchanged. Perhaps that was why Billings was so fond of her.

''I much prefer cricket,'' she said blandly. ''A more civilized game.'' She handed Brooke the glass.

''Can you see Claire sitting in the bleachers?''

Brooke demanded. "Surrounded by screaming, sweaty fans, watching a bunch of grown men swing at a little ball and run around in circles?"

"If I'm not mistaken," Billings said slowly, "there's a bit more to it than that."

"Sure, RBIs and ERAs and putouts and shutouts." Brooke heaved a long breath. "What the hell is a squeeze play?"

"I'm sure I have no idea."

"Doesn't matter." Brooke shrugged and gulped down some Perrier. "Claire has it in her head that watching this guy in action will give me some inspiration." She ran a fingertip down a shocking-orange ginger jar. "What I really need is a meal."

"You can get a hot dog and some beer in the park," Claire announced from the doorway.

Glancing up, Brooke gave a hoot of laughter. Claire was immaculately dressed in buff-colored linen slacks and tailored print blouse with low alligator pumps. "You're going to a ball game," Brooke reminded her, "not a museum. And I hate beer."

"A pity." Opening her alligator bag, Claire checked the contents before snapping it shut again. "Let's be on our way, then, we don't want to miss anything. Good night, Billings."

Gulping down the rest of her drink, Brooke bolted to her feet and raced after Claire. "Let's stop to eat on the way," she suggested. "It's not like missing the first act of the opera, and I had to skip lunch." She tried her forlorn orphan's look. "You know how cranky I get if I miss a meal."

"We're going to have to start putting you in front of the camera, Brooke; you're getting better all the time." With a slight frown at the low-slung Datsun, Claire maneuvered herself inside. She also knew Brooke's obsession with regular meals sprang from her lean adolescence. "Two hot dogs," she suggested, wisely buckling her seat belt. "It takes forty-five minutes to get to the stadium." Claire fluffed her silver-frosted brunette hair. "That means you should get us there in about twenty-five."

Brooke swore and rammed the car into first. In just over thirty minutes, she was hunting for a parking space outside of Kings Stadium. "...and the kid got it perfect on the first take," Brooke continued blithely, swerving around cars with a bullfighter's determination. "The two adult actors messed up, and the table collapsed so that it took fourteen takes, but the kid had it cold every time." She gave a loud war whoop as she spotted an empty space, swung into it, barely nosing out another car, then stopped with a jaw-snapping jerk. "I want you to take a look at the film before it's edited."

"What have you got in mind?" With some difficulty, Claire climbed out of the door, squeezing herself between the Datsun and the car parked inches beside it.

"You're casting for that TV movie, *Family in Decline.*" Brooke slammed her door then leaned over the hood. "I don't think you're going to want to look any further for the part of Buddy. The kid's good, really, really good."

"I'll take a look."

Together, they followed the crowd swarming toward the stadium. There was a scent of heated asphalt, heavy air and damp humanity—Los Angeles in August. Above them the sky was darkening so that the stadium lights sent up a white misty glow. Inside, they walked past the stands that hawked pennants and pictures and programs. Brooke could smell popcorn and grilled meat, the tang of beer. Her stomach responded accordingly.

"Do you know where you're going?" she demanded.

"I always know where I'm going," Claire replied, turning into an aisle that sloped downward.

They emerged to find the stadium bright as daylight and crammed with bodies. There was the continual buzz of thousands of voices over piped-in, soft-rock music. Walking vendors carried trays of food and drink strapped over their shoulders. Excitement. Brooke could feel the electricity of it coming in waves. Instantly, her own apathy vanished to be replaced by an avid curiosity. People were her obsession, and here they were, thousands of them, packed together in a circle around a field of green grass and brown dirt.

Something other than hunger began to stir in her.

"Look at them all, Claire," she murmured. "Is it always like this? I wonder."

"The Kings are having a winning season. They're leading their division by three games, have two potential twenty-game-winning pitchers and a third baseman who's batting three seventy-eight for the year." She sent Brooke a lifted-brow look. "I told you to do your homework."

"Mm-hmm." But Brooke was too caught up in the people. Who were they? Where did they come from? Where did they go after the game was over?

There were two old men, perched on chairs, their hands between their knees as they argued over the game that hadn't yet started. Oh, for a cameraman, Brooke thought, spotting a five-year-old in a Kings fielder's cap gazing up at the two gnarled fans. She followed Claire down the steps slowly, letting her eyes record everything. She liked the size of it, the noise, the smell of damp, crowded bodies, the color. Navy-blue-and-white Kings pennants were waved; children crammed pink cotton candy into their mouths. A teenager was making a play for a cute little blonde in front of him who pretended she wasn't interested.

Abruptly Brooke stopped, dropping her hand on Claire's shoulder. "Isn't that Brighton Boyd?"

Claire glanced to the left to see the Oscar-winning actor munching peanuts from a white paper bag. "Yes. Let's see now, this is our box." She scooted in, then lifted a friendly hand to the actor before she sat. "This should do very well," Claire observed with a satisfied nod. "We're quite close to third base here."

Still looking at everything at once, Brooke dropped into her chair. The Colosseum in Rome, she thought, must have had the same feel before the gladiators trooped out. If she were to do a commercial on baseball, it wouldn't be of the game, but of the crowd. A pan, with the sound low—then gradually increase it as the camera closed in. Then, *bamm!* Full volume, full effect. Clichéd or not, it was quintessentially American.

''Here you go, dear.'' Claire disrupted her thoughts by handing her a hot dog. ''My treat.''

''Thanks.'' After taking a healthy bite, Brooke continued with her mouth full. ''Who does the advertising for the team, Claire?''

''Just concentrate on third base,'' Claire advised as she sipped at a beer.

''Yes, but—'' The crowd roared as the home team took the field. Brooke watched the men move to their positions, dressed in dazzling white with navy-blue caps and baseball socks. They didn't look foolish, she mused as the fans continued to cheer. They looked rather heroic. She focused on the man on third.

Parks's back was to her as he kicked up a bit of dust around the base. But Brooke didn't strain to see his face. At the moment, she didn't need it—his build was enough. Six one, she estimated, a bit surprised by his height. No more than a hundred and sixty pounds—but not thin. She leaned her elbows on the rail, resting her chin on her hands.

He's lanky, she thought. He'll show off clothes well. Parks dipped for a grounder then returned it to short. For an instant, Brooke's thoughts scattered. Something intruded on her professional survey that she quickly brushed aside. The way he moved, she thought. Catlike? No. She shook her head. No, he was all man.

She waited, unconsciously holding her breath as he fielded another grounder. He moved loosely, apparently effortlessly, but she sensed a tight control as he stepped, bent, pivoted. It was a fluid action—feet, legs, hips, arm. A dancer had the same sort of nonchalant perfection after practicing a basic routine for years. If she could keep him moving, Brooke mused, it wouldn't matter if the man couldn't say his own name on camera.

There was an unexpected sexuality in every gesture. It was there even when he stood, idly wanting to field another practice ball. It might just work after all, Brooke reflected as her eyes roamed up his body, brushing over the blond curls that sprang around the sides and back of his cap. It might just…

Then he turned. Brooke found herself staring full into his face. It was long and lean like his body, a bit reminiscent of the gladiators she'd been thinking about earlier. Because he was concentrating, his full, passionate mouth was unsmiling; the eyes, almost the same shade as the navy hat that shaded them, were brooding. He looked fierce, almost warlike, definitely dangerous. Whatever Brooke had been expecting, it hadn't been this tough, uncompromisingly sexy face or her own reaction to it.

Someone called out to him from the stands. Abruptly, he grinned, transforming into a friendly, approachable man with an aura of easy charm. Brooke's muscles relaxed.

"What do you think of him?"

A bit dazed, Brooke leaned back in her chair and absently munched on her hot dog. "He might work," she murmured. "He moves well."

"From what I've been told," Claire said dryly, "you haven't seen anything yet."

As usual, Claire was right. In the first inning, Parks made a diving catch along the base line at third for the final out. He batted fourth, lining a long single to left field that he stretched into a double. He played, Brooke thought, with the enthusiasm of a kid and the diabolical determination of a veteran. She didn't have to know anything about the game to know the combination was unstoppable.

In motion, he was a pleasure to watch. Relaxed now, the first staggering impression behind her, Brooke began to consider the angles. If his voice was as good as the rest of him, she mused. Well...that was yet to be seen. After polishing off another hot dog, she resumed her position leaning against the rail. The Kings were ahead 2-1 in the fifth inning. The crowd was frantic. Brooke decided she would use some action shots of Parks in slow motion.

It was hot and still on the diamond. A fitful breeze fluttered the flag and cooled the spectators high up in the stands, but below, under the lights, the air was thick. Parks felt the sweat run down his back as he stood on the infield grass. Hernandez, the pitcher, was falling behind on the batter. Parks knew Rathers to be a power hitter who pulled to the left. He planted himself behind the bag and waited. He saw the pitch—a waist-high fast ball—heard the crack of the bat. In that one millisecond, he had two choices: catch the ball that was lined hard at him or end up with a hole in his chest. He caught it, and felt the vibration of power sing through his body before he heard the screams of the crowd.

A routine catch, most would say. Parks was surprised the ball hadn't carried him out of the stadium. "Got any leather left on your glove?" the shortstop called to him as they headed back to the dugout. Parks shot him a grin before he let his eyes drift up to the stands. His eyes locked on Brooke's, surprising them both.

In reaction, Parks slowed a bit. Now there was a face, he thought, a man wouldn't see every day. She looked a bit like a ravished eighteenth-century aristocrat with her wild mane of hair and English rose skin. He felt an immediate tightening in his stomach. The face exuded cool, forbidden sex. But the eyes... His never left them as he approached the dugout. The eyes were soft-gray and direct as an arrow. She stared back at him without a blink or a blush, not smiling as most fans would do if they were bold, or looking away if they were shy. She just stared, Parks thought, as if she were dissecting him. With simultaneous twinges of annoyance and curiosity, he stepped into the dugout.

He thought about her as he sat on the bench. Here, the atmosphere was subdued and tense. Every game was important now if they were to maintain their lead and win the division pennant. Parks had the personal pressure of having a shot at a four hundred batting average for the year. It was something he struggled not to think about and was constantly reminded of by the press. He watched the leadoff batter ground out and thought of the redhead in the box behind third base.

Why had she looked at him like that? As if she wondered how he would look on a trophy case. With a soft oath, Parks rose and put on his batting helmet. He'd better get his mind off the little number in the stands and on the game. Hernandez was slowing down, and the Kings needed some insurance runs.

The second batter bounced one to shallow right and beat out the ball. Parks went to stand on deck. He stretched his arms over his head, one hand on the grip, the other on the barrel. He felt loose and warm and ready. Irresistibly, his eyes were drawn to his left. He couldn't see Brooke clearly from this distance, but he sensed she watched him still. Fresh annoyance broke through him. When the batter flied out, Parks approached the box.

What was her problem, anyway? he demanded as he took a testing swing. It would have been simpler if he could have characterized her as a typical Baseball Annie, but there was nothing typical about that face—or about those eyes. Planting his feet, he crouched into position and waited for the pitch. It came in high and sweet. Parks took a cut at it just before the ball dropped.

Coolly, he stepped out of the box and adjusted his helmet before he took his batting stance again. The next ball missed the corner and evened the count. Patience was the core of Parks's talent. He could wait, even when the pressure was on, for the pitch he wanted. So he waited, taking another ball and an inside strike. The crowd was screaming, begging for a hit, but he concentrated on the pitcher.

The ball came at him, at ninety miles an hour, but he had it judged. This was the one he wanted. Parks swung, getting the meat of the bat on the ball. He knew it was gone the moment he heard the crack. So did the pitcher, who watched his two-strike pitch sail out of the park.

Parks jogged around the bases while the crowd roared. He acknowledged the slap of the first base coach with a quick grin. He'd never lost his childlike pleasure in hitting the long ball. As he rounded second, he automatically looked over at Brooke. She was sitting, chin on the rail, while the crowd jumped and screamed around her. There was the same quiet intensity in her eyes—no light of congratulations, no pleasure. Irritated, Parks tried to outstare her as he rounded third. Her eyes never faltered as he turned for home. He crossed the plate, exhilarated by the homer and furious with an unknown woman.

''Isn't that marvelous?'' Claire beamed over at Brooke. ''That's his thirty-sixth home run this season. A very talented young man.'' She signaled a roving concessionaire for another drink. ''He was staring at you.''

''Mm-hmm.'' Brooke wasn't willing to admit that her pulse rate had soared with each eye contact. She knew his type—good-looking, successful and heartless. She met them every day. "He'll look good on camera."

Claire laughed with the comfortable pleasure of a woman approaching fifty. "He'd look good anywhere."

Brooke's answer was a shrug as the game went into its seventh inning. She paid no attention to the score or to the other players as she watched Parks steadily. She remained, arms over the rail, chin on hands, booted feet crossed. There was something about him, she mused, something beyond the obvious attraction, the basic sexuality. It was that looseness of movement overlying the discipline. That's what she wanted to capture. The combination would do more than sell de Marco's clothes, it would typify them. All she had to do was guide Parks Jones through the steps.

She'd have him swinging a bat in immaculately sophisticated sports clothes—maybe riding through the surf in de Marco jeans. Athletic shots—that's what he was built for. And if she could get any humor out of him, something with women. She didn't want the usual adoring stares or knowing looks, but something fanciful and funny. If the script writers could pull it off and Jones could take any sort of direction. Refusing to look at the ifs, Brooke told herself she would make it work. Within the year, every woman would want Parks Jones and every man would envy him.

The ball was hit high and was curving foul. Parks chased after it, racing all the way to the seats before it dropped into the crowd four rows back. Brooke found herself face-to-face with him, close enough to smell the faint muskiness of his sweat and to see it run down the side of his face. Their eyes met again, but she didn't move, partly because she was interested, partly because she was paralyzed. The only thing that showed in her eyes was mild curiosity. Behind them there were shouts of triumph as someone snagged the foul as a trophy.

Enraged, Parks stared back at her. "Your name?" he demanded in undertones.

He had that fierce, dangerous look on his face again. Brooke schooled her voice to calmness. "Brooke."

"All of it, damn it," Parks muttered, pressed for time and furious with himself. He watched one thin eyebrow lift and found himself wanting to yank her out of the stands.

"Gordon," Brooke told him smoothly. "Is the game over?"

Parks narrowed his eyes before he moved away. Brooke heard him speak softly. "It's just beginning."

Chapter 2

Brooke had been expecting the call—after all, he had her name, and her name was in the book. But she hadn't been expecting it at six-fifteen on a Sunday morning.

Groggily, she groped for the phone as it shrilled, managing to grip the receiver as the cradle fell heavily to the floor. "'Lo," she mumbled without opening her eyes.

"Brooke Gordon?"

"Mmm." She snuggled back into the pillow. "Yeah."

"It's Parks Jones."

Instantly alert, Brooke opened her eyes. The light was soft and dim with dawn, early birds just beginning to chirp. She fumbled for the dented windup alarm beside her bed, then scowled at the time. Biting back a torrent of abuse, she kept her voice soft and sulky. ''Who?''

Parks shifted the receiver to his other hand and scowled. ''Parks Jones, third base. The Kings game the other night.''

Brooke yawned, taking her time about fluffing up her pillow. ''Oh,'' was all she said, but a smile flashed wickedly.

''Look, I want to see you. We're flying back after the game in New York this afternoon. How about a late dinner?'' Why was he doing this? he asked himself as he paced the small hotel room. And why, in God's name, wasn't he doing it with a bit more style?

''Dinner,'' Brooke repeated languidly while her mind worked fast. Wasn't it just like his type to expect a woman to have no plans that couldn't be altered to suit him? Her first instinct was to give him a cold refusal, then her sense of the ridiculous got the better of her. ''Well...'' She drew out the word. ''Maybe. What time?''

''I'll pick you up at nine,'' Parks told her, ignoring the maybe. When he couldn't get a woman out of his head for three days, he was going to find out why. ''I've got the address.''

''All right, Sparks, nine o'clock.''

''Parks,'' he corrected tersely and broke the connection.

Falling back on the pillow, Brooke started to laugh.

She was still in high good humor when she dressed that evening. Still, she thought it was too bad that the file she had read on Parks hadn't contained a bit more than all those baseball statistics. A few personal details would have given her more of an edge. What would Parks Jones have to say if he knew he was taking his future director to dinner? she wondered. Somehow Brooke didn't think he'd be too pleased when he learned she'd left out that little piece of information. But the whole scenario was too good to miss. And there was the fact that he'd touched off something in her that she wanted to get out of her system before they started to work together.

Wrapped in a bath towel, Brooke pondered her wardrobe. She didn't date often—her choice. Early experience had influenced her attitude toward men. If they were good-looking and charming, Brooke steered clear of them.

She'd been only seventeen when she'd met her first good-looking charmer. He'd been twenty-two and fresh out of college. When he'd come into the diner where she had worked, Clark had been quick with a joke and generous with a tip. It had started with a late movie once or twice a week, then an afternoon picnic in the park. It hadn't bothered Brooke that he wasn't working. He'd told her he was taking the summer off before he settled down to a job.

His family was well connected, genteel and Bostonian. The genteel, Clark had explained with an acerbic humor that had fascinated her, meant there were plenty of heirlooms and little ready cash. They had plans for him that he was consistently vague about with the carelessness of the young. He'd mentioned his family now and again—grandparents, sisters—

with a humor that spoke of an intimacy she envied almost painfully. Clark could make fun of them, Brooke realized, because he *was* one of them.

He'd needed a bit of freedom, he'd claimed, a few months to flow after the regimentation of college. He wanted to be in touch with the *real* world before he chose the perfect career.

Young and starved for affection, Brooke had soaked up everything he'd told her, believed every line. He had dazzled her with an education she had wished for but had never been able to have. He'd told her she was beautiful and sweet, then had kissed her as though he meant it. There had been afternoons at the beach with rented surfboards she'd hardly noticed that she'd paid for. And when she'd given him her innocence in a kind of panicked, shamed excitement, he had seemed pleased with her. He'd laughed at her naive embarrassments and had been gentle. Brooke had thought she'd never been happier.

When he'd suggested they live together, she'd agreed eagerly, wanting to cook and clean for him, longing to wake and sleep with him. The fact that her meager salary and tips now supported both of them had never crossed her mind. Clark had talked of marriage the same way he had talked of his work—vaguely. They were something for the future, something practical that people in love shouldn't dwell on. Brooke had agreed, rosily happy with what she'd thought was her first real home. One day they would have children, she had thought. Boys with Clark's handsome face, girls with his huge brown eyes. Children with grandparents in Boston who would always know who their parents were and where their home was.

For three months she'd worked like a Trojan, setting aside part of her small salary for the future Clark always talked of while he pursued what he called his studies and systematically rejected all the jobs in the want ads as unsuitable. Brooke could only agree. To her, Clark was much too smart for any manual labor, much too important for any ordinary position. When the right job came along, she knew he would simply stride into it then zoom to the top.

At times he'd seemed restless, moody. Because she had always had to steal her own privacy, Brooke had left him to his. And when he snapped out of it, he'd always been bursting with energy and plans. Let's go here, let's go there. Now, today. Tomorrow was always years away to Clark. To Brooke, for the first time in seventeen years, today was special. She had something—*someone*—who belonged to her.

In the meantime, she'd worked long hours, cooked his meals and hoarded her tips in a small apothecary jar on a shelf in the kitchen.

One night Brooke had come home from a late shift to find that Clark had gone, taking with him her small black-and-white television set, her record collection and her apothecary jar. A note was in its place.

Brooke,
Got a call from home. My parents are putting on the pressure—I didn't know it would start so

soon. I should have told you before, but I guess I kept thinking it would just go away. An old family tradition—a merger with my third cousin, as in matrimony. Hell, it sounds archaic, but it's the way my people work. Shelley's a nice girl, her dad's a connection of my dad's. I've been more or less engaged to her for a couple of years, but she was still at Smith, so it didn't seem important. Anyway, I'll slip into her family's business. Junior executive with a shot at the V.P. in five years or so. I guess I hoped I'd tell them to take a leap when the time came, but I can't. I'm sorry.

There's no fighting a wall of family and old money and stiff New England practicality, babe, especially when they keep reminding you that you're the heir apparent. I want you to know that these last couple of months I've had more breathing space than I've had in a long time, and I suppose than I'll have in an even longer time.

I'm sorry about the TV and stuff, but I didn't have the cash for the plane fare and the time wasn't right to tell my folks I'd already blown my savings. I'll pay you back as soon as I can.

I kept hoping it wouldn't have to be this way, but I'm backed into a corner. You've been great, Brooke, really great. Be happy.

Clark

Brooke had read the note twice before all the words registered. He'd gone. Her things hadn't mattered but he had. Clark was gone and she was alone—again—because she hadn't graduated from Smith or had a family in Boston or a father who could offer someone she loved a comfortable job so he'd choose her. No one had ever chosen her.

Brooke had wept until she was drained, unable to believe that her dreams, her trust and her future had been destroyed all in one instant.

Then she had grown up fast, pushing her idealism behind her. She wasn't going to be used ever again. She wasn't going to compete ever again with women who had all the advantages. And she wasn't going to slave in a steamy little diner for enough money to keep herself in a one-room apartment with dingy paint.

She had torn the note into tiny pieces, then had washed her face with icy water until all the traces of all the tears were gone.

Walking the pavement with all the money she had left in her pocket, she had found herself in front of Thorton Productions. She had gone in aggressively, belligerently, talking her way past the receptionist and into the personnel office. She'd come out with a new job, making hardly more than she had waiting tables, but with fresh ambition. She was going places. The one thing her betrayal by Clark had taught her was that she could depend on only one person: herself. No one was ever going to make her believe, or make her cry again.

Ten years later, Brooke drew a narrow black dress from her closet. It was a severely sophisticated outfit she had bought mainly for the cocktail circuit that went hand in hand with her profession. She fingered the silk, then nodded. It should do very well for her evening with Parks Jones.

As Parks drove through the hills above L.A. he considered his actions. For the first time in his career he had allowed a woman to distract him during a game—and this one hadn't even tried. For the first time, he had called a virtual stranger from three thousand miles away to make a date, and she didn't even know who the hell he was. For the first time, he was planning on taking out a woman who made him absolutely furious without having said more than a handful of words. And if it hadn't been for the road series that had followed that night game at Kings Stadium, he would have called her before this. He'd looked up her number at the airport on his way to catch a plane to New York.

He downshifted for the incline as he swung around a curve. All during the flight home, he had thought of Brooke Gordon, trying to pigeonhole her. A model or an actress, he had concluded. She had the face for it—not really beautiful, but certainly unique. Her voice was like something whispering through layers of smoke. And she hadn't sounded overly bright on the phone that morning, he reminded himself with a grimace as he stepped on the gas. There was no law that said brains had to go with intriguing looks, but something in her eyes that night… Parks shook off the feeling that he'd been studied, weighed and measured.

A rabbit darted out in front of him then stopped, hypnotized by his beams. Parks braked, swerved and swore as it raced back to the side of the road. He had a weakness for small animals that his father had never understood. Then, his father had understood little about a boy who chose to play ball rather than assume a lucrative position of power in Parkinson Chemicals.

Parks slowed to check his direction, then turned down the darkened back road that led to Brooke's tidy wooded property. He liked it instantly—the remoteness, the melodious sound of crickets. It was a small slice of country thirty-five minutes from L.A. Perhaps she wasn't so slow-witted after all. He pulled his MG behind her Datsun and looked around him.

Her grass needed trimming, but it only added to the rural charm of the house. It was a small, A-frame structure with lots of glass and a circular porch. He heard the tinkle of water from the narrow stream that ran behind the house. There was a scent of summer—hot, heavy blossoms he couldn't identify, and an inexplicable aura of peacefulness. He found himself wishing he didn't have to drive back down to a crowded restaurant and bright lights. In the distance a dog began to bark frantically, sending out echos to emphasize the openness. Parks climbed out of the car, wondering what sort of woman would choose a house so far from city comforts.

There was an old brass knocker in the shape of a hog's head at the right of the door. It made him grin as he let it bang. When she opened the door, Parks forgot all the doubts that had plagued him on his drive through the hills. This time he thought she looked like a seductive witch—fair skin against a black dress, a heavy silver amulet between her breasts. Her hair was pulled back at the temples with two combs, then left to fall wildly down to her hips. Her eyes were as misty as hell-smoke, the lids darkened by some subtle, glittering shadow. Her mouth was naked. He caught a drift of scent that brought him a picture of East Indian harems, white silk and dusky female laughter.

"Hello." Brooke extended her hand. It took every ounce of willpower to complete the casual gesture. How was she to have known her heart would start thudding at the sight of him? It was foolish, because she had already imagined what he would look like in sophisticated clothes. She'd had to if she was to plan how to film him. But somehow his body looked rangier, even more male in a suit coat and slacks—and somehow his face was even more attractive in the shadowed half-light of her front porch. Her plans to ask him in for a drink were aborted. The sooner they were in a crowd the better. "I'm starving," she said as his fingers closed over hers. "Shall we go?" Without waiting for his answer, she shut the door at her back.

Parks led her to the car then turned. In heels, she was nearly eye level with him. "Want me to put the top up?"

"No." Brooke opened the door herself. "I like the air."

She leaned back and shut her eyes as he started back down toward the city. He drove fast, but with the studied control she had sensed in him from the beginning. Since speed was one of her weaknesses, she relaxed and enjoyed.

''What were you doing at the game the other night?''

Brooke felt the smile tug at her mouth but answered smoothly, ''A friend had some tickets. She thought I might find it interesting.''

''Interesting?'' Parks shook his head at the word. ''And did you?''

''Oh, yes, though I'd expected to be bored.''

''I didn't notice any particular enthusiasm in you,'' Parks commented, remembering her calm, direct stare. ''As I recall, you didn't move through nine innings.''

''I didn't need to,'' she returned. ''You did enough of that.''

Parks shot her a quick look. ''Why were you staring at me?''

Brooke considered for a moment, then opted for the truth. ''I was admiring your build.'' She turned to him with a half smile. The wind blew the hair into her face, but she didn't bother to brush it aside. ''It's a very good one.''

''Thanks.'' She saw a flash of humor in his eyes that pleased her. ''Is that why you agreed to have dinner with me?''

Brooke smiled more fully. ''No. I just like to eat. Why did you ask me?''

''I liked your face. And it's not every day I have a

woman stare at me as if she were going to frame me and hang me on her wall.''

''Really?'' She gave him an innocent blink. ''I'd think that pretty typical in your profession.''

''Maybe.'' He took his eyes off the road long enough to meet hers. ''But then you're not typical, are you?''

Brooke lifted a brow. Did he know he'd given her what she considered the highest compliment? ''Perhaps not,'' she murmured. ''Why don't you think so?''

''Because, Brooke Gordon, I'm not typical either.'' He burst out of the woods and onto the highway. Brooke decided that she'd better tread carefully.

The restaurant was Greek, with pungent foods, spicy scents and violins. While Parks poured her a second glass of ouzo, Brooke listened to a waiter in a grease-splattered apron sing lustily as he served souvlaki. As always, atmosphere pulled at her. Caught up, she watched and absorbed while managing to put away a healthy meal.

''What are you thinking?'' Parks demanded. Her eyes shifted to his, disconcerting in their directness, seducing in their softness.

''That this is a happy place,'' she told him. ''The sort you imagine a big family running. Momma and Poppa in the kitchen fussing over sauces, a pregnant daughter chopping vegetables while her husband tends bar. Uncle Stefos waits tables.''

The image made him smile. ''Do you come from a large family?''

Immediately the light went out of her eyes. "No."

Sensing a boundary, Parks skirted around it. "What happens when the daughter has her baby?"

"She pops it in a cradle in the corner and chops more vegetables." Brooke broke a hunk of bread in half and nibbled.

"Very efficient."

"A successful woman has to be."

Leaning back, Parks swirled his drink. "Are you a successful woman?"

"Yes."

He tilted his head, watching the candlelight play on her skin. "At what?"

Brooke sipped, enjoying the game. "At what I do. Are you a successful man?"

"At the moment." Parks flashed a grin—the one that gave his face a young, rather affable charm. "Baseball's a fickle profession. A ball takes a bad hop—a pitcher blows a few by you. You can't predict when a slump will start or stop—or worse, why."

It seemed a bit like life to her. "And do you have many?"

"One's too many." With a shrug, he set his drink back on the table. "I've had more than one."

With her first genuine curiosity, Brooke leaned forward. "What do you do to get out of one?"

"Change bats, change batting stances." He shrugged again. "Change your diet, pray. Try celibacy."

She laughed, a warm, liquid sound. "What works best?"

"A good pitch." He, too, leaned forward. "Wanna hear one?"

When her brow rose again, he lifted a finger to trace it. Brooke felt the jolt shiver down to her toes. "I think I'll pass."

"Where do you come from?" he murmured. His fingertip drifted down her cheek, then traced her jawline. He'd known her skin would feel like that. Milkmaid soft.

"No place in particular." Brooke reached for her glass, but his hand closed over hers.

"Everyone comes from somewhere."

"No," she disagreed. His palm was harder than she had imagined, his fingers stronger. And his touch was gentler. "Not everyone."

From her tone, Parks realized she was speaking the truth as she saw it. He brushed a thumb over her wrist, finding her pulse fast but steady. "Tell me about yourself."

"What do you want to know?"

"Everything."

Brooke laughed but spoke with perfect truth. "I don't tell anyone everything."

"What do you do?"

"About what?"

He should have been exasperated, but found himself grinning. "About a job, for starters."

"Oh, I make commercials," she said lightly, knowing he would conclude she worked in front of the cameras. The game had a certain mischievous appeal for her.

"I'll be doing that myself soon," he said with a quick grimace. "Do you like it?"

"I wouldn't do it if I didn't."

He sent her a narrowed look, then nodded. "No, you wouldn't."

"You don't sound as though you're looking forward to trying it," Brooke commented, slipping her hand from his. Prolonged contact with him, she discovered, made it difficult to concentrate, and concentration was vital to her.

"Not when I have to spout some silly lines and wear somebody else's clothes." Idly, he toyed with a lock of her hair, wrapping it around his finger while his eyes remained on hers. "You've a fascinating face; more alluring than beautiful. When I saw you in the stands, I thought you looked like a woman out of the eighteenth century. The sort who had a string of anxious lovers."

With a low sound of humor, Brooke leaned closer. "Was that the first pitch, Mr. Jones?"

Her scent seemed intensified by the warmth of the candle. He wondered that every man in the room wasn't aware of it, and of her. "No." His fingers tightened briefly, almost warningly, on her hair. "When I make my first one, you won't have to ask."

Instinctively, Brooke retreated, but her eyes remained calm, her voice smooth. "Fair enough." She would definitely put him on film with women, she decided. Sultry brunettes for contrast. "Do you ride?" she asked abruptly.

"Ride?"

"Horses."

"Yeah," he answered with a curious laugh. "Why?"

"Just wondered. What about hang gliding?"

Parks's expression became more puzzled than amused. "It's against my contract, like skiing or racing." He didn't trust the light of humor in her eyes. "Should I know what game you're playing?"

"No. Can we have dessert?" She flashed him a brilliant smile he trusted less.

"Sure." Watching her, Parks signaled the waiter.

Thirty minutes later, they walked across the parking lot to his car. "Do you always eat like that?" Parks demanded.

"Whenever I get the chance." Brooke dropped into the passenger seat then stretched her arms over her head in a lazy, unconsciously sensual movement. No one who hadn't worked in a restaurant could fully appreciate eating in one. She'd enjoyed the food…and the evening. Perhaps, she mused, she'd enjoyed being with Parks because they'd spent three hours together and still didn't know each other. The mystery added a touch of spice.

In a few months, they would know each other well. A director had no choice but to get to the inside of an actor—which is what Parks would be, whether he liked it or not. For now, Brooke chose to enjoy the moment, the mystery and the brief companionship of an attractive man.

When Parks sat beside her, he reached over to cup her chin in his hand. She met his eyes serenely and with that touch of humor that was beginning to frustrate him. "Are you going to let me know who you are?"

Odd, Brooke mused, that he would have the same understanding of the evening she did. "I haven't decided," she said candidly.

"I'm going to see you again."

She gave him an enigmatic smile. "Yes."

Wary of the smile, and her easy agreement, Parks started the engine.

He didn't like knowing that she was playing him…any more than he liked knowing he'd have to come back for more. He'd known a variety of women—from icy sophisticates to bubbly groupies. There were infinite shadings in between, but Brooke Gordon seemed to fit none of them. She had both a haughty sexuality and a soft vulnerability. Though his first instinct had been to get her to bed, he now discovered he wanted more. He wanted to peel off the layers of her character and study each one until he understood the full woman. Making love to her would only be part of the discovery.

They drove in silence while an old, soft ballad crooned on the radio. Brooke had her head thrown back, face to the stars, knowing it was the first time in months she'd fully relaxed on a date and not wanting to analyze why. Parks didn't find it necessary to break a comfortable silence with conversation, nor had he found it necessary to slip in those predictable hints about how he'd like to end the evening. She knew there wouldn't be a wrestling match on the side of the road or an embarrassing, infuriating argument when they reached the front door. He was safe, Brooke decided, and closed her eyes. It seemed things were going to work very well after all. Her thoughts began to drift toward her schedule for the next day.

The motion of the car woke her, or rather the lack of motion. Brooke opened her eyes to find the MG parked in her drive, the engine quiet. Turning her head, she saw Parks sprawled in his seat, watching her.

"You drive very well," she murmured. "I don't usually trust anyone enough to fall asleep in a car."

He'd enjoyed the moments of quiet while he'd watched her sleep. Her skin looked ethereal in the moonlight, ghostly pale with a hint of flush in her cheeks. The wind had tossed her hair so that Parks knew how it would look spread on a pillow after a wild night of loving. Sooner or later he'd see it that way, he determined. After his hands had tangled it.

"This time you're staring," Brooke pointed out.

And he smiled—not the quick grin she'd come to expect, but a slow, unsettling smile that left his eyes dark and dangerous. "I guess we'll both have to get used to it."

Leaning over, he opened her door. Brooke didn't stiffen or shift away from the brush of his body against hers; she simply watched. As if, Parks mused, she were considering his words very carefully. Good, he thought as he stepped from the car. This time she'd have something to think about.

"I like this place." He didn't touch her as they

walked up the path to her house, though Brooke had expected him to take her hand or her arm. "I had a house in Malibu once."

"Not anymore?"

"Got too crowded." He shrugged as they walked up the porch steps. Their footsteps echoed into the night. "If I'm going to live out of the city, I want a place where I'm not forever stumbling over my neighbor."

"I don't have that problem here." Around them the woods were dark and quiet. There was only the bubbling sound of the stream and the music of tireless crickets. "There's a couple who live about a quarter mile that way." Brooke gestured to the east. "Newlyweds who met on a television series that folded." Leaning back against the door, she smiled. "We don't have any trouble keeping out of each other's way." She sighed, comfortably sleepy and relaxed. "Thanks for dinner." When she offered her hand, she wondered if he would take it or ignore it and kiss her. Brooke expected the latter, even wondered with a drowsy curiosity what the pressure of his lips on hers would be like.

Parks knew what she expected, and her lips, as they had from the first, tempted him. But he thought it was time this woman had something unexpected. Taking her hand, Parks leaned toward her. He saw from her eyes that she would accept his kiss with her own sultry reserve. Instead, he touched his lips to her cheek.

At the brush of his open mouth on her skin, Brooke's fingers tightened in his. Usually she viewed a kiss or embrace distantly, as from behind a camera, wondering dispassionately how it would appear on film. Now she saw nothing, but felt. Low, turbulent waves of sensation swept through her, making her tense. Something seemed to ripple along her skin, though he never touched her—just his hand over hers, just his lips on her cheek.

Slowly, watching her stunned eyes, Parks journeyed to her other cheek, moving his lips with the same feather-lightness. Brooke felt the waves rise until there was an echoing in her head. She heard a soft moan, unaware that it was her own. As hunger swept over her, Brooke turned her mouth toward his, but he glided up her skin, whispering over her eyelids so that they fluttered down. Drugged, she allowed him to roam over her face, leaving her lips trembling with anticipation, and unfulfilled. She tasted his breath on them, felt the warm flutter as they passed close, but his mouth dropped to her chin to give her a teasing touch of his tongue.

Her fingers went limp in his. Surrender was unknown to her, so she didn't recognize it. Parks did as he caught the lobe of her ear between his teeth. His body was throbbing, aching to press against hers and feel the yielding softness that came only from woman. Against his cheek, her hair was as silky as her skin, and as fragrant. It took every ounce of control to prevent his hands from diving into it, to keep himself from plundering the mouth that waited, warm and naked, for his. He traced her ear with his tongue and felt her shudder. Slowly, he brushed kisses up her temple and over her brow on his way to her other ear. He nibbled gently, letting his tongue slide over her skin until he heard her moan again.

Still he avoided her mouth, pressing his lips to the pulse in her throat, fighting the urge to move lower, to feel, to taste the subtle sweep of her breast beneath the black silk. Her pulse was jerky, like the sound of her breathing. High up in the mountains, a coyote called to the moon.

A dizzying excitement raced through him. He could have her now—feel that long, willowy body beneath his, tangle himself in that wild mane of hair. But he wouldn't have all of her. He needed more time for that.

''Parks.'' His name came throatily through her lips, arousing him further. ''Kiss me.''

Gently, he pressed his lips to her shoulder. ''I am.''

Her mouth felt as though it were on fire. She had thought she understood hunger, having felt it too often in the past. But she'd never known a hunger like this. ''Really kiss me.''

He drew away far enough to see her eyes. There was no light in them now; they were opaque with desire. Her lips were parted in invitation, her breath shuddering through them. He bent close, but kept his lips an aching whisper from hers. ''Next time,'' he said softly.

Turning, he left her stunned and wanting.

Chapter 3

''Okay, Linda, try to look like you're enjoying this.'' Brooke cast a look at her lighting director and got a nod. ''E.J., sweep up, starting at her toes—take your time on the legs.''

E.J. gave her a blinding white grin from his smooth mahogany face. ''My pleasure,'' he said affably and focused his camera on the actress's pink painted toenails.

''It's so hot,'' Linda complained, fussing with the strap of her tiny bikini. She was stretched out on a towel in the sand—long, blond and beautiful, with a rich golden tan that would hawk a popular suntan lotion. All Linda had to do was to look lush and lazy and purr that she had an *Eden* tan. The bikini would do the rest.

''Don't sweat,'' Brooke ordered. ''You're supposed

to be glowing, not wet. When we roll, count to six, then bring up your right knee—slow. At twelve, take a deep breath, pass your right hand through your hair. Say your line looking straight at the camera and think sex."

"The hell with sex, I'm roasting."

"Then let's get it in one take. All right. Speed. Roll film, and…action."

E.J. moved up from the manicured toenails, up the long, slender legs, over a rounded hip, golden midriff and barely confined bosom. He closed in on Linda's face—sulky mouth, pearly teeth and baby blues—then went back for a full shot.

"I've got an *Eden* tan," Linda claimed.

"Cut." Brooke swiped a hand over her brow. Though it was still morning, the beach was baking. She thought she could feel the sand burning through the soles of her sneakers. "Let's pump a little life into it," she suggested. "We've got to sell this stuff on one line and your body."

"Why don't you try it?" Linda demanded, falling onto her back.

"Because you're getting paid to and I'm not," Brooke snapped, then clicked her teeth together. She knew better than to lose her temper, especially with this one. The trouble was that since her evening with Parks, she'd been on a perpetual short fuse. Taking a deep breath, Brooke reminded herself that her personal life, if that's what Parks Jones was, couldn't interfere with her work. She walked over and crouched beside the pouting model. "Linda, I know it's miserable out here today, but a job's a job. You're a pro or you wouldn't be here."

"Do you know how hard I worked on this tan to get this lousy thirty-second spot?"

Brooke patted her shoulder, conveying sympathy, understanding and authority all at once. "Well then, let's make it a classic."

It was past noon before they were able to load up their equipment. E.J. reached in the back of the station wagon he used and pulled two iced drinks out of a chest cooler. "Here ya go, boss."

"Thanks." Brooke pressed the cold bottle against her forehead before she twisted off the top. "What was with her today?" she demanded. "She can be a problem, but I've never had to drag one line out of her like that before."

"Broke up with her man last week," E.J. informed Brooke before he took a greedy swallow of grape soda.

Grinning, Brooke sat on the tailgate. "Anything you don't know, E.J.?"

"Not a thing." He propped himself beside her, one of the few on the Thorton staff who wasn't leery of the Tiger-lady, as Brooke had been dubbed. "You're going to that fancy de Marco party tonight."

"Yeah." Brooke gave a slow, narrow-eyed smile that had nothing to do with the brilliance of the sun. The party would be her chance to cut Parks Jones down a few pegs. She could still remember how she had stood shaking on her porch in the moonlight after the echo of his engine had died away.

"It's going to be a kick working with Parks Jones." E.J. downed the rest of his soda in one swallow. "The man's got the best glove in the league and a bat that won't quit smoking. Knocked in two more RBIs last night."

Brooke leaned against the door frame and scowled. "Good for him."

"Don't you like baseball?" E.J. grinned, tossing his empty bottle into the back of the wagon.

"No."

"Ought to have some team spirit," he mused and gave her knee a friendly squeeze. "The better he does, the more punch the campaign'll have. And if he gets into the series—"

"If he gets into the series," Brooke interrupted, "we have to wait until the end of October before we can start shooting."

"Well." E.J. stroked his chin. "That's show biz."

Brooke tried to glare, then chuckled. "Let's get back. I've got a shoot in the studio this afternoon. Want me to drive?"

"Naw." E.J. slammed the tailgate then headed for the driver's seat. "I like living."

"You're such a wimp, E.J."

"I know," he agreed cheerfully. "I've got this thing about traveling at the speed of light." After adjusting mirror-lensed sunglasses on his face he coaxed the station wagon's engine into life. It sputtered and groaned temperamentally while he crooned to it.

"Why don't you buy a new car?" Brooke demanded. "You get paid enough."

He patted the wagon's dash when the engine caught. "Loyalty. I've been cruising in this little darling for seven years. She'll be around when that flashy machine of yours is nuts and bolts."

Brooke shrugged, then tilted back her head to drain the bottle. E.J. was the only one who worked under her who dared any intimacy, which was probably the reason she not only allowed it but liked him for it. She also considered him one of the best men with a camera on the West Coast. He came from San Francisco where his father was a high school principal and his mother owned and operated a popular beauty salon. She had met them once and wondered how two such meticulous people could have produced a free-wheeling, loose-living man with a penchant for voluptuous women and B movies.

But then, Brooke mused, she'd never been able to understand families. Always she viewed them with perplexity and longing, as only one on the outside could fully understand. Settling back on the carefully patched seat, she began to plot out her strategy for her afternoon session.

"Heard you took in a Kings game the other night." E.J. caught her swift, piercing look and began to whistle tunelessly.

"So?"

"I saw Brighton Boyd at a party a couple of nights ago. Worked with him on a TV special last year. Nice guy."

Brooke remembered seeing the actor in the box next to hers and Claire's. She dropped her empty bottle on the already littered floor. ''So?'' she repeated coolly.

''Big Kings fan,'' E.J. went on, turning the radio up loud so that he had to shout over the top 40 rock. ''Raved about Jones's homer—on a two-out, two-strike pitch. The man's a hell of a clutch hitter.'' While Brooke remained silent, E.J. tapped out the beat from the radio on the steering wheel. There was the glint of gold from a ring on his long dark fingers. ''Brighton said Jones stared at you like a man who'd been hit with a blunt instrument. That Brighton, he sure does turn a phrase.''

''Hmm.'' Brooke began to find the passing scenery fascinating.

''Said he came right over to your box chasing a foul. Had a few words to say.''

Brooke turned her head and stared into E.J.'s mirrored glasses. ''Are you pumping me, E.J.?''

''Hot damn! Can't pull anything over on you, Brooke; you're one sharp lady.''

Despite herself she laughed. She knew a ''no comment'' would only cause speculation she'd like to avoid. Instead she stretched her legs out on the seat and treated it lightly. ''He just wanted my name.''

''And?''

''And nothing.''

''Where'd you go with him?''

The faintest frown creased her brow. ''I didn't say I went anywhere with him.''

''He didn't ask your name because he was taking a census.''

Brooke gave him a cool, haughty look that would have discouraged anyone else. "You're a gossipy old woman, E.J."

"Yep. You go to dinner with him?"

"Yes," she said on a sigh of surrender. "And that's all."

"Not as bright as he looks, then." He patted her sneakered foot. "Or maybe he felt funny about starting something up with the lady who'll be directing him."

"He didn't know," Brooke heard herself say before she could stop herself.

"Oh?"

"I didn't tell him."

"Oh." This time the syllable was drawn out and knowing.

"I didn't think it was necessary," Brooke said heatedly. "It was strictly a social meeting, and it gave me the opportunity to plan how best to film him."

"Mm-hmm."

She turned back in her seat and folded her arms. "Shut up and drive, E.J."

"Sure thing, boss."

"As far as I'm concerned he can take his golden glove and smoking bat and sit on them."

E.J. nodded wisely, enjoying himself. "You know best."

"He's conceited and cold and inconsiderate."

"Must have been some evening," E.J. observed.

"I don't want to talk about it." Brooke kicked at the empty bottle on the floor.

"Okay," he said affably.

"He's the kind of man," she went on, "who thinks a woman's just waiting to fall all over him just because he's moderately attractive and successful and has an average mind."

"For a Rhodes scholar," E.J. mused as he slowed down for his exit.

"A what?"

"He's a Rhodes scholar."

Brooke's mouth fell open, then shut with a bang. "He is not."

E.J. shrugged agreeably. "Well, that's what it said in *Sports View*. That was supposed to be the main reason he didn't start playing professional ball until he was twenty-two."

"Probably just a publicity hype," she muttered, but she knew better. She rode the rest of the way to the studio in frowning silence.

The de Marco California villa was an eyeful. Brooke decided that it had the dubious ability of making Claire's mansion look simple and discreet. It was huge, E-shaped and dazzling white with two inner courtyards. One held a grottolike pool complete with miniature waterfall, the other a sheltered garden rich with exotic scents.

When Brooke arrived, she could hear the high liquid sounds of harps and mixed conversation. People were ranged through the house, spilling outdoors and clustered in corners. Passing through the gold-toned parlor, she caught the mingling, heady scents of expensive perfumes and spiced food. There was the glitter of diamonds, swirl of silks and flash of tanned, pampered skin.

Brooke caught snatches of conversations as she strolled through, searching for the main buffet.

"But darling, he simply can't carry a series anymore. Did you see him at Ma Maison last week?"

"She'll sign. After that fiasco in England, she's itching to come back to Hollywood."

"Can't remember a line if you feed it to him intravenously."

"Left her for the wardrobe mistress."

"My dear, have you ever seen *such* a dress!"

Hollywood, Brooke thought with halfhearted affection as she pounced on the remains of the pâté.

"I knew I'd find you here."

Brooke turned her head as she speared a chunk of smoked beef. "Hello, Claire," she managed over a mouthful of cracker. "Nice party."

"I suppose, as you always judge them by the menu." Claire gave her a long, appraising look. Brooke wore a buckskin jumpsuit, soft and smooth as cream, with a thick pewter belt cinched at her waist. She'd braided the hair at her temples and clipped it back over the flowing tousled mane, letting heavy pewter links dangle at her ears. Because she'd been distracted while applying it, she'd neglected her makeup and had only remembered to darken her eyes. As a result, they dominated her pale, sharp-featured face. "Why is it you can wear the most outlandish outfits and still look marvelous?"

Brooke grinned and swallowed. ''I like yours, too,'' she said, noting that Claire was, as always, stylishly neat in pale-blue voile. ''What have they got to drink in this place?''

With a sigh, Claire motioned to a roving, red-suited waiter and chose two tulip glasses of champagne. ''Try to behave yourself. The de Marcos are very old-fashioned.''

''I'll be a credit to the company,'' Brooke promised and lifted her hand in acknowledgment of a wave from a stand-up comic she'd directed in a car commercial. ''Do you think I could get a plate?''

''Gorge later. Mr. Jones's agent is here, I want you to meet him.''

''I hate talking to agents on an empty stomach. Oh, damn, there's Vera. I should have known she'd be here.''

Brooke answered the icy smile from the slim honey-haired model who was the current embodiment of the American look. Their paths had crossed more than once, professionally and socially, and the women had taken an instant, lasting dislike to each other. ''Keep your claws sheathed,'' Claire warned. ''De Marco's going to be using her.''

''Not with me,'' Brooke said instantly. ''I'll take the ball player, Claire, but someone else is going to hold the leash on that one. I don't like my poison in small doses.''

''We'll discuss it,'' Claire muttered then beamed a smile. ''Lee, we were just looking for you. Lee Dutton, Brooke Gordon. She's going to be directing

Parks.'' She placed a maternal hand on Brooke's arm. ''My very best.''

Brooke lifted an ironic brow. Claire was always lavish with praise in public and miserly with it behind closed doors. ''Hello, Mr. Dutton.''

Her hand was grabbed hard and pumped briskly. Discreetly, Brooke flexed her fingers while she made a swift survey. He was shorter than she was and rather round with thinning hair and startling black eyes. A creature of first impressions, she liked him on the spot.

''Here's to a long, successful relationship,'' he announced and banged his glass exuberantly against hers. ''Parks is eager to begin.''

''Is he?'' Brooke smiled, remembering Parks's description of his venture into commercials. ''We're just as eager to have him.''

Claire sent her a brief warning look as she tucked her arm through Lee's. ''And where is he? Brooke and I are both anxious to meet him.''

''He has a hard time getting away from the ladies.'' Lee gave the proud, apologetic smile of a doting uncle. But the eyes on Brooke were shrewd.

''How awkward for him,'' she murmured into her glass. ''But I suppose he manages to live with it.''

''Brooke, you really must try the pâté.'' Claire sent her a teeth-clenched smile.

''I did,'' Brooke returned easily. ''Tell me more about Parks, Mr. Dutton. I can't tell you what a fan I am.''

''Oh, you follow baseball?''

Brooke tilted her glass again. ''Why, we were in the park only a few weeks ago, weren't we, Claire?''

''As a matter of fact.'' Claire didn't bother to try to outstare Brooke this time but turned to Lee. ''Do you get to many games?''

''Not enough,'' he admitted, knowing a game was afoot and willing to play. ''But I happen to have a few tickets for Sunday's game,'' he said, making a mental note to arrange for some. ''I'd love to escort both you ladies.''

Before Brooke could open her mouth, Claire doled out subtle punishment. ''There's nothing we'd like better.''

He caught Brooke's quick scowl before she smoothed her features. ''Well, there's Parks now.'' Lee bellowed for him, causing heads to turn before conversation buzzed again.

Parks's first reaction was surprise when he saw Brooke standing beside his agent and the woman he knew was head of Thorton Productions. Then he experienced the same flare of reluctant desire he had felt on the other two occasions he'd seen her. He'd purposely let the days pass before he contacted her again, hoping the power of need would lessen. One glance at her told him it hadn't worked.

Apparently without hurry, he weaved through the crowd, stopping to exchange a few words when someone touched his arm, then gently disentangling himself. He'd learned, at an early age, how to keep from being cornered at a social occasion. In less than two minutes, Parks stood in front of Brooke.

Well done, Brooke thought. She answered Parks's smile cautiously, wondering what his reaction would be when they were introduced. She felt a jab of uneasiness then pushed it aside. After all, he'd been the one to wake her up at dawn and ask for a date.

"Parks, I want you to meet Claire Thorton, the lady who'll be producing your commercials." Lee laid his hand over Claire's in an unconsciously possessive gesture noticed only by Parks and Brooke. Parks was amused, Brooke annoyed.

"A pleasure, Ms. Thorton." He wanted to say he had expected a dragon from what he'd read of her professionally, not this soft-faced attractive woman with faded blue eyes. Instead, Parks smiled and accepted her hand.

"We're looking forward to working with you. I was just telling Mr. Dutton how much Brooke and I enjoyed your game against the Valiants a few weeks ago." Remembering his muttered demand for Brooke's name at the rail, Claire waited for the reaction.

"Oh?" So this was her friend, he thought, turning to Brooke. With her face, he concluded she must be a regular for Thorton's commercials. "Hello again."

"Hello." Brooke found her hand claimed and held. Taking a hasty sip of champagne, she waited for the bomb to drop.

"Claire tells me Ms. Gordon is her best," Lee told Parks. "Since you'll be working together closely, you'll want to get to know each other."

''Will we?'' Parks ran his thumb along Brooke's palm.

''Only my best director for a project this important,'' Claire put in, watching them closely.

Brooke felt his thumb stop its casual caress, then his fingers tightened. There was no change in his face. To prevent a quick gasp of pain, she swallowed the rest of her champagne. ''So you direct commercials,'' he said smoothly.

''Yes.'' She tugged once to free her hand, but he only increased his grip.

''Fascinating.'' Casually, he plucked the empty glass from her other hand. ''Excuse us.'' Brooke found herself being dragged through the crowd of jewels and silks. Immediately, she quickened her pace so that it appeared she was walking with him rather than being led.

''Let go of me,'' she hissed, giving a nodding smile to another director. ''You're breaking my hand.''

''Consider it a preview of things to come.'' Parks pulled her through the open French doors, hoping to find a quiet spot. There was a three-piece band in the garden playing soft, dancing music. At least a dozen couples were taking advantage of it. Parks swore, but before he could maneuver her through the garden to a more private spot, he heard someone call her name. Immediately, he dragged her into his arms.

The hard contact with his chest stole her breath, the arm tight around her waist prevented her from finding any more. Ignoring the choking sound she made, Parks began to sway to the music. ''Just wave to him,'' he ordered against her ear. ''I'm not about to be interrupted with small talk.''

Wanting to breathe again, Brooke obeyed. She was already planning revenge. When his grip lessened slightly, she drew in a sharp breath of air, letting it out on a string of abuse. ''You overgrown bully, don't think you can drag me around just because you're this year's American hero. I'll only take it once, and I'll only warn you once. Don't you *ever* grab me again.'' Brooke stomped hard on his foot and was rewarded by having her air cut off again.

''You dance beautifully, Ms. Gordon,'' Parks whispered in her ear. He bit none too gently on the lobe. Between the fury and pain, Brooke felt a stir deep in her stomach. Oh, no, she thought, stiffening. Not again. The band switched to an up-tempo number but he continued to hold her close and sway.

''You're going to have a lot of explaining to do when I faint from lack of oxygen,'' she managed. Who would have thought that lanky body would be so hard, or the limber arms so strong?

''You won't faint,'' he muttered, slowly maneuvering her toward the edge of the garden. ''And you're the one with the explaining to do.''

She was released abruptly, but before Brooke could take a breath, he was pulling her through a clump of azalea. ''Look, you jerk…'' Then she was back inside, dazed by bright lights and laughter. Without pausing, Parks dragged her through the center patio and into the adjoining courtyard.

There was no music here, except the liquid sound

of the water falling into the grotto, and only a few couples more intent on themselves than on a man pulling a furious woman in his wake. Parks drew her close to the pool and into the shadows behind the high wall. Brooke was effectively sandwiched between him and the smooth rocks.

"So you like to play games," he murmured.

For the first time she was able to lift her face and stare into his. Her eyes glittered in the moonlight. "I don't know what you're talking about."

"No?"

She had expected him to be annoyed, but she hadn't expected this smoldering fury. It was in his eyes, in the hard lines of his face, in the poised readiness of his body. When she felt her heart begin to thud uncomfortably, she became only more defensive. "You made all the moves," she tossed out. "You *demanded* that I give you my name. You called *me* at six o'clock in the morning for a date. All I did was let Claire drag me to a ball game."

She made an attempt to push by him and found herself pressed back against the wall by a firm hand on her chest. "You were sizing me up," he said slowly. "At the game, at dinner. Tell me, how did I come out?"

Brooke put her hand to his wrist, but was surprised when he let her push his hand away. She began a careless recital she knew would infuriate him. "You move more like a dancer than an athlete—it'll be a plus on film. Your build is good, it'll sell clothes. You can be charming at times, and your face is attractive without being handsome. That could sell anything. You have a certain sexuality that should appeal to women who'd like their men to have it, too. They're the primary target, as women still do the bulk of buying in ready-to-wear."

Her tone had been schooled to annoy. Even so, Parks couldn't prevent his temper from rising. "Do I get a rating?"

"Naturally." The bitten-off words pleased her enormously. It was a small payment for the scene on her porch, but it was payment. "Your popularity quotient is fair at the moment. It should get higher after the first commercial is aired. Claire seems to think if you could get into the World Series and do something outstanding, it would help."

"I'll see what I can do," he said dryly. "Now, why didn't you tell me who you were?"

"I did."

He leaned closer. She caught a trace of sharp cologne over the smell of wet summer leaves. "No, you didn't."

"I told you I make commercials."

"Knowing I'd conclude you were an actress."

"Your conclusions are your own problem," Brooke told him with a shrug. "I never said I was an actress." She heard a woman's laugh muffled in the distance and the rush of water into the pool beside her. The odds, she mused, were not in her favor at the moment. "I don't see what difference it makes."

"I don't like games," Parks said precisely, "unless I know the players."

"Then we won't play," Brooke countered. "Your job is to do what I tell you—no more, no less."

Parks controlled a wave of fury and nodded. "On the set." He caught the hair at her waist, then let it slide through his hands. "And off?"

"And off, nothing." She'd put more emphasis on the last word than she had intended to. It showed a weakness she could only hope he didn't notice.

"No." Parks stepped closer so that she had to tilt back her head to keep her eyes level with his. "I don't think I like those rules. Let's try mine."

Brooke was ready this time for the sneak attack on her senses. He wouldn't be permitted to seduce her, make her tremble with those feather-light teasing kisses on her skin. With a cool, hard stare, she dared him to try.

He returned the look as seconds dragged on. She caught the glint of challenge in his eyes but didn't see the slow curve of his lips. No man had ever been able to meet her stare so directly or for so long. For the first time in years, Brooke felt a weakness in her primary defense.

Then he did what he had wanted to do from the first moment he had seen her. Parks dove his hands into the lushness of her hair, letting them sink into the softness before he dragged her against him. Their eyes clashed a moment longer, even as he lowered his lips and savaged hers.

Brooke's vision blurred. She struggled to bring it back into sharp focus, to concentrate on that one sense to prevent her others from being overpowered. She fought not to taste the hot, demanding flavor of his lips, to feel the quick, almost brutal nip of his teeth that would tempt her lips to part. She didn't want to hear her own helpless moan. Then his tongue was plundering, enticing hers to answer in a seduction totally different from the teasing gentleness of his first embrace. She struggled against him, but her movements only caused more heat to flare from the friction of her body on his.

Gradually, the kiss altered. The hard pressure became sweet. He nibbled at her mouth, as if savoring the flavor, sucking gently, though his arms kept her pinned tight. She lost even her blurred vision, and her will to resist went with it.

Parks felt the change, her sudden pliancy. Her surrender excited him. She wasn't a woman to relinquish control easily, yet both times he had held her, he'd prized it from her. With gentleness, he realized, suddenly aware that the anger had fled from his body and his mouth. It was gentleness that won her, whereas force would only be met with force. Now he didn't want to think—not for a moment. He wanted only to lose himself in the soft give of her body, the white-silk scent that poured from her and the dusky flavor of her mouth. They were all the seduction of woman, only intensified by her surrender.

Brooke felt the liquid weight in her limbs, the slow insistent tug in her thighs before the muscles went lax. Her mouth clung to his, yearning for more of the magic it could bring with the gentle play of tongue and teeth. His hands began a slow exploration of her body, kneading over the soft material. When she felt him loosen the narrow zipper that ran from her throat to her waist, she roused herself to protest.

''No.'' The words came on a gasp of breath as his fingers slid along her skin.

Parks gathered her hair in one hand, drawing her head back so that his eyes met hers again. ''I have to touch you.'' Watching her, he glided his fingers over her breast, pausing briefly on the taut point before he roamed down to her flat, quivering stomach. ''One day I'll touch all of you,'' he murmured. ''Inch by inch. I'm going to feel your skin heat under my hands.'' His fingers trailed back to her breast, leaving a path of awakened flesh in their wake. ''I'm going to watch your face when I make love to you.''

Bending, he touched his lips to hers again, tasting her breath as it shuddered into his mouth. Very slowly, he drew up the zipper, letting his knuckles graze along her skin. Then he ran his hands up her back until their bodies fit together again.

''Kiss me, Brooke.'' He rubbed his nose lightly against hers. ''Really kiss me.''

Tingling from his touch, aroused by the whispered words, she pressed her open mouth to his. Her tongue sought his, hungry for the moist dark tastes that had already seeped inside of her. He waited for her demands, her aggressions, feeling them build as her body strained against his. With a groan of pleasure, Brooke tangled her fingers in his hair, wanting to drag him closer. When he knew his chain of control was on its last link, Parks drew her away. He'd learned more of her, but not enough. Not yet. And he wasn't going to forget that he had a small score to settle with her.

"When the camera's rolling, it's your game and your rules." He cupped her chin in his hand, wondering how many times he'd be able to walk away from her when his body was aching to have her. "When it's not," he continued quietly, "the rules are mine."

Brooke took a shaky breath. "I don't play games."

Parks smiled, running a fingertip over her swollen mouth. "Everyone does," he corrected. "Some make a career out of it, and they aren't all on ball fields." Dropping his hand, he stepped back from her. "We both have a job to do. Maybe we're not too thrilled about it at the moment, but I have a feeling that won't make any difference in how well you work."

"No," Brooke agreed shortly. "It won't. I can detest you and still make you look fantastic on the screen."

He grinned. "Or make me look like an idiot if it suited you."

She couldn't prevent a small smile from forming. "You're very perceptive."

"But you won't, because you're a pro. Whatever happens between us personally won't make you direct any differently."

"I'll do my job," Brooke stated as she stepped around him. "And nothing's going to happen between us personally." She looked up sharply when a friendly arm was dropped over her shoulder.

"I guess we'll just wait and see about that." Parks sent her another amiable grin. "Have you eaten?"

Brooke frowned at him dubiously. "No."

He gave her shoulder a fraternal pat. "I'll get you a plate."

Chapter 4

Brooke couldn't believe she was spending a perfectly beautiful Sunday afternoon at a ball game. What was more peculiar was that she was enjoying it. She was well aware that she was being punished for the few veiled sarcastic remarks she had tossed off at the de Marco party, but after the first few innings, she found that Billings was right. There was a bit more to it than swinging a bat and running around in circles.

During her first game, Brooke had been too caught up in the atmosphere, the people, then in her initial impressions of Parks. Now she opened her mind to the game itself and enjoyed. Being a survivor, whenever she was faced with doing something she didn't want to do, Brooke simply conditioned herself to *want* to do it. She had no patience with people who allowed themselves to be miserable when it was so simple to turn a situation around to your advantage. If it wasn't always possible to enjoy, she could learn. It pleased her to be doing both.

The game had more subtlety than she had first realized, and more strategy. Brooke never ceased to be intrigued by strategy. It became obvious that there were variables to the contest, dozens of ifs, slices of chance counterbalancing skill. In a game of inches, luck couldn't be overlooked. This had an appeal for her because she had always considered luck every bit as vital as talent in winning, no matter what the game.

And there were certain aspects of the afternoon, beyond the balls and strikes, that fanned her interest.

The crowd was no less enthusiastic or vocal than it had been on her first visit to Kings Stadium. If anything, Brooke reflected, the people were more enthusiastic—even slightly wild. She wondered if their chants and screams and whistles took on a tone of delirium because the score was tied 1-1, and had been since the first inning. Lee called it an example of a superior defensive game.

Lee Dutton was another aspect of the afternoon that intrigued her. He seemed—on the surface—a genial, rather unkempt sort of man with a faint Brooklyn accent that lingered from his youth. He wore a golf shirt and checked pants, which only accented his tubbiness. Brooke might have passed him off as a cute middle-aged man had it not been for the sharp black eyes. She liked him…with a minor reservation—he seemed inordinately attentive to Claire.

It occurred to Brooke that he found a great many

occasions to touch—Claire's soft manicured hands, her round shoulder, even her gabardine-clad knee. What was more intriguing to Brooke was that Claire didn't, as was her habit, freeze Lee's tentative advances with an icy smile or a stingingly polite word. As far as Brooke could tell, Claire seemed to be enjoying them—or perhaps she was overlooking them because of the importance of the de Marco account and Parks Jones. In either case, Brooke determined to keep an eye on her friend, and the agent. It wasn't unheard-of for a woman approaching fifty to be naive of men and therefore susceptible.

If she were to be truthful, Brooke would have to admit she enjoyed watching Parks. There was no doubt he was in his element in the field, eyes shaded by a cap, glove in his hand. Just as he had been in his element, she remembered, at the glossy party at the de Marco villa. He hadn't seemed out of place in the midst of ostentatious wealth, sipping vintage champagne or handling cocktail party conversation. And why should he? she mused. After their last encounter, Brooke had made it her business to find out more about him.

He'd come from money. Big money. Parkinson Chemicals was a third-generation, multimillion-dollar conglomerate that dealt in everything from aspirin to rocket fuel. He'd been born with a silver spoon in one hand and a fat portfolio in the other. His two sisters had married well, one to a restauranteur who had been her business partner before he became her husband, the other to a vice president of Parkinson attached to the Dallas branch. But the heir to Parkinson, the man who carried the old family name in front of the less unique Jones, had had a love affair with baseball.

The love affair hadn't diminished during his studies at Oxford under a Rhodes scholarship; it had simply been postponed. When Parks had graduated, he'd gone straight to the Kings' training camp—Brooke had to wonder how his family had felt about that—and there had been drafted. After less than a year on the Kings' farm team, he'd been brought up to the majors. There he had remained, for a decade.

So he didn't play for the money, Brooke mused, but because he enjoyed the game. Perhaps that was why he played with such style and steadiness.

She remembered, too, her impressions of him at the de Marcos'—charming, then ruthless, then casually friendly. And none of it, Brooke concluded, was an act. Above all else, Parks Jones was in complete control, on or off the diamond. Brooke respected that, related to it, while she couldn't help wondering how the two of them would juggle their need to be in charge when they began to work together. If nothing else, she mused as she crunched down on a piece of ice, it would be an interesting association.

Brooke watched him now as he stood on the bag at second while the opposing team brought out a relief pitcher. Parks had started off the seventh inning with a leadoff single, then had advanced to second when the next batter walked. Brooke could feel the adrenaline of the crowd pulsing while Parks talked idly with the second baseman.

"If they take this one," Lee was saying, "the Kings lock up the division." He slipped his hand over Claire's. "We need these runs."

"Why did they change pitchers?" Brooke demanded. She thought of how furious she would be if someone pulled her off a job before it was finished.

"There's two on and nobody out." Lee gave her an easy paternal smile. "Mitchell was slowing down—he'd walked two last inning and was only saved from having runs score by that rifle shot the center fielder sent home." Reaching in his shirt pocket, he brought out a cigar in a thin protective tube. "I think you'll see the Kings going to the bullpen in the eighth."

"I wouldn't switch cameramen in the middle of a shoot," Brooke mumbled.

"You would if he couldn't focus the lens anymore," Lee countered, grinning at her.

With a laugh, Brooke dove her hand into the bag of peanuts he offered her. "Yeah, I guess I would."

The strategy proved successful, as the relief man shut down the next three batters, leaving Parks and his teammate stranded on base. The crowds groaned, swore at the umpire and berated the batters.

"Now there's sportsmanship," Brooke observed, casting a look over her shoulder when someone called the batter, who struck out to end the inning, a bum—and other less kind names.

Lee gave a snort of laughter as he draped his arm casually over Claire's shoulders. "You should hear them when we're losing, kid."

The lifted-brow look Brooke gave Claire at the gesture was returned blandly. ''Enthusiasm comes in all forms,'' Claire observed. With a smile for Lee, she settled back against his arm to watch the top of the next inning.

Definitely an odd couple, Brooke mused; then she assumed her habitual position of elbows on rail. Parks didn't glance her way. He had only once—at the beginning of the game when he took the field. The look had been long and direct before he had turned away, and since then it was as though he wasn't even aware of her. She hated to admit it irked her, hated to admit that she would have liked to engage in that silent battle of eye to eye. He was the first man she *wanted* to spar with, though she had sparred with many since her first naive encounter ten years before. There was something exciting in the mind game, particularly since Parks had a mind she both envied and admired.

Lee was on target, as the Kings went to the bullpen when the starting pitcher walked two with one man out. Brooke shifted closer to the edge of her seat to watch Parks during the transition. What does he think about out there? she wondered.

God, what I wouldn't give for a cold shower and a gallon of beer, Parks thought as the sun beat down on the back of his neck. He'd been expecting the change of pitchers and was pleased with the choice. Ripley did well what a reliever was there to do—throw hard and fast. He gave a seemingly idle glance toward the runner at second. That could be trouble, he reflected, doing a quick mental recall of his opponent's statistics. The ability to retain and call out facts had always come naturally to Parks. And not just batting averages and stolen bases. Basically, he only forgot what he wanted to forget. The rest was stockpiled, waiting until he needed it. The trick had alternately fascinated and infuriated his family and friends, so that he generally kept it to himself. At the moment, he could remember Ripley's earned-run average, his win-loss ratio, the batting average of the man waiting to step into the batter's box and the scent of Brooke's perfume.

He hadn't forgotten that she was sitting a few yards away. The awareness of her kindled inside of him—a not quite pleasant sensation. It was more of an insistent pressure, like the heat of the sun on the back of his neck. It was another reason he longed for a cool shower. Watching Ripley throw his warm-up pitches to the catcher, Parks allowed himself to imagine what it would be like to undress her—slowly—in the daylight, just before her body went from limp surrender to throbbing excitement. Soon, he promised himself; then he forced Brooke to the back of his mind as the batter stepped up to the plate.

Ripley blew the first one by the batter—hard and straight. Parks knew that Ripley didn't throw any fancy pitches, just the fast ball and the curve. He was either going to overpower the hitters, or with the lineup of right-handers coming up, Parks was going to be very busy. He positioned himself another step back on the grass, going by instinct. He noted the base runner had a fat lead as the batter chipped the next pitch off. The runner was nearly at third before the foul was called. Ripley looked back over his shoulder at second, slid his eyes to first, then fired the next pitch.

It was hit hard, smashing into the dirt in front of third then bouncing high. There was never any opportunity to think, only to act. Parks leaped, just managing to snag the ball. The runner was coming into third in a headfirst slide. Parks didn't have the time to admire his guts before he tagged the base seconds before the runner's hand grabbed it. He heard the third base ump bellow, "Out!" as he vaulted over the runner and fired the ball at the first baseman.

While the crowd went into a frenzy, Brooke remained seated and watched. She didn't even notice that Lee had given Claire a resounding, exuberant kiss. The double play had taken only seconds—that impressed her. It also disconcerted her to discover that her pulse was racing. If she closed her eyes, she could still hear the cheers from the fans, smell the scent of sun-warmed beer and see, in slow motion, the strong, sweeping moves of Parks's body. She didn't need an instant replay to visualize the leap and stretch, the shifting of muscle. She knew a ball player had to be agile and quick, but how many of them had that dancerlike grace? Brooke caught herself making a mental note to bring a camera to the next game, then realized she had already decided to come back again. Was it Parks, she brooded, or baseball that was luring her back?

''He's something, isn't he?'' Lee leaned over Claire to give Brooke a slap on the back.

''Something,'' Brooke murmured. She turned her head enough to look at him. ''Was that a routine play?''

Lee snorted. ''If you've got ice water for blood.''

''Does he?''

As he drew on a cigar, Lee seemed to consider it. He gave Brooke a long, steady look. ''On the field,'' he stated with a nod. ''Parks is one of the most controlled, disciplined men I know. Of course''—the look broke with his quick smile—''I handle a lot of actors.''

''Bless them,'' Claire said and crossed her short, slim legs. ''I believe we all agree that we hope Parks takes to this, ah, alternate career with as much energy as he shows in his baseball.''

''If he has ten percent of this skill''—Brooke gestured toward the field—''in front of the camera, I'll be able to work with him.''

''I think you'll be surprised,'' Lee commented dryly, ''at just what Parks is capable of.''

With a shrug, Brooke leaned on the rail again. ''We'll see if he can take direction.''

Brooke waited, with the tension of the crowd seeping into her, as the game went into the bottom of the ninth inning. Still tied 1-1, neither team seemed able to break through the defensive skill of the other. It should have been boring, she mused, even tedious. But she was on the edge of her seat and her pulse was still humming. She wanted them to win. With a kind of guilty surprise, Brooke caught herself just before she shouted at the plate umpire for calling strike three on the leadoff batter. It's just the atmosphere, she told herself with a frown. She'd always been a sucker for atmosphere. But when the second batter came up, she found herself gripping the rail, willing him to get a hit.

"This might go into extra innings," Lee commented.

"There's only one out," Brooke snapped, not bothering to turn around. She didn't see the quick grin Lee cast at Claire.

On a three-and-two pitch, the batter hit a bloop single to center. Around Brooke, the fans went berserk. He might have hit a home run from the way they're reacting, she thought, trying to ignore the fast pumping of her own blood. This time Brooke said nothing as the pitcher was pulled. How do they stand the tension? she wondered, watching the apparently relaxed players as the new relief warmed up. Base runners talked idly with the opposition. She thought that if she were in competition, she wouldn't be so friendly with the enemy.

The crowd settled down to a hum that became a communal shout with every pitch thrown. The batter hit one deep, so deep Brooke was amazed at the speed with which the right fielder returned it to the infield.

The batter was content with a single, but the base runner had eaten up the distance to third with the kind of gritty speed Brooke admired.

Now the crowd didn't quiet, but kept up a continual

howl that echoed and reverberated as Parks came to bat. The pressure, Brooke thought, must be almost unbearable. Yet nothing showed in his face but that dangerous kind of concentration she'd seen once or twice before. She swallowed, aware that her heart was hammering in her throat. Ridiculous, she told herself once, then surrendered.

"Come on, damn it," she muttered, "smack one out of here."

He took the first pitch, a slow curve that just missed the corner. The breath that she'd been holding trembled out. The next he cut at, fouling it back hard against the window of the press box. Brooke clamped down on her bottom lip and mentally uttered a stream of curses. Parks coolly held up a hand for time, then bent to tie his shoe. The stadium echoed with his name. As if deaf to the yells, he stepped back into the box to take up his stance.

He hit it high and deep. Brooke was certain it was a repeat of his performance in her first game, then she saw the ball begin to drop just short of the fence.

"He's going to tag up. He'll tag up!" she heard Lee shouting as the center fielder caught Parks's fly at the warning track. Before Brooke could swear, the fans were shouting, not in fury but in delight. The moment the runner crossed the plate, players from the Kings' dugout swarmed out on the field.

"But Parks is out," Brooke said indignantly.

"The sacrifice fly scored the run," Lee explained.

Brooke gave him a haughty look. "I realize that"—only because she had crammed a few basic rules into her head—"but it hardly seems fair that Parks is out."

Chuckling, Lee patted her head. "He earned another RBI and the fleeting gratitude of a stadium full of Kings fans. He was one for three today, so his average won't suffer much."

"Brooke doesn't think much of rules," Claire put in, rising.

"Because they're usually made up by people who don't have the least idea what they're doing." A little annoyed with herself for becoming so involved, she stood, swinging her canvas bag over her shoulder.

"I don't know if Parks would agree with you," Lee told her. "He's lived by the rules for most of his life. Gets to be a habit."

"To each his own," she said casually. She wondered if Lee was aware that Parks was also a man who could seduce and half undress a woman behind the fragile covering of a rock wall in the middle of a crowded, glitzy Hollywood party. It seemed to her Parks was more a man who made up his own rules.

"Why don't we go down to the locker room and congratulate him?" Genially, he hooked his arms through Claire's and Brooke's, steamrolling them through the still cheering crowd.

Lee worked his way into the stadium's inner sanctum with a combination of panache and clout. Reporters were swarming, carrying microphones, cameras or notepads. Each one was badgering or flattering a sweaty athlete in the attempt to get a quote. In the closed-in area, Brooke considered the noise level to be every bit as high as it had been in the open stadium. Lockers slammed, shouts reverberated, laughter flowed in a kind of giddy relief. Each man knew the tension would return soon enough during the playoffs. They were going to enjoy the victory of the moment to its fullest.

"Yeah, if I hadn't saved Biggs from an error in the seventh inning," the first baseman told a reporter, deadpan, "it might have been a whole different ball game."

Biggs, the shortstop, retaliated by heaving a damp towel at his teammate. "Snyder can't catch a ball unless it drops into his mitt. The rest of us make him look good."

"I've saved Parks from fifty-three errors this season," Snyder went on blandly, drawing the sweaty towel from his face. "Guess his arm must be going. Thing is, some of the hitters are so good they just keep smacking the ball right into Parks's mitt. If you watch the replay of today's game, you'll see what fantastic aim they have." Someone dumped a bucket of water on his head, but Snyder continued without breaking rhythm. "You might notice how well I place the ball in the right fielder's mitt. That takes more practice."

Brooke spotted Parks, surrounded by reporters. His uniform was filthy, streaked with dirt, while his face fared little better. The smudges of black under his eyes gave him a slightly wicked look. Without the cap his hair curled freely, darkened with sweat. But his face and body were relaxed. A smile lingered on his lips as he spoke. That battlefield intensity was gone from his eyes, she noted, as if it had never existed. If she hadn't seen it, hadn't experienced it from him, Brooke would have sworn the man wasn't capable of any form of ruthlessness. Yet he was, she reminded herself, and it wouldn't be smart to forget it.

"With only four games left in the regular season," Parks stated, "I'll be satisfied to end up with a three eighty-seven average for the year."

"If you bat five hundred in those last games—"

Parks shot the reporter a mild grin. "We'll have to see about that."

"A little wind out there today and that game-winning sacrifice fly would've been a game-winning home run."

"That's the breaks."

"What was the pitch?"

"Inside curve," he responded easily. "A little high."

"Were you trying for a four-bagger, Parks?"

He grinned again, his expression altering only slightly when he spotted Brooke. "With one out and runners on the corners, I just wanted to keep the ball off the ground. Anything deep, and Kinjinsky scores…unless he wants the Lead Foot Award."

"Lead Foot Award?"

"Ask Snyder," Parks suggested. "He's the current holder." With another smile, Parks effectively eased himself away. "Lee." He nodded to his agent while running a casual finger down Brooke's arm. She felt the shock waves race through her, and only barely managed not to jerk away. "Ms. Thorton. Nice to see you again." His only greeting to Brooke was a slow smile as he caught the tip of her hair between his thumb and forefinger. She thought again it was wise to remember he wasn't as safe as he appeared.

"Hell of a game, Parks," Lee announced. "You gave us an entertaining afternoon."

"We aim to please," he murmured, still looking at Brooke.

"Claire and I are going out to dinner. Perhaps you and Brooke would like to join us?"

Before Brooke could register surprise at Claire having a date with Lee Dutton, or formulate an excuse against making it a foursome, Parks spoke up. "Sorry, Brooke and I have plans."

Turning her head, she shot Parks a narrowed look. "I don't recall our making any plans."

Smiling, he gave her a brief tug. "You'll have to learn to write things down. Why don't you just wait in your box? I'll be out in half an hour." Without giving her a chance to protest, Parks strolled off toward the showers.

"What incredible nerve," Brooke grumbled, only to be given a sharp but discreet elbow in the ribs by Claire.

"Sorry you can't join us, dear," she said sweetly. "But then you're not fond of Chinese food in any case. And Lee's going to show me his collection first."

"Collection?" Brooke repeated blankly as she was steered into the narrow corridor.

"We've a mutual passion." Claire gave Lee a quick and surprisingly flirtatious smile. "For Oriental art. Can you find your way back to the seats?"

"I'm not a complete dolt," Brooke muttered, while giving Lee a skeptical stare.

"Well then." Casually, Claire tucked her hand into Lee's beefy arm. "I'll see you Monday."

"Have a good time, kid," Lee called over his shoulder as Claire propelled him away.

"Thanks a lot." Stuffing her hands in her pockets, Brooke worked her way up, then out to the lower level, third-base box. "Thanks a hell of a lot," she repeated and stared out at the empty diamond.

There were a few maintenance workers scooping up the debris in the stands with humming heavy-duty cleaners, but other than that the huge open area was deserted. Finding it strangely appealing, Brooke discovered her annoyance waning. An hour before, the air had been alive, throbbing with the pulse of thousands. Now it was serene, with only the faintest trace of the crowd—the lingering odor of humanity, a whiff of salted popcorn, a few discarded cardboard containers. She leaned back against the rail, more interested in the empty stadium than the empty field.

When had it been built? she wondered. How many generations had crammed themselves into the seats and aisles to watch the games? How many thousands of gallons of beer had traveled along the rows of seats? She laughed a little, amused by her own whimsy. When a player stopped playing, did he come here to watch and remember? She thought Parks would. The game, she concluded, would get into your blood. Even she hadn't been immune to it…or, she thought wryly, to him.

Brooke tossed her head back, letting her hair fall behind her. The shadows were lengthening, but the heat still had the sticky, sweltering capacity of high afternoon. She didn't mind—she hated being cold. Habitually, she narrowed her eyes and let herself visualize how she would approach the stadium on film. Empty, she thought, with the echo of cheers, the sound of a ball cracking off a bat, a banner left behind to flutter in the breeze. She'd use the maintenance workers, sucking up the boxes and cups and bags. She might title it *Afterthought,* and there'd be no telling if the home team had left the field vanquished or victorious. What mattered would be the perpetuity of the game, the people who played it and the people who watched.

Brooke sensed him before she heard him—only an instant, but the instant was enough to scatter her thoughts and to bring her eyes swerving toward him. Immediately, all sense of the scene she had been setting vanished from her mind. No one else had ever had the power to do that to her. The fact that Parks did baffled her nearly as much as it infuriated her. For Brooke, her work was the one stability in her life—nothing and no one was allowed to tamper with it. Defensively, she straightened, meeting his stare head-on as he walked down to her in the loose, rangy stride that masked over a decade of training.

She expected him to greet her with some smart remark. Brooke was prepared for that. She considered he might greet her casually, as if his lie in the locker room had been perfect truth. She was prepared for that, too.

She wasn't prepared for him to walk directly to her, bury his hands in her hair and crush her against him in a long, hotly possessive kiss. Searing flashes of pleasure rocketed through her. Molten waves of desire overpowered surprise before it truly had time to register. His mouth pressed against hers in an absolute command that barely hid a trace of desperation. It was that desperation, more than the authority, that Brooke found herself responding to. The need to be needed was strong in her—she had always considered it her greatest weakness. And she was weak now, with the sharp scent of his skin in her senses, the dark taste of his mouth on her tongue, the feel of his shower-damp hair on her fingers.

Slowly, Parks drew away, waiting for her heavy lids to lift. Though his eyes never left hers, Brooke felt as though he looked at all of her once, thoroughly. "I want you." He said it calmly, though the fierce look was back on his face.

"I know."

Parks ran a hand through her hair again, from the crown to the tips. "I'm going to have you."

Steadying a bit, Brooke stepped out of his arms. "That I don't know."

Smiling, Parks continued to caress her hair. "Don't you?"

"No," Brooke returned with such firmness that Parks lifted a brow.

"Well," he considered, "I suppose it could be a very pleasant experience to convince you."

Brooke tossed her head to free her hair of his seeking fingers. "Why did you lie to Lee about our having plans tonight?"

"Because I'd spent nine long, hot innings thinking about making love to you."

Again he said it calmly, with just a hint of a smile on his lips, but Brooke realized he was quite serious. "Well, that's direct and to the point."

"You prefer things that way, don't you?"

"Yes," she agreed, settling back against the rail again. "So let me do the same for you. We're going to be working together for several months on a very big project that involves a number of people. I'm very good at my job and I intend to see that you're very good at yours."

"So?"

Her eyes flashed at his amused tone, but Brooke continued. "So personal involvements interfere with professional judgment. As your director, I have no intention of becoming your lover, however briefly."

"Briefly?" Parks repeated, studying her. "Do you always anticipate the length of your relationships beforehand? I think," he continued slowly, "you're more of a romantic than that."

"I don't care what you think," she snapped, "as long as you understand."

"I understand," Parks agreed, beginning to. "You're evading the issue."

"I certainly am not!" Temper flared, reflecting in her stance and her eyes as well as her voice. "I'm telling you straight out that I'm not interested. If that bruises your ego, too bad."

Parks grabbed her arm when she would have swept by him. "You know," he began in a careful tone that warned of simmering anger, "you infuriate me. I can't remember the last time a woman affected me that way."

"I'm not surprised." Brooke jerked her arm out of his hold. "You've been too busy devastating them with your charm."

"And you're too worried about being dumped to have any kind of a relationship."

She made a quick, involuntary sound, as if she'd been struck. Cheeks pale, eyes dark, she stared at him before she shoved him aside to race up the stairs. Parks caught her before she'd made it halfway. Though he turned her back to face him firmly, his touch was gentle.

"Raw nerve?" he murmured, feeling both sympathy and guilt. It wasn't often he lost control enough to say something he'd have to apologize for. Eyes dry and hurting, Brooke glared at him. "I'm sorry."

"Just let me go."

"Brooke." He wanted to pull her into his arms and comfort, but knew she wouldn't accept it. "I am sorry. I don't make a habit of punching women."

It wasn't charm, but sincerity. After a moment,

Brooke let out a long breath. ''All right. I usually take a punch better than that.''

''Can we take off the gloves—at least for the rest of the day?'' How deep was the hurt? Parks wondered. And how long would it take to win her trust?

''Maybe,'' Brooke returned cautiously.

''How about dinner?''

She responded to the smile before she realized it. ''My weakness.''

''We'll start there, then. How do you feel about tacos?''

She allowed him to take her hand. ''Who's buying?''

They sat outdoors at a busy fast-food franchise with tiny metal tables and hard stools. Sounds of traffic and blaring car radios rolled over them. Brooke relaxed when she ate, Parks noted, wondering if she were consciously aware of the dropping of guards. He didn't think so. The relaxation was the same when she sat in an elegant restaurant with wine and exotic food as it was in a greasy little take-out with sloppy tacos and watered-down sodas in paper cups. After handing her another napkin, Parks decided to do some casual probing.

''Did you grow up in California?''

''No.'' Brooke drew more soda through her straw. ''You did.''

''More or less.'' Remembering how skilled she was in evading or changing the subject, Parks persisted. ''Why did you move to L.A.?''

"It's warm," she said immediately. "It's crowded."

"But you live miles out of town in the middle of nowhere."

"I like my privacy. How did your family feel about you choosing baseball over Parkinson Chemicals?"

He smiled a little, enjoying the battle for control. "Stunned. Though I'd told them for years what I intended to do. My father thought, still thinks, it's a phase. What does your family think about you directing commercials?"

Brooke set down her cup. "I don't have any family."

Something in her tone warned him this was a tender area. "Where did you grow up?"

"Here and there." Quickly, she began to stuff used napkins into the empty cups. Parks caught her hand before she could rise.

"Foster homes?"

Eyes darkening with anger, Brooke stared at him. "Why are you pressing?"

"Because I want to know who you are," he said softly. "We could be friends before we're lovers."

"Let go of my hand."

Instead of obliging, Parks gave her a curious look. "Do I make you nervous?"

"You make me furious," she tossed back, evading one truth with another. "I can't be around you for more than ten minutes without getting mad."

Parks grinned. "I know the feeling. Still, it's stimulating."

"I don't want to be stimulated," Brooke said evenly. "I want to be comfortable."

With a half laugh, Parks turned her hand over, brushing his lips lightly over the palm. "I don't think so," he murmured, watching her reaction over their joined hands. "You're much too alive to settle for comfortable."

"You don't know me."

"Exactly my point." He leaned a bit closer. "Who are you?"

"What I've made myself."

Parks nodded. "I see a strong, independent woman with lots of drive and ambition. I also see a woman who chooses a quiet, isolated spot for her home, who knows how to laugh and mean it, who forgives just as quickly as she angers." As he spoke Parks watched her brows lower. She wasn't angry now, but thoughtful and wary. He felt a bit like a man trying to gain the confidence of a dove who might fly away at any time or choose to nestle in the palm of his hand. "She interests me."

After a moment, Brooke let out a long breath. Perhaps if she told him a little, she considered, he'd leave it at that. "My mother wasn't married," she began briskly. "I'm told that after six months she got tired of lugging a baby around and dumped me on her sister. I don't remember a great deal about my aunt, I was six when she turned me over to social services. What I do remember is being hungry and not very warm. I went into my first foster home." She shrugged then pushed away the debris that littered the table. "It wasn't too bad. I was there for little more than a year before I got shuffled to the next one. I was in five altogether from the age of six to seventeen. Some were better than others, but I never belonged. A lot of that may have been my fault."

Brooke sighed, not pleased to remember. "Not all foster parents take in children for the money. Some of them—most of them," she amended, "are very kind, loving people. I just never felt a part, because I always knew it would be temporary, that my sister or brother of the moment was real and I was…transient. As a result I was difficult. Maybe I challenged the people whose home I was placed in to want me—for me, not out of pity or social obligation or the extra dollars my living with them would bring in.

"My last two years in high school I lived on a farm in Ohio with a nice couple who had an angelic son who would yank my hair when his mother's back was turned." A quick grimace. "I left as soon as I graduated from high school, worked my way cross-country waiting tables. It only took me four months to get to L.A." She met Parks's quiet, steady look and suddenly flared. "Don't feel sorry for me."

The ultimate insult, he mused, taking her rigid hand in his. "I wasn't. I was wondering how many people would have had the guts to try to make their own life at seventeen, and how many would have the strength to really do it. At the same age I wanted to head for the Florida training camps. Instead I was on a plane heading for college."

"Because you had an obligation," Brooke countered. ''I didn't. If I had had the chance to go to college...'' She trailed off. ''In any case, we've both had a decade in our careers.''

''And you can have several more if you like,'' Parks pointed out. ''I can't. One more season.''

''Why?'' she demanded. ''You'll only be...''

''Thirty-five,'' he finished with a wry smile. ''I promised myself ten years ago that's when I'd stop. There aren't many of us who can play past forty like Mays.''

''Yes, it's obvious you play like an old man,'' she returned dryly.

''I intend to stop before I do.''

Taking a straw, she began to pleat it while she studied him. ''Quit while you're ahead?''

''That's the idea.''

That she could understand. ''Does giving it up with half your life ahead of you bother you?''

''I intend to do something with the second half, but at times it does. Other times I think about all those summer evenings I'll have free. Do you like the beach?''

''I don't get there often, but yes.'' She thought about the long, hot commercial she'd just filmed. ''With occasional exceptions,'' she added.

''I have a place on Maui.'' Unexpectedly he leaned over, caressing her cheek with fingers that were whisper soft and undeniably possessive. ''I'm going to take you there one day.'' He shook his head as Brooke started to speak. ''Don't argue, we do that too much. Let's go for a drive.''

"Parks," Brooke began as they rose, "I meant what I said about not getting involved."

"Yeah, I know." Then he kissed her long and lingeringly while she stood with her hands filled with paper plates and cups.

Chapter 5

It was three days before Brooke heard from Parks. She was aware that the last four-game series in the regular season would be played out of town. She knew, too, from what she told herself was simply a casual glimpse at the sports section, that Parks had knocked in three more RBIs in the first two games. In the meantime, she was busy looking over the story board for his first block of commercials.

The word had come down that the first thirty-second spot would be filmed before the league playoffs, in order to capitalize on Parks's exposure in the competition. That left Brooke little time to prepare, with an already demanding schedule of studio and location shoots, editing and preproduction meetings. But challenge, like food, was vital to her.

Closed off in her office, with a half an hour's leeway before she was due at the studio, Brooke ran over the final script for the initial de Marco commercial. Casually slick, she thought, approving. It had minimal dialogue and soft sell—Parks at the plate, swinging away while dressed in de Marco's elegant sports clothes, then a slow dissolve to the next scene with him dressed in the same suit, stepping out of a Rolls with a slinky brunette on his arm.

"Clothes for anytime—anywhere," Brooke muttered. The timing had been checked and rechecked. The audio, except for Parks's one-line voice-over, was already being recorded. All she had to do was to guide Parks through the paces. The salesmanship hinged on her skill and his charm. Fair enough, she thought and reached for her half cup of cold coffee as a knock sounded at her door. "Yeah?" Brooke turned the script back to page one, running through the camera angles.

"Delivery for you, Brooke." The receptionist dropped a long white florist's box on her cluttered desk. "Jenkins said to let you know the Lardner job's been edited. You might want to check it out."

"Okay, thanks." Curiously, Brooke frowned over the top of the script at the flower box. Occasionally, she received a grateful phone call or letter from a client when they were particularly pleased with a commercial—but not flowers. Then there'd been that actor in the car spot last year, Brooke remembered. The one who was on his third wife. He'd alternately amused and annoyed Brooke by sending her batches of red roses every week. But six months had passed since she had convinced him that he was wasting her time and his money.

More likely it was one of E.J.'s practical jokes, she considered. She'd probably find a few dozen frog legs inside. Not one to spoil someone's fun, Brooke pulled off the ribbon and lifted the lid.

There were masses of hibiscus. Fragrant, dew-soft pink-and-white petals filled the box almost to overflowing. After the first gasp of surprise, Brooke dove her hands into them, captivated by their purely feminine scent and feel. Her office suddenly smelled like a tropical island: heady, exotic, richly romantic. With a sound of pleasure, she filled her hands with the blooms, bringing them up to her face to inhale. In contrast to the sultry scent, the petals seemed impossibly fragile. A small white card fluttered down to her littered desk.

Letting the flowers drift back into the box, Brooke reached for the envelope and tore it open.

I thought of your skin.

There was nothing else, but she knew. She shuddered, then chided herself for acting like a mooning teenager. But she read the line three times. No one had ever been able to affect her so deeply with such simplicity. Though Parks was a thousand miles away, she could all but feel those lean, strong fingers trace down her cheek. The flood of warmth, the flash of desire told her she wasn't going to escape him—had never truly wanted to. Without giving herself any time for doubts or fears, Brooke picked up the phone.

"Get me Parks Jones," she said quickly. "Try Lee Dutton, he'll have the number." Before she could change her mind, Brooke hung up, burying her hands in the flowers again.

How was it he knew just what buttons to push? she wondered, then discovered at that moment she didn't care. It was enough to be romanced—and romanced in style. Lifting a single bloom, she trailed it down her cheek. It was smooth and moist against her skin—as Parks's first kiss had been. The ringing phone caught her dreaming.

"Yes?"

"Parks Jones on line two. You've got ten minutes before they need you in the studio."

"All right. Hunt me up a vase and some water, will you?" She glanced at the box again. "Make that two vases." Still standing with the blossom in her hand, Brooke punched the button for line two. "Parks?"

"Yes. Hello, Brooke."

"Thank you."

"You're welcome."

She hesitated, then let herself speak her first thought. "I feel like a teenager who just got her first corsage."

Dropping flat on his back on the bed, he laughed. "I'd like to see you with some of them in your hair."

Experimentally she held one up over her ear. Unprofessional, she thought with a sigh, and contented herself with the scent of them. "I've a shoot in the studio in a few minutes; I don't think the lights would do them much good.''

''You have your practical side, don't you, Brooke?'' Parks flexed the slight ache in his shoulder and closed his eyes.

''It's necessary,'' she muttered but couldn't quite bring herself to drop the blossom back in the box. ''How are you? I wasn't sure you'd be in.''

''I got in about half an hour ago. They cut us down five to two. I went oh for three.''

''Oh.'' She frowned, not quite sure what she was supposed to say. ''I'm sorry.''

''I didn't seem to have any rhythm—it'll pass.'' Before the play-offs, he added silently. ''I thought of you, maybe too much.''

Brooke felt an odd twist of pleasure that was difficult to pass off. ''I wouldn't want to be responsible for a slump, particularly when I remember some of the remedies.'' His chuckle sounded faint and weary. ''Are you tired?''

''A bit. You'd think with the division wrapped up we'd glide through this last series. Last night we went eleven innings.''

''I know.'' She could have bitten off her tongue. ''I caught the highlights on the late news,'' she said breezily. ''I'll let you sleep, then. I just wanted to thank you.''

Her inadvertent admission had his lips twitching, but he didn't bother to open his eyes. With them closed, he had no trouble bringing her face into focus. ''Will I see you when I get back?''

"Of course. We'll be shooting the first segment on Friday, so—"

"Brooke," he interrupted firmly, quietly. "Will I see you when I get back?"

She hesitated, then looked down at the mass of pink-and-white hibiscus on her desk. "Yes," she heard herself saying. Pressing the flower to her cheek, she sighed. "I think I'm going to make a very big mistake."

"Good. I'll see you Friday."

The trick to being a good director, Brooke had always thought, was to be precise without being too technical, brisk without losing sympathy, then to split yourself up into several small parts so that you could be everywhere at once. It was a knack she had developed early on—on the job—without the formalized training of many of her colleagues. Perhaps because she had worked so many of the other aspects of filming, from timing a script to setting the lights to mixing sound, she was fiercely precise. Nothing escaped her eye. Because she knew actors were often overworked and insecure, she had never quite lost her sympathy for them even when she was ready to rage at a consistently flubbed line. Her early experience at waiting tables had taught her the trick of moving fast enough to all but be two places at once.

On a set or in a studio, she had complete self-confidence. Her control was usually unquestioned because it came naturally. She never thought about being in charge or felt the need to remind others of it; she simply *was* in charge.

With a copy of the script in one hand, she supervised the final adjustments on the lights and reflectors. The ball diamond, she had noted immediately, had an entirely different feel at home plate than it had from the stands. It was like being on an island, cupped amid the high mountain of seats, with the tall green wall skirting the back. The distance from plate to fence seemed even more formidable from this perspective. Brooke wondered how men with sticks in their hands could continually hit a moving ball over that last obstacle.

She could smell the grass, freshly trimmed, the dusty scent of dirt that had dried in the sun and a whiff of E.J.'s blatantly macho cologne. "Give me a reading," she ordered the lighting director as she glanced up at the thick clouds in the sky. "I want a sunny afternoon."

"You got it." The lights were focused as Brooke stepped behind camera one to check for shadows on the plate.

Parks loitered at the tunnel entrance a moment, watching her. This was a different woman from the one who he had treated to tacos—different still from the one he had held in his arms at the de Marco party. Her hair was trained back in one long braid, nothing like the flowing, gypsylike mane he was used to seeing. She wore jeans that were white at the stress points, a plain T-shirt the color of scrambled eggs, dusty tennis shoes and winking sapphires at her ears.

But it wasn't her hairstyle or the apparel that denoted the difference. It was the assurance. He'd seen it before, but each time it had been underlying. Now she sparked with it, gesturing, ordering while men and women set about giving her exactly what she demanded. No one questioned her. And, he considered, it was patently obvious that she wouldn't have permitted it.

Grimacing, he tugged at the sleeve of the thin silk shirt he wore. Who the hell would play ball in an outfit like this? he wondered with a glance at the creaseless cream slacks. The rules of this game were hers, he reminded himself, then stepped into the light.

"Bigelow, get these cables secure before somebody breaks a leg. Libby, see if you can scrounge up some ice water, we're going to need it. Okay, where's..." Turning at that moment, Brooke spotted Parks. "Oh, there you are." If she felt any personal pleasure at seeing him, she hid it well, Parks thought wryly as she turned to shout an order at her assistant. "I'm going to want you to stand at the plate so we can check the lighting and camera angles."

Without a word, Parks complied. You might as well get used to it, he told himself. You've got yourself locked into hawking somebody else's clothes for the next two years. He stuffed his hands in his pockets, cursed Lee briefly and stood in the batter's box. Someone stuck a light meter next to his face.

"You gonna wipe out the Valiants in the playoffs?" the technician demanded.

"That's the plan," Parks returned easily.

"I've got fifty bucks on it."

This time Parks grinned. "I'll try to keep that in mind."

"Detrick." Brooke gave the technician a jerk of her head to send him on his way as she approached Parks. "Okay, this is the easy part," she began. "No dialogue, and you're doing what you're best at."

"What's that?"

Brooke lifted a brow at the loaded question but continued smoothly. "Swinging a bat. Since the pitching coach has agreed to throw you a few, you should feel comfortable."

"Ever stood in the box without a helmet?" he countered.

"It wouldn't go with your outfit," she said mildly. She gave him a deliberately slow study—eyes sweeping up, then down, then back up again. "And it looks good."

"I like yours, too." His smile was quick and dangerous. "I'm going to like unbinding your hair."

"Makeup!" she called abruptly. "Give him a dusting, he's going to glow."

"Wait a minute," Parks began, deftly catching the wrist of the woman with the powder.

"No sweating on camera," Brooke drawled, pleased with his reaction. "All I want you to do is what you usually do when you're in uniform. Take your regular stance," she continued. "A couple of those test swings. After you hit the ball, I want one of those grins before you toss the bat aside."

"What grins?" Reluctantly, Parks released the makeup artist's wrist and suffered the powder.

With humor dancing in her eyes, Brooke gave him a singularly sweet smile. "One of those boy-on-the-beach grins. Quick, lots of teeth, crinkles at the corners of the eyes."

He narrowed them dangerously. "I'm going to get you for this."

"Try to keep the strikes to a minimum," she went on blithely. "Every strike's a take. You don't have to hit it out of the park, just *look* like you have. Got it?"

"Yeah, I got it." Annoyed, he nodded to the pitching coach as he walked by.

"You look real cute, Jones."

"Just try to get it near the plate," Parks retorted. "Do I get a bat?" he demanded of Brooke. "Or do I just pretend?"

For an answer, Brooke turned and shouted to her assistant. "Let's have the bat, E.J., are you set? Just roll the film—no sweeps, no pans, no close-ups. Remember, we're selling the clothes."

"This is aluminum."

Distracted, Brooke turned back to Parks. "What?"

"This bat is aluminum."

When he held it out, Brooke automatically took it from him. "Yes, it appears to be." As she started to pass it back to him, Parks shook his head.

"I use wood. A two seventy-seven A."

She started to come back with a curt remark, then stopped herself. If she was accustomed to anything, it was temperament. "Get Mr. Jones the bat he prefers," she told her assistant, tossing the first one to him. "Anything else?"

For a moment, he regarded her keenly. "Does everybody jump when you say?"

"Damn right. Keep that in mind for the next couple of hours, and we shouldn't have any problems."

His look sharpened fractionally. "While the cameras are on," he returned in a voice only she could hear.

Turning, she walked to stand behind the camera. Automatically, E.J. stepped back so that she could check the angle herself. Brows drawn together, Brooke stared at Parks through the lens as her assistant handed him another bat. "Okay, Parks, would you take your stance?" Her frown deepened as he leaned slightly over the plate, feet planted, knees bent, shoulders lined toward the mound. The frown vanished. "Good," she decided, moving back so that E.J. could take her place.

"Ten bucks says he pulls one to left center."

A brief nod was Brooke's acceptance of the bet. "Parks, when I say action, I want you to take your stance again, then those testing swings. Keep your eye on the mound—*don't* look at the camera. Just forget we're here." With the first smile Parks had seen that morning, Brooke turned to the pitching coach. "Are you all set, Mr. Friedman?"

"All set, sweetheart. I'll try not to blow it by you, Jones."

Parks gave a snort of laughter. "Just see if you can

make it to the plate.'' He gestured to his uncovered head. ''And keep it low.''

Brooke took a last glance around, assuring herself everyone was in position. ''Let's do one for time. Set?'' She held up her hand, waiting for absolute silence. ''Roll film, and…action.''

She watched Parks crouch into position, then take two loose swings. The deep-blue silk of his shirt caught the light, accenting the play of muscles beneath. Hands on her hips, Brooke counted off the seconds and waited. Parks shifted his weight as the ball came toward him, tensed his muscles then checked his swing. The ball smashed into the pads behind him.

Just barely, Brooke controlled the need to swear. ''Cut.'' Battling her annoyance, she walked to him. ''Is there a problem, Parks?''

''Pitch was outside.''

''Like hell,'' Friedman called from the mound. ''It caught the corner.''

Immediately the crew split themselves up, arguing in favor of the batter or the pitcher. Ignoring them for the moment, Brooke gave her attention to Parks. ''This isn't the bottom of the ninth, you're just supposed to hit the ball. You'll notice,'' she continued, gesturing behind her, ''there aren't any fielders, no fans, no press.''

Parks set the bat, barrel down in the dirt, and leaned on the handle. ''You want me to swing at a bad pitch?''

Brooke met the amused blue eyes levelly. ''The

quality of the pitch is immaterial,'' she countered as the argument raged behind them. ''Just hit the ball.''

With a shrug, he hefted the bat again. ''You're the boss...at the moment.''

The look held, long and challenging, before Brooke turned back to the crew. ''Take two,'' she announced, effectively cutting off the debate.

This time Parks didn't check his swing but drilled the ball up the foul line at third. Without looking at E.J., Brooke held out her hand. ''Time,'' she requested as a ten-dollar bill was stuffed in her palm.

Parks noticed a tiny brunette with a stop watch and clip board. ''Twelve and a half seconds, Brooke.''

''Good. All right, let's go for it.''

''This one's going over the fence,'' E.J. pronounced in an undertone to Brooke. ''Bet ten?''

''Take three,'' she called out with a nod of assent. ''Roll film, and...action!'' A satisfied smile touched her lips as she studied Parks. He was either getting into the spirit of things, or his own competitive spirit was driving him. Either way, it was working for her. The look on his face as he crouched over the plate was exactly what she wanted—the steady intensity that bordered on fierceness. A pity she couldn't work in a close-up, she mused, then lost the thought as Parks took a full swing at the pitch.

Power. The word rippled through her as he connected with the ball. She saw the instant the shirt strained over his shoulders, was aware of the bunching of muscles in his thighs beneath the soft, expensive material. It wasn't necessary to follow the path of the ball to know where it had gone. She knew the flash of grin on Parks's face had nothing to do with her direction. It was sheer pleasure. Brooke kept the film rolling as his eyes followed the ball out of the park. Still grinning, he turned to her, then gave a deprecatory shrug.

She should have been angry that he had looked at the camera against her directions, but the movement, the expression was perfect. Even as she dug in her pocket for E.J.'s ten dollars, she decided to keep it in.

"Cut."

Spontaneous applause broke out, along with a few whistles. "Nice pitch, Friedman," Parks commented.

The coach tossed another ball in the air. "Just making you look good, Jones. The Valiants' pitchers won't be so friendly."

Brooke swiped the back of her wrist across her damp brow. "I'd like a couple more please. What was the time on that?"

"Fourteen seconds."

"Okay. The light's shifting, check the reading. Mr. Friedman, I'd like to get a couple more."

"Anything you say, sweetheart."

"Parks, I need a full swing like last time. No matter where the ball goes, look up and out—don't forget the grin."

Laying the bat on his shoulder, he drawled, "No, ma'am."

Brooke ignored him and turned away. "Lights?"

The technician finished the adjustments, then nodded. "Set."

Although she considered the third take close to perfect, Brooke ran through another three. Edited, this segment of the commercial would run twelve and a half seconds. That it took only three hours to set up and film showed that she ran a tight schedule.

"It's a wrap. Thanks," she added as she accepted the cup of ice water from her assistant. "We'll set up in front of the restaurant in..." She glanced at her watch. "Two hours, Fred, double-check on the Rolls and the actress. E.J., I'll take the film into editing myself." Even as she spoke, Brooke walked over to the mound. "Mr. Friedman." With a smile, she held out her hand. "Thank you."

He found her grip firm and her eyes soft. "My pleasure." With a chuckle, he tossed a spare ball into his mitt. "You know, in my day ball players plugged razor blades or beer. We endorsed bats and gloves." He cast a glance at Parks, who was signing a baseball for a technician. "No fancy designers would have asked us to sport his clothes."

Brooke shifted her eyes to Parks. He was laughing now, shaking his head at E.J. as the cameraman ticked off some point on his fingers. The casually elegant clothes suited him, as did the dark wood bat in his hand. "I'd hate to have him know I said it, Mr. Friedman," Brooke commented as she turned back to the coach, "but Parks is a natural."

With a shout of laughter, Friedman patted her on the back. "He won't hear it from me, sweetheart. Last thing my pitchers need is a third baseman with a big head. One more thing," he added before Brooke turned away. "I watched the way you run things." He gave her an expansive grin that revealed good dentures. "You'd make a hell of a coach."

"Thanks." Pleased with the compliment, Brooke made her way toward the plate, and Parks. "You did very well."

He regarded her extended hand with amusement, but accepted it. "For a rookie?" he countered.

When she started to remove her hand, Parks held it firmly, running a light fingertip over the inside of her wrist. He had the satisfaction of feeling her pulse jump then speed up. "I didn't anticipate any problems, as you were simply playing yourself." Behind her, technicians were taking down lights and coiling cable. She heard E.J. describing the new lady he was seeing in glowing, if exaggerated, terms. Using all her willpower, Brooke concentrated on the background noises instead of the feel of Parks's finger tracing over her skin. "The next scene should be fairly easy. We'll go over it on location this afternoon. If you have any questions—"

"Just one," Parks interrupted. "Come here a minute." Without waiting for agreement, he drew her toward the dugout, stepped inside then just through the door that led to the locker rooms.

"What's the problem, Parks?" Brooke demanded. "I have to get into editing before the next shoot."

"Are we finished here for now?"

With an impatient sigh, Brooke gestured to the equipment being packed. "Obviously."

"Fine." Pressing her back against the doorway, Parks covered her mouth with his.

It was a proprietary kiss with whispers of violence. The frustrations of the past hours seeped into it as he finally let them free. There was the annoyance of wanting her—of being too far away to touch for days, then being close enough, but not being permitted to. There was the exasperation of her cool professional treatment of him while he had fought an insistent growing desire. And there was the banked fury at being put in the position of taking orders from a woman who dominated his thoughts and denied his body.

Yet it was more agitating than soothing to press his body against the softness of hers. She filled him—the exotic scent, the ripe woman-taste of her mouth, the silken skin over the sharp, strong bones of her face. Almost desperately, he pressed closer, plunged deeper. He would *not* be filled. He would find that corner, that secret place that would open her for him so that he could have her at last—body and mind. To do that he needed the edge of control, over himself, and over Brooke. Her strength made it a challenge—his desire made it a necessity.

"Hey, Brooke, want a ride to the… Whoops." E.J. poked his head into the dugout then retreated. As Parks's lips freed hers, she could hear the cameraman whistling gleefully as he strolled away. Furious that she had completely lost track of time and place, Brooke shoved against Parks's chest.

"Let go of me!"

"Why?"

Apparently her ice-pick stare more amused than wounded him. "Don't you *ever* pull something like that when I'm working," she hissed, shoving a second time as Parks blocked her exit.

"I asked if we were finished," Parks reminded her, then backed her into the wall again.

"When we're on the job," Brooke said evenly, "I'm the director, you're the product." He narrowed his eyes at her choice of words, but she continued, full steam. "You'll do *exactly* what I tell you."

"The camera's not rolling, Brooke."

"I won't have my crew speculating, circulating gossip that can undermine my authority or my credibility."

His own temper rose in direct balance with need. She only aroused him more when she challenged. "Aren't you more afraid that you enjoy being touched by me? Doesn't it infuriate you that when I kiss you, you don't really give a damn who's in charge?" He bent his head so that his lips were only a breath from hers. "I took your orders all morning, Ms. Gordon. Now it's my turn."

Her lancelike stare didn't falter as the quiet words fluttered over her lips. With the tip of his tongue he traced them, enjoying their taste and her own suppressed passion. Merging desire stung the air—they both felt it, they both tried to rise above it in the struggle for dominance. Yet they both became aware that it was the desire that would win over each of them.

His lips rubbed over hers, without pressure or force,

taunting her to demand he stop, daring her to resist her own needs. Their eyes remained open and fixed on each other. Both pairs of irises darkened as passion tempted each of them to surrender.

"We have another shoot this afternoon," Brooke managed as she fought to keep her voice steady.

"When we're filming, I'll do what you tell me." He kissed her once, hard and quick. "Tonight," he added, dealing with his own heated blood, "we'll see."

Chapter 6

Brooke chose to shoot during the late-afternoon lull using day-for-night filters, rather than compete with the evening traffic. It was a quick scene, relatively simple and very glossy. The champagne-colored Rolls would drive up in front of the posh restaurant, Parks would alight, in the same outfit, but wearing a jacket—already sponged and pressed from the morning—then offer his hand to the sleekly dressed brunette. She would step from the car, showing considerable leg, then flash Parks a look before linking her arm through his. The scene would then fade out, with Parks's voice-over dubbed in, stating the motto for the campaign.

"De Marco. For the man who's going places."

The visual would be another twelve seconds, so that combined with the stadium segment, the intro and the tag at the end, the commercial would round out at thirty seconds.

"I want a long shot of the Rolls, E.J., then come in on Parks as he steps out. We don't want to lose the impact that he's wearing the same outfit he played ball in. Don't get hung up on the lady," she added dryly as she sent him a knowing look.

"Who me?" Pulling a Kings fielder's cap out of his back pocket, he offered it to Brooke. "Want to wear it? Team spirit?"

Placing one hand on her hip, Brooke stared at him without any change of expression. With a quick chuckle, E.J. fit the cap over his own modified Afro. "Okay, boss, I'm ready when you are."

As was her habit, Brooke rechecked the camera angle and the lighting before she signaled the first take. The Rolls cruised sedately to the curb. Brooke played the background music over in her head, trying to judge how it would fit. On cue, Parks climbed out, turning to offer his hand to the brunette still inside. Frowning, Brooke let the scene play out. It wasn't right. She saw why immediately but took the few minutes until the cut to work out how to approach Parks.

With a gesture, Brooke indicated that she would speak to Parks while the driver backed up the Rolls for the next take. Putting a hand on his arm, she led him away from the technicians. "Parks, you have to relax." Because handling fidgety actors was second nature to her, Brooke's voice and manner were markedly different from the morning session. Parks noted it and bristled anyway.

"I don't know what you mean."

She steered him well away from where a few interested pedestrians were loitering by a barricade. "Number one," she began, "you're plugging a good product. Try to believe in it."

"If I didn't think it was a good product, I wouldn't be doing this," he retorted, frowning over her shoulder at the huddle of lights.

"But you're not comfortable." When Brooke gave his shoulder a reassuring pat, Parks scowled at her. "If you insist on feeling like an idiot, it's going to show. Wait," she ordered as he started to speak. "This morning, you felt more at ease—the stadium, a bat in your hand. After the first couple of minutes, you started to play the game. That's all I want you to do now."

"Look, Brooke, I'm not an actor—"

"Who's asking you to act?" she countered. "God spare me from that." She knew she'd insulted him, so she tempered the comment with a smile. "Listen, you're a winner, out on the town in a chauffeured Rolls with a gorgeous woman. All I want you to do is have a good time and look rather pleased with yourself. You can pull it off, Parks. Loosen up."

"I wonder how you'd feel if someone asked you to field a line drive with twenty thousand people watching."

Brooke smiled again and tried not to think about the minutes ticking away. "You do that routinely," she pointed out, "because you concentrate on your job and forget those thousands of people."

"This is different," he muttered.

"Only if you let it be. Just let me see that same self-satisfied look on your face that you had when you hit that homer this morning. Pretend, Parks." Brooke straightened the collar of his shirt. "It's good for you."

"Did you know that Nina has the IQ of a soft-boiled egg?"

"Nina?"

"My date."

Brooke gave in to a sigh. "Stop being so temperamental; nobody's asking you to marry her."

Parks opened his mouth, then shut it again. No one had ever accused him of being temperamental. He'd never *been* temperamental. If his manager told him to take a three-and-one pitch, he took it. If the third base coach told him to steal home, he ran. Not because he was malleable, but because if he was signed with a team, he followed the rules. It didn't mean he always had to like them. With a quiet oath, he ran a hand through his hair and admitted that it wasn't so much what the orders were in this case, but who was laying them out. But then, the lights and cameras would eventually shut down.

"Fine, let's do it again." He gave Brooke the slow smile she'd learned not to trust before he walked toward the Rolls. Suspicious of his easy capitulation, Brooke turned back to stand beside E.J.

Parks gave her no more cause to complain, though

they were more than two hours shooting the segment. Brooke found that she had more trouble with the professional actress—and a couple of fans who recognized Parks—than she had with him. It took three takes before she convinced Nina that she wasn't looking for glowing and adoring, but for sleek and aloof. Brooke wanted the contrast and ran everyone through the twelve seconds until she was certain she had it.

Then there was the matter of two fans who sneaked through the barricade to get Parks's autograph while the camera was still rolling. Parks obliged them, and though Brooke simmered at the interruption, she noted that he dispatched the fans with the charm of a seasoned diplomat. Grudgingly, she had to admit she couldn't have done better herself.

"That's a wrap," Brooke announced, arching her back. She'd been on her feet for over eight hours, bolting down a half a sandwich between segments. She felt pleased with the day's work, satisfied with Parks's progress and ravenous. "You can break down," she told the crew. "Good job. E.J., I've scheduled the editing and dubbing for tomorrow. If you want to see what we're going to do to your film, you can come in."

"It's Saturday."

"Yeah." She pulled the bill of the fielder's cap over his face. "We'll start working at ten. Nina..." Brooke took the actress's slim, smooth hand. "You were lovely, thank you. Fred, make sure the Rolls gets back in one piece, or you'll have to face Claire. Bigelow, what's the new kid's name?" Brooke jerked her head at a young technician who was busily packing up lights.

"Silbey?"

With a nod, Brooke made a mental note of it. "He's good," she said briefly, then turned to Parks. "Well, you made it through the first one. We'll dub in the voice-over tomorrow. Any scars?"

"None that show."

"Maybe I shouldn't tell you that this one is the easiest on the schedule."

He met the humor in her eyes blandly. "Maybe you shouldn't."

"Where's your car?"

"Out at the stadium."

With a frown, Brooke checked her watch. "I'll give you a lift back there." She toyed with the idea of going by Thorton's first to take a quick look at the film, then discarded the idea. It would be better to look at it fresh in the morning. "I have to call Claire.... Well." Brooke shrugged. "That can wait. Any problems?" she asked to the crew in general."

"Tomorrow's Saturday," an aggrieved E.J. stated again as he packed up his equipment. "Woman, you just don't give a man a break."

"You don't have to come in," she reminded him, knowing he would. "Good night." With Parks beside her, Brooke started down the street.

"Do you make a habit of working weekends?" he asked, noting that after a long, hectic day she still moved as though she had urgent appointments to keep.

"When it's necessary. We're rushing this through to get it aired during the play-offs or, barring that, the series." She shot him a look. "You'd better be in it." Still walking, she began to dig in the purse slung over her shoulder.

"I'll try to accommodate you. Want me to drive?"

With the keys in one hand, Brooke looked up in surprise. "Have you been talking to E.J.?"

His brows drew together. "No. Why?"

"Nothing." Dismissing the thought, Brooke paused beside her car. "Why do you want to drive?"

"It occurs to me that I may have had to stand in front of that stupid camera off and on all day, but you haven't stopped for over eight hours. It's a tough job."

"I'm a tough lady," she responded with a trace of defensiveness in her voice.

"Yeah." He grazed his knuckles over her cheek. "Iron."

"Just get in the car," Brooke muttered. After rounding the hood, she climbed in, slamming the door only slightly. "It'll take a little while to get across town in this traffic."

"I'm not in a hurry." Parks settled comfortably beside her. "Can you cook?"

In the act of starting the car, Brooke frowned at him. "Can I what?"

"Cook. You know." Parks pantomimed the act of stirring a pan.

She laughed, shooting out of traffic with an exuberance that made Parks wince. ‘‘Of course I can cook.’’

‘‘How about your place?’’

Brooke zipped through a yellow light. ‘‘What about my place?’’ she asked cautiously.

‘‘For dinner.’’ Parks watched her shift into third as she scooted around a Porsche. ‘‘It seems to me I'm entitled after feeding you a couple times myself.’’

‘‘You want me to cook for you?’’

This time he laughed. She was going to fight him right down to the wire. ‘‘Yeah. And then I'm going to make love to you.’’

Brooke hit the brakes, stopping the car inches away from another bumper. ‘‘Oh, really?’’

‘‘Oh, really,’’ he repeated, meeting her dagger-eyed stare equably. ‘‘We both just punched out on the time clock. New game.’’ He fingered the end of her braid. ‘‘New rules.’’

‘‘And if I have some objection?’’

‘‘Why don't we talk about it someplace quiet?’’ With his thumb, he traced her lips. ‘‘Not afraid, are you?’’

The taunt was enough. When the light changed, Brooke hit the accelerator, weaving through Los Angeles traffic with grim determination.

‘‘Did you know that you drive like a maniac?’’ Parks observed.

‘‘Yes.’’

‘‘Just a passing comment,’’ he murmured, then settled back against the seat.

* * *

Despite the infuriated woman beside him, Parks had the same sensation of tranquility when Brooke zoomed up in her driveway, braking with a teeth-jarring jolt, that he had had the first time he had seen her house. There was a tang of fall in the air—that spicy, woodsy fragrance you never smelled in Los Angeles. Some of the leaves had turned so that splashes of red and amber and orange competed with the customary California green. The shadows of trees reflected in the glass of the windows as the sun dipped lower in the sky. Along the base of the house the flowers had been allowed to grow bushy and wild. Whether it had been by intent or lack of time, her unkempt garden was eye-catching and perfectly suited to the lonely mountain spot.

Without a word, Brooke slammed out of her side of the car. At a more leisurely pace, Parks followed suit. She was furious, Parks noted with a pleased grin. All the better. He didn't want an easy capitulation. From the first moment he had come into contact with her, he had looked forward to the struggle almost as much as he had looked forward to the outcome. He'd never had any doubt what that would be. When there was this much friction, and this much spark between a man and a woman, they became enemies or lovers. He had no intention of being Brooke's enemy.

Still keeping her stony silence, Brooke slipped the key into the lock and turned it. Walking inside, she left him to follow as he chose.

The fireplace caught his eye first. It was crafted from large stone, dominating one wall. The fire set was shiny brass, though dented and obviously old. Another wall was all glass, rising from either side of the door to the peak of the roof. Gazing at it, he felt not a loss of privacy but a basic sense of security. Rocking gently on his heels, he studied the rest of the main room.

A long armless sofa ranged in front of the fireplace, crowded with dozens of pillows. In lieu of a table a large, round hassock sat in front of it. Around this focal point a few chairs were scattered. All the colors were muted—ecrus, buffs, biscuits—set off by the surprising touches of huge, brilliant peacock feathers in a brass urn, a scarlet afghan tossed over the back of a chair, the vivid shades in the hooked rug on the planked floor.

A shelf had been built into the east wall. Ignoring Brooke's glare, Parks wandered to it. There was a small crystal butterfly that shivered in a rainbow of colors as the light struck it. There was a chipped demitasse set that had come from one of Brooke's yard sale jaunts along with a fat, grinning bear. Parks noted a piece of Wedgwood next to a pink monkey holding cymbals. It clapped them together gleefully when he flipped a switch. With a quick laugh, he flipped it off again. There were other treasures scattered haphazardly through the room, some priceless, some no more than department store whimsy.

Above his head, the second-floor balcony ran the length of the house. No closed-in spaces, he noted. He began to think the house itself would tell him more about Brooke than she would volunteer. The need for freedom of movement, the eclectic tastes, the combination of drab colors with the garish. It occurred to him that everything she owned would have been collected during the last ten years. But how much of the past had she brought with her?

Uncomfortable with Parks's silent, thorough survey, Brooke marched to a tiny corner cabinet to pull out a bottle. ''You're free to take a tour,'' she said abruptly. ''I'm going to have a drink.''

''Whatever you're having's fine,'' Parks said with infuriating amiability. ''You can show me around later.'' He proceeded to make himself at home on the low, spreading sofa. Leaning back, he glanced at the fireplace, observing by the ash that Brooke made good use of it. ''Fire'd be nice,'' he said casually. ''Got any wood?''

''Out back.'' Ungraciously, she stuck a glass under his nose.

''Thanks.'' After accepting it, Parks took her hand. ''Sit down,'' he invited with a pleasantness that put Brooke's teeth on edge. ''You've been on your feet all day.''

''I'm fine,'' she began, then let out a gasp of surprise as Parks yanked her down beside him. Realizing she should have been prepared for the move despite his outward mellowness only fanned her already strained temper. ''Who do you think you are,'' she began, ''barging in here, expecting me to whip up dinner then fall into bed with you? If you—''

''Hungry?'' Parks interrupted.

She sent him a searing look. ''No.''

With a shrug, he draped his arm behind her, propping his feet on the hassock. "You're usually ill-tempered when you are," he commented.

"I am *not* ill-tempered," Brooke raged. "And I am *not* hungry."

"Want some music?"

Brooke drew in a deep breath. How dare he sit there acting as though she were *his* guest? "No."

"You should relax." With firm fingers, he began to knead the base of her neck.

"I'm perfectly relaxed." She pushed his hand aside, disturbed by the sensation of warmth creeping down her spine.

"Brooke." Parks set his glass on the floor, then turned to her. "When you called me a few days ago, you accepted what you knew was going to happen between us."

"I said I would see you," she corrected and started to rise. Parks hand came back to her neck and held her still.

"Knowing what *seeing* me meant," he murmured. His eyes met the fury in her gaze for a moment, then drifted down to focus on her mouth. "You might have refused to let me come here tonight...but you didn't." Slowly, he brought his eyes back to hers in a long, intense look that had her stomach muscles quivering. "Are you going to tell me that you don't want me?"

She couldn't remember the last time she had felt the need to break eye contact. It took all her strength of will to keep from faltering. "I...I don't have to tell you anything. You might remember that this is my time, my house. And—''

''What are you afraid of?''

As he watched, the confusion in her eyes turned back to fury. ''I'm not afraid of anything.''

''Of making love to me,'' he continued quietly. ''Or to anyone?''

Angry color flooded her cheeks as she bolted up from the sofa. She felt a combination of rage and hurt and fear that she hadn't experienced in more than a decade. He had no right to bring the insecurity tumbling back over her, no right to make her doubt herself as a woman. Tossing her head, Brooke glared at him. ''You want to make love?'' she snapped. ''Fine.'' She turned on her heel and marched to the stairs leading to the second floor. Halfway up, she threw an angry look over her shoulder. ''Coming?'' she demanded, then continued on without waiting for his reply.

The fury carried her across the balcony and into her bedroom, where she stood in the center of the room, seething. Her gaze landed on the bed, but she averted it quickly as she heard the sound of Parks's footsteps approaching. It was all very simple, she told herself. They would go to bed and work this attraction or animosity or whatever it was out of their systems. It would clear the air. She sent Parks another killing look as he walked into the room. Fear prodded at her again. In defense, Brooke hastily began to undress.

It was on the tip of his tongue to tell her to stop, then Parks calmly followed her example. She was trembling and didn't even know it, he observed. For the moment, they would play it her way. As with the first night he had taken her out, Parks knew what Brooke expected. Though the angry fear urged him to comfort, he was aware that it would be refused. He didn't even glance over when she dropped her T-shirt into a heap on the floor. But he noticed that she had kept a small clutch of his hibiscus on her dresser.

Naked, Brooke stomped over to the bed and pulled off the quilt. Head high, brows arched, she turned to him. ''Well?''

He looked at her. The surge of sharp desire caused him to go rigid to control it. She was long and softly rounded with fragile, china-doll skin. The proud almost challenging stance was only accented by the overall frailty—until one looked at her eyes. Stormy, they dared him to make the next move.

Parks wondered if she knew just how vulnerable she was and vowed, even as he planned to conquer, to protect. Taking his time, he walked to her until they stood face-to-face. Though her eyes never faltered, he saw the quick nervous swallow before she turned toward the bed. Parks caught her braid in his hand, forcing her to turn back. The fury in her eyes might have cooled the desire of most men. Parks smiled, comfortable with it.

''This time,'' he murmured as he began to unbind the braid, ''I'll direct.''

Brooke stood stiffly as he slowly freed her hair. Her skin tingled, as if waiting for his touch—but he never touched her. Deliberately, Parks drew out the process, working his way leisurely up the confined hair until

Brooke thought she would burst. When he had finished, he spread it over her shoulders as if it were the only task he would ever perform.

"It's fabulous," Parks murmured, absorbed in its texture, at the way the slanting sunlight brought out the hidden gold within the red. Lifting a strand from her shoulder, he buried his nose in it, wanting to absorb the fragrance. Brooke felt her knees weaken, her muscles go lax. Would he ever touch her?

She kept her eyes on his face, trying to avoid a dangerous fascination with the tawny skin of his chest, the mat of dark-gold hair and cords of muscles she had glimpsed in his bare shoulders. If she allowed herself to look, would she be able to prevent herself from touching? But when she noticed the thin gold chain around his neck, curiosity drove her to follow it down to the small gold circle that dangled from it. Because of this, she didn't see him shift ever so slightly to press his lips against the curve of her shoulder. The touch was a jolt, a branding shock that had her jerking back even as his hands spanned her waist.

"Relax." Fingers kneaded gently into flesh; warm lips nibbled it over his words. "I won't take you anywhere you don't want to go." Slowly, he ran the whisper-soft kisses over her shoulder, loitering at her throat. His fingertips ran down to her hips then back up in a rhythmic caress that could never soothe, but only arouse. He knew what he did to her—she knew her response was no secret. In a last attempt to hold her own, Brooke pressed her hands against his chest, arching back.

Parks still held her waist, but made no attempt to draw her back. Over the desire in his eyes, Brooke caught the light of humor. ''Want me to stop?'' he asked quietly. There was a trace of challenge in the question. She realized abruptly that whatever response she gave, she would still lose.

''Would you?'' she countered, fighting the urge to run her suddenly sensitive fingertips over his naked chest.

It was his slow, dangerous smile. ''Why don't you ask me and see?'' Even as she opened her mouth to form an answer, his fastened on it. The kiss was soft and deep, the sort she knew a woman could drown in. Brooke had only the vague realization that her hands had crept up his chest to link around his neck, only the faintest knowledge that her body was melting into his. Then she was falling—or perhaps she was drowning—until the cool sheets were under her back and his weight was on her.

She didn't question how her body seemed to have become liquid, only reveled in the unaccustomed freedom of motion and space. His hands were so sure, so unhurried, as if he wished and waited for her total fluidity. With a deft caress, a strategic brush of lips, he was unlocking every restriction she had placed on herself. This pleasure was thick, fluent. Brooke luxuriated in it, no longer caring what she gave up in order to receive. Weightless, helpless, she could only sigh as he took his mouth on a lazy journey down her body.

The flick of his tongue over her nipple brought a

quick tug—not quite an ache—in her stomach. This pleasure was sharp, stunning. Then it was gone, leaving her dazed as he continued to range a moist trail over her.

His hands were never still, but moved so gently, almost magically, over her, that she could never pinpoint where the source of delight came from. It seemed to radiate through the whole of her, soothing, promising, luring. He caught the point of her breast between his teeth, causing a flash of heat to spring from her center out to her fingertips. But even as she gasped from it, arching, he moved on. He brushed his fingers over her inner thigh, almost absently, so that her skin was left heated then chilled. As fire and ice coursed through her, the sound of her own moan echoed in her head.

The quivering started—a drug wearing off. And the ache—unbearable, wonderful. She was no longer soothed, but throbbing and pleasure became exquisite torment. Suddenly her fingers were in his hair as she tried to press him closer. "Make love to me," she demanded as her breath started to tremble.

He continued with the same mind-destroying caresses. "Oh, I am," he murmured.

"Now." Brooke reached for him only to have him grip her wrists. His head lifted so that their eyes met. Even through a haze of passion she could see his intense concentration—that fierce warrior look.

"It's not so simple." He could feel her pulse hammering under his fingers, but he would give her no quick moment of pleasure. When he took her, she would never forget. Parks pressed his mouth to hers, not so gently. "I've only begun."

Still holding her wrists, he began a new journey over her, with his mouth only. As he captured her breast again, taking it into the heated moistness of his mouth, she could only writhe beneath him in a frenzy that had nothing to do with a desire to escape. The breezy patience had left him to be replaced by a demand that would accept only one answer. It seemed he would feed on her skin, nipping, suckling, licking until she was half-mad from need so long suppressed. It seemed he would taste, and taste only, for hours, assuaging a steady greed she was powerless to refuse.

The heat suffused her, enervated her. Her skin trembled and grew moist from it. Down the hollow between her breasts, over the lean line of ribs to the subtle curve of hip he traced kisses until he felt her hands go limp and her pulse rage.

When his tongue plunged into the warm core of her, she shuddered convulsively, crying out with the first delirious peak. But he was relentless. Even as she struggled for breath, his hands began a new journey of possession.

With hers free, Brooke gripped his shoulders, hardly aware of the tensing of his muscles. There was no part of her body he hadn't explored, exploited, in his quest to have all of her. Now her surrender became agility and drive. Neither of them knew that her true capitulation came when she began her own demands.

Her hands sped over him, touching all she could reach while she twisted, wanting to taste—his mouth, his shoulder, the strong line of his jaw. Parks thought her scent intensified until it dominated all his senses—weakening and strengthening him at once. Her skin was moist and heated wherever his mouth nestled, bringing him another tantalizing image of white silk and forbidden passion. Husky murmurs and quick breathing broke the early-evening hush.

He was no longer thinking, nor was she. They had entered a place where thoughts were only sensations; sharp, aching, sweet and dark. Even as she fastened her mouth on his, Brooke trembled.

Then he was deep inside her, so swiftly that she dug her nails into his flesh in shock and pleasure. They merged, body to body, heart to heart, while all the sensations concentrated into one.

Chapter 7

Brooke luxuriated in the soft, warm security. As she hung between sleep and wakefulness she thought it was winter, and that she slept beneath a thick downy quilt. There was no need to get up, no need to face the cold. She could lie there for a whole lazy day and do nothing. She felt utterly peaceful, completely unburdened and pleasantly languid. Wanting to enjoy the sensations more, she struggled to shrug off sleep.

It wasn't winter, but early fall. There was no quilt, only a tangle of sheets that half covered her naked body as she curled into Parks. With sleep cleared from her mind, Brooke remembered everything—the first revelation of lovemaking, the surprise of having the secret door open without resistance, the hours of passion that had followed. There had been little talk, as the urgency to give and take had grown beyond the control of either of them. Time after time, fulfillment had led to rekindled desire, and desire to demand, until they had fallen asleep, wrapped tightly together.

Now, Brooke could remember her own insatiable thirst, the boundless energy and strength that had filled her. She remembered, too, Parks's ability to arouse her to desperation with patience…and that she had driven him beyond patience with a skill she had been unaware of possessing. But beyond the passion and pleasure, Brooke remembered one vital thing. She had needed him. This was something she had refused herself for years. To need meant dependence, dependence meant vulnerability. A woman who was vulnerable would always be hurt.

The night was behind her and dawn was breaking. In the misty gray light, Parks's face was relaxed, inches from hers, so that the warmth of his breath fluttered over her cheek. His arm was around her, his fingers curled into her hair, as if even in sleep he had to touch it. Her arm reached around to lock him close. They had slept, if only for a few hours, in a classic pose of possessing and possessed. But which one, Brooke thought hazily, was which?

With a sigh, Brooke closed her eyes. Not knowing was dangerous. The hours she had spent not caring put the independence she had taken for granted in jeopardy.

It was time to think again before it was too late, before emotions dominated her—those perilous emotions that urged her to burrow closer to Parks's warmth. If she were ever to stop the need for him from growing beyond her control, she had to do it now.

Brooke shifted in an attempt to separate her body from his. Parks tightened his hold and only brought her closer. ''No,'' he murmured without opening his eyes. With sleepy slowness he ran his hand down the length of her naked back. ''Too early to get up.''

Brooke felt her breasts yield against his chest, felt the warmth in her stomach begin to smolder to heat. His lips were close—too close. The need to stay in the security of his arms was so strong it frightened her. Again Brooke tried to shift, and again Parks brought her back.

''Parks,'' she said, then was silenced by his lips.

Brooke told herself to struggle against the deep, musky morning kiss, but she didn't. She told herself to resist the gentle play of fingertips on her spine, but she couldn't. The gray dawn suddenly took on a rosy hue. The air seemed to grow thick. Even as he touched her, her skin quivered to be touched again. Don't! her brain shouted. Don't let this happen. But she was already sinking, and sinking quickly. She made a sound of protest that became a groan of pleasure.

Parks shifted so that his body lay across hers. Burying his face in her hair, he took his hand down the length of her; the slight swell of the side of her breast, the firm line of ribs and narrow waist, a flare of hip and long smooth thigh. He could feel the struggle going on inside her, sense her desire to separate herself from what had begun to happen between them since that first meeting of eyes. His quick flash of anger was tinged with unexpected hurt.

"Regrets already?" Lifting his head, he looked at her. Her eyes were dark, heavy with kindling passion. Her breathing was unsteady. But he knew she fought herself just as fiercely as she fought him. Her hands were on his shoulders, poised to push him away.

"This isn't smart," Brooke managed.

"No?" Controlling anger, ignoring the hurt, Parks brushed the hair from her cheek. "Why?"

Brooke met his eyes, because to look away would have admitted defeat. "It's not what I want."

"Let's be accurate." His voice was calm, his eyes steady. "It's not what you want to want."

"All right." Brooke shivered as his finger traced her ear. "It's not what I want to want. I have to be practical. We're going to be working together for quite a while. More technically, you'll be working for me. A solid professional relationship won't be possible if we're lovers."

"We are lovers," Parks pointed out, casually shifting so that the friction of his body on hers sent a shudder coursing through her.

"It won't be possible," Brooke continued, concentrating on keeping her voice steady, "if we go on being lovers."

Tilting his head, Parks smiled at her. "Why?"

"Because..." Brooke knew why. She knew dozens of logical reasons why, but no firm thought would form in her brain when he touched a light friendly kiss to her lips.

"Let me be practical a minute," Parks said after another quick kiss. "How often do you let yourself have fun?"

Brooke drew her brows together in annoyed confusion. "What do you mean?"

"You can work eight, twelve hours a day," Parks continued. "You can enjoy your job, be terrific at what you do, but you still need to throw a Frisbee now and again."

"Frisbee?" This brought on a baffled laugh that pleased him. The hands on his shoulders relaxed. "What are you talking about?"

"Fun, Brooke. A sense of the ridiculous, laziness, riding Ferris wheels. All those things that make working worthwhile."

She had the uncomfortable feeling she was being expertly led away from the subject at hand. "What does riding a Ferris wheel have to do with you and me making love?"

"Have you ever had a lover before?" Parks felt her stiffen but continued. "I don't mean someone you slept with, but someone you shared time with. I'm not asking you for any more than that." Even as he said it, Parks knew it wouldn't be true for long. He would ask for more, and she would fight him every step of the way. But then he had lived his life playing to win. "Throw a few Frisbees with me, Brooke. Ride a few waves. Let's see where it takes us."

Looking at him, she could feel her resistance melting. Before she could prevent it, her hand had lifted from his shoulder to brush at the hair that fell over his forehead. ''You make it sound so simple,'' she murmured.

''Not simple.'' He took her other hand and pressed his lips to the palm. ''Even fun isn't always simple. I want you...here.'' And his eyes came back to hers. ''Naked, warm, daring me to arouse you. I want to drive with you with the top down and the wind in your hair. I want to see you caught in the rain, laughing.'' He ran whispering kisses over her face, then paused at her lips to drink long and deep. ''I want to be with you, but I don't think it's going to be simple.''

Rolling over, Parks cradled her head on his chest, allowing her to rest and think while he brushed his hands through her hair. His words had touched her in tiny vulnerable places she couldn't defend. Was she strong enough, she wondered, to try things his way without losing control? Fun, she thought. Yes, they could give each other that. He challenged her. Brooke had to admit that she had come to enjoy even the friction. What had he said once? That they could be friends before they were lovers. Odd, she mused, that both had happened almost before she realized it. Only the niggling fear that she was already afraid of losing him kept her from relaxing completely.

''I can't afford to fall in love with you,'' she murmured.

An odd way to put it, Parks reflected as he continued to stroke her hair. ''Rule one,'' he drawled. ''Party A will not fall in love with Party B.''

Making a fist, Brooke punched his shoulder. ''Stop making me sound ridiculous.''

''I'll try,'' he agreed amiably.

''Fun,'' she murmured, half to herself.

''A three-letter word meaning amusement, sport or recreation,'' Parks recited in a blandly didactic tone.

With a chuckle, Brooke lifted her head. ''All right. I'll buy the Frisbee,'' she said before she pressed her mouth to his.

Parks cupped the back of her neck in his hand. ''It's still too early to get up,'' he murmured.

Brooke's low laugh was muffled against his lips. ''I'm not sleepy.''

With a reluctant sigh, he closed his eyes. ''Acting,'' he said thickly, ''takes a lot out of you.''

''Aw.'' Sympathetically, Brooke stroked his cheek. ''I guess you'd better conserve your strength.'' She pressed a kiss to his jaw, then his collarbone, before continuing down his chest. Her fingers tangled with the gold chain he wore. ''What's this for?''

Parks opened one eye to stare at the five-dollar gold piece that dangled from the chain Brooke held up. ''Luck.'' He shut his eyes again. ''My aunt gave it to me when I headed for the Florida training camp. She told my father he was a''—Parks reached back in his memory for the exact phrasing—''a stiff-necked old fool who thought in graphs and formulas, then gave me the gold piece and told me to go for it.''

Brooke turned the shiny circle over in her palm. So he carried a little piece of the past with him, too, she mused. ''Superstition?'' she asked as she dropped the chain and pressed her lips to his chest.

''Luck,'' Parks corrected, enjoying the feel of her

mouth on his skin, "has nothing to do with superstition."

"I see." She scraped her nails lightly down his side and heard his quick inhalation of breath. "Do you always wear it?"

"Mmm." She flicked her tongue over his nipple, bringing a low, involuntary groan from him. A sense of power whipped through her—light, freeing, tempting. His hands were buried in her hair again, seeking the flesh beneath. Brooke slid her body down, bringing them both a rippling slice of pleasure.

His scent was different, she discovered as she ran her lips over his skin. Different, she realized, because hers had mingled with it during the night. That was intimacy, as tangible as the act of love itself.

As the power stayed with her, she experimented. His body was strong and muscled beneath hers, tasting of man. He was taut and lean, his skin golden in the early-morning light. The palms that moved over her back were hard, calloused from his profession. Like the man, the body was disciplined, a product of that odd combination of pampering and outrageous demands any athlete subjects it to. She brushed her lips over the hard, flat stomach and felt the firm muscles quiver. Beneath her own smooth palms she could feel the sinewy strength of his thighs.

The knowledge of the pure physical strength he possessed excited her. With light touches and caresses, she could make this man breathe as though he had run to the point of collapse. With feathering kisses she could make this hardened athlete shudder with an inner weakness she alone was aware of. Though she didn't fully understand it, Brooke knew that she had given him something more than her body the night before, something more complex than surrender or passion. Without even knowing what the gift was, she wanted Parks to offer it in return.

Slowly, enjoying every movement of his body beneath hers, savoring each subtly different taste, she roamed up until her lips fastened greedily on his. How soft his mouth was. How nectarous, with a dark, secret cachet. Brooke savored it on her tongue, feeling it intensify until the draining, liquefying pleasure crept into her. Knowing she would lose that slim edge of control, she tore her mouth from his to bury it at his throat.

She felt the vibration of his groan against her lips, but she couldn't hear it. Her heartbeat raged in her head until all of her senses were confused. If it was morning, how could she feel this sultry night pleasure? If she was seducing him, how was she so thoroughly seduced? Her body pressed against his, matching itself to the slow, tortuous rhythm he set even as she raced tormenting kisses along his flesh. The heat seeping into her only seemed to add to the delirium of power, yet it wasn't enough. She was still searching for something so nebulous she wasn't certain she would recognize it when it was found. And desire, sharp bolts of desire, were causing everything but the quest for fulfillment to fade.

Parks gripped her hair in one hand to pull her head up. She had only a brief glimpse of his face—the eyes half-shut but darker and more intense than she had ever seen them—before he brought her mouth down to his and devoured. All will, all sense was seeping out of her.

"Brooke..." His hands were on her hips, urging her. "Now." The demand was wrenched from him, hoarse and urgent. She resisted, struggling to breathe, fighting to hold some part of herself separate. "I need you," he murmured before their lips met again. "I need you."

Then it was clear—for one breathless instant. She needed, and knew now she was needed in return. It was enough...perhaps everything. With a shuddering sound of relief and joy, she gave.

At nine fifty-five, Claire swept into the editing room. Neither the editors nor E.J. were surprised to see the head of Thorton Productions on the job on a Saturday morning. Anyone who had worked at Thorton more than a week knew that Claire wasn't a figurehead but an entity to be reckoned with. She wore one of her trim little suits, the color of crushed raspberries, and a trace of Parisian scent.

"Dave, Lila, E.J." Claire gave all three a quick nod before heading toward the coffeepot. A newer member of the staff might have scurried to serve the boss, but those lounging near the control board knew better.

"Made it myself, Ms. Thorton," E.J. told her as she poured. "It won't taste like the battery acid these two cook up."

"I appreciate that, E.J.," she said dryly. Just the

scent of it revived her. Claire inhaled it, telling herself only an old fool thought she could dance until three and still function the next day. Ah, but how nice it was to feel like a fool again, she thought with a slow smile. "I'm told that the shoot went well, with no major problems."

"Smooth as silk," E.J. stated. "Wait till you get a load of Parks knocking that sucker over the fence." He grinned reminiscently. "I won ten bucks off Brooke with that hit." His selective memory allowed him to forget that it had been his ten dollars in the first place.

Claire settled into a chair with a quiet sigh. "Is Brooke in yet?"

"Haven't seen her." E.J. began to whistle as he recalled Brooke leaving the location with Parks. Accustomed to his habits, Claire only lifted a brow.

"Are you set up, Dave?"

"Ready to run through it, Ms. Thorton. Want to see it from the top?"

"In a moment." Even as Claire checked her watch, she heard Brooke's voice in the corridor.

"As long as you understand you have absolutely no say in what gets cut and what stays in."

"I might have an intelligent comment to make."

"Parks, I'm serious."

His low chuckle rolled into the editing room just ahead of Brooke. "Morning," she said to the group at large. "Coffee hot?"

"E.J.'s special," Claire told her, watching Brooke over the rim of her mug as she sipped. She looked different, Claire thought, then slid her eyes to Parks. And there was the reason, she concluded with a small smile. ''Good morning, Parks.''

Her face remained bland and friendly, but he recognized her thoughts. With a slight nod, he acknowledged them. ''Hello, Claire,'' he said, abandoning formality as smoothly as he reached for a cup for himself. ''I hope you don't mind me sitting in on this.'' Taking the pot, he poured Brooke's coffee, then his own. ''Brooke has a few reservations.''

''Amateurs,'' Brooke said precisely as she reached for the powdered cream, ''have a tendency to be pains in the—''

''Yes, well I'm sure we're delighted to have Parks join us,'' Claire interrupted over E.J.'s chuckle. ''Run it through, Dave. Let's see what we've got.''

At her order, he flicked a series of buttons on the large control panel in front of him. Parks watched himself appear simultaneously on three monitors. He could hear Brooke's voice off camera, then the little man with the clapboard scooted in front of him announcing the scene and take.

''It's the third take that worked,'' Brooke announced as she settled on the arm of Claire's chair. ''Casey at the bat didn't like the first pitch.''

Her remark earned her a grin from Parks and a mild exclamation from Claire. ''The lighting's very good.'' Claire studied the second take through narrowed eyes.

''The new boy, Silbey. He's got a nice touch. The clothes sell it.'' Brooke sipped while gesturing with her free hand. ''Watch when he sets for the swing....

Yes.'' She gave a nod of approval. ''Nice moves, no apparent restriction. He looks comfortable, efficient, sexy.'' Intent on the screen, Brooke didn't notice the look Parks tossed at her. ''This is the one I want to use.'' She waited, silently, watching the replay of Parks's home run. The test swings, the concentration, the connection and follow-through, the satisfied grin and the shrug.

''I want to keep in the last bit,'' Brooke went on. ''That gee-whiz shrug. It sells the whole business. That natural cockiness is its own appeal.'' Parks choked over his coffee, but Brooke ignored him. ''As I see it, this segment is pretty clear-cut. The next I'm not so sure about. It's going to be effective....''

Cupping his mug in both hands, Parks sat down. For the next two hours he watched himself on the screens of the monitors, listened to himself being weighed, dissected, judged. Though the latter disconcerted him initially, he found that watching himself didn't bring on the feeling of idiocy he'd been certain it would. He began to think he might find some enjoyment out of his two-year stint after all.

Though he'd heard himself picked apart and put back together countless times over the years—coaches, sports critics, other players—Parks couldn't find the same level of tolerance at hearing Brooke speak so matter-of-factly about his face and body, his gestures and expressions. All in all, he thought, it was as though he were the salable product, not the clothes he wore.

They ran the film back and forth, while Claire listened to input and made occasional comments. Yes, they would have to work in close-ups in the next shoot, his face was very good. It would be smart to fill another thirty-second spot with action to exploit the way he moved, showing the durability of the clothes as well as the versatility. They might try tennis shorts if his legs were any good.

At this Parks shot Brooke a deadly glance, half expecting her to offer her personal opinion. She caught it, then smothered a chuckle with a fit of coughing. Over Claire's head she gave him an innocent smile and an unexpectedly lewd wink. The quick response of his own body caused him to scowl at her. She was dressed like a waif, in baggy chinos and a sweater, her hair braided back and secured with a rubber band. From across the room he could smell the elusive, promising scent of her perfume.

"We taped his voice-over this morning," she told Claire. "I think you'll find his voice is good, though how he'll handle real dialogue remains to be seen. Do we have the graphics for the tag-on, Lila?"

"Right here." She flipped a series of switches. On the monitor now was the de Marco logo of a black-maned lion against a cool-blue background. The signature line cartwheeled slowly onto the screen until it stopped below the cat. It held long enough for impact, then faded.

"Very classy," Brooke approved. "then it's agreed? The third take from the first segment, the fifth from the second."

"We saved you guys from a lot of splicing," E.J.

commented as he toyed with an unlit cigarette. ''You should be able to put this together with your eyes closed.''

''I'd appreciate it if you'd keep them open,'' Claire said as she rose. ''Let me know when it's cut and dubbed. E.J., a splendid job, as always.''

''Thanks, Ms. Thorton.''

She handed him her empty mug. ''On the camera work, too,'' she added. The editors snickered as she turned toward the door. ''Parks, I hope you didn't find all this too boring.''

''On the contrary...'' He thought of the objective discussions on his anatomy. ''It's been an education.''

She gave him a mild smile of perfect understanding. ''Brooke, my office, ten minutes.'' As an afterthought she glanced at her watch. ''Oh, dear. Perhaps you'd like to join us for lunch, Parks.''

''I appreciate it, but I have a few things I have to do.''

''Well then.'' Patting his arm, she smiled again. ''Best of luck in the play-offs.'' She slipped away, leaving Brooke frowning after her.

''I probably won't get any lunch now,'' she muttered. ''If you'd said yes, she'd have made reservations at Ma Maison.''

''Sorry.'' Parks drew her out in the corridor. ''Did that wink mean you approve of my legs?''

''Wink?'' Brooke stared at him blankly. ''I don't know what you're talking about. Winking during an editing session is very unprofessional.''

He glanced at the door she had closed behind her.

"The way you all talked in here, I felt that I was the product."

With a half laugh, Brooke shook her head. "Parks, you *are* the product."

His eyes came back to hers, surprising Brooke with the flare of anger. "No. I wear the product."

She opened her mouth, then closed it again on a cautious sigh. "It's really a matter of viewpoint," she said carefully. "From yours, from de Marco's, even from the consumers', the clothes are the product. From the viewpoints of your producer, your director, your cinematographer and so forth, you're as much the product as the clothes you wear because we have to see that both of you are salable. If I can't make you look good, what you're wearing might as well be flea market special."

He saw the logic but didn't care for it. "I won't be a commodity."

"Parks, you're a commodity every time you walk out on the diamond. This really isn't any different." Exasperated, she lifted her hands palms up. "You sell tickets to Kings games, baseball cards and fielder's caps. Don't be so damned sanctimonious about this."

"First it's temperamental, now it's sanctimonious," he muttered disgustedly. "I suppose what it comes down to is we look at this little...venture from two different perspectives."

Brooke felt a light flutter of fear inside her breast. "I told you," she said quietly, "that it would be difficult."

His eyes came back to her, recognizing the shield

she was already prepared to bring down. Parks ran a finger down her cheek. ''And I told you it would be fun.'' Leaning closer, he brushed his lips over hers. ''We're both right. I have some things to do. Can I meet you back here later?''

Relaxing, Brooke told herself she had imagined the fear. ''If you like. I'll probably be tied up until around five.''

''Fine. You can cook me that dinner you promised me last night.''

Brooke lifted her chin. ''I never promised to cook you dinner,'' she corrected. ''But perhaps I will.''

''I'll buy the wine.'' Parks sent her a grin before he turned away.

''Wait.'' After a moment, Brooke went after him. ''You don't have your car.''

Parks shrugged. ''I'll take a cab.'' He saw her hesitate then struggle with a decision.

''No,'' she said abruptly, digging in her bag. ''You can use mine.''

Parks took the keys, and her hand. He knew enough about her to realize offering the use of her car, or anything else important to her, wasn't a casual gesture. ''Thank you.''

Her color rose—the first truly self-conscious thing he had noticed about her. ''You're welcome.'' Quickly, she drew her hand from his and turned away. ''See you at five,'' she called over her shoulder without stopping.

Brooke felt a bit foolish as she rode the elevator to Claire's office. How could she have blushed over a simple thank-you for the loan of a car? She glanced up at the numbers flashing over the elevator door. Oh, he knew her too well, she realized, knew her too well when she'd hardly told him anything.

He didn't know she still had the copy of *Little Women* her second foster mother had given her. He didn't know that she had adored those temporary parents and had been devastated when a broken marriage had caused her to be placed in another foster home. He didn't know about the horrid little girl she had shared a room with during what she still considered the worst year of her life. Or the Richardsons, who had treated her more like a hired hand than a foster child. Or Clark.

With a sigh, Brooke rubbed her fingers over her forehead. She didn't like to remember—didn't like knowing that her growing feelings for Parks seemed to force her to face the past again. Oh, the hell with it, Brooke thought with a shake of her head. It *was* the past. And she was going to have enough trouble dealing with the present to dwell on it.

Steadier, she stepped out into the wide, carpeted corridor of Claire's floor. The receptionist, a pretty girl with lots of large healthy teeth, straightened in her chair at Brooke's approach. She'd worked on the top floor for over two years and was still more in awe of Brooke than of Claire.

"Good afternoon, Ms. Gordon."

"Hello, Sheila. Ms. Thorton's expecting me."

"Yes, ma'am." Sheila wouldn't have contradicted her if her life had depended on it.

Unaware of the impression she made, Brooke strode easily down the corridor and through a set of wide glass doors. Here, two secretaries, known as the twins only because of identical desks, labored away on word processors. The outer office was huge, scrupulously modern and cathedral quiet.

"Ms. Gordon." The first twin beamed a smile while a second one reached for the button on her intercom.

"She's expecting me," Brooke said simply and breezed by them into Claire's office. The door opened silently. Brooke was halfway across the pewter-colored carpet before she realized Claire was sound asleep at her desk. Totally stunned, Brooke stopped dead in her tracks and stared.

The chair Claire sat in was high-backed pale-gray leather. Her desk was ebony, gleaming beneath stacks of neat papers. The glasses Claire wore for reading were held loosely in her hand. A Chinese "literary painting" in color wash and ink hung on the wall to her right, while behind her L.A. sunshine poured through a plate-glass window. Unsure what to do, Brooke considered leaving as quietly as she had come, then decided it was best to stay. Walking to the squashy leather chair facing the desk, she sat, then gently cleared her throat. Claire's eyes snapped open.

"Morning," Brooke said brightly and grinned at Claire's uncharacteristic confusion. "You'd do better on the sofa if you want a nap."

"Just resting my eyes."

"Mm-hmm."

Ignoring the comment, Claire reached for the papers she had been reading before fatigue had won. "I wanted you to have a look at the script for the next de Marco spot."

"Okay." Brooke accepted the script automatically. "Claire, are you all right?"

"Don't I look all right?"

Deciding to take her literally, Brooke studied her. Except for the heavy eyes, she decided, Claire looked better than ever. Almost, Brooke mused, glowing. "You look marvelous."

"Well then." Claire smoothed her hair before she folded her hands.

"Didn't you sleep well last night?" Brooke persisted.

"As it happens, I was out late. Now the script."

"With Lee Dutton?" The thought went through her mind and out her lips before she could stop it. Claire gave her a tolerant smile.

"As a matter of fact, yes."

Brooke set the script back on the desk. "Claire," she began, only to be interrupted by a knock on the door.

"Your lunch, Ms. Thorton." A tray was wheeled in by twin number one.

The scent of hot roast beef had Brooke rising. "Claire, I misjudged you." Lifting the cover from a hot plate, she inhaled. "Forgive me."

"Did you think I'd let you go hungry?" With a chuckle, Claire stood to move to the sofa. "Brooke, dear, I've known you too long. Bring me my salad and coffee like a good girl."

Nibbling on a potato wedge, Brooke obeyed. "Claire, I really want to talk with you about Lee Dutton."

"Of course." Claire speared a radish slice. "Sit down and eat, Brooke, pacing's bad for my digestion."

Plate in hand, Brooke approached the couch. She set it on the low coffee table, picked up half a roast beef sandwich and began. "Claire, are you actually dating Lee Dutton?"

"Does dating seem inappropriate to you for someone of my age, Brooke? Pass me that salt."

"No!" Flustered, Brooke looked down at Claire's outstretched hand. She gave her the salt shaker then took a defiant bite of her sandwich. "Don't be ridiculous," she muttered over it. "I can see you dating all manner of fabulous men. I have trouble seeing you out on the town with Lee Dutton."

"Why?"

Brooke shifted her shoulders uncomfortably. This wasn't how she had intended it to go. "Well, he's nice enough, and certainly sharp, but he seems sort of…well." Brooke sighed and tried again. "Let's put it this way: I can see Lee Dutton in the neighborhood bowling alley. I can't picture you there."

"No…." Claire pursed her lips in thought. "We haven't tried that yet."

"Claire!" Exasperated, Brooke rose and began to

pace again. "I'm not getting through to you. Look, I don't want to interfere with your life—"

"No?" The mild smile had Brooke flopping back down on the couch.

"You matter to me."

Claire reached over to squeeze her hand. "I appreciate that, Brooke, I've been taking care of myself for a long time. I've even handled a few men."

A bit reassured, Brooke began to eat again. "I suppose if I thought you were really getting involved..."

"What makes you think I'm not?" At Brooke's gaping stare, Claire laughed.

"Claire, are you—are you..." She gestured, not quite certain she should put her thoughts into words.

"Sleeping with him?" Claire finished in her calm, cultured voice. "Not yet."

"Not yet," Brooke echoed numbly.

"Well, he hasn't asked me to." Claire took another bite of salad and chewed thoughtfully. "I thought he would by now, but he's quite conservative. Very sweet and old fashioned. That's part of his appeal for me. He makes me feel very feminine. You can lose that at times in this business."

"Yes, I know." Brooke picked up her iced tea and stared into it. "Do you—are you in love with him?"

"I think I am." Claire settled back against the gray-and-rose patterned sofa. "I was only in love once before, really in love. I was your age, perhaps a bit younger." Her smile was soft for a moment, a girl's smile. "In all the years in between, I've never met anyone I was attracted to enough, comfortable enough with, trusted enough, to think of marrying.''

Brooke took a long swallow of tea. She thought she understood Claire's phrasing all too well. ''You're thinking of marriage?''

''I'm thinking I'm almost fifty years old. I've built this up''—she gestured to indicate Thorton—''I have a comfortable home, a nice circle of friends and acquaintances, enough new challenges to keep me from dying of boredom, and suddenly I've found a man who makes me want to curl up in front of a fire after a long day.'' She smiled slowly and rather beautifully—not the girl's smile this time. ''It's a good feeling.'' She let her eyes slide to Brooke, who was watching her closely. ''I'd hate to see you have to wait twenty more years for it. Parks is a great deal more than mildly attracted to you.''

For the third time, Brooke rose to pace the room. ''We haven't known each other long,'' she began.

''You're a woman who knows her own mind, Brooke.''

''Am I?'' With a mordant smile, she turned back. ''Perhaps I do know how I think, how I feel. I don't really know Parks, though. What if I give too much? What's to stop him from getting bored and moving on?''

Claire met her eyes steadily. ''Don't compare him, Brooke. Don't make him pass tests for all those old hurts.''

''Oh, Claire.'' Passing a hand through her hair,

Brooke walked to stare out of the window. ''That's the last thing I want to do.''

''What's the first thing?''

''It's always been to have my own. To have my own so that nobody can come along and say, 'Whoops, you really only borrowed this, time to give it back.''' She laughed a little. ''Silly, I suppose I've never really shaken that.''

''And why should you?'' Claire demanded. ''We all want our own. And to get it, you and I both know there are a few basic risks involved.''

''I'm afraid I'm falling in love with him,'' Brooke said quietly. ''And the closer I get, the more afraid I am that it's all going to crumble under my feet. I have a feeling I need this defense...that if I fall in love with him, I need this edge of control, this little pocket of power, to keep myself from getting demolished. Is that crazy?''

''No. You're not the kind of woman who gives herself completely without asking for something back. You did that once, but you were a child. You're a woman who needs a strong man, Brooke. One strong enough to take, strong enough not to take all.'' She smiled as Brooke turned to face her. ''Give yourself a little time,'' she advised. ''Things have a way of falling into place.''

''Do they?''

Claire's smile widened. ''Sometimes it only takes twenty years.''

With a laugh, Brooke walked back to the sofa. ''Thanks a lot.''

Chapter 8

Brooke sat cross-legged on the softly faded Oriental rug in Claire's den. Sometime during the fourth inning she'd given up trying to sit in a chair. To her right, Lee and Claire sat on a two-cushioned brocade sofa. Billings had outdone herself by preparing her specialty, Beef Wellington, then had been mutely offended when Brooke had done little more than shift the food around on her plate. Though she chided herself for being nervous, Brooke had been able to do nothing but worry about the outcome of the play-offs since Parks had taken off for the Valiants' home stadium.

She'd been able to catch part of the first afternoon game on her car radio as she had driven to a location shoot. One of the production crew had thought ahead, bringing a portable radio with an earplug, and had kept up a running commentary between takes. Brooke had felt overwhelming relief when the Kings had taken the first game, then frustration and more nerves when they had lost the second. Now, she watched the third on the television set in Claire's small, elegant den.

"That man was out at second," Brooke fumed, wriggling impotently on the faded royal-blue rug. "Anyone with two working eyes could see that."

As she launched her personal attack, the Kings' manager, a squat man with the face of a dyspeptic elf, argued with the second base umpire. If she hadn't been quite so furious herself, Brooke might have admired the manager's theatrical gestures as he spun around, rolled his eyes to heaven and pointed an accusing finger in the umpire's face. The umpire remained unmoved and the call stood. With the Kings holding on to a thin one-run lead, a runner on second with one out boded ill.

When the next batter sent one sailing over the fence and the slim lead changed hands, Brooke groaned. "I can't stand it," she decided, pounding her fists on the rug. "I just can't stand it."

"Brooke's become involved in the game," Claire murmured to Lee.

"So I've noticed." He dropped a light kiss on her cheek. "You smell wonderful!"

The sensation of blood rising to her cheeks was pleasant. She had been romanced by suave masters of the game in the more than twenty-five years of her womanhood, but she couldn't remember one who had made her feel quite the way Lee Dutton could. If they had been alone, she would have snuggled closer, but remembering Brooke, she merely squeezed his hand. "Have some wine, dear," she said to Brooke as she reached for the iced bottle beside her. "Good for the nerves."

Because she was breathing a sigh of relief as the next batter struck out, Brooke didn't acknowledge the teasing tone. "That's three out," she said as she took the cool glass from Claire.

"Two," Lee corrected.

"Only if you believe a nearsighted umpire," she countered, sipping. When he chuckled, she sent a grin over her shoulder. "At least I didn't call him a bum."

"Give yourself a little time," Lee advised, winking at Claire as she handed him a glass.

"You know, some of the players—" Brooke began, then broke off with a gasp as a smoking line drive was hit toward third. Her stomach muscles knotted instantly. Parks dove sideways, stretching his arm out toward the speeding ball. He nabbed it in the tip of his glove just before the length of his body connected with the hard Astroturf. Brooke thought she could feel the bone-rattling jolt herself.

"He got it!" Lee broke out of his casual pose with a jerk that nearly upset Claire's wine. "Look at that, look at that! He got it!" he repeated, pointing at the television image of Parks holding up the glove to show the catch while he still lay prone. "That young sonofa—" He caught himself, barely, and cleared his throat. "Parks is the best with a glove in the league," he decided. ''In *both* leagues!'' He leaned forward to pound Brooke companionably on the back. ''Parks robbed him, kid. Stole a base hit from him as sure as God made little green apples.''

Because she watched Parks stand up and brush himself off, Brooke relaxed. ''I want to see it on replay,'' she murmured. ''Slow motion.''

''You'll see that play a dozen times before the night's through,'' Lee predicted. ''And again on the eleven o'clock news. Hey, lookie here.'' Grinning, he gestured to the set. ''That's what I call classy timing.''

Brooke shifted her concentration to the de Marco commercial. Of course she'd seen it a dozen times in the editing room, and again on television, but each time she watched, she searched for flaws. She studied the graphics as Parks's cool clear voice spoke out to her. ''It's perfect,'' she said with a smile. ''Absolutely perfect.''

''How's the next one coming?'' Lee asked Claire.

''It's just waiting for Parks to be available. We hope to shoot next week.''

He settled back again, one arm around Claire. ''I'm going to enjoy seeing that one play during the series.''

''They still have two games to win,'' Brooke reminded him. ''They're a run behind in this one, and—''

''The opera's not over till the fat lady sings,'' Lee said mildly.

Brooke swiveled her head to look at him. Claire was snug beside him, a crystal glass in one hand. Lee's paunch strained against the buttons of his checked shirt. The ankle of one leg rested on the knee of the other while his foot bounced up and down to some personal tune. Abruptly, Brooke saw them as a perfect match. "I like you, Lee," she said with a wide smile. "I really like you."

He blinked twice, then his lips curved hesitantly. "Well, thanks, kid."

She's just given us her blessing, Claire thought with an inward chuckle as she took Lee's hand in hers.

Brooke made her way through the airport crowd with steady determination. In addition to the usual flow of traffic at LAX, there were fans, mobs of fans, waiting to greet the incoming Kings team. Some carried handmade signs, others banners. There were, she noted with some amusement, a good number of truants in the Los Angeles school system that morning, not to mention a deficit in the work force. After the twelve-inning victory, Brooke thought the players deserved a bit of adulation. She also wondered if she'd ever be able to fight her way through so that Parks would see her. The impulse to surprise him, she realized, had not been practical. A truant father hoisted a truant second-grader onto his shoulders. Brooke grinned. Maybe not practical, but it was going to be fun.

Pushing her sunglasses atop her head, Brooke narrowed her eyes against the sun and waited for the plane to touch down. As it stopped being a dot in the sky and took on form, she began to experience the first flicker of nerves. She fidgeted nervously with her bag while she stood, crushed shoulder to shoulder, with excited fans.

He'll be tired, she thought as dozens of conversations buzzed around her. He's probably looking forward to going home and sleeping for twenty-four hours. Brooke ran a hand through her hair. I should have told him I was coming. She shifted her weight to the other foot, curled her fingers around the chain link in front of her and watched the plane glide to a stop.

The moment the door opened, the cheering started, building, rising as the first men began to deplane. They waved back, looking tired and somehow vulnerable without their uniforms. Men, she thought. Simply men suffering from jet lag and perhaps a few hangovers. Then she smiled, deciding that the gladiators might have looked precisely the same the day after a bout.

As soon as she saw him, she felt warm. Beside Brooke, a teenager grabbed her companion and squealed.

''Oh, there's Parks Jones! He's bee-utiful.''

Brooke swallowed a laugh as she thought of how Parks would react to the adjective.

''Every time I watch him, my knees get weak.'' The teenager pressed her lithe young body against the fence. ''Did you see him in the commercial? When he smiled, it was like he was looking right *at* me. I nearly died.''

Though she didn't take her eyes off Parks, Brooke smiled inwardly. My plan exactly, she thought, pleased with herself. Why do I feel like a woman watching her man come home from the wars?

Though her sharp director's eye had seen a group of tense and tired men, the fans saw heroes. They cheered them. Some of the players merely waved and moved on, but most came up to the fence to exchange words, jokes, a touch of hands. Brooke watched Parks walk toward the barrier with a man she recognized as Snyder, the first baseman. She wondered, by the intensity of their discussion, if they were outlining infield strategy.

''It would only take twenty-five or thirty cans of shaving cream to fill his locker,'' Snyder insisted.

''Takes too long and evaporates too fast,'' Parks commented. ''You've got to be practical, George.''

Snyder swore mildly and lifted his hand in acknowledgment to a shout in the crowd. ''Got a better idea?''

''Carbon dioxide.'' Parks scanned the crowd as they neared it. ''Quick and efficient.''

''Hey, yeah!'' Pleased, Snyder gave him a slap on the back. ''Knew your brains were good for something, Einstein.''

''And as long as I help you work out the mechanics,'' Parks added, ''my locker doesn't get filled with the thinking man's shaving cream.''

''There's that, too,'' Snyder agreed. ''Would you look at these people?'' His grin widened. ''Fantastic.''

Parks started to agree, then spotted a mass of red hair touched with gold in the sunlight. The fatigue drained as though someone had pulled a cork. ''Fantastic,'' he murmured and walked straight toward Brooke.

The teenager beside her made a moaning, melting sound and took a death grip on her friend's arm. ''He's coming over here,'' she managed in a choked whisper. ''Right over here. I know I'm going to die.''

Brooke tilted her chin up so that her eyes would stay level with his as he stopped on the other side of the fence. ''Hi.'' Parks's hand closed over hers on the metal wire. The simple contact was as intimate as anything she had ever known.

''Hi.'' Brooke smiled slowly, accepting the flare of desire and the sense of closeness without question.

''Can I get a lift?''

''Anytime.''

He pressed his lips to the fingers still curled around the wire. ''Meet me inside? I have to get my baggage.''

Out of the corner of her eye, Brooke saw the two teenage girls gawking. ''Great catch last night.''

He grinned before he stepped away. ''Thanks.''

Snyder caught him by the arm as Brooke melted back into the crowd. ''Hey, I like that catch better.''

''Off limits,'' Parks said simply, making his way down the line of fans and outstretched hands.

''Aw, come on, Parks, we're teammates. All for one and one for all.''

''Forget it.''

''The trouble with Parks,'' Snyder began to tell a grandfatherly type behind the fence, ''is he's selfish. I make his throws look good. I bite the bullet when he lines a hospital pitch at me. And what thanks do I get?'' He sent Parks a hopeful smile. ''You could at least introduce me.''

Parks grinned as he signed a snatch of paper a fan thrust through a hole in the fence. ''Nope.''

It took him nearly thirty minutes to get away from the crowd and through the terminal. Impatience was growing in him. The simple touch of fingers outside had whetted his appetite for a great deal more. He'd never been lonely on the road before. Even if there was a rain out or an off day away from home, you were surrounded by people you knew. You became as close as a family—close enough to spend endless evenings together or opt to spend one alone without bruising feelings. No, he'd never been lonely. Until this time.

Parks couldn't count the times he had thought of her over the last four days, but he knew that everything had suddenly slipped back into focus the moment he had seen her standing there. Now he saw her again.

Brooke leaned back against a pillar near the baggage belt, Parks's suitcase at her feet. She smiled but didn't straighten as she saw him. She'd hate to have him know just how crazily her pulse was racing. ''You travel light,'' she commented.

He cupped her face in his hand and, oblivious to the people milling around them, brought her close for a long, hard kiss.

''I missed you,'' he murmured against her mouth, then kissed her again.

There were enough of his teammates still loitering around to start up a chorus of approval.

"Excuse me." Snyder tapped Parks on the shoulder and grinned engagingly at Brooke. "I believe you've made a mistake. *I'm* George Snyder. This is our aging bat boy." He gave Parks an affectionate pat.

"How do you do." Brooke extended her hand and had it enveloped in a huge, hard palm. "Too bad about those two strikeouts last night."

There were several jeers as Snyder winced. "Actually, I'm luring the Valiants into complacency."

"Oh." Amused, Brooke gave him a big smile. "You did very well."

"Sorry, Snyder, time for your shot." Parks signaled to two teammates, who agreeably hooked their arms through Snyder's to haul him away.

"Aw, come on, Jones, give me a break!" Good-naturedly, Snyder let himself be dragged away. "I just want to discuss my strategy with her."

"Goodbye, George." Brooke waved as Parks bent to retrieve his bag.

"Let's get out of here."

With her fingers laced through his, Brooke had no choice but to follow. "Parks, you might have introduced me to your friends."

"Dangerous men," he stated. "All dangerous men."

With a chuckle, she matched her pace to his. "Yes, I could see that. Especially the one holding a toddler on each hip."

"There are a few exceptions."

"Are you one?"

Parks caught her around the waist and drew her close against him. "Uh-uh."

"Oh, good. Want to come home with me and tell me your strategy?"

"That's the best offer I've had today." After tossing his bag in the rear of her car, Parks sprawled in the passenger seat. Accustomed to her driving pattern now, he relaxed and began to unwind by rambling about the previous day's game. Brooke said little, pleased to listen, glad that she had arranged to take the day off so that they could have a few hours together, alone.

"The commercial aired during each play-off game, you know," she commented as they headed out of town.

"How'd it look?" Parks laid his head back against the seat. God, it was good to know he didn't have to go anywhere or do anything for twenty-four hours.

"Fantastic." As the road opened up, so did the Datsun's throttle. "And I have it from the source that it plays very well."

"Hmm?"

"A teenager girl in that mob today." With near perfect mimicry, Brooke related the girl's comments. She caught Parks's automatic grimace at the term *beeutiful* but swallowed a chuckle as she continued.

"Nice to know I devastate sixteen-year-old girls," he said dryly.

"You'd be surprised at the buying power of sixteen-year-old girls." With experienced ease, Brooke negotiated the curves on the narrowing road. ''Not so much directly, certainly, but indirectly through their parents. And since they'd like their teenage boyfriends to make their knees weaken, too, they'll push them toward de Marco jeans, shirts, belts, *ad infinitum.*'' Tossing her hair back, she slid her eyes to his. ''And you do have a great smile.''

''Yeah.'' He gave a modest sigh. ''I do.''

Brooke stopped in her driveway with a deliberate jerk that had him swearing. Wisely slipping from the car before he could retaliate, she headed up the path.

''Just for that,'' Parks began as he dragged his bag out of the back, ''I'm not going to give you the present I bought you.''

At the door, Brooke turned, her grin changing to a look of bewilderment. ''You bought me a present?''

Because she looked like a child who expected to be handed a brightly wrapped empty box, Parks treated it lightly. ''I did. But I'm seriously considering keeping it myself now.''

''What is it?''

''Are you going to open the door?''

Brooke shrugged, trying to pretend indifference as she turned the key. ''There's a fire laid,'' she said as she breezed inside. ''Why don't you light it while I get us some coffee?''

''Okay.'' Setting his bag down, Parks stretched travel-cramped muscles. With a wince, he pressed his fingers to the ribs still sore from their contact with Astroturf.

She'd brought some of her garden inside, he noted,

spotting the bowl of vibrant mums and zinnias on the side table across the room. The table, he observed, was Queen Anne; the bowl, dimestore special. Grinning, he went to the hearth. The combination suited her—the exquisite and the practical.

Parks struck a match and set it to the carefully rolled paper beneath the kindling. Dry wood caught with a crackle and a *whoosh*. He inhaled the smell that brought back flickering images of the past; evenings in the cozy parlor of his family home, camping trips with his uncle and cousins, weekends in England at the home of a college friend. He wanted to add to the pictures now with the memory of Brooke lying in his arms in front of the simmering fire while they made slow, endless love.

When he heard her returning, Parks stood, turning to face her as she entered with a tray holding a bottle and two glasses. "I thought you might want wine instead."

Smiling, Parks took the tray from her. "Yes." After setting the tray on the hassock, Parks lifted the bottle, examining the label with a lifted brow. "Is this a celebration?"

"A precelebration," Brooke countered. "I expect you to win tomorrow." She picked up both glasses, holding them out. "And if you don't, we'll have had the wine in any case."

"Seems fair." Parks poured pale-gold liquid into the stemmed glasses. Taking one from her, he clinked the rims together. "To the game?" he asked with a slow smile.

Brooke felt the quick nervous flutter in her stomach and nodded. ''To the game,'' she agreed and drank. Her eyes widened but remained steady when he reached out to take a handful of her hair.

''I saw this in the sunlight,'' he murmured. ''Even in that mob of people at the airport, I'm not sure what I would have done if that fence hadn't been in the way.'' He let it sift through his fingers. ''It was a long four days, Brooke.''

She nodded, taking his hand to draw him onto the sofa beside her. The curves of her body seemed to fit naturally against the lines of his. ''You're tense,'' she said quietly.

''Postseason games.'' He drew her closer, knowing the nerves would gradually drain before they built again the next day. ''Maybe the lucky ones are the players raking leaves in their backyards in October.''

''But you don't really think so.''

Parks laughed. ''No, I don't really think so. The play-offs pump you up until you're ready to explode, but the series…'' He trailed off with a shake of his head. He didn't want to let his mind run that far ahead. The rules were three out of five—they weren't there yet. For now he didn't want to think of it, but of the woman beside him, the quiet afternoon and the long evening ahead. He thought that he'd remember her this way, a little pensive, with the smell of woodsmoke and fall flowers mixing with her own perfume. His mind drifted lazily, comfortably, as he sipped the iced wine and watched the flames dance.

''Have you been busy?''

Brooke tilted her head in absent agreement. She didn't want to think of work any more than Parks did. "The usual," she said vaguely. "E.J. talked me into seeing a perfectly dreadful movie where the cast pranced around in mythological costumes and shot lightning bolts."

"*Olympian Revenge?*"

"It had a talking three-head dragon."

"That's the one. I caught it in Philadelphia last month when we had a rain out."

"I saw the mike in the frame three times."

Parks chuckled at her professional disdain. "Nobody else did," he assured her. "They were all asleep."

"Gross ineptitude keeps me awake." She leaned her head against his shoulder. It occurred to her how empty her home had been for the last few days, and how cozy it felt again. Brooke had never felt the need to share it before. In fact, she had always had a strong proprietary feeling about what was hers. Now, sitting quietly on the sofa, she realized she had already begun to give up her privacy, willingly and with total unawareness. Turning her head, she studied Parks's profile. "I missed you," she said at length.

He turned his head as well so that their lips were close, not quite touching. "I'd hoped you would." Then he shifted so that his mouth grazed her cheek. She trembled. Not yet, he told himself as the heat flared inside him. Not quite yet. "Maybe I'll give you that present after all."

Brooke's lips curved against his throat. "I don't believe you bought me anything at all."

Recognizing the ploy but willing to play, Parks rose. "You'll have to apologize for that," he said soberly as he walked to his suitcase. He flipped open the case then rummaged inside. When he stood again, Parks had a white box in his hands. Brooke regarded it curiously but with some of the wariness he had noted outside.

"What is it?"

"Open it and find out," he suggested, dropping it into her lap.

Brooke turned it over, examining the plain white box, testing it for weight. She wasn't a woman accustomed to spontaneous gifts and in the short time he had known her, Parks had already given her two. "You didn't have to—"

"You *have* to give your sister a Christmas present," he said mildly, sitting beside her again. "You're not my sister and it isn't Christmas."

Brooke frowned. "I'm not sure I understand the logic in that," she murmured then opened the lid. Packed in wads of tissue paper was a fat pink ceramic hippo with heavily lashed eyes, a flirtatious grin and varicolored polka dots. With a laugh, Brooke drew it out. "She's gorgeous!"

"She reminded me of you," Parks commented, pleased with the laugh and the look of humor in her eyes when she turned them to him.

"Is that so?" She held the hippo up again. "Well, she does have rather fetching eyes." Touched, she stroked the wide ceramic flank. "She really is sweet, Parks. What made you think of it?"

"I thought she'd fit into your menagerie." Seeing the puzzled look on her face, he gestured toward the shelf that held her monkey and bear. "Then there's that pig on the front door, the little carving of a jack rabbit in your bedroom, the china owl on the windowsill in the kitchen."

Comprehension came slowly. There were animals of varying types and materials scattered all through the house. She'd been collecting them for years without having the slightest idea what she was doing. But Parks had seen. Without an instant of warning to either of them, Brooke burst into tears.

Stunned, then alarmed, Parks reached for her, not having a clue what he would offer comfort for. Still, he'd seen enough tears from his sisters to know that logic often had nothing to do with tears. Ashamed, and unable to stem the flow, Brooke evaded his arms and rose. "No, no, please. Give me a minute. I *hate* to do this."

Even as he told himself to respect her wishes, Parks was going to her. Despite her resistance, he pulled her against him. "I can't stand to *see* you do it," he muttered; then, with a hint of exasperation, "Why are you doing it?"

"You'll think I'm stupid. I hate being stupid."

"Brooke." Firmly, he cupped a hand under her chin and lifted it. Tears rolled freely down her cheeks. Knowing no other remedy, he kissed her—the soft lips, the wet cheeks, the damp eyelids. What began as a blind effort to comfort grew to smoldering passion.

He could feel it build in him as his mouth sought hers again. His hands moved through her hair like those of a man making his tentative way through bolts of silk. She trembled against him—sobs or desire Parks was no longer sure as the kiss went deeper and deeper. She opened for him, more giving than he could remember. Her defenses were down, he reminded himself, fighting the impatience to fill his own needs quickly. His murmurs were quiet-pitched to soothe, his hands gently stroking to arouse.

Even recognizing her own vulnerability, Brooke didn't resist. She wanted to drift into that smoky, weightless world where every movement seemed to be in slow motion. She wanted to feel that fire and flash that left you breathless. She wanted the down-soft contentment that would lull you to sleep and linger in the morning.

As he lowered her to the floor, the scent of wood-smoke grew stronger. Brooke could hear the pop and hiss of the logs as flames ate at them. His long patient kisses held her suspended—half in the reality of the wool rug beneath her back, the red flickers of firelight and sun on her closed lids, half in the world of dreams lovers understand. While her mind floated, flirting with each separate sensation, he undressed her.

Parks took infinite care with the tiny round buttons of her blouse, as if he could wait until the seasons changed outside the tall windows. There was no time here, no winter, no spring, only one everlasting moment. Brooke slipped her hands under his shirt, fingertips gliding over the warmth and the strength. As patient as he, she drew the material up, over his shoulders, then discarded it.

Flesh against flesh, they lay before the fire while the sun streamed through the massive windows and pooled over them. Kisses grew longer, interrupted only for sighs, for murmurs. She tasted the mellow warmth of wine on his tongue and was intoxicated.

Slowly, his mouth never leaving hers, Parks began to explore her body. Tiny, needlelike chills ran over her flesh, chasing the path of his hands. Feeling the light graze of his knuckles against the side of her breast, Brooke moaned, a liquid sound of pleasure. He took his tongue deeper into her mouth, gently exploiting this small weakness until the drug took full effect. She was limp, languid, utterly his. Then and only then did he give his lips the freedom to taste her skin again. It was as pungent as her scent, and somehow more erotic.

With moist, open-mouthed kisses he savored her, entranced her. Then the quick pressure of his teeth on some sensitive spot would bring her sharply aware, gasping with the change. His lips would soothe again, lulling her back into pliancy. Again and again he yanked her toward the flame, then guided her back to the clouds, until Brooke was no longer certain which she most desired.

She felt him draw her slacks down over her hips while he pressed those soul-wrenching kisses along her stomach. A mindless excitement filled her, rendering her helpless to do any more than move as he requested. His breath was warm on her intimate flesh so that the long muscles in her thighs trembled then went lax.

Still his mouth moved slowly. The hands that had already discovered every secret point of pleasure continued to caress and linger, keeping her trapped beneath a thin sheet of silken passion. The power she had experienced before moved through her, but her mind was too dazed to recognize it. She felt herself balanced on a slender edge—desire's tightrope—and wanted to continue to walk it as much as she longed to fall headlong into the wild, churning sea below. Then he was above her again, his eyes looking down into hers for a long, long, moment before his lips descended. He was waiting, and she understood. Their mouths still clinging, Brooke guided him inside her.

Her moan melted into his mouth, hot and passionate. Though she was clinging to him now with a sudden, fierce strength, Parks moved slowly. Brooke felt herself fill, fill to the desperate point of explosion. Then the shudders, wracking, convulsive, until she seemed to slide back down some smooth cool path to the torrent again. Like a swimmer trapped in rushing white water, she was swept from peak to peak while he moved with tortuous slowness. She could feel the tight, tense control in him, hear it in the quick labored breaths that merged with hers as he prolonged the pleasure, and the agony. Then he murmured something—a prayer, a plea, an oath—and took them both tumbling off the tightrope.

* * *

He must have slept. Parks thought he had closed his eyes for only an instant, but when he opened them again, the slant of the sun was different. Brooke was beside him, her hair wrapping them to each other. Her eyes were wide and aware as she stared into his. She'd been watching him for nearly an hour. Parks smiled and pressed his mouth to her shoulder.

"Sorry. Did I fall asleep?"

"For a little while." She hid her face against his neck a moment. It was as though he had stripped off her flesh, exposing all her thoughts. She wasn't quite certain what she should do about it. "You must have been exhausted."

"Not anymore," he said truthfully. He felt alert, pumped with energy and…clean. The last made him give a quick shake of his head. He stroked a hand down her arm. "There was something I wanted to ask you before I got… distracted." Propping himself on his elbow, Parks looked down at her. "Why were you crying?"

Brooke moved her shoulders in a shrug and started to shift away. With a firm hand, Parks stopped her. He could feel the effort she was making to draw back from him, but he realized he could no longer permit it. Whether she knew it or not, she had given herself to him completely. He was going to hold her to it.

"Brooke, don't try to block me out," he said quietly. "It won't work anymore."

She started to protest, but the quiet, steady look in his eyes told her he spoke nothing less than the truth. That alone should have been a warning of where her heart was taking her. "It was a sweet thing to do," she said at length. "I'm not used to sweetness."

Parks lifted a brow. "That's part of it, perhaps. What's the rest?"

With a sigh, Brooke sat up. This time he let her. "I hadn't realized I'd been collecting." With both hands, she pushed her hair back, then wrapped her arms around her knees. "I overreacted when you pointed it out. I always wanted a dog, a cat, a bird, anything when I was growing up. It wasn't feasible the way I shifted around." She moved her shoulders again, causing her tumbled hair to shiver over her naked back. "It was kind of shattering to realize I was still compensating."

Parks felt a chord of sympathy and suppressed it. There was no quicker way to alienate her. "You've got your own home, your own life now. You could have anything you wanted." Reaching around her, he poured more wine for both of them. "You don't have to compensate." He sipped, studying her profile.

"No," she agreed in a murmur. "No, I don't."

"What kind of dog do you want?"

Brooke twirled the glass in her hand, then suddenly laughed. "Something homely," she said, turning to grin at him. "Something down-to-the-ground homely." She reached out, laying a hand on his cheek. "I didn't even thank you."

Parks considered, nodding solemnly as he took the glass from her hand. "No, you didn't." In a quick move, he had her rolling on top of him. "Why don't you thank me now?"

Chapter 9

Claire came down to give the set her final approval. At the far end of the studio, serenely indifferent to the piles of equipment, lights and shades, was a cozy living room scene. A deep, cushy sofa in shades of masculine brown was spotlighted as technicians made adjustments. On a table beside it was a Tiffany lamp which would appear to give the soft, sexy lighting the crew was working to achieve. Claire worked her way around cable and cases to a new angle.

Tasteful, she decided. And effective. De Marco was pleased with the first spot. So pleased, Claire thought with a mild grimace, that he had insisted his current inamorata appear in this one. Well, that was show business, she decided as she checked her watch. Brooke had moaned and groaned at the casting, then had given in with the mutter that at least he hadn't insisted they write her any dialogue.

The studio segment was being filmed first, though it would appear at the end of the ad when aired. Judging Parks's temperament, Brooke had decided to go with what would probably be the most difficult portion for him first, then ease him into the rest. And, Claire mused as she checked her watch, their luck was holding. The Kings would compete in the World Series the following week, giving the commercials just that much more impact.

Outside the studio, a long buffet had been set up in the hall. E.J., the production coordinator and the assistant cameraman were already making the most of it. Brooke was in the studio, nibbling on a hunk of cheese as she supervised the finer details.

''Damn it, Bigelow, that light's flickering again. Change the bulb or get a new fixture in here. Silbey, let me see what kind of effect we get with that new gel.''

Obediently, he hit a switch so that the light filtered through the colored sheet and came out warm and sultry. ''Okay, not bad. Sound?''

The sound technician walked under the boom mike. With her face innocently bland, she began to recite a nursery rhyme with a few interesting variations. At the polite volley of applause, she curtsied.

''Any problems?'' Claire asked as she moved to stand beside Brooke.

''We've smoothed them out. Your end?''

''Everyone's accounted for. The talent's changing.'' Absently, she straightened the hem of her sleeve. ''I got a glimpse of de Marco's lady. She's gorgeous.''

''Thank God,'' Brooke said with feeling. ''Are we expecting him?''

''No.'' Claire smiled at the resigned tone of Brooke's voice. She heartily disliked relatives, friends or lovers hanging around a shoot. ''He tells me Gina claims he would make her nervous, but he left no doubt she's to be given the royal, kid-glove treatment.''

''I won't bite her,'' Brooke promised. ''I ran through Parks's lines with him. He has it cold...if he doesn't fumble it on camera.''

''He doesn't appear to be a fumbler.''

Brooke smiled. ''No. And I think he's starting to enjoy this whole business despite himself.''

''Good. I have a script I want him to read.'' Above their heads on a ladder, someone cursed pungently. Claire's smooth features never registered she had even heard. ''There's a part, a small one, I think he's perfect for.''

Brooke turned to give Claire her full attention. ''A feature?''

She nodded. ''For cable. We won't be casting for another month or two, so he's got plenty of time to think about it. I'd like you to read it, too,'' she added casually.

''Sure.'' Mulling over the idea of Parks as an actor, Brooke turned to call out another instruction.

''You might like to direct it.''

The order froze in her throat. "What?"

"I know you're happy directing commercials," Claire went on as if Brooke weren't gaping at her. "You've always said you enjoy creating the quick and intense, but this script might change your mind."

"Claire"—Brooke might have laughed if she hadn't been stunned—"I've never directed anything more complex than a sixty-second spot."

"Like the promo for the new fall shows you filmed last summer? Three major network stars told me you were one of the best they'd ever worked with." It was said dryly, hardly like a compliment. "I've wanted to ease you into something like this for a long time, but I didn't want to push." Claire patted her hand. "I'm still not pushing, just read the script."

After a moment, Brooke nodded. "All right, I'll read it."

"Good girl. Ah, there's Parks now." Her eyes ran over him with professional discrimination. "My, my," she murmured, "he does wear clothes well."

He looked as though he had chosen the pale-blue cashmere sweater and slate-gray jeans at random, shrugging into them without a thought. That they fit with tailored precision wasn't nearly as important as the sense of rightness—that careless style that comes not from money but from basic class.

That he had, Brooke thought. Beneath the attractive face and athletic body was a sense of class that one was born with or one was not. It could never be taught. He held a glass of ginger ale in his hand, looking over the rim as he studied the room.

He found it crowded and cluttered and apparently disorganized but for the small island of order that was a sofa, table and lamp. He wondered fleetingly how anyone could work sanely around the coiled snakes of cable, huge black cases and poles of light. Then he saw Brooke. She could, he thought with a smile. She would simply steamroll over the chaos until she got exactly what she wanted. She might have wept like a child in his arms only a few nights before, but when she was on the job she was as tough as they came.

Perhaps, he mused, that was why he'd fallen in love with her—and perhaps that was why he was going to keep that little bit of information to himself for a while. If he'd nearly panicked when he'd realized it, Brooke would undoubtedly do so. She wasn't quite ready to sit trustingly in the palm of his hand.

Brooke moved toward him, eyes narrowed. Parks thought uncomfortably that she could always make him feel like a department store dummy when she looked at him that way. It was her director's look, appraising, searching for flaws, mulling over the angles.

"Well?" he said at length.

"You look marvelous." If she had noticed the faint irritation in his voice, she ignored it. Reaching up, she disheveled his hair a bit, then studied the effect. "Yes, very good. Nervous?"

"No."

Her face softened with a smile. "Don't frown, Parks, it won't help you get into the mood. Now..." Linking her arm in his, she began to lead him toward the set. "You know your lines, but we'll have cue cards in case you draw a blank, so there's nothing to worry about. The main thing we want is that sort of laid-back, understated machismo. Remember this is the end of the segment; the first scene you're on the field in uniform, then there's the business in the locker room while you're changing, then this. Soft lights, a little brandy, a beautiful woman."

"And I owe it all to de Marco," he said dryly.

"The woman in any case," she returned equably. "It's simply a statement that clothes suit a man's image. Hopefully, men will be convinced that de Marco's right for theirs. You'll sit here." Brooke gestured toward the end of the couch. "Give me that relaxed slouch of yours when you're unwinding. It's casual but not sloppy."

He frowned again, helplessly annoyed that she could dissect his every gesture and put a label on it. "Now?"

"Yes, please." Brooke stood back while Parks settled himself on the couch. "Yes, good.... Bring your elbow back just a bit on the arm. Okay." She smiled again. "That's what I want. You're getting very good at this, Parks."

"Thanks."

"You'll talk right into the camera this time," she told him, gesturing behind her to where the machine sat on a dolly. "Easy, relaxed. The girl will come up behind you, leaning over as she hands you the brandy snifter. Don't look at her, just touch her hand and keep talking. And smile,'' she added, looking at her watch. ''Where is the girl?''

On cue, Gina entered, tall and voluptuous, followed by a stern-looking blonde and two men in business suits. Better than the photo de Marco sent over, Brooke noted, and that had been impressive. The woman was young, but not too young, a ripe twenty-five, Brooke estimated, with large sloe eyes and raven hair. Her body was curvy, shown to advantage in a clingy low-cut gown that stopped just short of censorship. She wouldn't get aloof from this one, Brooke mused, watching Gina make her way across the studio. Heat vibrated in every movement. This time she would go for pure sex—for the five and a half seconds Gina was on screen. For a thirty-second television ad, it would be more than enough.

Ignoring the appreciative mutters and elbowing of her crew, Brooke walked to meet de Marco's lady. ''Hello.'' She extended her hand with a smile. ''I'm Brooke Gordon, I'll be directing you.''

''Gina Minianti,'' she purred in a voice that instantly made Brooke regret she'd have no lines.

''We're very pleased to have you, Ms. Minianti. Do you have any questions before we begin?''

Gina gave her a slight smile. *''Come?''*

''If there's anything you don't understand,'' Brooke began, only to have the blonde interrupt her.

''Signorina Minianti doesn't speak English, Ms. Gordon,'' she said briskly. ''Weren't you informed?''

''Doesn't—'' Breaking off, Brooke rolled her eyes to the ceiling. ''Lovely.''

‘‘I’m Mr. de Marco’s personal secretary. I’ll be glad to translate.’’

Brooke gave the blonde a long hard look, then turned around. ‘‘Places,’’ she called. ‘‘It’s going to be a long day.’’

‘‘A little stumbling block?’’ Parks murmured as she passed him.

‘‘Shut up and sit down, Parks.’’

Controlling a grin, he stepped forward to take Gina’s hand. ‘‘Signorina,’’ he began, then caught Brooke’s full attention when he continued in fluid Italian. Beaming, Gina answered in a rapid spate, gesturing freely with her other hand.

‘‘She’s excited,’’ Parks commented, knowing Brooke had stopped in her tracks behind him.

‘‘So I gathered.’’

‘‘She’s always wanted to do an American movie.’’ He spoke to Gina again, something that made her throw back her magnificent head and laugh throatily. Turning, she dismissed the blonde with a flick of the wrist and tucked her arm through Parks’s. When they faced her, the tawny Californian, the raven Italian, Brooke was struck with the perfection of the contrast. That five and a half seconds of film, she thought, was going to crackle like a forest fire—and sell one hell of a lot of de Marco merchandise.

‘‘You seem to speak Italian well enough to suit her,’’ Brooke commented.

‘‘Apparently.’’ He grinned again, noting that Brooke wasn’t the least jealous but appraising, as if he and Gina were already in a view screen. "She'd like me to interpret for her."

"All right, tell her we'll run through it once to show her what she needs to do. Let's have the lights!" Striding to the set, Brooke waited impatiently while Gina and Parks strolled behind her, heads close as he relayed Brooke's instructions. "Sit down, Parks, and tell her to watch closely. I'll run through it with you." Parks settled on the couch as she had instructed him. "Take it from the top, just as if the camera were rolling."

He began, talking easily, as if to a few friends on a visit. Perfect, Brooke thought as she picked up the prop brandy snifter and walked into camera range behind the couch. She leaned over, letting her cheek come close to his as she offered it. Without glancing from the camera, Parks accepted it, raising the fingers of his other hand to run down the back of Brooke's as it rested on his shoulder. She straightened slowly, moving out of camera range as he finished the dialogue.

"Now ask her if she understands what she's to do," Brooke ordered.

Gina lifted an elegant hand at Parks's question, silently communicating "of course."

"Let's try one." Brooke backed behind E.J. and the assistants who would dolly the camera platform forward for the close-ups. "Quiet on the set," she called, effectively cutting off a few discreet murmurs. "Roll film...." The clapper struck—Parks Jones for de Marco, scene three, take one. She narrowed her eyes at Parks. ''Action.''

He ran through it well enough for a first take, but Brooke decided he hadn't warmed to it yet. Gina followed instructions, bringing the snifter, leaning over him suggestively. Then she glanced up, startled, as the camera rolled in.

''Cut. Parks, explain to Gina not to look at the camera, please.'' She smiled at the woman, hoping she communicated patience and understanding. She needed a great deal of both by the fifth take. Instead of becoming more used to the camera, Gina seemed to be growing more unnerved. ''Five minutes,'' Brooke announced. The hot lights switched off, and the crew began a pilgrimage toward the buffet. With another smile, Brooke gestured for Gina to join her and Parks on the sofa. ''Parks, will you tell her she need only be natural. She's gorgeous, the few seconds she's going to be on film will make a tremendous impact.''

Gina listened with brows knit, then tossed Brooke a smile. ''*Grázie.*'' Taking Parks's hand, she launched into a long, emotional torrent that turned out to be an apology for her clumsiness and a request for something cold to calm her nerves.

''Bring Signorina Minianti some orange juice,'' Brooke demanded. ''Tell her she's not clumsy at all,'' Brooke continued diplomatically. ''Ah, tell her to try to imagine you're lovers, and when the camera turns off—''

''I get the idea,'' Parks said with a grin. When he

spoke to Gina again, she gave her throaty laugh then shook her head before she answered. ''She says she'll try to imagine it,'' Parks relayed to Brooke, ''but if she imagines it too well, Carlo will step on my face…or words to that effect.''

''We have to sacrifice for our art,'' Brooke told him dryly. ''Parks, it would help if you could put a little more steam into it.''

''Steam?'' he repeated, lifting a brow.

''A man who doesn't steam a bit with a woman like that hanging over his shoulder needs a transfusion.'' Rising, Brooke patted his shoulder. ''See what you can do?''

''Anything for art,'' he returned, sending her a wolfish grin.

As E.J. sat behind his camera again, Brooke walked to stand at his shoulder. ''Let's see if we can make one this time,'' she muttered.

''Boss, I can do this all day long.'' He focused his lens on Gina and sighed. ''I think I've died and gone to heaven.''

''De Marco might arrange it if you don't watch your step. Places!''

Better, she mused. Yes, definitely better as they completed the sixth take. But not perfect. She told Parks to ask Gina to give the camera a languid look before she slid Parks an under-the-lashes smile. The direction lost something in the interpretation. ''Cut. Here, tell her to stand next to the camera and watch again.'' Brooke took Gina's place, moving behind him as he spoke, cupping the snifter of lukewarm tea.

This time when Parks took it from her, he brought her other hand to his lips, pressing a soft kiss against it without breaking the rhythm of the dialogue. Brooke felt a jolt shoot up her arm and forgot to move away.

"Just seemed natural," Parks told her, linking his fingers through hers.

Brooke cleared her throat, aware that her crew was watching with avid interest. "Give it a try that way, then," she said matter-of-factly. She walked back to E.J., but when she turned, Parks's eyes were still on her. Brooke gave a quick, frustrated shake of her head. She knew that look. Slowly, the meaning crystal-clear, Parks smiled.

"Places!" Brooke called in her own defense.

It took three more takes before she got just what she wanted. A hot but self-satisfied Gina gave Parks two exuberant kisses, one on each cheek, then came over and chattered something at Brooke. Glancing up at Parks, Brooke saw that amused and all too innocent look on his face.

"Just say thank you," he advised.

"Thank you," Brooke said obediently as Gina took her hand and squeezed it. She swept off with her entourage. "What was I thanking her for?" Brooke used the sleeve of her shirt to dry the sweat on her forehead.

"She was complimenting your taste."

"Oh?"

"She said your lover was magnificent."

Dropping her arm, Brooke stared at him. "Really?" she said coolly.

Parks grinned, gave a deprecatory shrug then strolled off to see if anything was left at the buffet.

Hands on her hips, Brooke stared after him. She wouldn't give him the satisfaction of letting her own smile escape. "Location, one hour," she called out.

Brooke had been right in thinking that the third brief scene of the commercial would be the most difficult to film. She shot the second scene next, crowding lights, equipment and crew into the Kings locker room. Claire had arranged, with a little negotiating, to have a few of the better-known of Parks's teammates available for background or cameos. Once Brooke got them settled down so that they stopped waving at the camera or making fictitious announcements into the mike, it began to work. And work well.

Because of the relative ease with which the segment was progressing, Brooke found the headache growing at the base of her skull unexplainable. True, the locker room was noisy between takes, and after the first hour of many bodies under hot lights, it *smelled* like a locker room, but this headache was pure tension.

At first she simply ignored it; then, when that became impossible, she grew annoyed with herself. There was nothing to be tense about. Parks did what he was told, pulling the cashmere sweater over his naked chest for each take. And every time he smiled at her, Brooke felt the headache pulse.

By the time the crew was setting up for the scene on the diamond, Brooke had convinced herself she had it under control. It was just a nagging ache, something she would take care of with a couple of aspirin when she got home. As she watched the sound technician work on a mike, she felt a beefy arm slip over her shoulders.

"Hi." Snyder grinned down at her, drawing an automatic smile of response from Brooke. He was, she thought, about as dangerous as a cocker spaniel.

"Ready for the next scene, George? You did very well before. Of course, you won't be on camera this time."

"Yeah, I wanted to mention that you're making a big mistake using Parks. Too skinny." He flexed a well-muscled arm.

Brooke gave his biceps a nod of approval. "I'm afraid I don't have anything to do with the casting."

"Too bad. Hey, now that I'm a star, are you going to pick me up at the airport?"

"Forget it, Snyder." Before Brooke could answer, Kinjinsky strolled over, a bat in one hand, a ball in the other. "She's out of your league." He grinned at Brooke, jerking his head at his teammate. "He specializes in belly dancers."

"Lies." Snyder looked amazingly like an overgrown choirboy. "All lies."

"When my daughter grows up," Kinjinsky said mildly, "I'm going to warn her about men like him." Walking to the plate, he tossed the ball up in the air then drilled it out to center field.

"Kinjinsky's the best fungo hitter on the team," Snyder told Brooke. "Too bad he has such trouble with a pitched ball."

"At least I can make it from first to second in under two and a half minutes," Kinjinsky tossed back.

Snyder, well used to ribbing about his base running, feigned an offended look. "I have this genetic anatomical problem," he explained to Brooke.

"Oh." Playing along, she looked sympathetic. "That's too bad."

"It's called a lead foot," Parks commented as he came up behind them.

Hearing his voice had the headache she'd nearly forgotten drumming again. She turned to find him watching her and his teammates with a lazily amused smile. Parks wore full uniform, the blazing white that brought out the gold of his skin. The navy cap shaded his eyes, giving him a cocky, assured look. Quietly possessive, his eyes skimmed over her. This time Brooke felt a flutter in her stomach in addition to the throb at the base of her neck.

"Just keeping your woman entertained," Snyder said genially.

"Brooke's her own woman." But there was something unmistakably proprietary in the disclaimer.

Hearing it, Snyder realized there was something deeper here than he had imagined. So the lightning's finally hit the Iceman, he thought. Snyder had the wit to rib unmercifully and the nature of a man who mends the broken wings of small birds. "When she sees how good I come across on camera, you're going to be out of a job."

"De Marco doesn't have a line for sumo wrestlers," Parks countered.

"Gentlemen," Brooke spoke, cutting them off. "The crew's ready. George, if you'd take your place at first to give Parks his target."

"Ouch." He winced. "Try not to take that literally, Jones. I don't want to be on the disabled list next week."

"Mike." Brooke stepped over to Kinjinsky. "If you'll just hit them to Parks—don't make it too easy for him, I want to see a little effort."

With a grin, Kinjinsky tossed up another ball. "I'll see what I can do."

Nodding, Brooke walked toward the crew. "Places. Parks, any questions?"

"I think I can handle this one." He stepped up to third, automatically kicking up a bit of dust with his spikes.

She looked through the lens, feeling another flutter in her stomach as she focused on Parks. Shifting his weight to one hip, he grinned at her, Brooke stepped back, gesturing to E.J.

"Hey, boss, you okay?"

"Yes, I'm fine. Roll film."

It went perfectly. Brooke knew she could have used the first take without a hitch, but opted for two more. They were equally smooth. Kinjinsky blasted the ball at Parks, enough to make him dive or leap before Parks in turn fired the ball at Snyder on first.

"Third take's the winner," E.J. announced when Brooke called the session a wrap.

"Yes." Unconsciously, she rubbed the back of her neck.

"He shouldn't have even caught it," E.J. went on, watching Brooke as he began to load his equipment.

"He seems to excel at doing the impossible," she murmured.

"Headache?"

"What?" Glancing down, she found E.J. watching her steadily. "It's nothing." Annoyed, she dropped her hand. Parks was already in a conference on the mound with his two teammates. He had his glove hand on his hip, grinning at Snyder's newest concept for a practical joke. "It's nothing," Brooke repeated in a mutter, reaching for one of the sodas in the ice chest.

It had to be nothing, she told herself as she tipped the bottle and drank deeply. Whatever was rolling around inside her was just a product of fatigue after a long day's work. She needed aspirin, a decent meal and eight hours' sleep. She needed to stay away from Parks.

The minute the thought entered her head, Brooke was infuriated. He has nothing to do with it, she told herself fiercely. I'm tired, I've been working too hard, I've— She caught E.J.'s speculative stare and bristled.

"Would you get out of here?"

His face cleared with a wide grin. "On my way. I'll drop off the film at editing."

With a curt nod, Brooke strode out to the mound to thank Snyder and Kinjinsky. She heard the tail of Snyder's brainstorm, something about frogs in the bullpen, before Parks turned to her.

"How'd it go?"

"Very well." Heat was running along her skin now, too physical, too tangible. She gave her attention to his teammates. "I want to thank both of you. Without your help, it never would have gone so smoothly."

Snyder leaned his elbow on Kinjinsky's shoulder. "Just keep me in mind when you want something more than a pretty face in one of these commercials."

"I'll do that, George."

Parks waited through the rest of the small talk, adding comments easily though his concentration was all for Brooke. He waited until the ball players had wandered off toward the locker room before he took Brooke's chin in his hand. Closely, patiently, he examined her. "What's wrong?"

Brooke stepped away so that they were no longer touching. "Why should anything be wrong?" she countered. Her nerves had gone off like bells in her head at his touch. "It went very well. I think you'll be pleased with it when it's edited. With the two spots running throughout the series, we won't shoot another until November." Turning, she noted that most of the crew had gone. She found she wanted to be away before she and Parks were completely alone. "I have a few things to clear up back at the office, so—"

"Brooke." Parks cut her off cleanly. "Why are you upset?"

"I'm *not* upset!" Biting back fury, she whirled back to him. "It's been a long day, I'm tired. That's all."

Slowly, Parks shook his head. "Try again."

"Leave me alone," she said in a trembling undertone that told her, and him, just how close she was to the edge. "Just leave me alone."

Dropping his mitt to the ground, he took both her arms. "Not a chance. We can talk here, or we can go back to your place and hash it out. Your choice."

She shoved away from him. "There's nothing to hash out."

"Fine. Then let's go have dinner and see a movie."

"I told you I had work to do."

"Yeah." He nodded slowly. "You lied."

Sharp, bubbling anger filled her eyes. "I don't have to lie, all I have to do is tell you no."

"True enough," he agreed, holding on to his own temper. "Why are you angry with me?" His voice was calm, patient. His eyes weren't. The sun fell against his face, accenting that fierce sexuality.

"I'm not angry with you!" she nearly shouted.

"People usually shout when they're angry."

"I'm *not* shouting," she claimed as her voice rose.

Curiously, he tilted his head. "No? Then what are you doing?"

"I'm afraid I'm falling in love with you." Her expression became almost comically surprised after the words had tumbled out. She stared in simple disbelief, then covered her mouth with her hand as if to shove the words back inside.

"Oh, yeah?" He didn't smile as he took another step toward her. Something was scrambling inside his stomach like a squirrel in a cage. "Is that so?"

"No, I..." In defense, she looked around, only to

find that she was alone with him now. Alone in his territory. The stands rose up like walls to trap them inside the field of grass and dirt. Brooke backed off the mound. "I don't want to stay here."

Parks merely matched his steps to hers. "Why afraid, Brooke?" He lifted his hand to her cheek, causing her to stop her retreat. "Why should a woman like you be afraid of being in love?"

"I know what happens!" she said suddenly with eyes that were dark and stormy in contrast to the trembling tone.

"Okay, why don't you tell me?"

"I'll stop thinking. I'll stop being careful." She ran an agitated hand through her hair. "I'll give until I lose the edge, then when it's over I won't have anything left. Every time," she whispered, thinking of all the transient parents, thinking of Clark. "I won't let it happen to me again. I can't be involved with you for the fun of it, Parks. It just isn't working." Without being aware of the direction, Brooke had turned to pace to the third base bag. Parks felt the warmth of the gold piece against his chest and decided it was fate. Taking his time, he followed her. His percentage of errors at the corner was very small.

"You are involved with me, whether you're having fun at it or not."

She sent him a sharp glance. This wasn't the easygoing man but the warrior. Brooke straightened her shoulders. "That can be remedied."

"Try it," he challenged, calmly gripping her shirt in his hand and pulling her toward him.

Brooke threw her head back, infuriated, and perhaps more frightened than she had ever been in her life. "I won't see you again. If you can't work with me, take it up with Claire."

"Oh, I can work with you," he said softly. "I can even manage to take your orders without too much of a problem because you're damn good at what you do. I told you once before I'd follow your rules while the camera was on." He glanced around, silently relaying that there was no camera this time. "It's tough to beat a man on his own ground, Brooke, especially a man who's used to winning."

"I'm not a pennant, Parks," she said with amazing steadiness.

"No." With one hand still gripping her shirt, he traced the other gently down her cheek. "Pennants are won through teamwork. A woman's a one-on-one proposition. Seventh-inning stretch, Brooke. Time to take a quick breath before the game starts again." The hand on her cheek moved up to cup her neck. She wondered that he couldn't feel the sledgehammers pounding there. Then he smiled, that slow dangerous smile that always drew her. "I'm in love with you."

He said it so calmly, so simply, that it took her a moment to understand. Every muscle in her body went rigid. "Don't."

He lifted a brow. "Don't love you or don't tell you?"

"Stop." She put both hands on his chest in an attempt to push him away. "It's not a joke."

"No, it's not. What are you more afraid of?" he

asked, studying her pale face. "Loving or being loved?"

Brooke shook her head. She'd been so careful to keep from crossing that thin line—been just as careful to keep others from crossing from the other side. Claire had done it, and E.J., she realized. There was love there. But *in* love... How could a tiny, two-letter word petrify her?

"You could ask me when," Parks murmured, kneading the tense muscles in her neck, "and I couldn't tell you. There wasn't a bolt of lightning, no bells, no violins. I can't even say it snuck up on me because I saw it coming. I didn't try to step out of the way." He shook his head before he lowered his mouth to hers. "You can't wish it away, Brooke."

The kiss rocked her back on her heels. It was hard and strong and demanding without the slightest hint of urgency. It was as if he knew she could go nowhere. She could fight him, Brooke thought. She could still fight him. But the tension was seeping out of her, filling her with a sense of freedom she had thought she would never fully achieve. She was loved.

Feeling the change in her, Parks pulled back. He wouldn't win her with passion. His needs ran too deep to settle for that. Then her arms were around him, her cheek pressed against his chest in a gesture not of desire, but of trust. Perhaps the beginning of trust.

"Tell me again," she murmured. "Just tell me once more."

He held her close, stroking her hair while the breeze whispered through the empty stadium. "I love you."

With a sigh, Brooke stepped over the line. Lifting her head, she took his face in her hands. "I love you, Parks," she murmured before she urged his lips to take hers.

Chapter 10

Clubhouses have their own smell. Sweat, foot powder, the tang of liniments, the faint chemical aroma of whirlpools and the overlying fragrance of coffee. The mixture of odors was so much a part of his life, Parks never noticed it as he pulled on his sweat shirt. What he did notice was tension. That was inescapable. Even Snyder's determined foray of practical jokes couldn't break the curtain of nerves in the locker room that afternoon. When a team had spent months together—working, sweating, winning and losing—aiming toward one common goal, nothing could ease the nerves of facing the seventh game of the World Series.

If the momentum had been with them, the atmosphere would have been different. All the minor aches that plague the end of a season would barely have been noticed—the tired legs, the minor pulls. But the Kings had dropped the last two games to the Herons. A professional athlete knows that skill is not the only determining factor in winning. Momentum, luck, timing are all added for balance.

Even if the Kings could have claimed they'd fallen into a slump there might have been a little more cheer in the clubhouse. The simple fact was that they'd been outplayed. The number of hits between the opponents was almost even—but the Herons had made theirs count while the Kings had left their much needed runs stranded on base. Now it came down to the last chance for both teams. Then when it was over, they'd pick up their off-season lives.

Parks glanced at Snyder, who'd be on his charter boat in Florida the following week. Catching fish and swapping lies, he called it, Parks mused. Kinjinsky, getting heat applied to his ribs, would be playing winter ball in Puerto Rico. Maizor, the starting pitcher, would be getting ready to play daddy for the first time when his wife delivered in November. Some would go on the banquet circuit and the talk show circuit—depending on the outcome of today's game. Others would go back to quiet jobs until February and spring training.

And Parks Jones makes commercials, he reflected with a small grimace. But the idea didn't bring on the sense of foolishness it had only a few months before. It gave him a certain pleasure to act—though Brooke wouldn't call it that—in front of the camera. But he wasn't too thrilled with the poster deal Lee had cooked up.

He smiled a little as he drew on his spikes. Hype, Brooke had called it, saying simply it was part of the game. She was right, of course; she usually was about that aspect of things. But Parks didn't think he'd ever be completely comfortable with the way she could look him over with those calm eyes and sum him up with a few choice words. Wouldn't it disconcert any man to have fallen in love with a woman who could so accurately interpret his every expression, body move or careless word? Face it, Jones, he told himself, you could have picked an easier woman. Could have, he reflected, but didn't. And since Brooke Gordon was who and what he wanted, she was worth the effort it took to have her, and to keep her. He wasn't so complacent that he believed he had truly done either yet.

Yes, she loved him, but her trust was a very tenuous thing. He sensed that she waited for him to make a move so that she could make a countermove. And so the match continued. Fair enough, he decided; they were both programmed to compete. He didn't want to master her…did he? With a frown, Parks pulled a bat out of this locker and examined it carefully. If he had to answer the question honestly, he'd say he wasn't sure. She still challenged him—as she had from the very first moment. Now, mixed with the challenge were so many emotions it was difficult to separate them.

He'd been angry when Brooke wouldn't change her schedule and fly east during the games at the Herons' home stadium. And when he'd become angry, she'd become very cool. Her work, she had told him, couldn't be set aside to suit him or even herself…any more than his could. Even though he'd understood, Parks had been angry. He had simply wanted her there, wanted to know she was in the stands so that he could look up and see her. He had wanted to know she was there when the long game was over. Pure selfishness, he admitted. They both had an ample share of that.

With a grim smile Parks ran a hand down the smooth barrel of the bat. She'd told him it wouldn't be easy. Brooke had been her own person long before he had pushed his way into her life. Circumstances had made her the person she was—though they were circumstances she had still not made completely clear to him. Still it was that person—the strong, the vulnerable, the practical and the private, whom he had fallen for. Yet he couldn't quite get over the urge he had at times to shake her and tell her they were going to do it his way.

He supposed what epitomized their situation at this point was their living arrangement. He had all but moved in with her, though neither one of them had discussed it. But he knew Brooke considered the house hers. Therefore, Parks was living with her, but they weren't living together. He wasn't certain his patience would last long enough to break through that final thin wall—without leaving the entrance hole a bit jagged.

With a quiet oath he reached into the locker and

grabbed a batting glove, sticking it in his back pocket. If he had to use a bit of dynamite, he decided, he would.

"Hey, Jones, infield practice."

"Yeah." He grabbed his mitt, sliding his hand into its familiar smoothness. He was going to handle Brooke, he told himself. But first there was a pennant to win.

Alternately cursing and drumming her fingers against the steering wheel, Brooke cruised the parking lot in search of a space. "I knew we should've left earlier," she muttered. "We'll be lucky to get anything within a mile of the stadium."

Leaning back against the seat, E.J. interrupted his humming long enough to comment. "Still fifteen minutes before game time."

"When somebody gets you a free ticket," Brooke said precisely, "the least you can do is be ready when they pick you up. There's one!" Brooke gunned the motor and slipped between two parked cars with inches to spare. Hitting the brake, she glanced at her companion. "You can open your eyes now, E.J.," she said dryly.

Cautiously, one at a time, he did so. "Okay...." He looked at the car beside him. "Now how do we get out?"

"Open the door and inhale," she advised, wiggling out her side. "And hurry up, will you? I don't want to miss them taking the field."

"I've noticed your interest in baseball's increased

over the summer, boss.'' Thankful for his thin frame, E.J. squeezed out of the Datsun.

''It's an interesting game.''

''Yeah?'' Joining her, he grinned.

''Careful, E.J., I still have your ticket. I could scalp it twenty times before we reach the door.''

''Aw, come on, Brooke, you can tell your friend what's already in the papers.''

She scowled at that, stuffing her hands in her pockets. There'd been pictures of her and Parks, tantalizing little articles and hints in every paper she'd looked at for more than a week. In L.A., gossip carried quickly—a hot ball player and his attractive director were definitely food for gossip.

''I even caught a bit in one of the trades,'' E.J. went on, blithely ignoring the storm clouds in Brooke's eyes. ''Speculation is that Parks might take up, ah…show business,'' he said, giving her another grin, ''seriously.''

''Claire has a part for him if he wants it,'' Brooke returned, evading his obvious meaning. ''It's small but meaty. I didn't want to go into it in depth with Parks until after the series. He has enough on his mind.''

''Yeah, I'd say the man's had a few things on his mind for some time now.''

''E.J.,'' Brooke began warningly as she passed over her tickets.

''You know,'' he continued when they fought their way through the inside crowd, ''I've always wondered when somebody'd come along who'd shake that cool of yours a little."

"Is that so?" She didn't want to be amused, so she slipped her sunglasses down to conceal the humor in her eyes. "And you apparently think someone has?"

"Honey, you can't get within ten feet of the two of you and not feel the steam. I've been thinking..." He fussed with the front of his T-shirt as if straightening a tie. "As your close friend and associate, maybe I should ask Mr. Jones his intentions."

"Just try it, E.J., and I'll break all of your lenses." Caught between amusement and irritation, Brooke plopped down in her seat. "Sit down and buy me a hot dog."

He signaled. "What do you want on it?"

"All I can get."

"Come on, Brooke." He fished in his pocket for a couple of bills, exchanging them for hot dogs and cold drinks. "Buddy to buddy, how serious is it?"

"Not going to let up, are you?"

"I care."

Brooke glanced over at him. He was smiling, not the wisecracking grin she so often saw on his face, but a simple smile of friendship. It was, perhaps, the only weapon she had no defense against. "I'm in love with him," she said quietly. "I guess that's pretty damn serious."

"Grade-A serious," he agreed. "Congratulations."

"Am I supposed to feel like I'm walking on a cliff?" she demanded, only half-joking.

"Don't know." E.J. took a considering bite of his hot dog. "Never had the experience."

"Never been in love, E.J.?" Leaning back in her seat, Brooke grinned. "You?"

"Nope. That's why I spend so much time looking." He gave a heavy sigh. "It's a tough business, Brooke."

"Yeah." She took off his fielder's cap and swatted him with it. "I bet it is. Now shut up, they're going to announce the starting lineup."

A tough business, she thought again. Well, he wasn't far wrong, even if he had been joking. Looking for love was a lonely occupation, one she'd given up—or thought she'd given up—years before. Finding it—or having it tackle you from behind—was even tougher. Once it found you it clung, no matter how much you tried to shake it off. But she wasn't trying to shake it off, Brooke mused. She was just trying to understand how it fit and make a few adjustments. The fabric kept changing.

"Playing third and batting fourth, number twenty-nine, Parks Jones."

The already boisterous crowd went frantic as Parks jogged out on the field to take his place in the lineup. When he stood beside Snyder, he let his eyes drift over. They locked on Brooke's. With a smile, he gave the customary tip of his cap. It was a gesture for the crowd, but she knew it had been aimed at her personally. It was all the acknowledgment he would give her until it was over. It was all she expected.

"I'm going to outhit you today, Iceman," Snyder

warned, grinning at the crowd. "Then Brooke's going to realize her mistake."

Parks never took his eyes off her. "She's going to marry me."

Snyder's jaw dropped. "No kidding! Well, hey..."

"She just doesn't know it yet," Parks added in a murmur. He slapped hands with the right fielder, batting fifth. "But she will."

Brooke detected a change in Parks's smile, something subtle, but to her unmistakable. Narrowing her eyes, she tried to decipher it. "He's up to something," she muttered.

E.J. perfected a shot with a small still camera. "What?"

"Nothing." She swirled her drink so that ice chunks banged together. "Nothing."

A well-known blues singer stepped up to the mike to sing the national anthem. Two lines of athletes removed their caps. The crowd rose, silent for what would be the last time in more than two hours. The excitement was so tangible Brooke thought she could reach out into the warm October air and grab a handful of nerves. It built and built until it exploded with cheers and shouts and whistles as the last note of the song trembled. The Kings took the field.

Sportscasters are fond of saying that the seventh game of the World Series is the ultimate in sports events—the pinnacle test of teamwork and individual effort. This was no exception. In the first inning, Brooke saw the Kings' center fielder charge a ball, stretching forward to catch it on the run then holding on to it as the momentum carried him into a forward roll. She saw the Herons shortstop seem to throw heart and body after a ball to prevent it from going through the hole for a base hit. At the end of the fourth, the teams had one run apiece, each on solo home runs.

Brooke had seen Parks guard his position at third, stealing, as Lee would have put it, two certain base hits and starting the execution of a clutch double play. Watching him, Brooke realized he played this game just as he played every other—with total concentration, with steady determination. If he had nerves, if somewhere in his mind was the thought that this was *the* game, it didn't show. As he stepped up to bat, she leaned out on the rail.

Before he stepped into the box, Parks ran a hand up and down his bat as though checking for splinters. He was waiting for calm, not the calm of the shouting fans but inner calm. In his mind's eye he could see Brooke leaning on the rail, her hair tumbling over her shoulders, her eyes cool and direct. The knot of tension in his stomach eased.

When he stepped up to the plate his predominant thought was to advance the runner. With Snyder on first, he'd have to put it well out of the infield. And they'd be pitching him carefully. Both times he had come to bat, Parks had clipped a single through the hole between third and short.

Parks took his stance and looked directly into the pitcher's eyes. He watched the windup, saw the ball hurtling toward him, shifted his weight, then checked his swing. The slider missed the corner. Ball one.

Stepping out of the box, Parks knocked the bat against his spikes to clear them of dirt. Yeah, they were going to be careful what they gave him. But he could get Snyder to second just as easily on a walk as on a hit. The trouble was, second wasn't a sure scoring position for Snyder.

The second pitch missed, low and outside. Parks checked the signal from the third base coach. He didn't allow his eyes to drift over to where Brooke sat. Parks knew even that brief contact would destroy his concentration.

The next pitch came in on him, nearly catching him on the knuckles then bouncing foul. The crowd demanded a hit. Parks checked Snyder, who was keeping very cozy with the bag, before he stepped into the box again.

Hoping to even the count, the pitcher tried another fast curve. In that fraction of a second, Parks shifted his weight. Wrists square and unbroken, he connected, letting his hips bring the bat around. He had the satisfaction of hearing the ball crack off the bat before the crowd was on its feet, screaming.

The ball sailed over center field, and though three men gave chase, no one reached it before it smashed into the dirt of the warning track and bounced high over the wall. With the fans roaring on all sides, Parks settled for the ground-rule double. There was sweat trickling down his back, but he barely felt it. He thought once that if he'd pulled the ball a bit to the right, it would have gone over clean, scoring two. Then he forgot it.

With Snyder on third, he couldn't take a sizable lead, so he contented himself with putting only a couple of feet between himself and the bag. The odds that Farlo would sacrifice to score Snyder were slim. The outfielder could spray a ball to all fields, but he wasn't a power hitter. Parks crouched, shaking his arms to keep the muscles loose.

Farlo fell behind quickly, fouling off two pitches and frustrating the crowd. Parks simply refused to think of the possibility of being stranded on base again. The infield was playing them tight, looking for that ground ball that could be turned into a double play.

Parks saw the pitch, judged it to be a low curve and tensed. Farlo showed his teeth and smacked it to right field. Parks was running on instinct before he consciously told his feet to move. The third base coach was waving him on. Years of training had Parks rounding third at top speed and heading home without hesitation or question. He saw the catcher crouched, ready to receive the ball, shielding the plate like a human wall. It flashed through Parks's mind that the Herons' right fielder was known for his arm and his precision before he threw himself at the plate in a feet-first slide that had dirt billowing in the clouds. He felt the red flash of pain as his body connected with the catcher, heard his opponent's *whoosh* of air at the hit and saw the small white ball swallowed by the mitt.

They were a tangle of bodies and mutual pain as the umpire spread his arms. "Safe!"

The crowd went wild, stranger pounded on

stranger, beer sloshed over cups. Brooke found that E.J. had grabbed her for a quick dance. His camera cut into her chest but it was several moments before she felt it.

"My man!" E.J. shouted, whirling her into the man on her right, who tossed his box of popcorn into the air.

No, she thought breathlessly. *My* man.

At the plate, Parks didn't concentrate on the adulation of the crowd, but on drawing enough breath into his lungs so he could stand again. The catcher's knee had slammed solidly into his ribs. Rising, he gave his uniform a perfunctory brush then headed to the dugout, where his teammates waited for him. This time, he allowed his eyes to find her. She was standing, her arms still around E.J. But her face softened with a smile that was only for him.

Touching his cap, he disappeared into the dugout. The trainer had the cold spray ready for his ribs.

Parks had forgotten his aches long before he had taken his defensive position in the top of the ninth. The Herons had whittled their lead down to one run with some blood and guts baserunning in the seventh. Since then, both teams had held like rocks. But now, Maizor was in trouble.

With only one out, he had a runner on second and a power hitter coming to the plate. We could walk him and put him on, Parks considered as the catcher tipped back his mask on his way to the mound for a conference. But the Herons had more big bats in the lineup and a few pinch hitters who couldn't be underestimated. Parks sauntered over to the mound, noting as he did that Maizor was strung tight.

''Gonna go for him?'' Parks asked as the catcher chewed on a wad of gum the size of a golf ball.

''Yeah, Maizor's gonna take care of him, aren't you, Slick?''

''Sure.'' He turned the ball over and over in his hand. ''We all want a ride in Jones's new sports car.''

Parks took the mention of the Most Valuable Player Award with a shrug. They were still two outs away, and all three men knew it. ''One thing.'' He adjusted his cap. ''Don't let him hit it toward me.''

Maizor swore and grinned and visibly relaxed. ''Let's play ball.''

Over his shoulder, Maizor checked the runner on second. Satisfied that his lead wasn't too greedy, he fired the ball at the plate. Parks could almost hear the rush of the wind as the bat cut, just over the ball. Kinjinsky called out, telling him to bear down and do it again. He did, but this time the batter got a solid piece of it.

As if a button had been pushed, Parks went for it, lunging from his side as Kinjinsky dashed to cover him. He had only seconds to judge the speed and the height. Even as he let his body fall in the direction of the ball, he felt the runner pass him on his way to third. Landing on his knees, Parks caught in on the short bounce. Without taking the time to rise, he fired the ball toward third. Kinjinsky nabbed it and held his ground as the runner slid into him.

''Still trying to make the easy plays look hard,'' the

shortstop commented as they passed each other. They were both coated with dirt and sweat. "One more, baby, just one more."

Parks let the long, mixed roar of the crowd wash over him as he crouched at third. His face was utterly impassive. The tying run was on first. By the time the count reached three and two, being on the diamond was like being in the eye of a hurricane. Noise and turbulence whirled around them from the stands. On the field, the tension was dead silent.

Maizor went inside, handcuffing the batter. The ball was hit, drifting foul. Parks gave chase as it drifted toward the seats, running at full speed as though the wall weren't looming up in front of him. He could get it, he knew he could get it—if an excited fan didn't reach over and make a grab.

With his free hand, he caught the rail and lifted his glove. He felt the impact of the ball as he closed his leather over it. While the crowd started to scream, he found he was looking directly into Brooke's eyes. The foul had all but fallen into her lap.

"Nice catch." Leaning over, she kissed him full on the mouth.

Then one of his teammates had him around the waist, and the rest was madness.

Parks had more champagne dumped on him than he could possibly have drunk. It mixed with sweat and washed some of the grime away. Snyder had positioned himself on top of a locker and from there emptied two bottles on anyone in sight—reporters and league brass included. Accused of showboating, Parks was tossed, fully dressed, into the whirlpool. Grateful, he stripped and remained where he was with half a bottle of champagne. From there he gave interviews while the water beat the aches from his body and bedlam raged around him.

The pitch on his double had been an outside fast ball. Yeah, his slide into home had been risky, considering the arm of the right fielder, but he'd had a good lead. He continued to answer questions as Snyder, in a champagne-drenched uniform, was not so gently assisted into the whirlpool with him. Parks slid down farther in the soothing water and drained the cold wine straight from the bottle. Yes, the redhead in the stands was Brooke Gordon, his director on the de Marco commercials. Parks smiled as Snyder wisecracked the reporters' attention to himself. Teammates might poke and prod into each other's business, but they protected their own.

Parks closed his eyes a moment, just a moment. He wanted to recapture that instant when she had leaned over and touched her lips to his. Everything had been heightened in that split second of victory. He had thought he could hear each individual shout from the crowd. He'd seen the sunlight glint on the chipped paint of the railing, felt the baking heat as his hand had wrapped around it. Then he'd seen her eyes, close, soft, beautiful. Her voice had been quiet, conveying excitement, humor and love all in two words. When they had touched his, her lips had been warm and smooth, and for an instant that had been all he had felt. Just the silky texture of her lips. He hadn't even heard the last out called. When he'd been dragged back on the field by his teammates, she had simply lowered her chin to the rail and smiled at him. *Later.* He had heard her thought as clearly as if she had spoken it.

It took two hours to urge the last reporter out of the clubhouse. The players were quieting. The first rush of victory was over, replaced by a mellowness that would very quickly become nostalgia. The year was over. There'd be no more infield practice, batting practice, night rides on planes with card games and snoring. They were in a business where today was over quickly and tomorrow took all their efforts. Now there wasn't a tomorrow, but next year.

Some were sitting, talking quietly on the benches in the midst of the locker room litter, as Parks dressed. He glanced at the second-string catcher, a boy of barely nineteen, completing his first year in the majors. He held his shin guards in his hands as if he couldn't bear to part with them. Parks put his mitt into his duffel bag and felt suddenly old.

''How're the ribs?'' Kinjinsky asked as he slung his own bag over his shoulder.

''Fine.'' Parks gestured to the boy on the bench. ''The kid's barely old enough to vote.''

''Yeah.'' Kinjinsky, a ripe thirty-two, grinned. ''It's hell, isn't it?'' They both laughed as Parks closed his locker for the last time that year. ''See you in the spring, Jones. My woman's waiting for me.''

Parks zipped up his bag while the thought warmed

in him. He, too, had a woman, and it would take him thirty minutes to drive to the mountains.

"Hey, Parks." Snyder caught him before he'd reached the door. "You really going to marry her?"

"As soon as I can talk her into it."

Snyder nodded, not questioning the phrasing of the answer. "Give me a call when you set it up. I'm the best man."

With a smile, Parks held out a hand and shook the beefy one. "Damned if you're not, George." He walked into the corridor, closing the door on the clubhouse and the season.

When he emerged outside, it was dusk. Only a few fans lingered, but he signed autographs for them and gave them the time they wanted. Parks thought idly about picking up another bottle of champagne for himself and Brooke as he signed his name to the bill of a twelve-year-old's battered hat. Champagne, a fire burning low, candles. It seemed like a good setting to propose marriage. It was going to be tonight, because tonight he didn't think he could lose.

The parking lot was all but deserted. The overhead lights were just flickering on as twilight deepened. Then he saw her. Brooke was sitting on the hood of his car, spotlighted in the flood of a security light, her hair like tongues of flame around her strong-boned, delicate-skinned face. Love welled up in him, a fierce possessive love that took his breath away. Except for the lips that curved, she didn't move. He realized then she had been watching him for some time. He struggled to regain some control over his muscles before he continued toward her.

"If I'd known you were waiting here, I'd have come out sooner." He felt the ache in his ribs again, but not from the bruise this time. This was from a need he was still not quite used to.

"I told E.J. to take my car. I didn't mind waiting." Reaching up, she put both hands on his shoulders. "Congratulations."

Very deliberately, Parks set his bag down on the asphalt then dove his hands into her hair. Their eyes held briefly, endlessly, before he lowered his mouth and took what he needed.

His emotions were more finely tuned than he had realized. All the pleasure of victory, the weariness that came from winning it, the dregs of excitement and tension surfaced, to be doubled then swept away by one all-encompassing need. Brooke. How was he to have known that she would grow to be everything—and all things? A bit unnerved by the intensity, Parks drew away. A man couldn't win when his knees were buckling. He ran his knuckles down her cheek, wanting to see that very faint, very arousing clouding of her eyes.

"I love you."

At his words, Brooke rested her head against his chest and breathed deeply. She could smell his shower on him, some subtle soap fragrance that spoke of gymnasiums and locker rooms that were inhabited only by men. For some reason, it made her feel acutely a woman. The light grew dimmer as they remained, held close and silent.

"Too tired to celebrate?" she murmured.

"Uh-uh." He kissed her hair.

"Good." Drawing away, she slid from the hood. "I'll buy you dinner to start it off." Brooke opened the passenger door and smiled. "Hungry?"

Until that moment, Parks hadn't realized that he was starving. What little he'd eaten before the game had been devoured by nerves. "Yeah. Do I get to pick the place?"

"Sky's the limit."

Fifteen minutes later, Brooke gazed around the garishly colored Hamburger Heaven. "You know," she mused, studying the overhead lights that were shaped like sesame seed rolls. "I'd forgotten your penchant for junk food."

"A hundred percent pure beef," Parks claimed, picking up an enormous double-decker sandwich.

"If you believe that, you believe anything."

Grinning, he offered her a French fry. "Cynic."

"If you call me names, I won't read you the sports page." She put her hand over the folded paper she'd just bought. "Then you won't hear the accolades the press have heaped on you." When he shrugged, unconcerned, she opened the paper. "Well, I want to hear them." With one hand on her milk shake, Brooke began to thumb her way through. "Here… Oh." She stopped dead and scowled.

"What is it?" Parks leaned over. On the front page

were two pictures, side by side. The first was of his over-the-seats catch of the final out. The second was of Brooke's impulsive kiss. The caption read:

JONES SCORES...TWICE

"Cute," he decided, "considering I didn't score but snagged a pop fly." He twisted his head, skimming down the article which ran through the highlights of the game—critiques and praise. "Hmm.... 'And Jones ended it with a race to the rail, snagging Hennesey's long foul out of the seats in one of the finest plays of the afternoon. As usual, the MVP makes the impossible look routine. He got his reward from the luscious redhead—'" here he shot Brooke a brief glance "'—Brooke Gordon, a successful commercial director who's been seen with the third baseman on and off the set.'"

"I really hate that," Brooke said with such vehemence that Parks looked up in surprise.

"Hate what?"

"Having my picture splashed around that way. And this—this half-baked speculation. This, and that silly business in the *Times* a couple days ago."

"The one that called you a willowy, titian-haired gypsy with smoky eyes?"

"It's not funny, Parks." Brooke shoved the paper aside.

"It's not tragic, either," he pointed out.

"They should mind their own business."

Leaning back, Parks nibbled on a fry. "You'd probably be the first to tell me that being in the public eye makes you public property."

Brooke scowled at that, knowing they were precisely her words when they'd discussed the poster deal. "*You're* in the public eye," she countered. "It's the way you make your living. *I* don't. I work behind the camera, and I have a right to my privacy."

"Ever heard of guilty by association?" He smiled before she could retort. Instead of a curt remark, she let out a long sigh. "At least they're accurate," he added. "I've often thought of you as a gypsy myself."

Brooke picked up her cheeseburger, frowned, then bit into it. "I still don't like it," she muttered. "I think..." She shrugged, not certain how foolish she was going to sound. "I've always been a little overly sensitive about my privacy, and now...what's happening between us is too important for me to want to share with anyone who has fifty cents for a paper."

Parks leaned forward again and took her hand. "That's nice," he said softly. "That's very nice."

The tone of his voice had fresh emotion rising in her. "I don't want to hole up like a couple of hermits, Parks, but I don't want every move we make to be on the evening news, either."

With a bit more nonchalance than he was feeling at the moment, he shrugged and began to eat again. "Romance is news.... So's divorce, when it involves public people."

"It's not going to ease up with the de Marco campaign, either, or if you decide to take that part in the film.'' She took another French fry out of its paper scoop and glared at it. ''The hotter you are, the more the press will buzz around. It's maddening.''

''I could break my contract,'' he suggested.

''Don't be ridiculous.''

''There's another solution,'' he considered, watching Brooke swallow the French fry and reach for another.

''What?''

''We could get married. Want some salt for those?''

Brooke stared at him, then found she had to search for her voice. ''What did you say?''

''I asked if you wanted some salt.'' Parks offered her a tiny paper packet. ''No?'' he said when she neither answered nor moved. ''I also said we could get married.''

''Married?'' Brooke echoed stupidly. ''You and me?''

''The press would ease off after a while. Quietly married couples don't make news the same way lovers do. Human nature.'' He pushed his sandwich aside and leaned toward her. ''What do you think?''

''I think you're crazy,'' Brooke managed in a whisper. ''And I don't think this is funny.''

Parks gripped her arm when she started to scoot out of the booth. ''I'm not joking.''

''You—you want to get married so we won't get our picture in the paper?''

''I don't give a damn if we get our picture in the paper or not, you do.''

"So you want to get married to—to placate me." She stopped struggling against his hold on her arm, but her eyes filled with fury.

"I've never had any intention of placating you," he countered. "I couldn't placate you if I dedicated my life to it. I want to get married because I'm in love with you. I'm *going* to marry you," he corrected, suddenly angry, "if I have to drag you, kicking and screaming."

"Is that so?"

"Yes, that's exactly so. You might as well get used to it."

"Maybe I don't want to get married." Brooke shoved the food in front of them aside. "What about that?"

"Too bad." He leaned back, eyeing her with the same simmering temper with which she eyed him. "*I* want to get married."

"And that's supposed to be enough, huh?"

"It's enough for me."

Brooke crossed her arms over her chest and glared at him. "Kicking and screaming?"

"If that's the way you want it."

"I can bite, too."

"So can I."

Her heart was thudding against her ribs, but Brooke realized it wasn't from anger. No, it had nothing to do with anger. He was sitting there, across a laminated table littered with food from a twelve-year-old's fantasy, telling her he was going to marry her whether she liked it or not. Brooke discovered, somewhat to her own amazement, that she liked it just fine. But she wasn't going to make it easy for him.

"Maybe winning the series went to your head, Parks. It's going to take more than a temper tantrum to get me to marry you."

"What do you want?" he demanded. "Candlelight and soft music?" Annoyed that he had scuttled his own plans, he leaned over again and grabbed her hands. "You're not the kind of woman who needs scenery, Brooke. You know just how easy it is to come by and how little it means. What the hell do you want?"

"Take two," she said very calmly. "You know your motivation," she began in her cool director's voice, "but this time tone down the force and try for a little finesse. Ask," she suggested, looking into his eyes, "don't tell."

He felt the anger, or perhaps it had been fear, slide out of him. The hands that held hers gentled. "Brooke"—he lifted a hand and pressed her fingers to his lips—"will you marry me?" Parks smiled over their joined hands. "How was that?"

Brooke laced the fingers with hers. "Perfect."

Chapter 11

What was she doing? In a sudden panic, Brooke stared at herself in the free standing long-length mirror. How could things be happening so fast and be so much out of her control? A year ago—no, even six months ago—she hadn't known Parks Jones existed. In something under an hour, she would be married to him. Committed. For life. Forever.

From somewhere deep inside her brain came a panicked call to run and run fast. Brooke hadn't realized she'd made a move until she was summarily jerked back into place.

''Be still, Ms. Gordon,'' Billings ordered firmly. ''There are two dozen of these little buttons if there's one.'' She used a complaining tone, though privately she thought Brooke's choice of an ivory satin gown with its snug bodice and flowing skirt was inspired.

A good, traditional wedding dress, she decided, not one of those flighty trouser suits or miniskirted affairs in scarlet or fuchsia. Billings continued to fasten the range of tiny pearl buttons in back.

"Stand still now," she ordered again as Brooke fidgeted.

"Billings," Brooke said weakly, "I really think I'm going to be sick."

The housekeeper looked up at Brooke's reflection. Her face was pale, her eyes huge, made darker by the merest touch of slate-gray shadow. In Billings's staunch opinion, a bride was supposed to look ready to faint. "Nonsense," she said briskly. "Just a case of the flutters."

"Flutters," Brooke repeated, creasing her brow. "I never flutter. That's ridiculous."

The Englishwoman smiled fleetingly as Brooke straightened her shoulders. "Flutters, jitters, nerves—every woman born has them on her wedding day."

"Well, I don't," she claimed as her stomach muscles quivered.

Billings only sniffed as she finished her fastening. "There now, that's the last one."

"Thank God," Brooke muttered, heading for a chair before Billings caught her.

"No, you don't. You're not putting creases in that skirt."

"Billings, for heaven's sake—"

"A woman has to suffer now and again."

Brooke's opinion was a short four-letter word. Lifting a brow, Billings picked up a hairbrush from the vanity. "A fine way for a blushing bride to talk."

"I'm not a blushing bride." Brooke swept away before Billings could apply the brush. "I'm twenty-eight years old," she continued, pacing. "I must be crazy, I must be absolutely crazy. No sane woman agrees to marry a man in a fast-food restaurant."

"You're getting married in Ms. Thorton's garden," Billings corrected. "And it's quite a lovely day for it."

The practical tone caused Brooke to scowl. "And I should never have let her talk me into that, either."

"Hah!" The exclamation had Brooke's brows lifting. Billings gestured threateningly with the hairbrush. "Hah!" she said again, effectively closing Brooke's mouth. "No one talks you into anything. You're a hard-headed, stubborn, single-minded young woman, and you're shaking in your shoes because there's a hard-headed, stubborn, single-minded young man downstairs who's going to give you a run for your money."

"I certainly am not shaking in my shoes," Brooke corrected, insulted. Billings saw the faint pink flush rise to the pale cheeks.

"Scared to death."

Brooke stuck both fists on her hips. "I am most certainly not afraid of Parks Jones."

"Hah!" Billings repeated as she pulled over a foot-stool. Climbing on it, she began to draw the brush through Brooke's hair. "You'll probably stammer and quake when you take your vows, just like some silly girl who doesn't know her own mind."

"I've never stammered in my life." Enunciating each word precisely, Brooke glared at their twin reflections in the mirror. "And nothing makes me quake."

"We'll just see about that, won't we?" Rather pleased with herself, Billings arranged Brooke's mane of hair into a cunningly tumbled mass. In this, she secured a delicate clip of pale-pink-and-white hibiscus. She had fussed that lily of the valley or rosebuds would have been more suitable, but secretly thought the exotic flowers were stunning.

"Now, where are those lovely pearl drops Ms. Thorton gave you?"

"Over there." Still fuming, Brooke pointed to the tiny jeweler's box that held Claire's gift.

They should have eloped as Parks had suggested, Brooke thought. What had made her think she wanted all this fuss and bother? What had made her think she wanted to get married in the first place? As her nerves started jumping again, she caught Billings's ironic stare. Brooke lifted her chin.

"Well, put them on," the housekeeper ordered, holding the pink-blushed pearls in her palm. "It was very clever of Mr. Jones to send you flowers to match them."

"If you like him so much, why don't you marry him?" Brooke muttered, fastening the earrings with fingers that refused to stop trembling.

"I suppose you'll do," Billings said briskly, swallowing a lump in her throat. "Even without a proper veil and train." She wanted badly to press a kiss to Brooke's cheek, but knew it would weaken both of them. "Come along, then," she said instead. "It's time."

I could still call it off, Brooke thought as she let Billings draw her down the hall. There's still time. No one can make me go through with this. The little skips of nerves in her stomach had increased to thumps. There's absolutely nothing that can make me walk out into that garden. What was the phrase? she wondered. Marry in haste, repent at leisure? This was certainly haste.

It had only been four days since Parks had asked her. Four days. Maybe the big mistake had been in telling Claire. Good God, she'd never seen anyone move so fast once they'd gotten the bit between their teeth. Brooke decided she must have been in a state of shock to have let Claire sweep her along with plans and arrangements. An intimate ceremony in her terraced garden, a champagne reception. *Elope?* Claire had brushed that aside with a wave of her hand. Elopements were for silly teenagers. And wouldn't a three-piece ensemble be lovely? Brooke had found herself caught up. And now she was just caught.

But no, Brooke corrected as she and Billings reached the foot of the stairs. All she had to do was turn around and head for the door. She could get into her car and just drive away. That was the coward's way. Straightening her shoulders, Brooke rejected it. She wouldn't run, she would simply walk outside and explain very calmly she had changed her mind. Yes, that's all it would take. I'm very sorry, she practiced mentally, but I've decided not to get married after all. She'd be very calm and very firm.

"Oh, Brooke, you look lovely." And there was Claire, dressed in powder-blue silk with the sheen of tears in her eyes.

"Claire, I—"

"Absolutely lovely. I wish you'd let me have them play the wedding march."

"No, I—"

"It doesn't matter, as long as you're happy." Claire pressed her cheek to Brooke's. "Isn't it silly, I feel just like a mother. Imagine having your first pangs of motherhood at my age."

"Oh, Claire."

"No, no, I'm not going to get sloppy and sentimental and ruin my face." Sniffling, she drew away. "It's not every day I'm maid of honor."

"Claire, I want to—"

"They're waiting, Ms. Thorton."

"Yes, yes, of course." Giving Brooke's hand a quick squeeze, she went out on the terrace.

"Now you, Ms. Gordon." Brooke stood where she was, wondering if the coward's way wasn't basically sound. Billings put a firm hand on her back and pushed. Brooke found herself out on the terrace facing Parks.

He took her hand. He was firm as he brought hers to his lips. She noticed his eyes, smiling, sure. He was in a pearl-gray suit, more formal than anything she had seen him wear. But his eyes held that complete intensity she knew they had when he waited for a pitch. She found herself walking with him to the center of the terrace that was surrounded by flowers and the ornamental trees Claire loved.

Still time, Brooke thought as the minister began to speak in a calm, clear voice. But she couldn't open her mouth to stop what was already happening.

She'd remember the scent always. Jasmine and vanilla, and the sweet drift of baby roses. But she didn't see the flowers because her eyes were locked on Parks's. He was repeating the words the minister spoke, the traditional words spoken countless times by countless couples. But she heard them as if they were uttered for the first time.

Love, honor, cherish.

She felt the ring slip onto her finger. Felt, but again didn't see because she couldn't take her eyes from his. From the branches of a weeping cherry, a bird began to trill.

She heard her own voice, strong and assured, repeat the same promises. And her hand, with no trembling, placed the symbol of the promise on Parks's finger.

A pledge, a promise, a gift. Then their lips moved together, sealing it.

I was going to run, she remembered.

"I'd have caught you," Parks murmured against her mouth.

Astonished and annoyed, Brooke drew back. He was grinning at her, his hands still caught in her hair. To the confusion of the others in the quiet, fragrant garden, Brooke cursed then threw her arms around his neck and laughed.

"Hey." Snyder gave Parks a firm shove. "Give somebody else a chance."

Claire's idea of a small gathering was the epitome of a producer's understatement. Though Brooke didn't bother to count heads, she knew there were well over a hundred "absolutely essential guests." She found she didn't mind—the glitter was her gift to Claire. There was a bubbly fountain of champagne, a five-tiered pink-and-white cake and silver platters of food that for once Brooke had no interest in. Which turned out for the best, as she was swept from one person's arms to another, kissed, hugged and congratulated until it all became a blur of color and sound.

She met Parks's mother, a tiny, exquisite woman who kissed her cheek then burst into tears. His father crushed Brooke in a hug and murmured that now that Parks was married, he would stop the nonsense and come into the company. She found herself inheriting a family in a lump—a large, confusing family that didn't quite fit any of the imaginings of her youth. And through it all, she had barely more than glimpses of Parks as she was passed from cousin to cousin to be weighed, measured and discussed like a fascinating new acquisition.

"Leave the girl be a minute." A sturdy, pewter-haired woman swept the others aside with an imperious wave of her hand. "These Joneses are a silly bunch." She sighed, then summed Brooke up with one long look. "I'm your Aunt Lorraine," she said and extended her hand.

Brooke accepted the handshake, knowing instinctively the gesture was somehow more sincere and more intimate than all the kisses she had received. Then with a flash of insight, she knew. "The gold piece."

Lorraine smiled, pleased. "Told you about that, did he? Well, he's a good boy...more or less." A straight, no-nonsense brow lifted. "And he won't bully you, will he?"

With a grin, Brooke shook her head. "No, ma'am, he won't."

Lorraine nodded, giving Brooke's hand a quick pat. "Good. I'll expect a visit in six months. It takes a couple that long to work out the first kinks. Now, if I were you, I'd get my husband and sneak out of this rabble." With this advice, she strode away. Brooke had her first twinge of genuine kinship.

Even so, it seemed like hours before they could slip away. Brooke had intended to steal back upstairs and change, but Parks had seen his opportunity and had pulled her outside, bundled her into his car and driven off. Now he stopped the car in the driveway of the A-frame and sighed.

"We made it."

"It was rude," Brooke mused.

"Yeah."

"And very smart." Leaning over, she kissed him. "Especially since you managed to cop a bottle of champagne on the way."

''Quick hands,'' he explained as he stepped from the car.

Brooke chuckled, but felt a fresh ripple of unease as they walked up the path. Parks's hand was closed over hers. She could feel the slight, unfamiliar pressure of her wedding ring against her skin. ''One problem,'' she began, pushing the feeling aside. ''You dragged me out of there without my purse.'' She glanced at the door, then back at Parks. ''No keys.''

Parks reached in his pocket and drew out his own. A faint frown creased her brow as she remembered he had a key to the door now. A key to her life. Though he noticed her reaction, Parks said nothing, only slipping the key into the lock. It opened silently. He swept her up into his arms, and with her laughter, the subtle disharmony was forgotten.

''I hadn't realized you were such a traditionalist,'' Brooke murmured, nuzzling at his neck, ''but...'' She trailed off at the sound of high, sharp yapping. Astonished, she looked down to see a small brown dog with a black muzzle racing around Parks's feet, making occasional dives for his ankles. ''What's that?'' she managed.

''Your wedding present.'' With his toe, he nudged the puppy, sending him rolling over on his back. ''Homely enough?''

Brooke stared down at the pushed-in mongrel face. ''Oh, Parks,'' she whispered, close to tears. ''You fool.''

''E.J. should've dropped him off about an hour ago, if he was on schedule. Guy at the pound thought I was crazy when I told him I wanted something down-to-the-ground homely.''

''Oh, I love you!'' Brooke squeezed his neck fiercely then wriggled out of his arms. In her satin wedding dress, she knelt on the floor to play with the puppy.

She looked young, Parks thought, too young, as she buried her face in the little dog's fur. Why would he constantly expose her vulnerabilities then be uncertain how to handle them? There was so much sweetness in her, and yet, was he somehow more comfortable with the vinegar she could serve him? It was the mix, Parks thought as he knelt to join her, the fascinating mix he couldn't resist.

''Our first child.'' Brooke chuckled when the puppy lay in exhausted slumber on the rug.

''He has your nose.''

''And your feet,'' she retorted. ''He's going to be enormous from the size of them.''

''Maybe you can cast him in a few dog food commercials,'' he commented as he drew Brooke to her feet. Gently he kissed her cheek, then trailed his lips over her chin to the other one. He felt the sudden tremble of her breath on his skin. ''Champagne's getting warm,'' he murmured.

''I'm not thirsty.''

He was leading her slowly toward the stairs, still planting those soft, whispering kisses over her face on the journey, leaving her lips—her heating, seeking lips—subtly tormented. And they started to climb the stairs, without rush or hurry, while Parks began unfastening that long range of tiny buttons.

"How many are there?" he murmured against her mouth.

"Dozens," Brooke answered, loosening his tie as they reached the halfway point.

His fingers were nimble. Before they reached the door of the bedroom, he had the gown loosened to her waist. Brooke pushed the jacket from his shoulder, and with her teeth nipping at his neck, tugged his shirt from the waistband of his pants.

"Are you ever going to kiss me?" she demanded breathlessly.

"Mm-hmm." But he only drove her mad by running his lips over her shoulder as he nudged the satin aside. Then he drew it from her, running his hands slowly down her body until the material was only a pool of white at her feet. He toyed with the bits of lace she wore, tiny, filmy wisps designed to torment men. And even as they tormented him, Parks fought for control. There was always that last struggle for control before he found he was lost in her.

Her fingers slid down his naked ribs to brush over his stomach before she found the hook to his trousers. She heard his quick, indrawn breath before his hands became more demanding. Needing, wanting, she pulled him with her onto the bed.

Why should there be such desperation when they were now so securely bound to each other? Though neither of them understood it, they both felt it. The urgency to touch, taste. To possess. Gentleness was abandoned while hungry, primitive passion took its place. The teasing kisses stopped with a hard, burning pressure of mouth on mouth. Her hands sought, as skillfully as his, to find weaknesses. Every moan brought a fresh thrill of arousal, each sigh an increase of tortuous desire until neither knew if the sounds were from pleasure or desperation. And both refused to succumb to the fire.

He found her breast taut and firm. Greedily, his mouth sought it, sending a tearing thread of delight into the core of her. Even as she moaned in surrender, her hands pressed him closer, her body moving sinuously under his until he was lost in the taste of her.

Flesh heated against flesh. The pace quickened. Faster, faster until they were breathless and clinging but still not ready to yield. She ran her hands over his damp back, over the roping of muscles that accented his superior strength. But physical strength meant nothing in the inescapable quicksand of passion. They were both trapped in it, both equally incapable of freeing themselves.

With sudden strength, she shifted, so that they were tangled together, side by side. Her mouth fastened on his, devouring as eagerly as she was devoured, taking as mindlessly as she was taken. Her hair fell over them, curtaining their faces so that Parks couldn't breathe without breathing her. If he had been capable of thought, he might have imagined himself absorbed by her. But there was no thought for either of them, and the need had grown too great to be resisted.

She went willingly when he shifted her, drawing

his mouth down to hers even as he entered her with something close to violence. Then there was only speed and heat, driving them beyond everything but each other.

"Should I need you more each time?" Brooke wondered aloud.

"Mmm." Parks didn't want to move from the warm comfort of her body. It yielded under his, pressed deep into the mattress. "Just don't stop."

It was dusk. The light filtering through the windows was soft—and soon it would be night. Her wedding night. Yet she still felt only like a lover. How would it be to feel like a wife? Lifting her hand, she stared at the band on her finger. It was encrusted with diamonds and sapphires that glowed softly in the room's twilight. "I don't want it to be different tomorrow," she thought aloud. "I don't want it to change."

Parks raised his head. "Everything changes. You'll get mad if I use all the hot water for my shower. I'll get mad if you've drunk the last of the coffee."

Brooke laughed. "You have a way of simplifying things."

"Those are the nuts and bolts of a relationship, Mrs. Jones," he claimed and kissed her.

The eyes that had begun to close for the kiss opened wide. "Jones," she repeated. "I'd forgotten about that part of it." She considered for a minute. "It makes me think of your mother…though of course she was very nice."

Parks gave a muffled chuckle. "Don't worry. Just remember she lives three hundred miles away."

Brooke rolled over until she lay on top of him. "You have a very nice family."

"Yeah, and we don't want to get tangled up with them any more than we have to."

"Well..." Brooke laid her head on his chest. "No. At least not too soon," she added, thinking of his aunt. She relaxed again as he began to lazily stroke her hair. "Parks?"

"Hmm?"

"I'm glad we decided to come here instead of flying off somewhere."

"We'll go to Maui for a couple of weeks around Christmas. I want you to see my place there."

Brooke thought of her schedule if she decided to take Claire up on the feature for cable. Somehow or other, she'd managed to get the two weeks. "I love you."

His hand stopped a moment, then pressed her closer. They were three words she didn't say often. "Did I tell you how beautiful you looked when Billings shoved you out on the terrace?"

Brooke's head shot up. "You saw that?"

Grinning he traced her ear with his fingertip. "Funny, I didn't expect you to be as terrified as I was."

Brooke regarded him a moment, then a smile curved on her lips. "Were you really?"

"A half hour before the wedding, I'd run up a list of all the reasons why we should call it off."

She lifted a brow. "Were there many?"

"I lost count," he told her, ignoring the narrowing of her eyes. "I could only think of one good reason to go through with it."

"Oh, really?" Her chin came up as she tossed her head. "And what was that?"

"I love you."

Brooke dropped her forehead onto his. "That's it, huh?"

"The only one I could think of." He slid a hand down to her hip. "Though one or two others are beginning to occur to me."

"Mmm. Like it being good for the campaign." She began to nuzzle, just behind his ear.

"Oh, sure. That's top on my list." He groaned when the first shudder rippled through him. "Right next to having somebody to sort my socks."

"You can forget that one," Brooke murmured, moving down to his shoulder. "But there's always having an in with the director when you do that part for cable."

"Haven't decided to do it." His legs tangled with hers as they altered positions. "Have you?"

"Not yet." Her thoughts began to drift as he cupped her breast. "But you should."

"Why?"

Lazily, her eyes opened to look into his. "I shouldn't tell you."

Intrigued, he propped himself on his elbow and toyed with her hair. "Why not?"

She sighed a little, while managing to convey a

shrug. "The last thing you need is someone feeding your ego."

"Go ahead." He kissed her nose. "I can take it."

"Damn it, Parks, you're good."

He stopped in the action of twining her hair around his finger and stared at her. "What did you say?"

Brooke shifted again. "Well, I don't mean you can *act,*" she began. "Don't start getting delusions."

He grinned, enjoying her ironic lift of brow. "That's more like it."

"You have good camera presence," she went on. "Do you have any idea how many big stars stay big simply by playing themselves?" Parks grunted, more interested in the curve of her shoulder. "You know how to play yourself, Parks," Brooke persisted, drawing him back for a moment. "And if you were to stick to parts, at least for a while, that suited you…well, when you really are ready to retire from baseball you could walk right into a movie career."

He started to laugh, then stopped when he saw the look in her eyes. "You're not joking."

Brooke stared at him, then let out a long breath. "I'm really going to hate myself when I've got to deal with you as a director in a couple of weeks, but you're very, very good, and you should think about it. And if you get a star complex when I tell you to run through some business on camera a half a dozen times, I'll…"

"What?" he challenged.

"Something," Brooke said ominously. "Something despicable."

He gave her a wicked grin. "Promise?"

Since she couldn't stop the laugh, she rolled him over forcibly so that she was lying across him again. "Yeah. And now I'm going to make love to you until your bones dissolve."

"Is this in my contract?" he demanded.

"You better believe it."

Chapter 12

Though it was November, Los Angeles was suffering from a heat wave that fried tempers and melted patience. Brooke's was no exception. She and Parks had had ten long, isolated days before she had begun work again—but they hadn't been trouble-free. Nothing's trouble-free, Brooke reminded herself as she knotted her blouse beneath her breasts. What fool thought a honeymoon would be? She had, she admitted ruefully as the camera crane was unloaded. But then how much thought had she really given to adjustments, to changes and, as Parks had termed it, the nuts and bolts business that made up a marriage?

She had accepted his name, and though she would keep her own professionally, it was Brooke Jones that she would sign to all legal documents. He had given up his apartment and moved into her house. She had his name, he had her key. Why did she feel she was tallying a balance sheet? Frustrated, Brooke wiped her forearm over her brow.

Was that what marriage was, she wondered, a series of checks and balances? With her marriage barely three weeks old, she should be blissfully happy, glowing. Instead, Brooke felt frustrated, annoyed and unsettled—perhaps more unsettled because she knew Parks was no more blissfully happy than she.

With a shake of her head, she told herself to put it aside. Bringing her personal problems to work wouldn't solve them—and more than likely it would make them worse, since she was directing Parks.

"Let's go up, E.J., I want to see the angle." Sitting in the basket beside him, she gave the crane operator a nod to take them up.

Below them, the beach spread gold. The surf kicked up, white and frothy, catching the glint of the sun and rainbowing through the lens. She thought she could feel the heat steam from the metal casing of the camera. "All right, I'll want a wide shot when he starts, then zoom in, but not too tight. At this angle, we'll get a good profile of the horse. The palomino's a nice contrast with the jeans. Set the speed. I want it slow enough so they see every muscle ripple."

"On Parks or the horse?" E.J. asked with a grin.

"On both," Brooke answered curtly, nodding to be brought down. Wiping her palms on the seat of her pants, she strode over to where Parks waited. He wore nothing but snug, low-slung de Marco jeans. "We're ready for you."

"All right." Parks gave her a long, steady look as he hooked his thumbs in his front pockets. He wasn't sure why he was dissatisfied, or why he felt the need to annoy her. The friction had been growing between them for the past few days, building and shifting like some electric storm. But there'd been no boom of thunder, no slash of lightning to release the pressure. "What do you want?"

"You've seen the script," she reminded him.

"Aren't you going to give me my motivation?"

"Don't be a smart aleck, Parks," she snapped. "It's too damn hot."

"Just want to make sure I've got the right mood so you won't make me do it a half dozen times."

Temper flared in her eyes and was forcefully suppressed. She wouldn't let him taunt her into a public sniping. "You'll do it two dozen times if I feel it's necessary," she said as calmly as possible. "Now get on the horse, gallop straight down the beach in the shallows. And enjoy it."

"Is that an order?" he murmured, deceptively mild.

"It's a direction," she returned evenly. "I'm the director, you're the talent. Got it?"

"Yeah, I got it." Catching her close, he crushed her mouth with his. He felt the dampness of her blouse under his palm, the angry rigidity of her body and the yielding softness of her breasts. Why was he angry? he wondered even as his temper inched higher. Why did he feel he was dragging her close and shoving her away at the same time? "Got that?" he demanded as he turned and swung onto the horse.

She glared at him, a half-naked man astride a golden horse, as he smiled down at her with the cocky assurance she both loved and detested. Making him pay for that small victory would be a pleasure. Turning on her heel, Brooke strode back to her crew. "Take one," she ordered, then waited, turning ideas for vengeance over in her mind. She took the bullhorn her assistant handed her. "Places!" Parks led the palomino into the surf. Brooke stared at him, forcing herself to put her personal feelings on hold while she thought and felt and saw only as a director. "Roll film, and…action!"

He's magnificent, Brooke thought with a twin surge of pride and irritation. He took the horse into an easy, rolling gallop, kicking up the surf so that the streams of water rose high. Beads glistened on his skin, darkly tanned so that he and the palomino merged into one golden form. Parks's hair and the horse's mane lifted in the wind the motion caused. Strength, an elegance of movement and the simplicity of two beautiful animals. Brooke didn't need special effects to show her how it would look in slow motion.

"Cut. E.J.?"

"Fantastic," he called down. "Sales of de Marco jeans just went up ten percent."

"Let's make sure." Pulling her damp shirt away from her back, Brooke walked to where Parks waited, astride the horse. It had been fantastic, she mused, but not perfect. Spotting her, Parks broke off his conversation with the palomino's trainer.

"Well?"

''It looked pretty good. Let's do it again.''

''Why?''

Ignoring the question, she absently patted the gelding's smooth throat. ''I want you to look down the beach as you ride…all the way down.'' She didn't want that comfortable, free-wheeling sexuality this time, but a dash of aloofness, the solitary-man appeal flavored with the sensuality any female over twelve would recognize.

He shifted in the saddle, his eyes never leaving hers. ''Why?''

''Ride the horse, Parks,'' she countered. ''Let me sell the jeans.''

Very slowly, he dismounted. The trainer quickly remembered something he had to do somewhere else. Behind them, the crew became very busy. Parks held the reins in one hand while he and Brooke measured each other. ''Ever considered asking?'' he said quietly.

''Ever considered following directions?'' she tossed back.

He felt the salt spray drying on his skin. ''Too bad you've never been a team player, Brooke.''

''This isn't a ball game,'' she retorted, firing up. ''We all have our jobs to do. Yours is whatever I tell you it is.''

The flash of anger in his eyes suited her mood. She wanted a fight, a rip-roaring screamer that would tear through the tension of their last few days together. Planting her feet, Brooke prepared to attack and defend.

"No," he said with a sudden deadly calm that put her at a disadvantage, "it's not. My job is to endorse de Marco."

"And that's what I'm telling you to do." She forced herself to match his tone, though she badly wanted to shout. "If you want to be a prima donna, wait until after we wrap. Take your complaints and talk to your agent."

His hand snaked out to grab her arm before she could stalk away. "I'm talking to my wife."

Heart hammering in her throat, she looked down at the hand that held her. "Your director," Brooke icily corrected, meeting his eyes. "My crew's hot, Parks. I'd like to finish this before someone faints from heat exhaustion."

His grip tightened. But he saw that her face was flushed from the heat and damp with sweat. "We're not finished with this," he told her as he released her arm. "This time, you're going to take a good hard look at the rules." Swinging onto the horse, Parks rode away before she could think of an appropriate comment.

Brooke frowned after him as she stalked back to the crane. "Take two."

He could have given no logical, succinct explanation for his anger. Parks only knew he was furious. He had only one motivation as he stalked down the corridors to Brooke's office—to have it out with her. He wasn't certain what *it* was, but he would have had it out with her on location if she hadn't been gone before he'd realized it. Though he wasn't thrilled about coming to terms with her in her office, he'd had plenty of experience in meeting a challenge on the opposition's home field. All it meant was that he would take the offensive first.

Brushing by her secretary without a word, Parks pushed open the door to Brooke's office. Empty.

"I'm sorry, Mr. Jones." The secretary hurried up to him, warned by the dangerous light in his eye. "Ms. Gordon…Mrs. Jones isn't in."

"Where?" Parks demanded curtly.

"I— Perhaps Ms. Thorton's office. If you'll wait, I'll check for you…." But he was already heading out with a long, determined stride that had her chewing on the nail of her forefinger. It looked like Brooke was in trouble. And some people have all the luck, the secretary mused before she went back to her desk.

In less than five minutes, Parks walked by the twins in Claire's outer office and opened her door without knocking. "Where's Brooke?" he demanded, not bothering to greet Claire or his agent.

"Good afternoon, Parks," Claire said easily. "Tea?" She continued to pour Lee's cup as if a furious man weren't at that moment glaring at her.

Parks gave the classic little tea service a brief glance. "I'm looking for Brooke."

"You've missed her, I'm afraid." Claire sipped her tea, then offered Lee a plate of macaroons. "She was in and out a half an hour ago. Would you like a cookie, Parks?"

''No....'' He managed to get a tenuous hold on his manners. ''Thanks. Where did she go?''

Claire nibbled on a macaroon, then dusted her fingers on a pink linen napkin. ''Didn't she say she was going home, Lee?''

''Yep. And she wasn't in any better mood than Parks is.'' He sent his client a bland smile before he wolfed down a cookie.

''No, she wasn't, was she?'' Claire folded her hands on her lap. ''Tell me, dear, are you two having a tiff?''

''No, we're not having a tiff,'' Parks muttered, not certain what they were having. It occurred to him suddenly how cozy his agent and his producer were on the small two-cushioned sofa. ''What are you two having?'' he countered.

''Tea.'' Claire smiled her dry smile.

''Why don't you have a seat and cool off,'' Lee invited. ''You look like you've just played nine full innings.''

''We were shooting on the beach,'' Parks murmured. Did Lee Dutton have his arm around Claire Thorton, or was he seeing things?

''It went well?'' Claire asked, noting his expression, amused by the reason for it.

''Apparently Brooke was satisfied.''

''Apparently,'' Claire murmured, then shot him a level stare. ''When are you and Brooke going to relax and enjoy yourselves?''

Parks's speculative look changed to a frown. ''What do you mean?''

"I mean I've never in my life seen two people spend so much time poking at each other."

"Is that what you call it?" Parks muttered, stuffing his hands in his pockets.

"For want of a better term." Claire set her teacup carefully in its saucer. "I realize, of course, that the power game is a founding part of your relationship, and provides its own stimulation, but don't you think it's time you became a family as well as opponents?" Keeping her eyes level, Claire settled into the crook of Lee's arm.

Parks stared at her for nearly a full minute. Power game, he repeated silently. Well yes, it was an intricate part of what they were to each other. They had both looked for strength, challenge, and would have walked the other way if they hadn't found the combination. But as for the rest—a family… Was that what was niggling at the back of his mind?

Wasn't it true that he couldn't resolve himself to the fact that they were living in *her* house, surrounded by *her* things? He still felt uncomfortably like a guest. Even as fresh annoyance grew, he remembered their discussing a trip to Maui. He had told Brooke he wanted her to see *his* place. But… Even as he searched for an excuse, he knew he wouldn't find one.

Turning, Parks paced to the window and scowled out. "I don't think Brooke's ready for a family relationship." The brief, undignified answer Claire gave him had Parks turning back, half-amused. Lee merely reached forward and snatched another cookie.

"She's looked for one all of her life. If you know

anything about her, you know that.'' Suddenly angry, Claire rose. ''Is it possible for two people to live together and not understand the other's needs, the other's hurts? How much has she told you about how she grew up?''

''Barely anything,'' Parks began. ''She—''

''How much did you ask?'' Claire demanded. ''Don't tell me you didn't want to pry,'' she said quickly, cutting him off. ''You're her husband, it's your business to pry. You can be civilized enough to respect her privacy and never touch on what she really needs from you.''

''I know that she needs to know she can make her own place,'' he tossed back. ''I know that it doesn't matter if it's a chipped cup or a Hepplewhite table, as long as it's hers.''

''Things!'' Claire raged. ''Yes, she needs things. God knows she never had them as a child, and the child in her still hurts because of it. But they're only a symbol of what she really wants. Brooke walked in here, an eighteen-year-old adult with nothing more than a few dollars in her pocket and a lot of guts. Someone she thought she loved had taken everything from her, and she wasn't ever going to let that happen again.'' Her mouth tightened, her eyes frosting over at the memory. ''It's your job to show her that it won't.''

''I don't want to *take* anything from her,'' Parks retorted heatedly.

''But you want her to give,'' Claire shot back.

''Of course I do, damn it. I love her.''

"Then listen to me. Brooke's struggled all her life to have something of her own, to have some*one* of her own. She has the things. She's earned them. If you want to share them with her, share her life, you'd better have something pretty special to offer in return. Love isn't enough."

"What is?" Parks tossed back, furious at being lectured by someone half his size.

"You'd better figure it out."

Parks measured her another moment. "All right," he said coolly and left without another word.

Lee rose from the sofa to stand beside Claire. Her pampered skin was flushed with temper, her faded blue eyes icy. "You know," he mused as he studied her, "I've never seen you in full gear before."

"I don't often lose my temper." Claire fluffed at her hair. "Young people," she stated, as if the two words explained everything.

"Yeah." Taking her shoulders, he turned her to face him. "They don't know a good thing when they've got it." His puckish round face creased with a grin. "How'd you like to spend the rest of your life with an overweight theatrical agent?"

The ice melted from Claire's eyes, but the flush remained. "Lee, I thought you'd never ask."

Parks was fighting his way through L.A. traffic when he heard the first report of the fire. His anger at Claire, his frustration that she had spoken no more than the truth, was switched off instantly as he caught the tail end of a news broadcast reporting brush fires in Liberty Canyon—less than an hour away from Brooke's isolated A-frame. No, there wasn't anger now, but a sick sense of fear that had his palms slipping damply on the wheel.

Had she gone home? he wondered frantically as he sped around a cruising Ferrari. Would she have the television set on, the radio, or would she be in one of her solitary moods? After a hot, enervating day on location, she would often simply shower and sleep for an hour. Recharging, he had called it jokingly. Now the idea terrified him.

As he drove higher, he began to scent the fragrance of dry leaves burning. A faint haze of smoke rose into the sky to the east. Thirty minutes, Parks estimated as he pressed his foot on the accelerator. Forty, if they were lucky. It would take him nearly half that to get there.

There was no wind to hurry the fire along, he reminded himself, fighting to keep calm. They weren't calling it a firestorm…not yet. Brooke was probably already packing up her most important things—he might even meet her on the road on her way down. Any minute she could come zipping around one of the curves in the road leading back down the mountain. They'd get a hotel, talk this business out. Claire was right, he hadn't dug deep enough. Once he had promised himself he would learn the whole woman. It was long past time to make good on the promise.

Parks could almost taste the smoke now, the thick black smoke that led the way for the fire. He saw a pack of small animals—rabbits, raccoons, a fox—race down the road on the other side in their migration to lower elevation. It was close, then, he thought, too close. Why in God's name wasn't she speeding down the road toward safety? He drove the last fifteen miles in a blur of speed and fear.

Parks only took the time to register that Brooke's car was in the driveway before he was out of his own and racing toward the house. She had to be asleep, he decided, not to know the fire was closing in. Even without the radio on, the haze of smoke and smell of burning brought the news. He burst through the front door, calling her name.

The house was silent. There was no sound of hurried movement, of drawers slamming, nothing to indicate frantic packing. Parks was racing up the stairs two at a time when he heard the dog barking. He swore, but kept going. He'd forgotten the dog completely in his fear for Brooke. And the fear grew again when he saw the bed was empty. He was racing through the second floor, still calling, when a movement outside the window caught his eye.

Rain? he thought, pausing long enough to stare. No, water—but not rain. Going to the window, he saw her. Relief was immediately overlapped by irritation, and irritation by fury. What the hell was she doing standing in the backyard watering the lawn when the smoke was thick enough to block out the trees to the east?

With a quick jerk, he pulled up the window and shouted through the screen. "Brooke, what the hell are you doing?"

She jolted, then looked up. "Oh, Parks, thank God!

Come down and help, there isn't much time. Close the window!'' she shouted. ''The sparks could get inside. *Hurry!*''

He moved, and moved quickly, intending on shaking her until she rattled then dragging her to the car. Halfway down the stairs, he leaped over the banister and headed to the back door. ''What the hell are you doing?'' he demanded again. Then, instead of shaking her, he found he was holding her tight enough to make her bones crack. If he hadn't heard the radio, if she'd been sleeping… *If.* A thousand ifs ran through his mind as his mouth came down frantically on hers.

It was the sudden howl of wind that brought him back. A sudden ripple of terror ran down his spine. The wind would speed the fire and feed the flames. Brush fire became firestorm. ''We've got to get out of here.''

He had dragged her nearly two feet before he realized she was fighting him. ''No!'' With a show of pure strength, Brooke broke away from him then picked up the hose she had dropped.

''Damn it, Brooke, we can't have more than fifteen minutes.''

He took her arm again and again she broke away. ''I know how much time there is.'' She aimed the spray of water toward the house again, soaking the wood. The sound drummed in the air over the growing fierceness of the wind.

For the first time, Parks noticed that she was wet and filthy and wearing only a bathrobe. She'd just been stepping from the shower when the special report on the radio had warned her of the approaching fire. He looked at the dirt and grass stains on the silk of her robe and realized what she'd been doing. The land around the house had been cleared. She'd done it with her hands. He saw the scratches and dried blood on them and on her legs and ankles. Now, with the puppy barking frantically around her, she was wetting down the house.

"Are you crazy!" he demanded as the first flash of admiration was drowned in fresh fury. Parks grabbed her arm again, ripping the shoulder seam of her robe. "Do you know what a firestorm is?"

"I know what it is." Her elbow connected with his ribs as she struggled away. "If you won't help, stay out of my way; half the house hasn't been wetted down yet."

"You're getting out of here." Parks pulled the hose out of her hand and started dragging her. "If I have to knock you unconscious."

Brooke shocked them both by planting her fist solidly on his jaw. The blow was enough to free her so that she stumbled back, losing her balance and landing on all fours.

"I said stay out of my way," she hissed, then choked as the smoke clogged her lungs.

Parks dragged her to her feet. His eyes were as wild with fear and fury as hers. "You idiot, are you going to fight a firestorm with a garden hose? It's wood and glass!" he shouted as he shook her. "Wood and glass," he repeated, coughing as he threw a hand toward the house. "Is it worth dying for?"

"It's worth fighting for!" she shouted back against smoke and wind as the tears started to flow. "I won't give in to the fire, I *won't!*" She began fighting him again, more desperately than before.

"Damn it, Brooke, stop!" He took her shoulders until his fingers bit into her flesh. "There isn't time."

"The fire won't have it. Not our home, don't you understand?" Her voice rose, not in hysteria but in fierce determination. "Not *our* home."

Parks stopped shaking her, again finding that his arms had wrapped around to hold her close. Understanding flooded through him, and in its wake came every emotion he'd ever experienced. Is that what Claire had meant, he wondered, when she'd said love wasn't enough? Love was enough for beginning, but sustaining took every feeling a human being was capable of. *Our home,* she had said. And with the two words Brooke had cemented everything.

He drew her away. The tears were streaming, her breath was labored. Her eyes were rimmed with red but steady. He knew he had never felt more for another, and never would. And suddenly he knew that questions and answers weren't necessary for him to know the whole woman. Without speaking, he let her go and picked up the hose himself. Brooke stayed where she was while he turned the water onto the house. With the back of her wrist, she wiped the stinging tears from her face.

"Parks..."

He turned, smiling the grim gladiator smile. "It's worth fighting for." Brooke let out a shuddering sigh as she closed her hand over his. "We'll need towels to breathe through, a couple of blankets. Get them while I hose down the rest of the house."

It seemed like hours passed while they worked together, soaking the wood and each other, the dog, again and again while the smoke grew thicker. The wind screamed, threatening to rip the blanket Parks had tossed over her out of her hands. The heat, Brooke thought. She wouldn't be able to bear the heat. But the flames still held off. There were moments she almost believed the fire would veer away, then she would be choking on the smoke and taking her turn with the hose until she couldn't think at all. There was only one goal—to save the house she'd shared with Parks—the symbol of everything she had ever needed. Home, family, love.

With the towels pressed to their faces, they worked their way around and around the house, soaking the roof, the sides, all the surfaces the heat seemed to dry again so quickly. They no longer spoke, but worked systematically. Two pairs of arms, two sets of legs, working with one mind—to protect what was theirs.

Parks saw the flames first, and was almost too awed to move. It wasn't a furnace, he thought, or an oven. It was hell. And it was racing toward them. Great, greedy towers of fire belched out of the main body like spears. And in the midst of unbearable heat, he felt the icy sweat of human fear.

"No more." In a quick move, he grabbed Brooke's arm and scooped up the puppy.

"What are you doing? We can't leave now." Stumbling and choking, Brooke fought to free herself.

"If we don't leave now, we could be dead." He pushed Brooke into his car and shoved the puppy into her arms. "Damn it, Brooke, we've done all we can." His hands were slick with sweat as he turned the key. "Nothing you can buy is worth dying for."

"You don't understand!" With the back of her hand she smeared grime and tears together on her face. "Everything—everything I have is back there. I can't let the fire take it all—everything that means anything to me."

"Everything," he repeated in a murmur. Parks stopped the car to stare at her with red-rimmed, stinging eyes. "All right, if that's how you feel, I'll go back and do what I can." His voice was curiously flat and emotionless. "but, by God, you stay here. I won't risk you."

Before she could take in what he'd said or what he was doing, he was gone. For a moment, the hysteria had complete control. She trembled with it, unable to move or think. The fire was going to take her home, all her possessions. She'd be left with nothing, just as she had been so many times before. How could she face it again after all the years of struggling, of work, of wanting?

The puppy squirmed in her arms and whimpered. Blankly, Brooke stared down at him. What was she doing sitting there when her house was in danger? She had to go back, go back and save…Parks.

Fear froze her, then had her springing from the car

and racing through the smoke. She'd sent him back—he'd gone back for her. For what? she thought desperately. What was she trying to save? Wood and glass—that's what he'd called it. It was nothing more. He was her home, the real home she'd searched for all her life. She shouted for him, sobbing as the smoke blocked everything from view.

She could hear the fire—or the wind. Brooke was no longer certain one was separate from the other. All that was clear now was that if she lost him now, she truly lost everything. So she shouted his name again and again, fighting her way through the smoke to get to him.

For an instant she could no longer breathe, no longer be certain where she was or where to run. An image flashed through her mind, one of herself as a young girl approaching a small two-story house where she would spend a year of her life. She couldn't remember the names of the people who would be her parents for those twelve months, only that sense of disorientation and loneliness. She'd always felt as lonely going in as she had coming out. She'd always been separate, always an outsider, until she'd met Parks.

She saw him racing back to her, misted through the curtain of smoke. Before she could separate one image from another, she was in his arms.

"What happened?" he demanded. "I heard you shouting, I thought—" He buried his face against her neck a moment as the fear ebbed. "Damn it, Brooke, I told you to stay in the car."

"Not without you. Please, let's go." She was dragging on his arm, pulling him back down the road toward the car.

"The house—"

"Means nothing," she said fiercely. "Nothing does without you." Before he could react, Brooke was climbing into the driver's seat herself. The moment Parks was beside her, she started down the twisting road.

After nearly a mile, the smoke thinned. It was then Brooke felt the reaction set in with shudders and fresh tears. Pulling off the road, she laid her head on the steering wheel and wept.

"Brooke." Gently, he brushed a hand over her wet, tangled hair. "I'm sorry. I know the house was important to you. We don't know yet that it's gone or beyond repair. We can—"

"Damn the house!" Lifting her head, she looked at him with eyes that were both angry and desolate. "I must've been crazy to act that way. To send you back there when..." Trailing off, she swore and slammed out of the car. Slowly, Parks got out and followed her.

"Brooke."

"You're the most important thing in my life." She turned to him then, taking deep breaths to keep the tears back. "I don't expect you to believe that after the way I behaved, but it's true. I couldn't let go of the house, the things, because I'd waited so long to have them. I needed the identity they gave me." Because the words were painful, she swallowed. "For so long everything I had was only mine on loan. All I could think of was that if I didn't keep that house, those things, I'd be lost again. I don't expect you to understand—''

''I will understand.'' He took her face in his hands. ''If you'll let me.''

She let out a long, shuddering breath. ''I never belonged anywhere, to anyone. Ever. It makes you afraid to trust. I always told myself that there'd be a day when I'd have my own things, my own place—I wouldn't have to share them, I wouldn't have to ask. It was something I promised myself because I couldn't have survived without that one hope. I forgot to let go of that when I didn't need it anymore.''

''Maybe.'' He stroked a thumb over her cheek. ''Or maybe you had without realizing it. Back there, you called it *our* home.''

''Parks.'' She reached up to place her hands on him. ''I don't care if the house is gone, if everything in it's gone. I have everything I need, everything I love, right here in my hands.''

They were wet, filthy, exhausted. Alive. Parks looked at her blackened face and matted hair, the red-rimmed eyes. She'd never looked more beautiful to him. Throats raw from smoke, eyes stinging, he reached for her. Together, they fell to the grass.

Brooke was laughing and weeping as he kissed her. Her face was streaked with soot and tears, but his lips raced wildly over it. Passion met passion. Bruises were unfelt as they touched each other while a need, as volatile as the fire they had challenged, raged through them. When the tatters of her robe were gone, his sodden clothes joined it, they lay tangled, naked on the grass. Again and again, their mouths clung, drawing the strength and victory of the moment from each other, climbing beyond the smoke and stench of the fire left behind to a clean, bright world.

She knew she had never been so aware, so stunningly alive. Her body seemed to hum from a thousand pulses that grew more erratic as he touched her. With her arms tight around him, his body pressed against hers, she felt the sensation of absolute trust. He would protect, she would defend, against any outside forces that threatened. During the fire, they had ceased to be a man and a woman. They had become a unit. Somewhere beneath the swirling passion, Brooke felt peace. She had found her own.

They made love while the smoke broke into mists above their heads. And when they were spent, they clung still, unwilling to break the unity so newly discovered.

"You've hurt yourself," Parks murmured, touching a bruise on her shoulder.

"I don't feel hurt." She buried her lips at his throat and knew she would never forget the smell of smoke and ash and loving. "I hit you."

"Yeah, I noticed."

Hearing the grin in his voice, she closed her eyes. "You were only thinking of me. I'm sorry."

"Now you're thinking of us." He pressed his lips to her temple. "I'm glad."

"We won," she whispered.

Parks lifted his head to look down at her. Taking his thumb, he rubbed a streak of soot from her skin. It was the color of her eyes, he thought, seeing it on his own flesh. ''We won, Brooke.''

''Everything.''

His lips curved before he brought them down to hers. ''Everything.''

She cradled his head on her shoulder, gently stroking his hair. Tiny pieces of ash continued to float above her like memories. ''I said once I didn't want anything to change.... I was afraid to let it change. I was wrong.'' Closing her eyes, she let herself absorb his closeness. ''It's not quite the same now.''

''Better,'' he murmured. ''It makes a difference. It'll always make a difference.''

She sighed, knowing the contentment she had always searched for was irrevocably bound up in one man, one love. ''But we'll still play the game, won't we?''

This time when he lifted his head, he grinned. Brooke's lips curved in response. ''By our own rules.''

* * * * *

THE NAME OF THE GAME

To Faye Ashley.
Now you'll have to leave me the bracelet.

Chapter 1

"Marge Whittier, this is your chance to win *ten thousand dollars*. Are you ready?"

Marge Whittier, a forty-eight-year-old schoolteacher and grandmother of two from Kansas City squirmed in her chair. The lights were on, the drum was rolling and the possibility of her being sick was building. "Yes, I'm ready."

"Good luck, Marge. The clock will start with your first pick. Begin."

Marge swallowed a lump of panic, shuddered with excitement and chose number six. Her sixty seconds began to dwindle, and the tension grew as she and her celebrity partner picked their brains for the right answers. They leaped over such questions as who founded psychoanalysis and how many yards in a mile, then came to a screeching halt. What element do all organic compounds contain?

Marge went pale, and her lips quivered. She was an English teacher and a bit of a history and movie buff, but science wasn't her long suit. She looked pleadingly at her partner, who was better known for her wit than for her wisdom. Precious seconds ticked away. As they fumbled, the buzzer sounded. Ten thousand dollars flowed through Marge's sweaty fingers.

The studio audience groaned their disappointment.

"Too bad, Marge." John Jay Johnson, the tall, sleekly polished host, laid a sympathetic hand on her shoulder. His rich, rolling voice expressed just the right combination of disappointment and hope. "You were so close. But with eight correct answers you add another eight hundred dollars to your total. An impressive one." He smiled at the camera. "We'll be back after this break to total up Marge's winnings and to give you the correct answer to the stumper. Stay with us."

The music was cued. John Jay kept his avuncular smile handy. He used the timed ninety-second break to come on to the pretty celebrity panelist.

"Pompous jerk," Johanna muttered. The pity was that she was too aware his smooth looks and slick manner were keeping *Trivia Alert* up in the ratings. As producer, she'd learned to accept John Jay as part of the set. She checked the second hand of her watch before walking over to the losers. Putting on a smile of her own, she commiserated and congratulated as she eased them along. She needed them in camera range for the finish.

"Coming up on five," she announced, and signaled for applause and music. "And cue."

John Jay, his arm around Marge and his three-thousand-dollar caps gleaming, closed the show.

They were one big happy family as the assistant director shut off his stopwatch. "That's a wrap."

Kiki Wilson, Marge's partner and the current star of a popular situation comedy, chatted a few moments longer with Marge in a way that would have the schoolteacher remembering her warmly for years to come. When Kiki rose, her smile was still firmly in place as she walked the few steps to John Jay.

"If you ever pull something like that again," she said quietly, "you'll need a paramedic."

Knowing she was referring to his quick—and, if he did say so, clever—hand maneuver just before the end of the break, John Jay smiled. "Just part of the service. About that drink, sweetheart..."

"Kiki." In a smooth move that didn't appear nearly as rushed and harassed as it was, Johanna swung over and scooted the actress away. "I want to thank you again for agreeing to do the show. I know how hectic your schedule must be."

Johanna's warm voice and soothing manner brought Kiki's blood pressure down slightly. "I enjoyed it." Kiki pulled out a cigarette and tapped it absently against an enameled case. "It's a cute show, moves fast. And God knows the exposure never hurts."

Though Johanna didn't smoke, she carried a small gold lighter. Pulling it out, she lit Kiki's cigarette. ''You were wonderful. I hope you'll consider coming back.''

Kiki blew out smoke and regarded Johanna. The lady knew her job, Kiki admitted. Even though she looked like some cuddly little model for shampoo or yogurt. It had been a long day, but the catered dinner break had been first-class, the studio audience generous with their applause. In any case, her agent had told her that *Trivia Alert* was *the* up-and-coming game show of the year. Considering that, and the fact that Kiki had a good sense of humor, she smiled.

''I just might. You've got a good crew, with one notable exception.''

Johanna didn't have to turn to know where Kiki's narrowed gaze had landed. With John Jay it was either love or disgust, with little middle ground. ''I have to apologize for any annoyance.''

''Don't bother. There are plenty of jerks in the business.'' Kiki studied Johanna again. Quite a face, she decided, even with the minimal makeup. ''I'm surprised you don't have a few fang marks.''

Johanna smiled. ''I have very thick skin.''

Anyone who knew her would have attested to that. Johanna Patterson might have looked soft and creamy, but she had the energy of an Amazon. For eighteen months she had slaved, hustled and bargained to get and keep *Trivia Alert* on the air. She wasn't a novice in the entertainment business, and that made her all the more aware that behind the scenes and in the boardrooms it was still a man's world.

That would change eventually, but eventually was too long a wait. Johanna wasn't patient enough to wait for doors to open. When she wanted something badly enough, she gave them a push. For that she was willing to make certain adjustments herself. The business of entertainment was no mystery to her; nor were the deals, the concessions or the compromises. As long as the end product was quality, it didn't matter.

She'd had to swallow pride and sacrifice a principle or two to get her baby off and running. For example, it wasn't her name, but her father's logo that flashed importantly at the end of the show: Carl W. Patterson Productions

His was the name the network brass related to, and his was the one they trusted. So she used it—grudgingly—then ran things her way.

Thus far, the uneasy marriage was into its second year and holding its own. Johanna knew the business—and her father—too well to take for granted that it would continue.

So she worked hard, tying up loose ends, hammering out solutions to problems and delegating carefully what couldn't be handled personally. The success or failure of the show wouldn't make or break her, financially or professionally, but she had more than money and reputation tied up with it. She had her hopes and her self-esteem.

The studio audience had been cleared. A few technicians remained on the set, either gossiping or tidying up last-minute business. It was just past eight o'clock, and moving into hour fourteen for Johanna.

"Bill, do you have the dupes?" She accepted the copies of the day's tape from her editor. Five shows were produced and recorded in one full-day session. Five costume changes for the celebrity panelists—Johanna had a policy against referring to them as guest stars. Five wardrobe trips for John Jay, who insisted on a change from underwear out for each show. His natty suits and coordinated ties would be sent back to the Beverly Hills tailor who provided them free in exchange for the plug at the end of each show.

His job was over, but Johanna's was just beginning. The tapes would be reviewed, edited and carefully timed. Johanna would oversee each step. There would be mail to go through, letters from home viewers who hoped to be chosen as contestants, more letters from people who disagreed with certain answers. She'd go head-to-head with her research coordinator to check facts and select new questions for upcoming shows. Though she couldn't personally interview and screen each potential contestant, she would go over her contestant coordinator's selections.

The game-show scandals of the fifties were long over, but no one wanted a repeat of them. Standards and Practices was very strict, their rules and regulations very clear. Johanna made it a habit never to relax her own, and to check each detail herself.

When screened contestants arrived at the studio for a day's taping, they were turned over to staff members who sequestered them from the crew, the audience and their prospective partners. They were entertained and soothed, literally cut off from the show until their turn came to participate.

Questions were locked in a safe. Only Johanna and her personal assistant had the combination.

Then, of course, there were the celebrities to deal with. They would want their favorite flowers and choice of beverage in their dressing rooms. Some would go with the flow and make her life easier, and others would be difficult just to show they were important. She knew—and they knew she knew—that most of them appeared on morning game shows not for the money or the fun but for the exposure. They were plugging series and specials, placating their networks or scrambling to keep their face familiar to the public.

Fortunately, a good percentage of them had fun once the ball was rolling. There were still more, however, who required pampering, cajoling and flattery. She was willing, as long as they helped her keep her show on the air. When a woman had grown up with artistic temperaments and the wheeling and dealing of the entertainment business, very little surprised her.

"Johanna."

Regretfully Johanna put her fantasy of a hot bath and a foot massage on hold. "Yes, Beth?" She slipped the tapes into her oversize tote and waited for her assistant. Bethany Landman was young, sharp and energetic. Just now she seemed to be bubbling over. "Make it good. My feet are killing me."

"It's good." A bouncy dark contrast to Johanna's

cool blond looks, Bethany gripped her clipboard and all but danced. "We've got him."

Johanna secured the tote on the shoulder of her slim violet-blue jacket. "Who have we got and what are we going to do with him?"

"Sam Weaver." Beth caught her lower lip between her teeth as she grinned. "And I can think of a lot of things we could do with him."

The fact that Bethany was still innocent enough to be impressed by a hard body and tough good looks made Johanna feel old and cynical. More, it made her feel as though she'd been born that way. Sam Weaver was every woman's dream. Johanna wouldn't have denied him his talent, but she was long past the point where sexy eyes and a cocky grin made her pulse flutter. "Why don't you give me the most plausible?"

"Johanna, you have no romance in your soul."

"No, I don't. Can we do this walking, Beth? I want to see if the sky's still there."

"You read that Sam Weaver's done his first TV spot?"

"A miniseries," Johanna added as they wound down the studio corridor.

"They aren't calling it a miniseries. Promotion calls it a four-hour movie event."

"I love Hollywood."

With a chuckle, Bethany shifted her clipboard. "Anyway, I took a chance and contacted his agent. The movie's on our network."

Johanna pushed open the studio door and breathed in the air. Though it was Burbank air and therefore far from fresh, it was welcome. "I'm beginning to see the master plan."

"The agent was very noncommittal, but..."

Johanna stretched her shoulders, then searched for her keys. "I think I'm going to like this *but*."

"I just got a call from upstairs. They want him to do it. We'll have to run the shows the week before the movie and give him time to plug it every day." She paused just long enough to give Johanna a chance to nod. "With that guarantee they'll put on the pressure and we've got him."

"Sam Weaver," Johanna murmured. There was no denying his drawing power. Being tall, lanky and handsome in a rough sort of way didn't hurt, but he had more than that. A bit part in a feature film five, maybe six years before had been a springboard. He'd been top-billed and hot box office ever since. It was more than likely he'd be a pain in the neck to work with, but it might be worth it. She thought of the millions of televisions across the country, and the ratings. It would definitely be worth it.

"Good work, Beth. Let's get it firmed up."

"As good as done." Bethany stood by the spiffy little Mercedes as Johanna climbed in. "Will you fire me if I drool?"

"Absolutely." Johanna flashed a grin as she turned the key. "See you in the morning." She drove the car out of the lot like a bullet. Sam Weaver, she thought as she turned the radio up and let the wind whip her hair. Not a bad catch, she decided. Not bad at all.

* * *

Sam felt like a fish with a hook through his mouth, and he didn't enjoy the sensation. He slumped in his agent's overstuffed chair, his long, booted legs stretched out and a pained scowl on the face women loved to love.

"Good Lord, Marv. A game show? Why don't you tell me to dress like a banana and do a commercial?"

Marvin Jablonski chomped a candied almond, his current substitute for cigarettes. He admitted to being forty-three, which made him a decade older than his client. He was trim and dressed with a subtle flair that spoke of wealth and confidence. When his office had consisted of a phone booth and a briefcase, he'd dressed the same. He knew how vital illusions were in this town. Just as he knew it was vital to keep a client happy while you were manipulating him.

"I thought it was too much to expect that you'd be open-minded."

Sam recognized the touch of hurt in Marv's tone—the poor, self-sacrificing agent, just trying to do his job. Marv was far from poor and he'd never been into personal sacrifice. But it worked. With something like a sigh, Sam rose and paced the length of Marv's glitzy Century City office. "I was open-minded when I agreed to do the talk-show circuit."

Sam's easy baritone carried a hint of his native rural Virginia, but his reputation in Los Angeles wasn't that of a country gentleman. As he paced, his long-legged stride made the observer think of a man who knew exactly where he was going.

And so he did, Marv thought. Otherwise, as a selective and very successful theatrical agent he would never have taken the struggling young actor on six years before. Instinct, Marv was wont to say, was every bit as important as the power breakfast. "Promotion's part of the business, Sam."

"Yeah, and I'll do my bit. But a game show? How is guessing what's behind door number three going to boost the ratings for *Roses*?"

"There aren't any doors on *Trivia*."

"Thank God."

Marv let the sarcasm pass. He was one of the few in the business who knew that Sam Weaver could be maneuvered with words like *responsibility* and *obligation*. "And it'll boost the ratings because millions of sets are tuned in to that half-hour spot five days a week. People love games, Sam. They like to play, they like to watch and they like to see other people walk out with a free lunch. I've got miles of facts and figures, but let's just say that most of those sets are controlled by women." His smile spread easily, shifting his trim, gray-flecked mustache. "Women, Sam, the ones who buy the bulk of the products the sponsors are hyping. And that fizzy little soft drink that's the major sponsor for *Roses* also buys time on *Trivia*. The network likes that, Sam. Keeps things in the family."

"That's fine." Sam hooked his thumbs in the pockets of his jeans. "But we both know I didn't take the TV deal to sell soda pop."

Marv smiled and ran a hand over his hair. His new

toupee was a work of art. "Why did you take the deal?"

"You know why. The script was gold. We needed the four hours to do it right. A two-hour feature would have meant hacking it to bits."

"So you used TV." Marv closed his fingers together lightly, as if he were shutting a trap. "Now TV wants to use you. It's only fair, Sam."

Fair was another word Sam had a weakness for.

A short four-letter epithet was Sam's opinion. Then he said nothing as he stared out at his agent's lofty view of the city. He wasn't so many years off the pavement that he'd forgotten what it felt like to have the heat bake through his sneakers and frustration run through his blood. Marv had taken a chance on him. A calculated risk, but a risk nonetheless. Sam believed in paying his dues. But he hated making a fool of himself.

"I don't like to play games," he muttered, "unless I set the rules."

Marv ignored the buzzer on his desk; it was the prerogative of a man in demand. "You talking politics or the show?"

"Sounds to me like they've been lumped together."

Marv only smiled again. "You're a sharp boy, Sam."

Sam turned his head just a fraction. Marv had been hit by the power of those eyes before. They were one of the reasons he'd signed an unknown when he'd been in a position to refuse the business of well-established luminaries. The eyes were big, heavy lidded and blue. Electric blue, with the power of a lightning bolt. Intense, like his long-boned, narrow face and firm mouth. The chin wasn't so much cleft as sculpted. The kind of chin that looked as though it could take a punch. The nose was a bit crooked, because it had.

California sun had tanned the skin a deep brown and added the interest of faint lines. The kind that made a woman shiver, imagining the experiences that had etched them there. There was a mystery about his face that appealed to females, and a toughness that drew approval from other men. His hair was dark and left long enough to go its own way.

It wasn't a face for a poster in a teenager's room, but it was the kind that haunted a woman's secret dreams.

"How much choice do I have on this?" Sam asked.

"Next to none." Because he knew his client, Marv decided it was time to bare the truth. "Your contract with the network ties you to promotion work. We could get around it, but it wouldn't be good for you, this project or any future ones."

Sam didn't give a damn if it was good for him. He rarely did. But the project was important. "When?"

"Two weeks from today, I'll move the paperwork through. Keep it in perspective, Sam. It's one day out of your life."

"Yeah." One day, he thought, could hardly make much difference. And it wasn't easy to forget that a decade before he'd have considered an offer to do a game show as much of a miracle as manna from heaven. "Marv..." He paused at the door. "If I make an ass out of myself, I'm going to dump Krazy Glue on your hairpiece."

It was strange that two people could have business in the same building, often ride the same elevator, but never cross paths. Sam didn't make the trip from Malibu to his agent's office often. Now that his career was on the rise he was usually tied up in rehearsals, script meetings or location shoots. When he had a few weeks, as he did now, he didn't waste it battling L.A.'s traffic or closing himself up inside Century City's impressive walls. He preferred the seclusion of his ranch.

Johanna, on the other hand, made the trip to her Century City office daily. She hadn't taken a personal vacation in two years, and she put in an average of sixty hours a week on her show. If anyone had tagged her as a workaholic she would have shrugged off the label. Work wasn't an illness, as far as Johanna was concerned; it was a means to an end. The long hours and dedication justified her success. She was determined that no one accuse her of riding on Carl Patterson's coattails.

The offices maintained by *Trivia*'s staff were comfortable but understated. Her own was large enough to prevent her from feeling claustrophobic and practical enough to make the statement that this was a place of business. She arrived like clockwork at eight-thirty, broke for lunch only if it included a meeting,

then worked straight through until she was finished. Besides her almost maternal devotion to *Trivia*, she had another concept on the back burner. A word game this time, an idea that was nearly refined enough to take to the network brass.

Now she had her jacket slung over her chair and her nose buried in a week's worth of potential questions passed on to her by Research. She had to get close to the words because she refused to wear the reading glasses she needed.

"Johanna?"

With little more than a grunt, Johanna continued to read. "Did you know Howdy Doody had a twin brother?"

"We were never close," Bethany said apologetically.

"Double Doody," Johanna informed her with a nod. "I think it's a great one for the speed round. Did you catch today's show?"

"Most of it."

"I really think we should try to lure Hank Loman back. Soap stars are a big draw."

"Speaking of big draws…" Bethany set a stack of papers on Johanna's desk. "Here's the contract for Sam Weaver. I thought you'd like to look it over before I run it up to his agent."

"Fine." She shuffled papers before drawing the contract close enough to focus on it. "Let's send him a tape of the show."

"The usual fruit and cheese for the dressing room?"

‘‘Um-hmm. Is the coffee machine fixed?’’

‘‘Just.’’

‘‘Good.’’ She took a casual glance at her watch. It was a simple affair with a black leather band. The diamond-encrusted one her father’s secretary had picked out for her last birthday was still in its box. ‘‘Listen, you go on to lunch. I’ll run these up.’’

‘‘Johanna, you’re forgetting how to delegate again.’’

‘‘No, I’m just delegating me.’’ Rising, she shook the creases out of her pale rose jacket. After picking up the remote channel changer from her desk, she aimed it at the television across the room. Both picture and sound winked off. ‘‘Are you still seeing that struggling screenwriter?’’

‘‘Every chance I get.’’

Johanna grinned as she shrugged into her jacket. ‘‘Then you’d better hurry. This afternoon we need to brainstorm over the home viewer’s contest. I want that rolling by next month.’’ She picked up the contracts and slipped them and a cassette into a leather portfolio. ‘‘Oh, and make a note for me to slap John Jay’s wrist, will you? He charged a case of champagne to the show again.’’

Bethany wrote that down enthusiastically and in capital letters. ‘‘Glad to do it.’’

Johanna chuckled as she swung out the door. ‘‘Results of the contestant screening by three,’’ she continued. ‘‘That tech’s wife—Randy’s wife—she’s in Cedars of Lebanon for minor surgery. Send flowers.’’

Johanna grinned over her shoulder. ''Who says I can't delegate?''

On the ride up in the elevator, Johanna smiled to herself. She was lucky to have Beth, she thought, though she could already foresee the time when her assistant would be moving up and out. Brains and talent rarely settled for someone else's dream. She liked to think she'd proved that theory for herself. In any case, Johanna had Beth now, and with the rest of her bright young staff, Johanna was on her way to establishing her own niche in the competitive world of daytime television.

If she could get her new concept as far as a pilot, she had no doubt she could sell it. Then maybe a daytime drama, something with as much action as heartache. That story was already in its beginning stages. In addition to that, she was determined to have a nighttime version of *Trivia* syndicated to the independents. She was already on the way to achieving her five-year goal of forming her own production company.

As the elevator rose, Johanna automatically smoothed down her hair and straightened the hem of her jacket. Appearances, she knew, were as important as talent.

When the doors opened, she was satisfied that she looked brisk and professional. She passed through the wide glass doors into Jablonski's offices. He didn't believe in understatement. There were huge Chinese-red urns filled with feathers and fans. A sculpture of what might have been a human torso gleamed in brushed brass. The carpet was an unrelieved white and, Johanna's practical mind thought, must be the devil to keep clean.

Wide chairs in black and red leather were arranged beside glass tables. Trade magazines and the day's papers were set in neat piles. The setup told her Jablonski didn't mind keeping clients waiting.

The desks in the reception area followed the theme in glossy red and black. Johanna saw an attractive brunette seated at one. Perched on the corner of the desk and leaning close to the brunette was Sam Weaver. Johanna's brow lifted only slightly.

She wasn't surprised to see him flirting with one of the staff. Indeed, she expected that kind of thing from him and others like him. After all, her father had had an affair with every secretary, receptionist and assistant who had ever worked for him.

He'd been the tall, dark and handsome type, too, she thought. Still was. Her only real surprise at running into Sam Weaver was that he was one of that rare breed of actor who actually looked better in the flesh than on the screen.

He packed a punch, an immediate one.

Snug jeans suited him, she acknowledged, as did the plain cotton shirt of a working man. No gold flashed, no diamonds winked. He didn't need them, Johanna decided. A man who could look at the receptionist the way Sam was looking at that brunette didn't need artifice to draw attention to him.

"She's beautiful, Gloria." Sam bent closer to the snapshots the receptionist was showing off. From Johanna's angle it looked as though he were whispering endearments. "You're lucky."

"She's six months old today." Gloria smiled down at the photograph of her daughter, then up at Sam. "I was lucky Mr. Jablonski gave me such a liberal maternity leave, and it's nice to be back at work, but boy, I miss her already."

"She looks like you."

The brunette's cheeks flushed with pride and pleasure. "You think so?"

"Sure. Look at that chin." Sam tapped a finger on Gloria's chin. He wasn't just being kind. The truth was, he'd always gotten a kick out of kids. "I bet she keeps you busy."

"You wouldn't believe—" The still-new mother might have been off and running if she hadn't glanced up and seen Johanna. Embarrassed, she slid the pictures into her drawer. Mr. Jablonski had been generous and understanding, but she didn't think he'd care to have her spending her first day back on the job showing off her daughter. "Good afternoon. May I help you?"

With a slight inclination of her head, Johanna crossed the room. As she did, Sam swiveled on the desk and watched her. He didn't quite do a double take, but damn near.

She was beautiful. He wasn't immune to beauty, though he was often surrounded by it. At first glance she might have been taken for one of the hordes of slim and leggy California blondes who haunted the beaches and adorned glossy posters. Her skin was gold—not bronzed, but a very pale and lovely gold. It set off the smoky blond hair that fluffed out to tease the shoulders of her jacket. Her face was oval, the classic shape given drama by prominent cheekbones and a full mouth. Her eyes, delicately shaded with rose and violet, were the clear blue of a mountain lake.

She was sexy. Subtly sexy. He was used to that in women as well. Maybe it was the way she moved, the way she carried herself inside the long loose jacket and straight skirt, that made her seem so special. Her shoes were ivory and low-heeled. He found himself noticing even them and the small, narrow feet they covered.

She didn't even glance at him, and he was glad. It gave him the chance to stare at her, to absorb the sight of her, before she recognized him and spoiled the moment.

"I have a delivery for Mr. Jablonski."

Even her voice was perfect, Sam decided. Soft, smooth, just edging toward cool.

"I'll be happy to take it." Gloria gave her most cooperative smile.

Johanna unzipped her portfolio and took out the contracts and tape. She still didn't look at Sam, though she was very aware he was staring. "These are the Weaver contracts and a tape of *Trivia Alert.*"

"Oh, well—"

Sam cut her off neatly. "Why don't you take them in to him, Gloria? I'll wait."

Gloria opened her mouth, then shut it again to clear

her throat as she rose. ‘‘All right. If you’d just give me a moment,’’ she said to Johanna, then headed down the corridor.

‘‘Do you work for the show?’’ Sam asked her.

‘‘Yes.’’ Johanna gave him a small and purposefully disinterested smile. ‘‘Are you a fan, Mr.—?’’

She didn’t recognize him. Sam had a moment to be both surprised and disconcerted before he saw the humor of it and grinned. ‘‘It’s Sam.’’ He held out a hand, trapping her into an introduction.

‘‘Johanna,’’ she told him, and accepted the handshake. His easy reaction made her feel petty. She was on the verge of explaining when she realized he hadn’t released her hand. His was hard and strong. Like his face, like his voice. It was her reaction to them, her quick and intensely personal reaction to them, that drove her to continue the pretense and blame it on him.

‘‘Do you work for Mr. Jablonski?’’

Sam grinned again. It was a fast, crooked grin that warned a woman not to trust him. ‘‘In a manner of speaking. What do you do on the show?’’

‘‘A little of this, a little of that,’’ she said, truthfully enough. ‘‘Don’t let me keep you.’’

‘‘I’d rather you did.’’ But he released her hand because she was tugging at it. ‘‘Would you like to have lunch?’’

Her brow lifted. Five minutes ago he’d been cuddling up to the brunette; now he was inviting the first woman who came along to lunch. Typical. ‘‘Sorry. I’m booked.’’

''For how long?''

''Long enough.'' Johanna glanced past him to the receptionist.

''Mr. Jablonski will have the contracts signed and returned to Ms. Patterson by tomorrow afternoon.''

''Thank you.'' Johanna shifted her portfolio and turned. Sam laid a hand on her arm and waited until she looked back at him.

''See you.''

She smiled at him, again disinterestedly, before she walked away. She was chuckling when she reached the elevators, unaware that she'd tucked the hand he'd held into her pocket.

Sam watched her until she'd turned the corner. ''You know, Gloria,'' he said, half to himself, ''I think I'm going to enjoy playing this game after all.''

Chapter 2

On the day of a taping, Johanna was always on the set by nine. It wasn't that she didn't trust her staff. She did. She simply trusted herself more. Besides, last week they'd had a few mechanical glitches with the moving set that swung the contestants and their counters stage center for play, then off again for the championship round. Small problems like that could delay taping anywhere from five minutes to two hours. By checking everything through personally beforehand, she sweetened the odds.

All the lights on the display board had to be tested, and the dressing rooms had to be primped and fresh coffee and cookies arranged for the prospective contestants.

They weren't due until one, but experience told Johanna that most would arrive early so they could chew their nails in the studio. Soothing them was one job she gladly delegated. The celebrities were also due at one so they could do a run-through and still have plenty of time for hair, makeup and wardrobe.

John Jay would arrive at two to complain about the suits that had been selected for him. Then he would close himself in his dressing room to sulk before his makeup call. When he was suited up, powdered and sprayed he would emerge, ready to shine for the cameras. Johanna had learned to ignore his artistic temperament—for the most part—and to tolerate the rest. There was no arguing with his popularity quotient. It was largely due to him that the line would form outside the studio for tickets for the day's taping.

Johanna checked off her duties one by one, then double-checked everyone else's. Over the years, efficiency had grown from a habit to an obsession. At noon she downed something that resembled a shrimp salad. The taping should start at three and, if God was in his heaven, be over by eight.

Fortunately, the female celebrity was a repeater who had done *Trivia* at least a dozen times, along with numerous other game shows. That gave Johanna one less headache. She hadn't given Sam Weaver a thought.

So she told herself.

When he arrived, she would turn him and his entourage over to Bethany. It would give her assistant a thrill and keep God's gift to women out of her hair.

She only hoped he could handle the game. The questions were fun, for the most part, but they weren't always easy. More than once she'd had a celebrity grumble and complain because an inability to answer had made him or her look stupid. Johanna made it a policy to see that each show's batch of questions contained the obvious and amusing, as well as the challenging.

It wouldn't be her fault if Sam Weaver turned out to have an empty head. He would only have to smile to gain the audience's forgiveness.

She remembered the way he'd smiled at her when she'd asked if he worked for Jablonski. Yes, that was all it would take to make every woman at home and in the studio turn to putty—except her, of course.

"Check the bell." Johanna stood in the middle of the set and directed her sound technician. At her signal the bright, cheery beep of the winning bell rang. "And the buzzer." The flat drone of the loser sounded. "Bring up the lights in the winner's circle." She nodded in satisfaction as the bulbs flashed.

"The contestants?"

"Sequestered." Bethany checked her clipboard. "We have the accountant from Venice returning from last week. He's a three-game winner. First challenger's a housewife from Ohio in town visiting her sister. Nervous as hell."

"Okay, see if you can help Dottie keep them calm. I'll give the dressing rooms a last check."

Mentally calculating her time as she went, Johanna scooted down the corridor. Her female celebrity was Marsha Tuckett, a comfortable, motherly type who was part of the ensemble of a family series in its third year. A nice contrast for Sam Weaver, she thought. Johanna made sure there were fresh pink roses on the dressing table and plenty of club soda on ice. Satisfied the room was in order, she walked across the narrow hall to the next room.

Because she hadn't thought roses appropriate for Sam Weaver, she'd settled on a nice leafy fern for the corner. As a matter of course she checked the lights, plumped the pillows on the narrow daybed and made certain the towels were fresh and plentiful. A last look showed her nothing he could find fault with. Carelessly she stole a mint from the bowl on the table and popped it into her mouth, then turned.

He was in the doorway.

"Hello again." He'd already decided to make it his business to find her, but he hadn't expected to be quite so lucky. He stepped into the room and dropped a garment bag negligently over a chair.

Johanna pushed the candy into the corner of her mouth. The dressing room was small, but she couldn't recall feeling trapped in it before. "Mr. Weaver." She put on her best at-your-service smile as she offered a hand.

"It's Sam. Remember?" He took her hand and stepped just close enough to make her uncomfortable. They both knew it wasn't an accident.

"Of course. Sam. We're all delighted you could join us. We'll have our run-through shortly. In the meantime, you can let me or one of the staff know if you need anything." She looked past him, puzzled. "Are you alone?"

"Was I supposed to bring someone?"

"No." Where was his secretary, his assistant, his gofer? His current lover?

"According to my instructions, all I needed was five changes. Casual. Will this do to start?"

She studied the navy crewneck and the buff-colored slacks as though it mattered. "You look fine."

She'd known who he was all along, Sam thought. He wasn't so much annoyed as curious. And she wasn't comfortable with him now. That was something else to think about. Making a woman comfortable wasn't always a goal. After reaching for a mint himself, he rested a hip against the dressing table. It was a move that brought him just a little closer. Her lipstick had worn off, he noticed. He found the generous and unpainted shape of her mouth appealing.

"I watched the tape you sent."

"Good. You'll have more fun if you're familiar with the format. Make yourself comfortable." She spoke quickly but not hurriedly. That was training. But she wanted out, and she wanted out now. That was instinct. "One of the staff will be along to take you to Makeup."

"I also read credits." He blocked the door in an offhand way. "I noticed that a Johanna Patterson is executive producer. You?"

"Yes." Damn it, he was making her jittery. She couldn't remember the last time anyone had been able to make her nervous. Cool, controlled and capable. Anyone who knew her would have given that description. She glanced deliberately at her watch. "I'm sorry I can't stay and chat, but we're on a schedule."

He didn't budge. "Most producers don't hand-deliver contracts."

She smiled. Though on the surface it was sweet, he saw the ice underneath and wondered at it. "I'm not most producers."

"I won't argue with that." It was more than attraction now, it was a puzzle that had to be solved. He'd managed to resist any number of women, but he'd never been able to resist a puzzle. "Since we missed lunch before, how about dinner?"

"I'm sorry. I'm—"

"Booked. Yeah, so you said." He tilted his head just a bit, as if to study her from a new angle. It was more than the fact that he was used to women being available. It was the fact that she seemed bound and determined to brush him off, and not very tactfully. "You're not wearing any rings."

"You're observant."

"Involved?"

"With what?"

He had to laugh. His ego wasn't so inflated that he couldn't take no for an answer. He simply preferred a reason for it. "What's the problem, Johanna? Didn't you like my last movie?"

"Sorry. I missed it," she lied, smiling. "Now if you'll excuse me, I've got a show to see to."

He was still standing at the door, but this time she brushed past him. And against him. Both felt a jolt, unexpected and tingling.

Annoyed, Johanna kept walking.

Intrigued, Sam kept watching.

She had to admit, he was a pro. By the middle of the taping of the first show, Sam had gotten in a casual and very competent plug for his new miniseries *No Roses for Sarah.* So effective, that Johanna knew she'd tune in herself. The sponsors and the network brass would be delighted. He'd charmed his partner, the mother of two from Columbus, who had walked onto the set so tense that her voice had come out in squeaks. He'd even managed to answer a few questions correctly.

It was hard not to be impressed, though she worked at it. When the lights were on and the tape was rolling he was the embodiment of that elusive and too often casually used word: *star.* John Jay's posturing and flashing incisors shifted to the background.

Not all entertainers were at ease in front of a live audience. He was. Johanna noted that he was able to turn on just the right amount of enthusiasm and enjoyment when the cameras were rolling, but also that he played to the studio audience during breaks by joking with his competitor and occasionally answering a question someone shouted out at him.

He even seemed to be genuinely pleased when his partner won five hundred in cash in the bonus speed round.

Even if he was just putting on a good face, Johanna couldn't fault him for it. Five hundred dollars meant a great deal to the mother of two from Columbus. Just as much as her moment in the sun with a celebrated heartthrob.

"We've got a very tight game going here, folks." John Jay smiled importantly at the camera. "This final question will determine today's champion, who will then go to the winner's circle and try for ten thousand dollars. Hands on your buzzers." He drew the card from the slot on his dais. "And the final question, for the championship, is...who created Winnie the Pooh?"

Sam's finger was quick on the trigger. The woman from Columbus looked at him pleadingly. John Jay called for a dramatic silence.

"A. A. Milne."

"Ladies and gentlemen, we have a new champion!"

As the cheers got louder and his partner threw her arms around his neck, Sam caught Johanna's look of surprise. It was easy to read her mind and come up with the fact that she didn't see him as a man who could read and remember storybooks—especially not classic children's books.

John Jay said the official goodbyes to the accountant from Venice and broke for a commercial. Sam had to all but carry his partner to the winner's circle. As he settled back in his chair, he glanced at Johanna.

"How'm I doing?"

"Sixty seconds," she said, but her voice was friendlier because she saw he was holding his partner's hand to calm her.

When the minute was up, John Jay managed to

make the woman twice as nervous as he ran down the rules and the possibilities. The clock started on the first question. They weren't so difficult, Sam realized. It was the pressure that made them hard. He wasn't immune to it himself. He really wanted her to win. When he saw she was beginning to fumble, he blanked out the lights and the camera the way he did during any important scene. The rules said he could answer only two questions for her. Once he did, letting her keep her viselike grip on his hand, she was over the hump.

There were ten seconds left when John Jay, his voice pitched to the correct level of excitement, posed the last question. ''Where was Napoleon's final defeat?''

She knew it. Of course she knew it. The problem was to get the word out. Sam inched forward in the impossibly uncomfortable swivel chair and all but willed her to spit out the word.

''Waterloo!'' she shouted, beating the buzzer by a heartbeat. Above their heads, *$10,000* began to flash in bold red lights. His partner screamed, kissed him full on the mouth, then screamed again. While they were breaking for a commercial, Sam was holding her head between her knees and telling her to take deep breaths.

''Mrs. Cook?'' Johanna knelt down beside them and monitored the woman's pulse. This wasn't the first time a contestant had reacted so radically. ''Are you going to be all right?''

''I won. I won ten thousand dollars.''

"Congratulations." Johanna lifted the woman's head far enough to be certain it was merely a case of hyperventilation. "We're going to take a fifteen-minute break. Would you like to lie down?"

"No. I'm sorry." Mrs. Cook's color was coming back. "I'm all right."

"Why don't you go with Beth? She'll get you some water."

"Okay. I'm fine, really." Too excited to be embarrassed, Mrs. Cook managed to stand, with Johanna taking one arm and Sam the other. "It's just that I've never won anything before. My husband didn't even come. He took the kids to the beach."

"You'll have a wonderful surprise for him," Johanna said soothingly, and kept walking. "Take a little breather, then you can start thinking about how you're going to spend that money."

"Ten thousand dollars," Mrs. Cook said faintly as she was passed over to Beth.

"Do you get a lot of fainters?" Sam asked.

"Our share. Once we had to stop taping because a construction worker slid right out of his seat during the speed round." She watched a moment longer until she was satisfied Bethany had Mrs. Cook under control. "Thanks. You acted quickly."

"No problem. I've had some practice."

She thought of women fainting at his feet. "I'll bet. There'll be cold drinks and fresh fruit in your dressing room. As long as Mrs. Cook's recovered, we'll start the tape in ten minutes."

He took her arm before she could move away. ‘‘If it wasn't my last movie, what is it?''

‘‘What is what?''

‘‘All these little barbs I feel sticking into my heart. You have a problem with me being here?''

‘‘Of course not. We're thrilled to have you.''

‘‘Not we. You.''

‘‘I'm thrilled to have you here,'' she corrected, wishing he didn't make it a habit to stand almost on top of her. Her low heels brought her eyes level with his mouth. She discovered it wasn't the most comfortable view. ‘‘This series of contests, like your movie, will be shown during the May sweeps. What could be better?''

‘‘A friendly conversation, over dinner.''

‘‘You're persistent, Mr. Weaver.''

‘‘I'm puzzled, Ms. Patterson.''

Her lips very nearly twitched. There was something cute about the way he drawled her last name. ‘‘A simple no shouldn't puzzle a man who obviously thinks so well on his feet.'' Deliberately she looked at her watch. ‘‘Half your break's up. You'd better change.''

Because things ran smoothly, they were able to tape three shows before the dinner break. Johanna began to have fantasies about finishing on time. She kept them to herself, knowing how easy it was to jinx success. The dinner spread wasn't elaborate, but it was plentiful. Johanna didn't believe in pinching pennies over such minor matters as food. She wanted to keep her celebrities happy and her contestants at ease.

During the break she didn't sit, but grabbed a plate and a few essentials and kept herself available. The audience had been cleared, and new ticketholders would be allowed in for the two final tapings. All she had to do was avoid any crises, keep the energy level up and make certain John Jay didn't proposition any of the females on set.

With the first in mind, Johanna kept her eyes on the new challenger, a young woman from Orange County who appeared to be about six months pregnant.

"Problem?"

She'd forgotten that her other prerequisite had been to avoid Sam Weaver. Reminding herself to keep the celebrities happy, she turned to him as she plucked a small chilled shrimp from her plate. "No, why?"

"You don't relax, do you?" Without expecting an answer, he chose a slim carrot stick from her plate. "I've noticed you're watching Audrey like a hawk."

She wasn't surprised that he already knew the expectant mother by her first name. "Just being cautious." She bit into the shrimp and unbent enough to smile at him. After all, the day was nearly over. "During one of my early shows we had an expectant mother go into labor in the winner's circle. It's not an experience you forget."

"What did she have?" he asked, testing.

"A boy." Her smile became more generous as her eyes met his. It was one of her best memories. "By the time she was halfway to the hospital the staff had a pool going.'' She swallowed the last of the shrimp. "I won.''

So she liked to bet. He'd keep that in mind. "I don't think you have to worry about Audrey. She's not due until the first part of August.'' He caught Johanna's curious look. "I asked,'' he explained. "Now, can I ask you a question? Professional,'' he added when he sensed her withdrawal.

"Of course.''

"How often do you have to wind John Jay up?''

She had to laugh, and she didn't bother to object when he snitched a cube of cheddar from her plate. "Wind down's more like it. He's harmless, really. Only he thinks he's irresistible.''

"He told me the two of you were...cozy.''

"Really?'' She glanced briefly over in the show's host's direction. The haughty look was so casual and innate that Sam grinned. "He's also an optimist.''

He was glad to hear it. Very glad. "Well, he does his job. Somehow he manages to hit the note between cheerleader and father confessor.''

Covering her personal opinion with her professional one was an old habit. To her, entertainment was first and last a business. "Actually, we're lucky to have him. He hosted another show about five years back, so he's not only familiar but also has a strong appeal to the home viewer.''

"Are you going to eat that sandwich?''

Without answering, Johanna took half of the roast-beef-and-Swiss and handed it to him. "Are you enjoying yourself so far?"

"More than I'd expected." He took a bite. So she had a taste for hot mustard. He was fond of spice himself, and in more than food. "Will you be offended if I tell you I kicked a bit about doing it?"

"No. I'm the first to admit that the show isn't Shakespeare, but it serves its purpose." Leaning against a wall, she watched one of the crew heap on a second helping. "What have you found appealing about it?"

He avoided the obvious answer. Her. The one he gave was equally true. "I got a kick out of seeing those people win. Of course, I developed a soft spot for Mrs. Cook. Why do you do it?"

She avoided several possible answers. The one she settled on was true enough. "I enjoy it." When he offered her his glass of sparkling water and lime, she accepted without thinking. She was relaxed, optimistic about the rest of the day and, though she didn't realize it, comfortable in his company.

"I hesitate to point this out, but it looks like we're having dinner after all."

She looked at him again, slowly, gauging him and her reaction to him. If she'd had a different background, different memories, fewer disillusionments, she would have been flattered. More, she would have been tempted. He had a way of looking at her as though they were alone; as though, if they'd been in a room with hundreds of other people, he would have picked her, and only her, out.

Trick of the trade, she told herself, disliking her own cynicism.

"Isn't it handy we got that out of the way?" She handed him back his glass.

"Yeah. It should make it easier for us to do it again."

Casually she signaled to the crew to begin clearing up. "I don't want to rush you, but we'll start taping again in fifteen minutes."

"I never miss my cue." He shifted his body just enough to prevent her from walking by him. He had the moves, Johanna thought. Very smooth. Very slick. "I get the impression you like to play games, Johanna."

There was a dare in his voice. She caught it, and was trapped. Though her voice was cool again, she stood her ground and met his gaze. "Depends on the stakes."

"Okay, how's this? If I win the next two games you'll have dinner with me. I set the time and the place."

"I don't like those stakes."

"I haven't finished. If I lose I come back on the show within six months. No fee." That had her attention, he noted, pleased with himself. He hadn't misjudged her dedication to her show or her weakness for a dare.

"Within six months," she repeated, studying him to assess whether he could be trusted. Not an inch, she decided, on many matters. But she didn't see him as a man to welch on a bet.

"Deal?" He made his voice deliberately challenging as he held out a hand.

It was too good a bet to turn down. His eyes were too mocking to ignore. "Deal." She set her palm against his, then removed it and stepped away. "Ten minutes, Mr. Weaver."

Johanna had a very bad feeling when Sam and his teammate took the first game. Since the conception of the show, she'd had a strict personal policy against rooting for either side. It didn't matter that no one could read her thoughts. She knew them, and prejudice of any kind was unprofessional. She certainly would never have imagined herself actually rooting against a certain team. She did now.

It was because she wanted him back on the show, she told herself when the last taping of the day began. The producer, not the woman, had made the bet. It was ridiculous to think that she was afraid, even uneasy, about having a meal with him. That would only be a small annoyance—like a spoonful of bad-tasting medicine.

But she stood behind camera two and cheered inwardly when he opposing team took the lead.

He didn't show nerves. Sam was much too skilled an actor to show nerves in front of a camera. But they dogged him. It was the principle, he told himself. That was the only reason he was so determined to win and make Johanna pay the price. He certainly wasn't infatuated. He'd been around too long to be infatuated just because a woman was beautiful. And aloof, his mind added. And contrary and stubborn. And damn sexy.

He wasn't infatuated. He just hated to lose.

By the beginning of the final round, the two teams were neck and neck. The studio audience was loud and raucous, the contestants wired. Johanna's stomach was in knots. When Sam turned and winked at her during the commercial break she nearly bared her teeth.

Positions jockeyed back and forth. Professionally Johanna knew that when the show aired it would pull the television audience in. That was, after all, the name of the game. Personally, she'd hoped for a landslide, however boring.

When the final question came up, she held her breath. Sam was quick to push the button, but his partner was quicker. He nearly swore. The expectant mother from Orange County had more than her own fate in her hands.

"Surrender, Dorothy!" she shouted. When the lights went on, Sam took her face in his hands and kissed her. Hard. Audrey would be able to dine out on the moment for months. Sam kept his arm around her as they walked toward the winner's circle. Once she was settled, he strolled casually over to Johanna and bent closer to her ear.

"Saturday night, seven. I'll pick you up."

She only nodded. It was hard to speak when your teeth were clenched.

Johanna found several vital tasks to perform after the taping was completed. She did not, as was her habit, say a personal thank-you to both guest stars. That job was handed over to Bethany. She made herself scarce for thirty minutes so that she could be sure Sam Weaver was off and out of her hair. Until Saturday.

She couldn't quite drum up the job-well-done mood the end of the day usually brought her. Instead she made a list of details to see to the following day that would keep her occupied from the time she got up until she crawled back home again. Business as usual, she told herself, and broke the tip off her pencil.

"Everybody's happy," Beth told her. "The questions we didn't use in the speed round are locked back in the safe. The contestants we didn't get to are ready and willing to come back next week. Your dupes." She handed Johanna the tapes. "We've got some great shows. Especially the last one. Even the techs were getting into it. They loved Sam." Bethany pushed back a lock of hair. "And you know how jaded techs can be. Anyway, it's nice to know that besides being gorgeous and sexy he's got some smarts."

Johanna grunted and dropped the tapes in her carryall.

Bethany tilted her head. "I was going to ask you if you wanted to take some of the leftover fruit home, but it looks more like you'd prefer raw meat."

"It's been a long day."

"Uh-huh." Beth knew her boss better. Johanna had pulled a roll of antacids out of her bag and had popped two of them. A sure sign of trouble. "Want to have a drink and talk about it?"

Johanna had never made it a habit to confide in anyone. There simply hadn't been enough people in her life she could trust. Johanna knew Beth. Her assistant was young and energetic, but she was also trustworthy. She was also the closest thing Johanna had ever had to a foul-weather friend.

"I'll pass on the drink, but how about walking me out to my car?"

"Sure."

The sun hadn't set. Johanna found something reassuring about that after having been inside all day. She'd put the top down, she thought, and take the drive home through the Hills fast. Maybe a bit recklessly. She had a taste for the reckless, a taste she usually controlled. It came from her father. But tonight it might do her good to give in to it for a little while.

"What did you think of Sam Weaver?"

Bethany cocked a brow. "Before or after I stopped drooling?"

"After."

"I liked him," she said simply. "He didn't expect the red carpet, he wasn't condescending and he wasn't snickering behind his hand at the contestants."

"Those are all negative virtues," Johanna pointed out.

"Okay, I liked the way he joked around with the crew. And the way he signed autographs as though he wanted to instead of acting as though he were granting a favor.'' She didn't add that she'd asked for one herself. ''He acted like somebody without making sure everybody remembered that *somebody* was in all capital letters.''

''Interestingly said,'' Johanna murmured. ''Are you still keeping that little book with the list of celebrity panelists?''

Beth colored a bit. She was in the business, but that didn't stop her from being a fan. ''Yeah. Sam gets five stars.''

Johanna's lips twitched a bit at her assistant's top rating. ''I guess I should be relieved to hear it. I'm having dinner with him on Saturday.''

Bethany's mouth went into the O position. There were stars in her eyes. She simply couldn't help it. ''Wow.''

''It's confidential.''

''Okay,'' Bethany said, and Johanna knew she was as good as her word. ''Johanna, I know you were raised in the business and Cary Grant probably bounced you on his knee, but doesn't it give you a tingle?''

''It gives me a pain,'' Johanna stated bluntly as she pulled open her car door. ''Actors aren't my type.''

''Too general.''

''Okay, blue-eyed lanky actors with a drawl aren't my type.''

''You're sick, Johanna. Very, very sick. You want me to go as proxy?''

She chuckled as she lowered herself into the car. ''No. I can handle Sam Weaver.''

"Lucky you. Listen, not to pry or anything..."

"But?"

"You will remember the details? I might want to write a book or something."

"Go home, Beth." The engine sprang to life as she twisted the key. Yes, she definitely wanted power and speed tonight.

"Okay, just let me know if he always smells so good. I can live on that."

Shaking her head, Johanna roared out of the lot. She hadn't been interested enough to notice what Sam Weaver had smelled like.

Like a man, her memory informed her. He'd smelled very much like a man.

Chapter 3

It was only dinner. Nothing to worry about. Certainly nothing, after several days to put it in perspective, to be annoyed about. They would no doubt go to one of L.A.'s flashier restaurants, where Sam could see and be seen. Between the pâté and the double chocolate mousse he would greet and chat with the other glamorous types who patronized that kind of eatery.

Meat houses, her second stepmother had called such places. Not because of the menu but because of the flesh exposed. Darlene had been one of the most honest and least affected of her father's attachments.

If she wanted to stretch a point, Johanna could consider it a business dinner. She found she wanted to stretch a point. She could tolerate this, as she had tolerated many other meals, as a part of the game everyone who wanted to remain part of the business learned to play. Since it was business, she would be charming and chatty, even gracious, until it was over and she could close the door on the entire episode.

She didn't like persistent men.

She didn't like men with reputations.

She didn't like Sam Weaver.

That was before the flowers arrived.

Johanna had spent Saturday morning gardening and half-hoping Sam Weaver wouldn't find her address. He hadn't called to ask her for it or to confirm plans. Waiting for him to do just that had left her jumpy and out of sorts all week. That was just one more sin to lay at his door.

It was her habit whenever she worked outside to take her cordless phone with her. Business could crop up even on weekends. Today, however, she pretended to have forgotten it and spent a warm and pleasant morning tending a plot of columbine.

This was her respite, even her vice, in a way. The flowers she planted were nurtured and cared for. They rewarded her by renewing themselves year after year. Their continuity soothed her. This, as was the case in other areas of her life, was something she'd done with her own hands. Whatever rewards she reaped, whatever failures she suffered, were her own.

The flowers lasted. The people in her life rarely did.

Her jeans were scruffy at the knees and her hands stained with mulch when the delivery man pulled up. Johanna shaded her eyes as she rose.

"Miz Patterson?"

"Yes."

"Sign here, please." The deliveryman met her halfway across her lawn, handing her first his clipboard and then a long white box embossed with a florist's name and tied with a red satin ribbon. "Nice garden you got there," he said with a tip of his hat as he climbed back into the truck.

She was a sucker for flowers. Without waiting to go in and wash up, Johanna opened the box. They were roses. Not a dozen red or two dozen pink, but one long-stemmed sample of every color she'd ever seen, from the purest white to the deepest red, and all the pinks and golds between. Charmed, she lowered her face to the box to draw in their scent.

Heady. Roses were always heady, lush and unashamedly sensual.

It wasn't her birthday. In any case, her father—or rather her father's secretary—wasn't imaginative enough to have thought of such a sweet and charming gift. Though her fingertips were soiled, she pulled open the card that had come with the box. I don't know your favorite color. Yet. Sam.

She wanted to shrug it off. Pretty gestures came so easily to some. It would have taken only a casual order to an assistant to have them delivered. How well she knew it. So he'd found her, she thought with a shrug as she started back across the lawn. The deal was still on, and she'd live up to her end of it.

She tried, really tried, to set them aside and go back to work on the buds she'd planted herself. But she couldn't dismiss the roses, didn't have the heart to dampen her own pleasure. She was smiling when she sniffed the flowers again. Smiling still when she went into the house to arrange them.

He hadn't looked forward to an evening quite so much in a long time. It was easy to compare it to a winning poker hand or a successful day at the track. He'd never cared half as much for the purse as for the winning. He'd have preferred to think of it in those terms, but the truth was that he was looking forward to spending a few hours in Johanna Patterson's company.

Maybe he was intrigued because she was so disinterested. Sam took a turn sharp and fast while the radio blared through the open windows. What man didn't appreciate a challenge? If she'd taken him at his word on their first meeting, they might have enjoyed a pleasant lunch and an easy hour. He'd never know if that would have been the end of it. The fact that she'd refused, and had continued to refuse, only made him more determined to wear her down.

Women came easily to him. Too easily. Sam wouldn't deny he'd gone through a stage when he'd taken advantage of that. But his background, and what many might have considered the rather quaint and traditional values that had gone into it, had surfaced again.

The press could beat the drum of his romantic adventures all they liked. The truth was, he *was* a romantic. Rolling from one bed to the next had never been his style.

There were two Sam Weavers. One was intensely private, guarded about matters like family and relationships, the things that really mattered. The other was an actor, a realist who accepted that the price of fame was public consumption. He gave interviews, didn't bother to dodge the paparazzi and was always willing to sign an autograph. He'd learned to shrug off whatever reports were exaggerations or outright lies. They were the public Sam's problem. The private one couldn't have cared less.

He wondered, given what he now knew about Johanna Patterson's background, which Sam Weaver she would understand.

She was the only child of the respected producer Carl Patterson, the product of his first, and reportedly most tempestuous marriage. Her mother had disappeared or, as some reports put it, "gone into seclusion," after the marriage had failed. Johanna had grown up in the luxury of Beverly Hills, had attended the best schools. Some rumors stated that she adored her father, others that there was no love lost between them. In either case, she was the only offspring Patterson had after four marriages and numerous affairs.

He was surprised that she lived back in the Hills. He'd expected some slick condo in the city or a wing in her father's Beverly Hills estate. The sharp professional woman he'd met seemed out of place so far from the action. He was more surprised when he found the house.

It was tiny. Like a dollhouse, but without the gingerbread. Hardly more than a cabin, it was rustic and sturdy, with the wood unpainted and the panes of glass sparkling in the evening sun. There wasn't much land before the trees and the hills took it over. What was there was uneven and rocky. To compensate—more, to enhance it—flowers and budding vines were everywhere. The dashing little Mercedes parked in the driveway looked as though it had been left there by mistake.

Hands in pockets, he stood beside his own car and looked again. She didn't have any close neighbors, and the view was nothing to write home about, but it seemed as though she'd carved out her own corner of the mountainside. He knew about that. Appreciated it.

When he reached the door, he caught the scent of sweet peas. His mother planted them each spring, outside the kitchen windows. Johanna opened the door and found him smiling.

"Brigadoon," he said, and watched her polite smile turn to an expression of puzzlement. "I was trying to think what your place reminded me of. Brigadoon. Like it's only here once every hundred years."

Damn him, she thought, feeling almost resigned. She'd barely managed to put the roses in perspective and here he was, charming her again. "I wasn't sure you'd find it."

"I have a good sense of direction. Most of the time." He glanced toward the flowers that flanked both sides of her house. "From the looks of things, the roses were overkill."

"No." It would have been petty not to let him know they'd pleased her. "It was sweet of you to send them.'' He wasn't wearing a dinner suit, but a breezy linen shirt and pleated slacks. Johanna was glad she'd guessed right when she'd bypassed glitz for the subtler lines of a slim-skirted white dress. ''If you'd like to come in a minute, I'll get my jacket.''

He did, though he thought it would be a shame to cover up her arms and shoulders. The living room was small enough to be cozy. She'd arranged deep chairs by a white bricked fireplace and had added dozens of pillows. It made Sam think that when Johanna was finished with work she liked to take off her shoes and snuggle in.

''This isn't what I expected.''

''No?'' She pulled on a sizzling tomato-red jacket. ''I like it.''

''I didn't say I didn't like it, I said it wasn't what I expected.'' He noted his roses had been given a place of honor on the mantel, tucked prettily in a clear, widemouthed vase that glinted at the bottom with colored pebbles. ''Do you have a favorite?''

She glanced at the roses. ''No. I just like flowers.'' The clusters of rubies at her ears glinted as she adjusted them. ''Shall we go?''

''In a minute.'' He crossed to her, noticing with some interest the way she stiffened up. Despite it, he took her hand. ''Are you going to be a good sport about this?''

She let out a little sigh. ''I've thought about it.''

''And?'' It was the easy curving of his lips that made her relax.

''I decided I might as well.''

"Are you hungry?"

"Some."

"Mind a bit of a ride?"

Curious, she tilted her head. "No, I suppose not."

"Good." He kept her hand in his as they walked outside.

She should have known he was up to something. They didn't drive into the city as she'd expected. Rather than comment, Johanna let the conversation flow as she wondered how to handle him. Actors were a tricky bunch. They knew how to set the stage, how to read their lines, how to put on whatever face was most appropriate to the situation. At the moment, it seemed Sam had chosen to be the casually friendly companion a woman could relax with. Johanna wasn't ready to give him an inch.

He drove fast, just faster than the law allowed and just under the edge of safety. Even when they left the freeway for a road that was rough and sparsely populated, he continued at the same steady clip.

"Mind if I ask where we're going?"

Sam negotiated a lazy turn. He'd wondered how long it would take before she asked. "To dinner."

Johanna turned to study the landscape. The land rolled by, wide and dusty. "Something over an open fire?"

He smiled. She'd used her haughty tone again, and damned if he didn't enjoy hearing it. "No, I thought we'd eat at my place."

His place. The thought of dining privately with him

didn't alarm her. She was too confident of her ability to handle whatever situation cropped up. She was more curious about the fact that he would have a *place* this far from the glitz. "You have a cave?"

Because there was amusement in her voice now, his smile widened. "I can do a little better than that. I only eat in restaurants when it's necessary."

"Why?"

"Because you end up doing business, or being stared at. I wasn't in the mood for either tonight." Pebbles spit from under the tires as he turned to drive through a plain wooden gate.

"That's part of the game, isn't it?"

"Sure, but there has to be a reason to play it." He whizzed by a pretty white house with blue shutters, giving two blasts of his horn. "My foreman and his family live there. If he knows it's me he won't come looking for trespassers."

They passed barns and sheds, and she was surprised that they looked as though they had a purpose other than a decorative one. She spotted paddocks with split-rail fencing and dark, rich dirt. A dog—or what sounded like a pair of them—began to bark.

The road forked, and then she saw the ranch house. It, too, was white, but the shutters were gray and the three chimneys it boasted were brick weathered to a dusky rose. It was low and spreading, shaped like an H turned on its side. For all its size, it didn't overpower. There were rockers on the porch, sturdy wooden ones that gave the impression that someone sat in them often. Window boxes had been freshly painted a bright, sassy red. Tumbling out of them were pansies and bushy impatiens. Though the air here was hot and dry, they were thriving and well tended.

Johanna stepped out of the car to turn a slow circle. It certainly looked like a working ranch. "Quite a place."

"I like it," he said, mimicking her earlier remark.

She acknowledged that with a quick, though cautious, smile. "It must be inconvenient to commute."

"I keep a place in L.A." He shrugged it off as though it were no more than a storage closet. "The best thing about finishing a film is being able to come back here and dig in for a while. Before I got hooked on acting, I'd wanted to come west and work on a ranch." He took her arm as they walked up the two wooden steps to the porch. They creaked. For some reason, Johanna found that endearing. "I was lucky enough to do both."

She glanced at the pansies, with their arrogant Alice-in-Wonderland faces. "Do you raise cattle?"

"Horses." He'd left the door unlocked. It was a habit he'd grown up with. "I bought the place about three years ago. Convinced my accountant that it'd be a great tax shelter. It made him feel better."

The hardwood floors were polished to a high gloss, scattered with hand-hooked rugs in muted pastels. In the entrance a collection of pewter—bowls, spoons, mugs, even a dented candlestick—was arranged on a waist-high table. The early twilight crept through the windows.

It had a good feel, a solid feel. Though she would never had admitted it out loud, Johanna had always felt strongly that houses had their own personalities. She'd selected her own house because it had made her feel warm and comfortable. She'd left her father's because it had been possessive and dishonest.

"Do you get to stay here often?" she asked him.

"Not often enough." He glanced around at the walls, which he'd painted himself. The house, like his career, was something he never took for granted. Though he'd never known poverty, he'd been taught to appreciate security, and that nothing replaced sweat for earning it. "Would you like a drink, or would you rather go for dinner?"

"Dinner," she said firmly. She knew better than to drink, socially or otherwise, on an empty stomach.

"I was hoping you'd say that." In the casual way he had, he took her hand and led her down the hall. The wing of the house ran straight. At the end it opened up into a large country kitchen. Copper pots hung from hooks over a center island. The room was flanked by counters and cabinets on one side and a small stone hearth on the other. A ribbon of windows gave an open view of dusk settling over a brick terrace and a mosaic pool. She'd thought to find a servant or two busily preparing the evening meal. Instead, all she found was the scent of cooking.

"It smells wonderful."

"Good." Scooping up two hot pads, Sam bent down to the oven. "I left it on warm." He drew out a casserole of bubbly lasagna.

Food wasn't something that usually excited her, but now the scent alone drew her over to his side. How long had it been since she'd seen someone take a homemade meal out of an oven? "It looks wonderful, too."

"My mother always told me food tastes better if it looks good." He picked up a long loaf of Italian bread and began slicing.

"You didn't cook this."

"Why not?" He glanced over his shoulder, amused that she was frowning again. She looked so thoughtful that he was tempted to run a fingertip down the faint line that formed between her brows. "Cooking's a very manageable skill if you approach it properly and have the right incentive."

Johanna stuck with carryout or prepackaged microwave meals. "And you have both?"

"I wanted to be an actor, but I didn't have any desire to be a starving actor." He poured garlic butter over the bread, set the oven, then slid it in. "After I came to California, I kicked around from audition to audition and from greasy spoon to greasy spoon. A couple of months of that and I called home and asked my mother for some recipes. She's a great cook." Sam drew the cork from a bottle of wine, then set it aside to breathe. "Anyway, it took me a lot less time to figure out how to sauté trout than it did for me to get a memorable part."

"Now that you've had a number of memorable parts, what's your incentive?"

"To cook?" He shrugged and took a leafy spinach

salad from the refrigerator. ''I like it. We're about ready here. You want to grab the wine? I thought we'd eat outside.''

The trouble with Hollywood, Johanna thought as she followed him out, was that things were never what they seemed. She'd been sure she had Sam Weaver pegged. But the man she'd assessed and dismissed wouldn't have copied recipes from his mother.

Nor was he the type, she thought as she set the wine down, who would have prepared a charming dinner for two, alfresco, with pretty blue stoneware plates and thick yellow candles. It was every bit as friendly as it was romantic. The romance she'd expected, and she knew just how to discourage it. The offer of friendship was another matter.

''Light those candles, will you?'' He glanced around briefly, checking the way a man did when he was already certain things were just as he wanted them to be. ''I'll get the rest.''

Johanna watched him go back inside. Did someone who walked like that, she wondered—as though he were heading toward a shoot-out—really prepare spinach salad? She struck a match and held it to the wick of the first candle. Apparently so. There were more important things to lie about than cooking. She held the match to the second candle, then deliberately blew it out. She wouldn't have called avoiding three on a match superstitious. Just practical.

She heard the music he put on, something low and bluesy, with a lot of sax. While he brought out the rest of the meal, she poured the wine.

His instincts had been right, Sam thought as they settled at the wicker table. He'd been on the verge of making dinner reservations at some tony restaurant when he'd pulled back. He'd cooked for women before, but never here. He never brought anyone to the ranch, because the ranch was home. Private. Off limits to the press and the public, it was both refuge and sanctuary from a world he was a voluntary member of—when he chose to be. At the time, he hadn't been sure why he'd wanted to break his own rule with Johanna. Now he began to understand.

At the ranch he could be himself—no pretenses, no roles. Here he was Sam Weaver from Virginia, and here he was most comfortable. He didn't have to be *on* here. And he wanted to be himself with Johanna.

She wasn't without pretenses, he mused as he watched her. Not entirely. Unless he missed his guess, most of her resentment had faded, but not her distrust. He'd already decided to ease his curiosity and find the reason for it.

Maybe she'd been stung in an affair that had gone sour. Broken hearts often mended jaggedly. If she had been betrayed by a man she'd cared for and trusted, it would be logical that she would put up some defences. It might take some time before he could wear them down, but he had a feeling it would be worth it. He'd start with what he believed was the focus of her life: her work.

''Were you happy with the taping the other day?''

''More than.'' She was too fair-minded not to give him his due. ''You were really good, not just as far as the answers went, but overall. A lot of times you can have people zip right through the questions and be a dead bore.'' She broke off a piece of bread, then nibbled at the crust. He'd hit the right tone. It was always easy for her to relax when the subject was business. ''And, of course, it was a coup to have you.''

''I'm flattered.''

She studied him again with those cool blue eyes. ''I doubt it would be that easy to flatter you.''

''An actor always wants to be wanted. Well, to a point, anyway,'' he added with another quick grin. ''Do you know how many game shows I've turned down in the last couple of days?''

She smiled and sipped her wine. ''Oh, I could hazard a guess.''

''How'd you get into it? Producing?''

''Heredity.'' Her lips tightened only briefly. After taking a second sip, she set her glass down. ''I guess you could say I like pulling the strings.''

''You'd have learned young with Carl Patterson as your father.'' He saw it, very briefly but very clearly. More than resentment, less than pain. ''He's produced some of the best, and most successful television shows, as well as an impressive number of features. Being second-generation can be a strain, I imagine.''

''You get past it.'' The lasagna was cheesy and rich with spices. Johanna concentrated on it. ''This really is terrific. Your mother's recipe?''

''With some variations.'' So her father was off limits. He could respect that—for now. "How about the show itself? How did that get started?"

"With the flu." At ease again, she smiled and took another bite.

"Care to elaborate?"

"I had the flu, a nasty bout of it, a couple of years ago. I had to stay in bed for a week, and since it hurt my eyes to read, I lay there hour after hour and watched television. The game shows hooked me." She didn't object when he topped off her glass. The wine was very mellow and dry, and she knew her limit right down to the swallow. "You get involved, you know, in the games, and the people playing them. After a while you start rooting for them, tensing up in an effort to help them. When someone wins, the vicarious thrill is automatic. And then you have the advantage of almost always being smarter at home, because there's no pressure. That's a nice smug feeling."

He watched her as she spoke. She was animated now, the way she'd been while she'd rushed around the set making sure things fell into place. "So after your bout with the flu you decided to produce one."

"More or less." She could remember running into the brick wall of the network brass and ultimately having to appeal to her father. "In any case, I had the concept, and the experience in producing. I'd done a couple of documentaries for public television and had worked on a prime-time special. With a little string-pulling, we got a pilot done. Now we're only a couple of ratings points from being on top. I'm waiting for the go-ahead to start evening syndication."

"What happens then?"

"The demographics open. You get the kids who've finished their homework, the business crowd who want to put their feet up for a half hour. You up the ante. Give away some cars, bigger bucks."

She was surprised to discover she'd cleared her plate. Usually she ate a few bites, then ended up picking at the rest, impatient for the meal—and the time sitting down—to be over.

"Want some more?"

"No. Thanks." She picked up her wine as she studied him. "I know I lost the bet, but it looks as though I got the best part of the deal."

"Not from where I'm sitting."

The shades came down. Just like that. One compliment, however offhand, and she pulled back. Seeing it, Sam rose and offered a hand. "Want to walk? There's enough moonlight."

There was no point in being ungracious, Johanna told herself. She hated it when she became prickly over something unimportant. "All right. The only ranches I've ever seen have been on the back lot."

He bundled up the last of the bread, then handed it to her. "We'll go by the pond. You can feed the ducks."

"You have ducks?"

"Several overfed ducks." He slipped an arm around her shoulders to steer her. She smelled like the evening they walked through, quiet and promising. "I like looking at them in the morning."

"Your Jake in *Half-Breed* would have eaten them for breakfast."

"So you did see my last movie."

She took a quick nip at the tip of her tongue. "Oh, was that your last one?"

"Too late. You've already boosted my ego."

When she looked at him, his smile was appealing and too easy to respond to. *He* was too easy to respond to. In self-defense she looked back at the house.

"It's lovely from out here, too. You live all alone?"

"I like a little solitude now and then. Of course, I've got a few hands who look after things while I'm working, and Mae comes in a couple times a week to scoop at the dust." His hand slipped down to take hers. "My family comes out a few times a year and shakes everything up."

"Your parents visit you here?"

"Them, my brother, my two sisters, their families. Assorted cousins. The Weavers are a large and loud bunch."

"I see." But she didn't. She could only imagine. And envy. "They must be proud of you."

"They were always supportive, even when they thought I was crazy."

The pond was almost a quarter mile from the house, but the going was easy. It was obvious he walked the path often. She caught the scent of citrus, then the stronger scent of water. The moonlight struck it, highlighting the grass which had been left to grow ankle-high. Sensing an audience, several brown and speckled ducks paddled over to the water's edge.

"I've never had the nerve to come out here empty-handed," he told her. "I think they'd follow me home."

Johanna opened the linen cloth and broke off a crust of bread. It didn't even hit the water before it was gobbled up. She laughed; it was a low, delighted sound deep in her throat. Immediately she tore off another piece and, tossing this one farther out, watched a drake zoom in on it.

"I've always wanted to watch them from underneath so I could see their feet scramble." She continued to break off and toss. Ducks pursued the bread in groups and squabbled over it with bad-tempered quacks and competitive pecks. "My mother and I used to go out and feed the ducks. We'd give them silly names, then see if we could tell them apart the next time."

She caught herself, amazed that the memory had surfaced, stunned that she'd shared it. Her hand closed into a fist over the bread.

"There was a pond about five miles away when I was a kid," Sam said, as if he hadn't noticed her change in mood. "We used to ride our bikes to it during the summer, after we'd stolen a pack of crackers or whatever from the kitchen. We'd toss it out for the ducks—and a couple of pushy swans—and accidentally fall in as often as possible." He glanced out over the water. "Looks like someone's had a family."

She followed his gaze and saw a brown duck gliding along, trailed by a long shadow. As it came closer, Johanna saw that the shadow wasn't a shadow, it was fluffy ducklings. "Oh, aren't they sweet?" She crouched down for a closer look, forgetting about the hem of her skirt. The babies followed Mama on their evening swim, straight as an arrow. "I wish there was more light," she murmured.

"Come back when there is."

Johanna tilted her head up. In the moonlight his face was stronger, more attractive, than it had a right to be. The eyes, eyes that invariably drew women in, were as dark as the water. And, as with the water, Johanna didn't know what lay beneath the surface. Turning away again, she continued shredding the bread and tossing it.

He liked the way her hair haloed around her face, stopping just inches from her shoulders. A man could fill his hands with it. It would be soft, like the hand she rarely offered but he continued to take. It would carry that same subtle scent.

Her skin would be like that, on the back of her neck beneath all that heavy blond hair. He had an urge to touch it now, to skim his fingers over it and see if she trembled.

The ducks stopped their chatter when the last of the bread was consumed. A few hopefuls hung around the edge of the pond for a minute longer, then, satisfied the treat was done, glided away. Into the sudden silence came a night bird's song, and the rustle of a rabbit running into the brush.

"It's a lovely spot," she said, rising and brushing the crumbs from her fingers. "I can see why you like it so much."

"I want you to come back."

It was said very simply, so it shouldn't have meant so much. Johanna didn't back away, because that would have been admitting it did. If her heart was beating a little faster, she could pretend otherwise. She reminded herself that things often seemed more important in the moonlight than they did in the day.

"We had a bet. I lost." She said it lightly, already aware that the tone wouldn't matter. "But that's been paid up tonight."

"This has nothing to do with bets or games." He touched her hair as he'd wanted to. "I want you to come back."

She should have been able to shrug it off, to nip it before whatever was beginning to grow would blossom. It wasn't as easy as it should have been to dredge up the cool smile and the careless refusal. She looked at him, really looked at him, and could think of only one thing to say.

"Why?"

His lips curved. She watched the smile move slowly over his face, the angles shifting, the shadows playing. "Damned if I know. But when you do come back, maybe we'll both have an answer. Meanwhile, why don't we get this one question out of the way?"

He leaned toward her. She'd told herself she didn't want to be kissed. She wouldn't like it. She wasn't a demonstrative person, and for her a kiss wasn't merely a touching of lips. Even though she'd grown up in a world where a kiss was nothing more than a handshake—and often less binding—to her it was a personal thing that meant affection, trust, warmth.

She'd told herself she wouldn't be kissed. But that had been before the moonlight and the bird's song. That had been before he'd touched her.

Her eyes were wary. He saw that even as he brushed his lips lightly over hers. He'd meant it to be light, casual, hardly more than a peace offering. She was so cool and lovely, and so firmly on guard, that he'd been unable to resist.

An easy kiss. A friendly kiss. That was where he'd meant to begin and end it. That was before he'd tasted her.

He drew back, not quite sure of his footing. He hadn't been prepared for whatever had rushed into him, not for the punch of it. With the water lapping beside them, he stared down at her. Moonlight was on her face, and he touched her cheek where the light played. She didn't move. He couldn't know that her own stunned reaction had left her rooted to the spot.

He touched her again, drawing his fingers back through her hair until they gripped it. Still she didn't move. But when his lips came to hers again, hard, hungry, she met passion with passion.

She'd never wanted it to be like this. Desire raced through her, pushing her to keep pace with it. His mouth ran along her jaw, across her face, making her shiver with pleasure, but she twisted until their lips joined again.

A craving she'd never known she had…a dream she'd never allowed into her waking hours…that was what he was. Wherever his hands touched, they lingered, as if he couldn't get enough. Lost in the first wave of pleasure, she pressed against him.

No, he couldn't get enough. He pulled her head back and deepened the kiss. She tasted like the night, dark, haunted. The thin silk under her jacket teased and shifted until he had to force back the urge to tear it away. He wanted her, all of her. There, in the tall, damp grass, he wanted to discover all her secrets and make them his own.

She was breathless when they drew apart. That frightened her. Caution and control had been hard-learned lessons, and she always, without exception, applied them to all the areas of her life. She'd lost them both in the flash of an instant, in the brush of his lips.

She had to remember what he was: an artist, both in his craft and with his women. More, she had to remember what *she* was. There was no room in her life for reckless passion in the moonlight.

He reached for her again, just to trace his knuckles along her cheek. Because even that affected her, she moved aside.

"This isn't the answer for either of us." She didn't like hearing the strain in her own voice, or the lingering huskiness he'd caused.

"It was a lot more than I bargained for," he admitted. The defenses were going up again. He took her hand before she could withdraw behind them completely. "I felt something the first time I saw you. Now I begin to see why."

"Lust at first sight?"

"Damn it, Johanna."

She'd hated herself the moment she'd said it, but she couldn't back down. If she backed down, she'd give in. "Let's let it go, Sam. I'll be honest and say that was more than nice, but I'm just not interested in the sequel."

Anger stirred. He knew his own temper well enough to take things slow. He'd never decked a woman. Yet. "What are you interested in?"

She recognized barely restrained fury when she heard it. It was almost a relief. If he'd been kind, if he'd been the least bit persuasive, she would have crumbled. "My job." She tried for a smile and almost managed it. "That's really enough complications for me."

"Lady, anybody who can kiss like that is just asking for complications."

She hadn't known she could kiss like that. She certainly hadn't known she'd wanted to. And what was even more unnerving was that she wanted to kiss him again. "I suppose that's a compliment. Shall we just say it was an interesting evening and leave it at that?"

"No."

"That's the best I can do."

He touched her hair again. It wasn't a testing gesture this time, it was a possessive one. "Okay. You'll learn as you go along."

She couldn't pretend to be amused, because he was

frightening her. It wasn't a fear that he would drag her to the ground and finish what they'd both started, but it was a fear that he would prove to be stronger-willed and much more determined than she.

Stay out of his way, her mind warned her. And get started on it now.

"It was much too nice an evening to end it with an argument. I appreciate the meal and the walk. Now it's getting late, and since it's a long drive, we should be going."

"All right." He was much too annoyed to fight with her. Better, he thought, that he do exactly as she asked, then reevaluate the situation. Turning homeward, he reached out to guide her so that she wouldn't stumble. When she jerked at his touch, he smiled again, and most of his annoyance left him.

"The longest trips are often the most eventful, don't you think?"

She thought it best to leave that question unanswered.

Chapter 4

"Just how many cases of Diet Zing do we have?" Johanna waited for Bethany to run down her list.

"Considering what the crew pinched, about a hundred and fifty cases. We're square on the porto-vacs and the gift certificates and, of course, the encyclopedias." Bethany turned over the list of parting gifts. Though she thought it odd that Johanna was staring out the window rather than checking off her own list, she didn't comment. "About the home viewers' contest," Bethany began.

"Hmmm?"

"The home viewers' contest?"

"Oh." Johanna swore at herself, then pulled her gaze away from the window and her mind away from Sam Weaver. Daydreaming was always a waste of time, but it was a sin during office hours. "I want to get that nailed down this morning.'' She unlocked the top drawer of her desk and pulled out a file. ''I have several potential questions. Research put in a lot of extra time on it last week. The idea is to have John Jay announce a different one every day, somewhere during the program.'' She glanced down the list again to satisfy herself. ''I don't want him to do it at the same time every day, particularly not at the beginning. If we're going to draw people in, I want them to watch all day, all week. Is the deal on the car set?''

''Almost. We're going with the American product and tying it in with the drawing the week of the Fourth of July.''

''Fine, but I want two.''

''Two what?''

''Two cars, Beth. Watch *Trivia Alert* and win.'' She smiled a bit and tapped the end of her pencil on the desk. ''Two luxury cars. One should be a convertible. People in Omaha with two kids don't usually buy convertibles. Let's make it a red one, at least for the ads. We'll have the full-sized car in white and John Jay in a blue suit.''

''Hit them over the head with patriotism?''

''Something like that. See if we can bring the total value up to fifty thousand.''

''Sure.'' Bethany blew her bangs away from her eyes. ''I'll use charm. And if that doesn't work I'll use Mongo the enforcer.''

''Use the ratings,'' Johanna suggested. ''I want a big ad in the *TV Guide* and the Sunday supplements. Black and white for the guide, color for the supplements.'' She waited while Bethany made her notes. ''The ten-second spot at ten is already set. We'll tape it as soon as the cars are delivered. We have to pick five questions from the list.'' She handed Bethany a copy. ''And the list doesn't go out of this office.''

Bethany skimmed down. ''Where did Betty meet the leader of the pack?'' Lips pursed, she glanced up. ''Betty who?''

''Brush up on your girl groups. Early-sixties rock and roll.''

Bethany merely made a face. ''These are pretty tough.''

That was exactly what she'd wanted to hear. ''They're worth fifty thousand.''

Giving a quiet murmur of agreement, she checked another question. ''Johanna, how could anyone know how many witches were burned at the stake in Salem?''

''None.'' Sitting back, Johanna ran the pencil through her fingers. ''They were hanged.''

''Oh. Well, so far I'm batting a thousand.'' When Johanna's phone rang, Bethany took another hard look at the questions.

''Mr. Weaver's on the line, Ms. Patterson.''

Johanna opened her mouth and was surprised when nothing came out.

''Ms. Patterson?''

''What? Oh, tell Mr. Weaver I'm in a meeting.''

When she hung up, Beth glanced over. ''I wouldn't have minded waiting.''

''I doubt he's calling to discuss the show.'' Telling

herself to dismiss it, Johanna picked up her list and made her eyes focus. ‘‘What do you think about number six?’’

‘‘I don’t know that answer, either. Johanna…’’ Outgoing and candid herself, Bethany nonetheless understood and respected her boss’s restraint. ‘‘Did everything go okay the other night?’’

It would have been foolish to pretend to misunderstand. ‘‘It went fine. Very pleasant.’’ Johanna dug into her pocket for a roll of antacids. ‘‘I’m leaning toward numbers one, four, six, nine and thirteen.’’

Beth looked at each one, decided she might have an inkling about question thirteen, then nodded. ‘‘Let’s go for them.’’ She handed the list back so that Johanna could lock them up. ‘‘Could we pretend we’re out of the office, maybe at home with our feet up and a nice bottle of wine already half-gone?’’

Johanna turned the key and pocketed it. ‘‘Do you have a problem, Beth?’’

‘‘No, but I’d swear you did.’’

‘‘I’m fine.’’ Johanna began to stack and straighten papers on her desk. ‘‘We had a friendly dinner, some pleasant conversation, and that was that. I have no idea why Sam’s calling me at the office, but I don’t have time to chat with him.’’

‘‘I didn’t mention Sam,’’ Bethany pointed out. ‘‘You did. I only mentioned a problem.’’ She smiled sympathetically. ‘‘I get the feeling they’re the same thing.’’

Johanna rose and, with her hands in the deep pockets of her skirt, walked to the window. ''He just can't get it through his head that I'm not interested.''

''Are you? Not interested, I mean,'' Bethany supplied when Johanna turned her head.

''I don't want to be interested. It's the same thing.''

''No. If you weren't interested you'd be able to smile, maybe pat him on the head and say thanks but no thanks. Not wanting to be interested means you are and you get around it by avoiding phone calls and making excuses.''

Johanna pushed a thumb into the ivy geranium hanging in a basket at her window. The soil was moist. She'd watered it herself that morning. ''How did you get to be an expert?''

''Unfortunately, most of it comes from observation rather than execution. He seems like a nice guy, Johanna.''

''Maybe, but I don't have room for men right now, and less than none for actors.''

''That's a hard line.''

''It's a hard town.''

Bethany wasn't willing to buy that. True, she'd only lived in L.A. for three years, but it still fascinated her. To her it remained the town where dreams could be chased and caught. ''I hope you're not going to break my heart and tell me he's a jerk.''

''No.'' With a reluctant smile, Johanna turned again. ''No, he's not a jerk. Actually, you're right, he's a very nice guy, charming, easy to talk to—'' She caught herself. ''For an actor.''

‘‘He makes my insides tingle,’’ Bethany confessed, unashamed and artless.

Mine, too, Johanna thought. Which was precisely why she wasn’t going to see him again. ‘‘You’re supposed to be concentrating on your screenwriter,’’ she said briskly, then stopped when she saw Beth’s expression. ‘‘Trouble?’’

‘‘He dumped me.’’ She shrugged her shoulders in an unconcerned gesture. Johanna only had to look at Beth’s eyes to see how much she was hurting. ‘‘It’s no big deal, really. We weren’t serious.’’

Maybe he wasn’t, Johanna thought with a mixture of sympathy and resignation. ‘‘I’m sorry. Everyone has spats, Beth.’’

Bethany understood that, had even expected it. She hadn’t expected deceit. ‘‘We went a little beyond that. It’s better this way, really it is. I thought he was interested in me, you know, but when I found out he was more interested in my position—’’ She caught herself, swore silently, then smiled. ‘‘Doesn’t matter. He was just one of the many toads you have to go through to find the prince.’’

‘‘What about your position?’’ It never took Johanna long to put two and two together. Screenwriter, assistant producer. Toss in ambition and it added up perfectly. ‘‘Did he want you to hawk a script?’’

Uncomfortable, Bethany shifted. ‘‘Not exactly.’’

‘‘Spit it out, Beth.’’

‘‘All right. He had the idea that I could influence you to influence your father to produce his screenplay. When I told him it wouldn’t work, he got mad, then

I got mad, and one thing led to another.'' She didn't add that it had been ugly. She didn't have to.

''I see.'' Why were there so many creeps in this world? Johanna wondered. So many users. ''I am sorry, Beth.''

''Bruises fade,'' Beth said easily, though she was aware hers would last a long time. ''Besides, I've got the satisfaction of hoping he sells nothing but commercial jingles for the next ten or twenty years.''

''Do yourself a favor,'' Johanna advised her. ''Fall in love with an insurance salesman.'' She glanced toward the door as her secretary popped a head in.

''Telegram, Ms. Patterson.''

With a murmured thank-you, Johanna took it. Stupid, she told herself as her fingers tensed on the paper. It had been almost twenty-five years since she'd gotten that brief and heartbreaking telegram from her mother. She hadn't even been old enough to read it herself. Shoving back the memory, she tore the envelope open.

I can be as stubborn as you. Sam.

Johanna scowled at the single line, read it twice, then crumpled it into a ball. But instead of tossing it in the wastebasket, she shoved it into her pocket.

''Bad news?'' Bethany asked.

''A weak threat,'' Johanna said, picking up her remote. ''The show's starting.''

The damn woman was making him crazy. Sam groomed the mare, who'd been bred only hours before to his prize stud. She was still skittish and prone to nip. High-strung, pedigreed and temperamental, she reminded Sam of Johanna. That made him smile, if a bit grimly. He didn't think Johanna would appreciate being compared to a horse, not even a purebred.

She hadn't returned one of his calls. *Miss Patterson is unavailable. Miss Patterson is in a meeting.*

Miss Patterson is avoiding you like the plague.

He was beginning to feel like a gawky teenager with a crush on the class princess. More than once he'd told himself to write her off, to find some less complicated woman to spend an evening with.

The mare turned her head and took aim at his shoulder. Sam merely shifted out of range and continued to stroke and soothe. He didn't want to spend the evening with a less complicated woman. He wanted to spend it with Johanna. Just a test, he told himself, to see if whatever had happened by the pond would happen again. And if it did, what the hell was he going to do about it?

He was better off not seeing her again. A man had a lot more freedom when he cluttered up his life with many women than when he found himself concentrating on only one. He wasn't trying to concentrate on her, he reminded himself. He just couldn't get her out of his head.

What secrets did she have tucked away inside her? He had to find out.

When she'd kissed him…there had been no secrets there. She'd been open, passionate and as honest as a man could hope for. It hadn't been ordinary. He knew what it was to kiss a woman for pleasure, for obligation or because the script called for it. That moment with Johanna had been nothing so simple as pleasure, and it had been nothing so casual as obligation. The reaction—his *and* hers—hadn't been in any script.

She'd been as stunned as he was, and as unnerved. Didn't she want to know why?

The hell with what she wanted, Sam decided as he shut the stall door. *He* had to know why. Whether she wanted to or not, Johanna was going along for the ride.

She was beat. Johanna downed two aspirin and a carton of yogurt at her kitchen sink. Her afternoon had been taken up by back-to-back meetings, and though she should have been celebrating the nighttime syndication of *Trivia*, she'd opted for a quiet evening at home. She'd have to set up a party for the crew next week. They deserved it. And she'd see that Beth got a raise. For tonight, she didn't want to think about production meetings or sponsors. Her flowers needed tending.

The sun was warm on her face and arms as she walked outside to her garden. The roses that climbed the trellis along the side of the house needed pinching off. Snapdragons and hollyhocks needed weeding. Some of the taller and heavier-bloomed plants would require staking. Pleased with the scents and colors, she dug in.

She'd spent many quiet afternoons with the gardener on her father's estate, learning the names of the plants and the care they required. He'd let her have a plot of her own and had shown her how to turn soil and plant seeds, how to separate at the roots and prune. She'd learned how to blend plants for color, texture, height and flowering periods from him. On rainy days, or during cold snaps, he'd let her explore the greenhouse, where fragile seedlings had been nursed or exotic bulbs forced for early blooming.

The scents there had never been forgotten, the sultriness, the heat, even the damp smell of watered soil. He'd been a kind man, a little stoop-shouldered and thick through the middle. During one brief fantasy she'd imagined he was her father and they'd gone into business together.

She hadn't known until she'd heard him talking with another servant that he'd felt sorry for her.

All the servants had felt sorry for her—the little girl who was only brought out and paraded at her father's whim. She'd had a three-story dollhouse, a tea set of English china and a white fur coat. There had been ballet lessons and piano lessons and French taught by a private tutor. Other little girls would have dreamed of having what Johanna had only had to lift a hand for.

At six, her picture had been splashed across the press. She'd worn a red velvet dress that had skimmed her ankles and a tiny diamond tiara as flower girl at her father's second wedding. A Hollywood princess.

The bride had been an Italian actress who enjoyed having tantrums. Her father had spent a good deal of that two-year union on the Italian Riviera. Johanna had spent most of it in the gardens of his Beverly Hills estate.

There had been a scandal and a mudslinging divorce. The actress had kept the Italian villa, and her father had had a blistering affair with the lead in his next production. Johanna, at age eight, had already developed a cool and all-too-adult view of relationships.

She preferred her flowers. She didn't like wearing gloves. She felt that she got a better sense of the soil and the fragile roots with her hands uncovered. When she managed to squeeze in time for a manicure, she was usually met with shock and dismay. As a matter of routine, Johanna kept her nails clipped short and didn't bother with enamel.

Unfeminine. That was what Lydia had called her. Lydia had been one of her father's more vocal and longer-lasting distractions. Lydia had been palely beautiful and unceasingly selfish. Fortunately, she hadn't wanted to marry Carl Patterson any more than he had wanted to marry her.

Send the girl to the nuns in Switzerland, darling. Nothing like nuns for teaching a girl a little femininity and grace.

Johanna, at twelve, had lived in terror that she would be sent away, but Lydia had been replaced before she'd managed to pressure Carl into paying the tuition.

Unfeminine. The word still cropped up in Johanna's head from time to time. She usually ignored it; she'd found her own style of womanhood. But now and again, like an old scar, the word caused an itch.

On her hands and knees, she brushed through her patio dahlias, back to the freesia that would bloom in another few weeks. With care and precision, she pulled out any weeds that had had the audacity to sprout. It had been a dry spring, and after testing the soil she decided she'd give everything a good soak before calling it a day.

She heard the car but didn't bother to glance up, because she expected it to drive by. When it didn't, Johanna had just enough time to look around before Sam swung out of the driver's side.

She said nothing and remained kneeling, speechless.

He was furious. The long drive from his ranch had given him plenty of time to work on his temper. Here he was chasing after some cool-eyed go-to-hell blonde and all he could think of when he saw her was how she'd looked in the moonlight.

It was dusk now, the light soft and tenuous. She was kneeling in front of a bank of flowers like some pagan virgin sacrifice. She didn't rise, and her hands were stained with soil and grass. The air smelled like sin, dark and rich.

"Why the hell do you have a secretary and an answering machine if you don't intend to answer messages?"

"I've been busy."

"What you are is rude."

She hated that. Hated knowing it was true. "I'm

sorry.'' She put on her coolest and most professional smile. ''The show's going into syndication and I've been tied up with meetings and paperwork. Was there something important?''

''You know damn well it's important.''

She spent the next ten seconds carefully wiping the worst of the dirt from her hands onto her jeans and staring at his boots. ''If there's a problem with your contract—''

''Cut it, Johanna. We've done our business. That's over.''

She looked at him then. ''Yes, that's right.''

He stuck his hands in his pockets. If he'd had them free much longer he might have throttled her. ''I don't like feeling like a fool.''

''I'm sure you don't.'' She rose, careful to keep an arm's length of distance between them. ''I'm losing the light, Sam. If there's nothing else...'' The rest of the words slid down her throat when he grabbed her by her shirtfront.

''You're going to turn away from me once too often,'' he said quietly. Much too quietly. ''I've always considered myself fairly even-tempered. Seems I was wrong.''

''Your temperament's not my problem.''

''The hell it isn't.'' To prove his point, he yanked her against him. Her hands came up automatically for balance and defense. But his mouth was already on hers.

There was no testing kiss this time, no friendly overture. There was only the outpouring of urgency and demand that had clawed inside him for days. She didn't struggle. He hated to think of what he might have done if she had. Instead, she went very still, and for a moment nearly fooled them both into thinking she was unaffected.

Then she moaned. The sound went from her mouth into his, filled with surrender and despair. Before the sound had died her arms were around him, her fingers digging into his shoulders.

Twilight deepened, cooling the air, but she felt only the heat from his body as she pressed against him. He smelled of horses and leather. Dazed, she thought that the scent must be part of some deeply buried fantasy. Knight on white charger. But she didn't want to be rescued. Like a fool, she'd thought she could escape, from him, from herself. It only took a moment to show her how firmly she was already bound.

He brushed his mouth across her face, drawing in the taste, the softness. Her lips skimmed his jaw as she, too, searched for more. He tightened his arms around her. He'd thought he'd understood what it was to ache for a woman. Nothing had ever come close to this. He hurt everywhere, with a pain more erotic than anything he'd ever imagined. The more he touched, the more he hurt. The more he hurt, the more he was driven to touch.

"I want you, Johanna." His hands were in her hair now, as if he couldn't trust them to wander over her again. "I haven't been able to stop thinking about you for days. For nights. I want to be with you. Now."

She wanted it, too. A shudder ran through her as

she clung to him. She wanted him. She wanted to let go of her control, of her caution, and just feel—the way he could make her feel. Somehow she already knew that he could bring her things she'd never believed in. Once he did, she'd never be the same.

For a moment longer, she held on. Regret, more than she'd ever known, replaced desire as she drew away. With an effort she managed a smile as she glanced at the smudges on his shoulders. "My hands were dirty."

He took them both. "Let's go inside."

"No." Gently she drew her hands from his. "It wouldn't work, Sam. *We* wouldn't work."

"Why?"

"Because I wouldn't want it to. I wouldn't let it work."

He took her chin in his hand. "Bull."

"I wouldn't." She wrapped her fingers around his wrist. The pulse was fast there, as fast as her own. "I'm attracted to you, I won't deny that. But it can't lead anywhere."

"It already has."

"Then it can't lead any farther. Believe me when I say I'm sorry, but we're both better off facing up to it now."

"I'm sorry, too, but I can't accept it." He moved his hand to her cheek in a gesture that pierced her with its tenderness. "If you're expecting me to walk away and leave you alone, you're going to be disappointed."

She took a deep breath and met his eyes squarely. ''I'm not going to sleep with you.''

His brow lifted. ''Now, or ever?''

The last thing she'd expected to do was laugh, but the chuckle bubbled out. ''Good night, Sam.''

''Hold on. We're not finished.'' There was amusement in his voice as he gestured toward her front steps. ''Why don't we sit down? It's a nice night.'' When she hesitated, he lifted his hands, palms out. ''No contact.''

''All right.'' She wasn't completely at ease with it but felt perhaps she owed them both that much. ''Would you like a drink?''

''What have you got?''

''This morning's coffee.''

''I'll skip it, thanks.'' He settled comfortably next to her, hip to hip. ''I do like your place, Johanna,'' he began, wondering if he would be able to understand her better through it. ''It's quiet, private, well looked-after. How long have you had it?''

''About five years.''

''Did you plant all this?''

''Yes.''

''What are those?''

She looked over to the edge of one of her borders. ''Soapwort.''

''Ugly name for such a pretty thing.'' The little pink flowers looked delicate, but he could see that they spread exactly as they chose. ''You know, it occurs to me that we don't know each other very well.'' He leaned back against the next step, stretching his legs out. Johanna thought he looked very much at home.

"No," she said cautiously. "I suppose we don't."

"You believe in dating?"

She hooked her hands around her knees and smiled. "It's a nice occupation for teenagers."

"You don't figure adults can pull it off?"

On guard again, she moved her shoulders. "Most people I know have lovers, not boyfriends."

"And you don't have either."

"I like it that way."

The way she said it made him glance back at the little pink flowers again. "Why don't we shoot for another term, like companion?" He turned to study her profile. "We could try being companions for a while. That's an easy, uncomplicated term. No strings."

It sounded that way, but she knew better. "I meant what I said before."

"I'm sure you did." He crossed his feet at the ankles. "That's why I figured you wouldn't be afraid to get to know me better."

"I'm not afraid," she said immediately, showing him that he'd hit the right button.

"Good. There's a benefit Friday night at the Beverly Wilshire. I'll pick you up at seven."

"I don't—"

"You support raising funds for the homeless, don't you?"

"Of course I do, but—"

"And since you're not afraid, it wouldn't bother

you to be my companion. It's formal,'' he continued smoothly. ''I don't care much for that kind of evening myself, but it's for a good cause.''

''I appreciate the offer, but I simply couldn't manage to get home from work and change in time for a formal function at the Wilshire by seven.'' And that, she thought, should be the end of that.

''All right, I'll pick you up at your office. That way we can make it seven-thirty.''

She let out a huge breath, then shifted so that she could look at him directly. ''Sam, why are you trying to maneuver me this way?''

''Johanna…'' He took her hand and kissed her fingers, too quickly for her to object. ''I can maneuver much better than this.''

''I'll just bet.''

Delighted, he grinned. ''I love it when you use that tone. It's so proper. Makes me want to muss you up.''

''You didn't answer my question.''

''Which question? Oh, that one,'' he finished when she narrowed her eyes. ''I'm not trying to maneuver you, I'm trying to make a date with you. No, not a date,'' he corrected. ''No dates for adults. We can't call it a meeting, that's too businesslike. How about encounter? You like encounter?''

''I don't think so.''

''One thing I've found out about you already, Johanna, is that you're a hard woman to please.'' He stretched out again with a sigh. ''But that's all right. I can sit right here until you come up with the right choice of words. Stars are coming out.''

Involuntarily she glanced up. She often sat out by herself in the evening. She'd been content to look at the stars alone. Somehow the night seemed more appealing with him there, and that worried her. Depending on someone else for your contentment was a big mistake.

"It's getting chilly," she murmured.

"Are you asking me in?"

She smiled, then rested her elbow on her knee. "It's not that chilly." They were silent for a moment. Then the silence was broken by a nighthawk. "Why aren't you down in the city at some club being seen with some up-and-coming actress with lots of teeth?"

As if he were thinking it through, Sam rested his elbows on the back of the step. "I don't know. Why aren't you down in the city at some club being seen with some hotshot director with a perfect tan?"

Still pouting a bit, she kept her head still but shifted her gaze over to him. "I asked you first."

"I love acting," he said after a moment. His voice was so calm and serious that she turned her head again. "I really love it when it all comes together—the script, the moves, the crew. And I don't mind being paid well for it, either. I've got a couple of weeks before we start shooting. Once we do, there are going to be a lot of very long and very demanding days. I don't want to waste the little time I have in a club." He touched her hair. They both remembered he'd promised there would be no contact, but she didn't object. "Are you going to come back and feed my ducks, Johanna?"

It was a mistake, she told herself as she smiled at him. A stupid one. At least she was making it with her eyes open. ''I think I can make it Friday night, if you don't mind leaving the benefit a bit early. I'll have put in a full day at the office.''

''Seven-thirty, at your office?''

''Fine. No strings?''

''Deal.''

The minute he leaned toward her, she held up a hand. ''Don't kiss me, Sam.''

He backed off, not without effort. ''Now, or ever?''

She rose and brushed off the seat of her jeans. ''Now, anyway. I'll see you tomorrow.''

''Johanna.'' She paused at the top of the steps and looked back. ''Nothing,'' he told her. ''I just wanted to look at you again. Night.''

''Drive carefully. It's a long trip.''

He threw her a grin over his shoulder. ''It's getting shorter all the time.''

Chapter 5

By five-thirty the offices were like a tomb. Johanna was happy enough to have an extra hour to herself. Paperwork that never seemed to diminish during the normal working day could be gotten through in an uninterrupted hour. Questions for Monday's taping had been chosen and checked, but Johanna took the time to go over them herself to be certain they were as entertaining as they were educational.

She answered a pile of memos, read and signed letters and approved a stack of bills. The beauty of game shows, she thought as she worked, was that they were cheap to produce. In a big week they could give away over fifty thousand dollars and still come in at a fraction of the cost of a thirty-minute situation comedy.

She was still determined to get her other concept

on the air, and was ready to make her pitch for the pilot so that when things clicked the show could debut in the fall. And they would click, Johanna promised herself. One more success, one more solid success, and her own production company could begin its struggle for survival.

Garden Variety Productions. She could already see the logo. Within two years others would see it, as well. And remember it.

She'd continue to do the games, of course, but she'd begin to expand her own horizons, as well. A daytime drama, a couple of prime-time movies, a weekly series. She could already see it building, step by step. But for now she had to concentrate on getting through the rest of the day. And the evening.

After her desk was cleared, Johanna brought out her secret. She'd hidden the bag in her bottom drawer, behind the office stationery. There'd been enough commotion over her bringing an evening dress to the office. Now Johanna pulled the box from the bag, opened it, then read the instructions through twice. It didn't seem that complicated. She'd make it an adventure, she told herself, even if it was silly. She'd told herself it was silly even as she'd let the clerk talk her into buying them.

Johanna set her equipment in orderly lines, with the instructions handy, then examined her hands, back, then palms. The clerk hadn't been wrong about her nails being a mess. And what was wrong with trying something new? Johanna picked up the first fake fingernail and began to file it. She tested it often, placing it on her short, unpainted thumbnail until she was satisfied that the length wasn't extravagant. Only nine more to go, she thought, and began to attack the rest.

As she worked, she slipped out of her shoes and curled her legs under her. It was a position she never would have permitted herself to take if anyone had been in the office. Alone, she switched to it without thinking. Once she had ten uniformly filed nails on her blotter, she went on to the next stage.

The instructions told her it was easy, quick and neat. Johanna peeled off the adhesive and pressed it against her nail. Easy. With the tweezers she carefully caught the tip of the backing and began to peel it off. The adhesive rolled into a ball. Patiently Johanna removed it and tried again. The third time she managed to make it stick. Pleased, she picked up the first nail and aligned it carefully over her own. After pressing down, she examined the result.

It didn't look like her thumb, but it was rather elegant. After she painted it with the Shell-Pink Fizz enamel the clerk had sold her, no one would know the difference.

It took her twenty minutes to complete one hand, and she had to resort to digging out her reading glasses—something else she never would have done unless completely alone. She was swearing at the clerk, at herself and at the manufacturer when the phone rang. Johanna hit line one and popped the nail off her index finger.

"Johanna Patterson," she said between her teeth.

"It's John Jay, honey. I'm so glad you're a workaholic."

Johanna glared at her naked index finger. "What is it?"

"I've got a teeny little problem, sweetheart, and need you to come to my rescue." When she said nothing, he cleared his throat. "Listen, it seems my credit card's at the limit and I'm in a bit of an embarrassment. Would you mind talking to the manager here at Chasen's? He says he knows you."

"Put him on." Disgusted, she ran her hand through her hair and popped off another nail. It took less than two minutes to squeeze John Jay out of his embarrassment. After she hung up the phone, Johanna looked at her hand. Two of the nails she'd meticulously placed were gone, and her fingers were smeared with adhesive. Letting out a long breath, she began to remove the rest.

She was an intelligent, capable woman, she reminded herself. She was a hop and a skip away from being thirty and she held down a complex and demanding job. She was also probably the only woman in the country who couldn't attach fake nails.

The hell with it. She dumped everything, including the bottle of enamel, into the trash.

She did what she could with her hair in the women's lounge. Then, because she was feeling unfeminine and klutzy, she went dramatic with her makeup. Dressed only in thigh-high stockings and tap pants, she unzipped the garment bag. She'd only worn the gown once before, a year ago. It was strapless and clingy, a far cry from her usual style. With a shrug, Johanna stepped into it, and shimmied it up, then fought to reach the zipper. She swore again and wondered why she'd allowed herself to be talked into going out at all. Once the dress was secured, she tried to see as much of herself as possible in the waist-high mirrors.

It was a good fit, she decided as she turned to the side. And the color—which, she remembered grimly, would have matched the enamel now in the trash—was flattering. Though she couldn't see it, the hem skimmed her knees in the front, then graduated down to full-length in the back. Johanna changed her everyday earrings for pearl-and-diamond circles, then clasped on a matching choker.

As good as it gets, she thought, and zipped her office clothes in the bag. She'd have her secretary send them to the cleaners on Monday. With the bag slung over her arm, she started back to her office. She'd been wise to have Sam meet her here, Johanna decided. Not only did it make it less like a date, there was the added security that she'd have to be dropped off back in the parking garage so that she could drive herself home.

The coward's way. She shrugged her shoulders with a touch of annoyance as she walked. The safe way, she corrected. Whatever she was feeling for Sam was a little too fast and a little too intense. Having an affair wasn't in her plans, professionally or personally. She'd simply lived through too many of her father's.

Her life would never be like his.

As far as Sam Weaver was concerned, she would be sensible, cautious and, above all, in complete control of the situation.

Oh, God, he looked wonderful.

He was standing in her office by the window, his hands in the pockets of his tux and his thoughts on something she couldn't see. Pleasure, hardly comfortable, slammed into her. If she'd believed in happily-ever-afters, she would have believed in him.

He hadn't heard her, but he'd been thinking about her hard enough, deeply enough, that he'd known the moment she'd stepped into the doorway. He turned, and his image of her dissolved and reassembled.

She looked so fragile with her hair swept up off her neck and her shoulders bare. The business-first office had suited the woman he'd first met. The pretty garden and isolated house had suited the woman who'd laughed with him beside the pond. But this was a new Johanna, one who seemed too delicate to touch.

As ridiculous as it made him feel, he had to catch his breath. "I thought you'd skipped out."

"No." When she realized her knuckles were turning white clutching her summer bag, she relaxed them. "I was changing." Because she wanted badly to act natural, she made herself move to the closet. "I'm sorry if I'm a bit behind. I got caught up. Work," she said, and with a quick glance made certain the fiasco of plastic nails and polish was out of sight.

"You look wonderful, Johanna."

"Thanks." She shut the closet door, trying to take

the compliment with the same ease with which it was given. "So do you. I'm ready whenever you are."

"I need another minute." He crossed to her, catching the quick surprise in her eyes just before he covered her bare shoulders with his hands and kissed her. He lingered over the kiss, struggling to keep the pressure light, the demand minimal. "Just wanted to see if you were real," he murmured.

She was real, all right, so real that she could feel her own blood pumping hot and quick. "We should go."

"I'd rather stay here and neck. Well, maybe some other time," he added when he saw her brow lift. With her hand in his, he started out of the office toward the elevators. "Listen, if this is really boring we could leave early. Take a drive."

"Hollywood galas are never boring." She said it so dryly that he laughed.

"You don't like them."

"I don't often find it necessary to attend them." She stepped into the elevator as the door opened.

"It's hard to be a part of a world and ignore it at the same time."

"No, it's not." She'd been doing it for years. "Some of us do better behind the scenes. I saw one of the early ads for your miniseries," she continued, changing the subject before he had a chance to probe. "It looked good, very classy, very sexy."

"That's marketing," he said dismissively as the elevator reached the underground parking garage. "It's not really sexy. It's romantic. There's a difference."

There was indeed, but it surprised her that he knew it. ''When you've got your shirt off and your chest is gleaming, people think sex.''

''Is that all it takes?'' He opened the passenger door of his car. ''I can be out of this cummerbund in under five seconds.''

She swung her legs into the car. ''Thanks, but I've already seen your chest. Why television?'' she asked when he'd joined her. ''At this point in your career, I mean.''

''Because the majority of people won't sit still in a theater for four hours, and I wanted to do this movie. The small screen's more personal, more intimate, and so was this script.'' The car's engine echoed in the nearly empty garage as he backed up and began to drive out. ''The character of Sarah is so fragile, so tragic. She's so absolutely trusting and naive. It knocked me out the way Lauren pulled it off,'' he added, referring to his co-star. ''She really found the essence of that innocence.''

And, according to the press, he and Lauren had had as many love scenes away from the cameras as they had in front of them. It would be wise, Johanna reminded herself, to remember that. ''It's not usual to hear an actor talk about a character other than his own.''

''Luke's a bastard,'' Sam said simply as he stopped at a light. ''An opportunist, a womanizer and a heel. A very charming, glib-tongued one.''

''Did you capture his essence?''

He studied Johanna before the light changed. "You'll have to watch and tell me."

Deliberately she turned away. "What's your next project?"

"It's a comedy."

"I didn't know you did comedy."

"Obviously you missed my tour de force as the Raisin Crunch man a few years ago."

The chuckle welled up. "I'm embarrassed to say I did."

"That's all right. I'm embarrassed to say I didn't. That was right before I did the Mano cologne commercials. 'What woman can resist a man who smells like a man?'"

She would have laughed again if she hadn't remembered her own reaction to everything about him, including his scent. "Well, no one can say you haven't paid your dues."

"I like to think I have, and I'm also aware that the Mano campaign got me a reading for *Undercover*."

She was sure it had. Johanna hadn't missed those particular ads. In them, Sam had been blood-pumpingly sexy, intensely male and cocky enough to make a woman's mouth water. His character in *Undercover* had been precisely the same, but with an underlying depth that had surprised both the audience and the critics.

"Those kind of breaks don't happen very often," she said aloud. "When they do, they're usually deserved."

"Well..." He drew the word out. "I think that was a compliment."

She shrugged. "I've never said you weren't good at what you do."

"Maybe we could turn that around and say the problem from the outset has been that I am." She said nothing, but he thought that was answer enough.

Her brow creased a bit as they drove up to the well-lit limousine-adorned Beverly Wilshire. "Looks like quite a crowd."

"We can still go back to your office and neck."

She gave him a brief, very bland look as one of the uniformed staff opened her door. The moment she was on the curb, strobe lights and cameras flashed.

She hated that. She didn't have the words to explain even to herself how much she hated it. With a gesture that could be taken for one of aloofness rather than panic, she turned away. Sam slipped an arm around her and by doing so caused a dozen more flashes.

"They hound you less if you smile and cooperate," he murmured in her ear.

"Mr. Weaver! Mr. Weaver! What can you tell us about your upcoming television miniseries?"

Sam aimed his answer at the crowd of reporters and personalized it with a smile even as he started to walk. "With a quality script and a cast that includes Lauren Spencer, I think it speaks for itself."

"Is your engagement to Miss Spencer off?"

"It was never on."

One of the reporters got close enough to grab Johanna's arm. "Could we have your name, Miss?"

"Patterson," she said, and shook him off.

"Carl Patterson's girl," she heard someone in the crowd say. "That's the old man's daughter. Ms. Patterson, is it true your father's marriage is on the rocks? How do you feel about him being linked with a woman half his age?"

Saying nothing, Johanna swept through the front doors into the lobby.

"Sorry." Sam kept his arm around her. She was trembling a bit with what he took for anger.

"You had nothing to do with it." She only needed a moment, she thought, to calm down. Yes, there was anger, but there was also that stomach-churning distress that swooped down on her whenever she was confronted with cameras and demanding questions about her father. It had happened before and would happen again, as long as she was the daughter of Carl W. Patterson.

"You want to slip into the bar and get a drink? Sit in a dark corner for a minute?"

"No. No, really, I'm fine." As the tension eased, she smiled up at him. "I'd hate to go through that as often as you must."

"It's part of the job." But he lifted her chin with a finger. "Are you sure you're okay?"

"Of course. I think I'll just—"

But her plans for a brief escape were scotched when several people walked over to greet Sam.

She knew them, some by sight, others by reputation. Sam's co-star in his last feature was with her husband and happily pregnant with her first child. The elite of the press who had been permitted inside took the photo opportunity.

As they inched their way to the ballroom, others came by to renew an acquaintance or be introduced. Through her father she knew a great many of them herself. There were cheeks to be kissed, hugs to be given, hands to be shaken. A veteran actor with a silver mane of hair and a face that still graced billboards squeezed her. With an affection she felt for few, Johanna hugged him back. She'd never forgotten how he had come up to her room and entertained her with stories long ago, during one of her father's parties.

''Uncle Max, you're even more handsome than ever.''

His laugh was low and gravelly as he kept his arm around her. ''Jo-Jo. Looking at you makes me feel old.''

''You'll never be old.''

''Mary will want to see you,'' he said, speaking of his longtime and only wife. ''She's run off with a safari to the ladies' room.'' He kissed her cheek again, then turned to size up Sam. ''So you've finally broken down and taken on an actor. At least you've chosen a good one. I've admired your work.''

''Thank you.'' After six years in the business, Sam had thought he was immune to being starstruck. ''It's an honor to meet you, Mr. Heddison,'' he said, and he meant it. ''I've seen everything you've ever done.''

''Little Jo-Jo always had taste. I'd like to work with

you sometime. Not many of this generation I'd say that to.''

''Tell me when and where.''

With his eyes narrowed, Max gave a slow nod. ''I've a script I've been considering. Maybe I'll send it along and let you have a look. Jo-Jo, I'd like to see your pretty face more often.'' He kissed her again, then strode off to find his wife.

''I believe you're speechless,'' Johanna commented when Sam only continued to watch Max's back.

''There's not another actor alive I admire more than Max Heddison. He doesn't socialize much, and the couple of times I've seen him I didn't have the nerve to wangle an introduction.''

''You, shy?''

''Intimidated is a mild way to put it.''

Johanna took his hand again, touched that he could be. ''He's the kindest man I know. Once for my birthday he gave me a puppy. My father was furious—he hates dogs—but he couldn't say anything because it was from Uncle Max.''

''Jo-Jo?''

She shot him a look. ''Uncle Max is the only one who has ever, or who will ever, call me that.''

''I like it.'' He ran a finger down her nose. ''It makes me wonder how you'd look in pigtails and a straw hat. Oh, God.'' She saw his expression change from one of amusement to resignation just before he was enveloped by slim white arms.

''Oh, Sam, I just can't believe how long it's been.'' The woman with the gypsy mane of red curls turned her face just enough to let the camera get her best side. "Darling, where *have* you been hiding?"

"Here and there." He managed, with considerable skill, to untangle himself. "How are you, Toni?"

"Well, how do I look?" She threw back her magnificent head and laughed. Johanna noted that her dress was cut to the lowest degree that the law would allow. "I've been so terribly busy I've lost touch. I've just started filming and could barely fit this little event into my schedule. It's so boring not being able to see friends."

"Johanna Patterson, Toni DuMonde."

"It's nice to meet you." Johanna knew DuMonde's reputation as a mediocre actress who traded more on sex appeal than talent. She'd married well twice, and both husbands had boosted her career.

"Any friend of Sam's—" she began, then stopped. "You aren't Carl's daughter, are you?" Before Johanna could answer, she threw her head back again, making sure her hair cascaded as she laughed. "What a riot! Darling, I've just been dying to meet you!" Placing a hand on Johanna's shoulder, she scanned the room. Her eyes, sharp and tawny, skimmed over minor celebrities, smiled at those worth noticing and narrowed when focused on a rival. When she found her objective, her smile turned up several hundred kilowatts. Johanna noticed the flashy diamond on her left hand as she signaled.

"This is such a happy coincidence," Toni continued. "I'm sure you'll understand how very delighted I am. Sweetheart, look who I found."

Johanna looked at her father as Toni snuggled against him. The move was calculated so that the diamond on her finger winked hard and cold and in plain sight.

"Johanna, I didn't realize you were attending." Carl brushed his cheek against hers, as he would have with any of his hundreds of acquaintances.

He was a tall man, with broad shoulders and a flat stomach. He'd allowed his face to line because he had a fear of going under the knife, even cosmetically. But he'd never permitted his body to sag. At fifty-five, Carl W. Patterson was in his prime. Women were as drawn to him now as they had been thirty years before. Perhaps more, as power added to his sex appeal.

"You're looking well," Johanna told him. Sam noted that there was none of the warmth here that there had been when she'd greeted Max Heddison. "Carl Patterson, Sam Weaver."

"A pleasure." Carl took Sam's hand in his hefty, well-manicured one. "I've kept my eye on your career. Word is you're starting a film with Berlitz soon. We go back a ways."

"I'm looking forward to it."

"Isn't this cozy?" Toni put in, clipping her free hand through Sam's arm. "The four of us running into each other this way. We'll have to get a table together, won't we, Carl? After all, I'll want to get to know your daughter, now that we're going to be family."

Johanna didn't freeze. She didn't even react. By this time she was past being surprised by her father.

"Congratulations." She winced only slightly when a camera flashed, catching the four of them together.

"We haven't set the date yet." Toni beamed up at Carl. "But we plan to make it soon—well, as soon as a few minor matters are taken care of."

Which would be the legal disposal of his fourth wife, Johanna surmised. Fortunately, she was no longer affected by the whims or variable presence of stepmothers. "I'm sure you'll be very happy."

"We intend to be." Carl patted Toni's hand, looking at her rather than at his daughter.

"Do let's get a table, Carl, and have a drink to celebrate." Toni kept a casual grip on both men. So casual that it was barely noticeable when Sam removed her hand and took Johanna's. Hers was ice-cold and rigid.

"I'm sorry, we can't stay long." Sam's smile was charming and faintly apologetic.

"Oh, pooh, you've time for one quick drink before this place turns into a zoo." Toni trailed her fingertips up Carl's arm. "Darling, you'll have to insist."

"No need to insist." She wouldn't be ill, Johanna told herself. She wouldn't even be upset. Neither did she smile as she looked up at her father. "The least I can do is drink to your happiness."

"Wonderful." Toni thought it more than wonderful to be seen with a man as important as Carl and a man as attractive as Sam at the same time. "Now, Johanna darling, you mustn't believe all those naughty things you must have read about Sam and me. You know how people in this town love to talk." She turned to be escorted inside and shot a smile over her shoulder, daring Johanna not to believe every word.

"Why in the hell are you doing this?" Sam demanded.

"Because it's part of the game." Chin up, Johanna stepped into the ballroom.

The room was full of babble. It glittered as such events are meant to, and it would make excellent copy in *People*. It would raise a great deal of money—a hundred, perhaps a hundred and fifty thousand dollars—while making the evening worth the price of the meal. And the food was lavish.

She didn't eat. Johanna barely noticed what was placed in front of her, though Toni cooed over each course and made noises about calories. The ring on her hand flashed triumphantly every time she moved her fingers. She made coy little remarks about Sam behaving like a gentleman with her almost-stepdaughter, giggled delightedly about having a daughter the same age as herself and snuggled kisses on Carl's cheek when she wasn't flirting elsewhere.

He was dazzled by her. Johanna sipped champagne and watched her father preen whenever the redhead stroked his ego. She'd never known him to be dazzled by a woman before. Desirous, covetous, infuriated, but never dazzled.

"Just a teeny bit more," Toni said when Carl poured more wine. "You know how silly I get when I drink too much." She shot him an intimate look that promised she could get a great deal more than silly.

"Isn't this a wild crowd?" She waved cheerily to someone at another table. "God, what a hideous dress. All those diamonds don't make up for plain bad taste, do they? Sam, darling, I heard Lauren's seeing some French race-car driver. Did she break your heart?"

"No," he said flatly, and shifted away when she patted his knee.

"That's because you always do the heartbreaking. Be very careful with this man, Johanna dear, better women than I have shed a tear over him."

"I'm certain," Johanna said sweetly, and sipped more champagne.

"Tell me, why haven't you had your daddy put you in the movies?" Toni gave her a cool woman-to-woman look over her glass.

"I don't act."

"What do you do?"

"Johanna produces daytime television," Carl put in. "The latest reports that crossed my desk were excellent, by the way."

"Thank you."

"Evening syndication is moving forward?"

"Yes, we just finalized it. I would have sent you a memo, but I thought you were out of town."

"We just spent two weeks on the most dismal location shoot in Arizona." Toni patted Carl's hand. "Thank God Carl was there to be sure I wasn't worn to a frazzle. Sam, I've heard the most marvelous things about your television thing. That'll be aired in a couple of weeks, won't it?"

He smiled at her again and nodded. He knew she'd tested for the part of Sarah and had yet to forgive him for not pulling strings to get it for her.

"We really should do a movie together, with Carl producing."

When hell freezes over, Sam thought. "I really hate to cut this short, but Johanna and I are already late." He rose before anyone could protest and offered a hand. "A pleasure meeting you, Mr. Patterson, and my compliments on your finest production." Taking Johanna by the hand, he grinned at Toni. "Don't ever change, darling."

"Good night," Johanna said to her father. "Best wishes." She didn't object to Sam's supporting arm as he guided her out of the ballroom. "You didn't have to cut your evening short on my account," she began.

"I didn't cut it short, and I'm not leaving only on your account. I don't like socializing with piranhas like Toni." He drew out the claim check for his car and handed it to the boy on the curb. "Besides, you look like you could use some fresh air."

"I'm not drunk."

"No, but you were heading there."

"I never get drunk, because I don't like to be out of control."

Truer words had never been spoken, he was certain. "Fine, but I'm going to get you something to eat anyway." He handed the boy who brought his car a twenty and ushered Johanna in himself. "Could you handle a burger?"

"I'm not hungry."

Stubborn, he thought, and just this side of sulking. "Okay, I want a burger."

She started to snap and realized just in time that she was being nasty. "Sam, I appreciate it, but I really don't want anything. Why don't you just drop me off so I can get my car?"

"You had five glasses of wine. I counted." He'd nursed one the moment he'd seen what kind of mood she was in. "I'm driving you home—after we eat."

"I can't leave my car in town."

"I'll have someone drop it off to you tomorrow."

"That's too much trouble. I can—"

"Johanna..." He pulled over to the curb and waited until she looked at him. "Let me be a friend, okay?"

She shut her eyes, wanting badly to do something else she never allowed herself. To cry, hard and long and for no reason at all. "Thanks. I guess I could use some food and some air."

In his tux, Sam ran into a bright fast-food restaurant, ordered burgers, fries and coffee, signed half a dozen autographs and ran out again. "Life's rarely simple anymore," he told Johanna as he tucked the bag between her feet. "The little girl behind the counter wanted to pay for them, and I know damn well she stuck her phone number in the bag. She must have been all of nineteen."

"You should have let me go in."

"We all have our crosses to bear." He headed out. "Johanna, I don't make it a habit to pay attention to what's said about me in print—unless it's a review—but I'd like to make an exception and tell you that Toni and I were never together."

"Sam, it's none of my business."

"Whether you think it's your business or not, I'd like you to believe me. If you've already got a picture of her and me, it's bad enough. When you add that to the fact that she's apparently going to marry your father, it's ludicrous."

Johanna opened her eyes and studied him as he drove. It hadn't occurred to her before. She'd been too wrapped up in her own thoughts and feelings to notice. But she saw it now. "She embarrassed you. I'm sorry."

"I just didn't like her implying—" Implying, hell, he thought. She'd practically taken out an ad. "I'd feel better if you understood there'd never been anything between us." He wanted to say more but found it difficult to say what he thought about the woman who was going to become a part of Johanna's family. "Anyway, it wasn't quite the evening I had in mind."

In a little while he pulled up at the crest of a hill. Below, spread out like a game of lights, was the Los Angeles Basin. He put the top down. Far off in the distance she heard the call of a coyote.

"We're not dressed for burgers, but I got plenty of napkins." He reached down for the bag and the back of his hand brushed her calf. "Johanna, I have to tell you something."

"What?"

"You have incredible legs."

"Give me a hamburger, Sam," she said, and took off her shoes.

"Smells better than the veal medallions."

"Is that what we had?"

"No, that's what you didn't have. Here's the ketchup." He passed her a handful of little plastic bags, then waited until he was satisfied she was eating. If he'd ever seen anyone more miserable than Johanna had been at that pretty, flower-bedecked table with stars glittering in every corner, he couldn't remember. The worst of it was that she'd been struggling to be valiant about it.

"Want to talk about it?" When she only shrugged, he pressed a little harder. "I take it you didn't know your father was planning to get married again."

"I didn't know he was planning to get divorced again. He doesn't check these things through with me."

"Are you fond of your current stepmother?"

"My father's current wife," she corrected automatically, which told him a great deal. "I don't know, I've only met her a couple of times. I think she moved back to New York a few weeks ago. I was just surprised because he doesn't usually stack one marriage on top of the other. Generally there's a space of a year or two between legal contracts."

"He'll have a few months to get to know Toni better. He could change his mind."

"I'm sure he knows exactly what she is. One thing Carl isn't is stupid."

"Sometimes if you tell someone when you're angry with them it loosens things up."

"I'm not angry with him, not really."

He brushed his knuckles along her cheek. "Hurt?"

She shook her head, unable to trust herself to speak for a moment. "He lives his own life. He always has. And that makes it easier for me to live mine."

"You know, I had some real matches with my father." He shook the bag of fries, urging them on her.

"Did you?"

"God, did we fight." With a laugh, Sam opened his coffee and began to sip. "The Weavers have tempers. We like to yell. I think I spent most of the years between fifteen and twenty going head-to-head with my old man. I mean, just because I plowed the car through Greenley's fence was no reason to confiscate my license for six weeks, was it?"

"I imagine Greenley thought it was. Did you ever get your own way?"

"I figure that was about seventy-five, twenty-five, with him holding the lion's share. I probably got as much as I did because he was busy yelling at my brother or one of my sisters."

"It must be different, having a big family. I always imagined…"

"What?"

The wine cushioned embarrassment. Without it, she might never have said it out loud. "I sometimes thought it would be nice when I was little to have brothers and sisters… I don't know, grandparents to visit, family squabbles. Of course, I had stepsiblings from time to time. Things were usually finished before we'd gotten used to each other."

"Come here." He shifted over so he could put an arm around her. "Feel any better?"

"A lot." She sighed and rested her head. "I appreciate it."

Her hair smelled like the air outside the windows. Clean, quiet. The urge to turn his face into it was natural, and he did it without thinking. "I wish you hadn't had so much wine."

"Why?"

"Then it wouldn't be against the rules for me to seduce you."

She surprised herself by turning her face to his. She didn't like the word "seduce." It implied a lack of will. But just now it sounded liberating, and more than tempting. "You live by the rules?"

"Not many of them." He brought his hand to her hair. "I want to make love with you, Johanna, but when I do I want you to have your wits about you. So for now I'll settle for a little less."

He nipped at her lower lip, testing its softness, experimenting with tastes. Here was warmth, just edging toward heat, and acceptance, only a step away from surrender.

Of all the visions and fantasies he'd already had of being with her, the one that was the strongest was of him just holding her like this, with the stars overhead and the night breezes blowing cool and clean.

She could have pulled away. His touch was so gentle she knew he would never have pushed. Not this time. There would be others. She already accepted that. On another night when the breeze was just ruffling the leaves he'd hold her like this, and his mood wouldn't be as patient. Nor, she was afraid, would hers. Something had taken root, no matter how hard she'd tried to pull it free. With a little sigh, she brought a hand to his face.

It was torture, but he ran his hand along her bare shoulders. He wanted to take the feel of her with him when he drew away. Just as he would take the taste of her, the scent of her skin, with him on the long, lonely trip home.

"I wish I knew what I was feeling," she murmured when she could speak again. It wasn't the wine. It would have been a lie to blame it on anything so ordinary. Her eyes were heavy, a bit dazed. Her mouth was soft. Just by looking at her Sam knew he could have her. One more easy nudge and they would be lovers.

He reminded himself about rules and fragile women.

"We're going to have to talk about it." He kissed her again, briefly. "Then we're going to have to do something about it. But right now I'm going to take you home."

Chapter 6

Johanna considered Saturdays the day the work force had been given to catch up on everything their jobs had forced them to ignore during the week. Rather than a day off, she thought of it as an alternate. Saturdays weren't for sleeping late—even if you were slightly hung over and punchy. They were for weeding the garden, marketing, dealing with personal correspondence and bookkeeping. Her Saturdays, like the rest of her days, had a routine she rarely varied. Johanna depended on organization because a well-ordered life was a safe one.

She dealt with the cleaning first. Though she'd never thought of herself as particularly domestic, Johanna had never considered hiring someone to do the housekeeping. The house was her personal life, and as in all areas of that life, she preferred to handle it herself.

The vacuuming and dusting, the scrubbing down and polishing up, were never mundane chores. There was a certain basic pleasure in them, but more compelling was the feeling that her house, her things, deserved her attention. It was as simple as that. She could haul a bucket and dust rags from room to room with the same dedication and enjoyment she put into reading contracts or balancing budgets.

She preferred the radio loud so that she could hear it in whatever corner of the house she decided to tackle first. This was a day for both production and solitude. Over the years, Johanna had developed a dependency on both.

She did think about the car, and thinking of that naturally turned her thoughts to Sam. She hoped he didn't forget his promise to have someone drop it off, but if he did she'd simply forgo her Saturday marketing and have Bethany pick her up on Monday morning.

Johanna never depended on promises or other people's memories.

But she did think of him, and if her thoughts weren't completely comfortable she couldn't forget that he'd been kind, and gentler than she'd expected. She remembered, a little too well, how she'd felt when she'd kissed him. Full, edgy, tempted. Just a little more tempted each time she was with him to throw away the pact she'd made with herself so many years ago. The pact said no relationships that couldn't be controlled, by her, from the outset—no dependencies, no promises, long- or short-term.

It was a sensible pact, unwritten but binding. The fact that Sam had nearly lured her into forgetting it worried her. But it made her wonder more.

Just what was it about him that made her lose a bit of ground every time they were together? She could discount his looks, however delightful they were. She might appreciate a great physique, but she wouldn't swoon over one.

Not that she was swooning over Sam Weaver, Johanna reminded herself as she poured hot water into her bucket. She thought very little of women who built fantasies or relationships around cleft chins and bulging biceps.

Nor was it his reputation. That, in fact, worked against him. Johanna dunked her mop in hot, soapy water, then began to wash her kitchen floor. The fact that he was an actor was a strike against him. The fact that he was an actor with a reputation with women was a bigger one.

Of course, she knew that such reports were usually exaggerated and often outright lies. But there were times… There were times, Johanna thought as she swiped the mop back and forth, that the press didn't even come close to making rumor as outrageous as the truth.

The press had never known her truth. Her mother's truth. With the care and firmness of experience, she locked that thought away.

So it wasn't his looks or his reputed way with

women. It certainly wasn't his fame. Growing up as she had, Johanna had had to tolerate vicarious fame all her life. It wasn't his talent, either, though she certainly respected that. She knew people were often drawn to talent and power. Her father, and the stream of women in his life, were proof of that. They were also drawn to wealth and position. Johanna was too ambitious and had spent too much time trying to perfect her own skills to be swayed by anyone else's.

So if it wasn't one of the attributes he was so obviously endowed with, just what was it that was making her think about him when she shouldn't?

It hadn't started with that first kiss. It would have been easy to blame it on basic sexual attraction, but Johanna preferred honest self-analysis. The seed of something had been there from that first meeting. If not, she wouldn't have gone out of her way to give him a hard time.

Defense mechanism, Johanna thought, recognizing and acknowledging it.

There was his charm, of course. She wrung out the mop and began to rinse. It wasn't stylized or deliberate. That she would have been immune to. It was natural, easy, even friendly. The roses had managed to turn the key in an old, well-guarded lock. The kiss had managed to blow it open briefly, just long enough to give her cause for alarm.

Alarm. Yes, that was what she'd felt overlaying every other emotion he'd drawn out of her. Now that she'd admitted it, she had to decide what to do about it.

She could ignore him. But she didn't believe that would do much good. She could—cautiously—go along with his suggestion that they get to know each other better. Slowly. And she could stick to her guns and not get involved beyond a wary friendship.

The solution had to be in there somewhere, she thought. She'd come up with it, and the next time she had to deal with him she'd be prepared.

She was incredible. Sam stood in the kitchen doorway and watched her mop the kitchen floor. He'd knocked, but the music she had blaring in the other room had drowned out the sound. Since the door hadn't been locked, he'd simply walked in and wandered through until he'd found her.

Johanna Patterson. She was just a bit different every time he saw her. Sophisticated one minute, wonderfully simple the next. Alluring, then cool. Nervous, then tough. A man could take years getting to know all of her. Sam figured he had time.

Right now she was dressed in faded cotton pants rolled up at the ankles and a big man-styled shirt pushed to her elbows. Her feet were bare, and her hair was pinned up untidily. She handled the mop with smooth, easy strokes, not skimming over the job and not swearing over it. He imagined she took to such things as housekeeping with the same steady drive she took to everything else. He liked that, and he liked her for it.

He knew exactly why he was attracted to Johanna. She was beautiful, but that wouldn't have been enough. She was smart, but though he respected a sharp mind that wouldn't have kept him coming back. She was vulnerable. Normally that would have made him take a cautious step back instead of these continued steps forward. She had an edge to her that in another few years might become hard. But now, just now, Johanna was a cautious woman with a few bruises who wasn't easily impressed by status. The combination was more than enough to keep pulling him toward her.

And she'd rather he didn't, Sam thought. On the surface, at least, she'd have preferred that he step out of her life and stay out. But deep down, he believed, she was looking for someone, for something, just as he was.

He wasn't naive enough to believe it was so just because that was what he wanted, but he was determined to find out.

He stood where he was as the strokes of the mop brought her closer. When she rammed into him, he took her arm to keep her from overbalancing.

Johanna whirled around, automatically gripping the mop like a weapon. The relief when she saw him turned quickly to anger.

"How the hell did you get in here?"

"The door," he told her easily. "It wasn't locked. I did knock. I guess you didn't hear me."

"No, I didn't." She was shouting to be heard over the music. "Apparently you took that as an invitation."

"I took it to mean you didn't hear me." He held

up the keys she'd given him the night before. "I thought you'd want your car back."

"Thanks." She stuffed them in her pocket. It wasn't anger nearly as much as it was embarrassment. She didn't care to be sneaked up on unaware.

"You're welcome." He handed her a bouquet of painted daisies and snapdragons. As he'd suspected they would, her eyes softened. "I stole them from Mae's garden. I figured she wouldn't notice."

"They're pretty." With a sigh that was only partially one of resignation, she took them. "I do appreciate you bringing my car back." She knew she was weakening, and she struggled not to. "You've caught me at a bad time. I can't even offer you a drink because the floor's wet, and I'm really busy."

"I'll take you out for one. Better, let's go have some lunch."

"I can't. I've only half finished here, and I'm not dressed to go out. Besides, I—"

"Look fine," he finished for her. "You'd better put those in water. They're starting to droop."

She could have been rude. Johanna knew she was capable of it, but she found she hadn't the heart. Instead, she said nothing. She plucked an old square bottle from a shelf and went into the bathroom to fill it. As she did, she heard the volume of the music go down several notches. He was in the living room studying her collection of antique glass when she came back.

"My mother used to have some plates like this green stuff here. Depression glass, right?"

"Yes."

"I thought that meant it made her sad. I could never figure out why she kept it."

She wouldn't be amused, Johanna told herself. At least not very. "Sam, you really shouldn't keep whoever followed you up waiting outside."

"No one followed me up." He hooked his thumbs in his pockets and smiled. Some might have thought the look sheepish, but Johanna wasn't fooled.

"Now I suppose you want me to drive you back."

"Sooner or later."

"I'll call you a cab," she said, turning to the phone. "I'll even pay for it."

He put his hand over hers on the receiver. "Johanna, you're being unfriendly again."

"You're being pushy."

"Yeah, but subtleties don't work with you." He reached over to stick a loose pin back in her hair. He'd have preferred to have pulled it out, and the rest of them besides, but bided his time. "So how about lunch?"

"I'm not hungry."

"So, we'll take a drive first." He skimmed his hand from her hair to her cheek. "I really think we should, because if we stay in here too much longer I'm going to want to make love with you, and since I figure you're not ready, a drive's a better idea."

Johanna cleared her throat and took another stab at persuasion. "I appreciate your logic, but I don't have time for a drive, either."

"You've got an appointment?"

"No," she said, then wished she could bite off her tongue. "That is, I—"

"You already said no." He watched her eyes narrow and thought she was almost as pretty annoyed as she was amused. You're already sunk waist-deep, Sam, he told himself. Another few steps and you're over your head. But what the hell. "It's too nice a day to stay indoors cleaning a house that's already clean enough."

"That's my business."

"Okay, then I'll wait for you to finish before we go out."

"Sam—"

"I'm persistent, Johanna. You told me so yourself."

"I'll drive you home," she said, giving up.

"Not good enough." He caught her again, this time by the shoulders. There was something about the way he spread his fingers over her, about the way his palm fit so truly over her. His expression had changed just enough to make her uneasy. The amusement was gone, but it hadn't been replaced by anger. She wouldn't have been uneasy about anger. This was determination, solid and unshakable. "I want to spend the day with you. You know damn well I want to spend the night with you, as well, but I'll settle for the day. Give me five reasons why not and I'll walk down to the freeway and hitch a ride."

"Because I don't want to."

"That's a statement, not a reason. And I don't buy it, anyway."

"Your ego won't buy it."

"Suit yourself." Refusing to be annoyed, he sat on the arm of her couch, absently picked up one of her pillows and began to toss it. "Look, I've got all day. I don't mind sitting around until you've stopped fussing with your imaginary dust. Hell, I'll even give you a hand, but then we're going to have to get out of here, because being alone with you for long periods of time isn't easy." She opened her mouth, but he continued before she could make a suggestion. "I keep wanting to touch you, Johanna, in all kinds of interesting places."

"We'll go out," she said quickly, before she could admit she wanted it, too.

"Good idea. Listen, why don't I drive?"

She started to protest even that—on principle—then decided he'd be less likely to give her trouble if he had his eyes on the road. "Fine." After switching off the radio, she dumped the keys back in his hands. "It'll take me a few minutes to change."

"You look fine," he said again, and took her hand. "I happen to like this Johanna every bit as much as the others I've met over the last couple of weeks."

She decided not to ask him what he was talking about. "We'll have to make it a very informal lunch, then."

"It will be." He opened the door of the car for her. "I promise."

He was as good as his word.

The hot dog dripped mustard, and the noise level was intense. Johanna sat almost in the shade and watched pink elephants circle overhead. It wasn't a dream, or the last remnants of a hangover. It was Disneyland.

"I don't believe this." She took another bite of the hot dog as a boy in mouse ears dashed by, yelling for his parents to hurry up.

"Pretty great, isn't it?" Sam wore sunglasses and a low-brimmed cowboy hat that Johanna was forced to admit suited him. So did the chinos and the simple T-shirt. The disguise wasn't very imaginative, and it would have been transparent as glass if anyone had looked closely enough. Sam had told her that the best place to be anonymous was a crowd. They certainly had one.

"You come here for lunch often?"

"Great hot dogs in Fantasyland." He took an enormous bite to prove his point. "Besides, I'm hooked on the Haunted Mansion. It's terrific, don't you think?"

"I don't know. I've never been in it."

"Never?" His tone of quick astonishment wasn't feigned. Wanting a better look, he tipped down his tinted glasses and studied her. "You grew up here, didn't you?"

She only shrugged. Yes, she'd grown up a short drive from Anaheim, but neither her father nor her succession of stepmothers or "aunts," as she'd been taught to call the other women in her father's life, had been inclined to take a day trip to an amusement park.

"You're not telling me you've never been to Disneyland at all?"

"It's not a requirement."

He pushed his glasses back on his nose as she wiped her hands on a napkin. He remembered the impersonal non-kiss her father had given her the night before. His family was always, had always been, demonstrative, both physically and vocally. No, Disneyland, like other small pleasures, wasn't a requirement. But it should be.

"Come on, your education's lacking."

"Where are we going?"

"To take Mr. Toad's Wild Ride. You're going to love it."

Oddly enough, she did.

It was fast and foolish and certainly designed for the younger set, but Johanna found herself gasping and giggling as the car swerved and twisted through the tunnels. She'd barely put her foot on the ground again before Sam was dragging her off to the next line.

They rode down a mountain in a raft, and the final waterfall drop surprised a scream out of her. Wet and breathless, she didn't even protest when he pulled her along again. By the time they'd done Fantasyland to his satisfaction, she'd been spun, twirled, flown and floated. The Mad Hatter's Tea Party had left her giddy and weak-kneed and without the least notion that she was being educated.

He bought her mouse ears with her name stitched across the front, using her own hairpins to secure it even when she grumbled.

"Looks cute," he decided, then kissed her. She

might not have known it, Sam thought, but she was more relaxed than he'd ever seen her. "I think you're ready for the Haunted Mansion."

"Does it spin?"

"No, it strikes terror into your heart. That's why you're going to hang on to me and make me feel brave." He swung an arm around her shoulders and began to walk. Johanna had already discovered he knew the park very well.

"You really do come here a lot, don't you?"

"When I first came to California I had two priorities. Get a job—an acting job—and go to Disneyland. Whenever my family comes out we always spend at least one day here."

Johanna looked around as they walked. There were families, so many families. Infants and toddlers pushed in strollers, children with sticky faces riding piggyback and pointing toward the next adventure.

"I guess it is an amazing place. Everything seems real while it's going on."

"It is real when it's going on." He stepped to the back of the line, undaunted by its length. After a moment's hesitation, he took a chance. "I was Pluto for six weeks."

"Pluto?"

"The dog, not the planet."

"I know who Pluto is," she murmured. Absently adjusting her hat, she frowned at him. "You actually worked here?"

"In a dog suit. A very hot dog suit—no pun intended. It paid my first month's rent."

"What exactly did you do?" The line shifted up.

"Marched in the parade, posed for pictures, waved and sweated a lot. I really wanted to be Captain Hook, because he gets to have sword fights and look evil, but Pluto was all that was open."

Johanna tried to imagine it, and nearly could. "I always thought he was cute."

"I was a terrific Pluto. Very lovable and loyal. I did cut it from my résumé after a while, but that was on Marv's suggestion."

"Marv? Oh, your agent?"

"He thought playing a six-foot dog was the wrong image to project."

While Johanna thought that one through, they were ushered inside. The spiel was camp and full of bad puns, but she couldn't help being pulled in. The pictures on the walls changed, the room shrank, the lights went out. There was no turning back.

By the time they were in their tram and starting on the tour she was, so to speak, entering into the spirit of things.

The producer in her couldn't fail to be impressed by the show. Holograms, music and elaborate props were blended to entertain, to raise goose pimples and nervous chuckles. Not so scary that the toddlers in the group would go home with nightmares, but not so tame that the adults felt cheated out of the price of a ticket, Johanna decided as she watched ghosts and spirits whirl around in a dilapidated, cobweb-draped dining room.

Sam had been right about one thing. It was real

while it was going on. Not everything in life could be trusted to be the same.

She didn't have to be prodded any further, not to visit a pirate's den and dodge cannon fire, nor to take a cruise up the Amazon or a train ride through Indian territory. She watched mechanical bears perform, ate dripping ice cream and forgot she was a grown woman who had been to Paris and dined in an English manor but had never been to Disneyland.

By the time they started back to the car she was exhausted, but in the most pleasant way she could remember.

"I did not scream," she insisted, holding the small stuffed Pluto he'd bought her in a headlock.

"You never stopped screaming," Sam corrected. "From the minute that car started moving through Space Mountain until it stopped again. You've got excellent lungs."

"Everyone else was screaming." In truth, she hadn't a clue whether she'd screamed or not. The car had taken its first dive, and planets had raced toward her. Johanna had simply squeezed her eyes shut and held on.

"Want to go back and do it again?"

"No," she said definitely. "Once was quite enough."

Sam opened the car door but turned before she could climb in. "Don't you like thrills, Johanna?"

"Now and again."

"How about now?" He cupped her face in his hands. "And again later."

He kissed her as he'd wanted to do since he'd seen her studiously mopping her floor that morning. Her lips were warm, as he'd known they would be, but softer, incredibly softer, than he'd remembered. They hesitated. There was a sweetness in that, a sweetness that was its own allure.

So he lingered, longer than he'd intended. He wanted, more than was wise. When she started to back away, he gathered her closer and took, more than either of them had expected.

It wasn't supposed to be like this, Johanna told herself even as she stopped resisting both of them. She was supposed to be strong, in charge, reachable only when and if she chose to be. With him, he only had to touch… No, he only had to look and she began losing ground.

All her careful analysis that morning was blown to dust the minute his mouth was on hers.

I don't want this. Her mind tried to cling to that thought while her heart beat out steadily: But you do, yes, you do. She could almost feel herself separating into two parts, one aloof, one almost pitifully vulnerable. The most frightening thing was that this time she was more than afraid that vulnerability would be the stronger.

"I want to be alone with you, Johanna." He said it against her lips, then again against her cheek as he trailed kisses there. "Anywhere, anywhere at all as long as it's only you and me. I haven't been able to get you out of my system."

"I don't think you've been trying."

"You're wrong." He kissed her again, feeling her renewed resistance swerve toward passion. That was the most exciting, the most irresistible thing about her, the way she wanted, held back and wanted again. "I've actually given it a hell of a shot. I kept telling myself you're too complicated, too uptight, too driven." He felt her lips move into a frown and was seduced into nibbling on them. "Then I find ways to see you again."

"I'm not uptight."

He sensed her change of mood but could only be amused by it. Johanna, outraged, was fascinating. "Lady, half the time you're like a spring that's wound to the limit and just waiting to bust out. And I damn well intend to be there when you do."

"That's ridiculous. And don't call me lady." She snatched the keys from him, decided she'd do the driving this time.

"We'll see about that." He climbed into the car and nearly managed to stretch out his legs and get comfortable. "Going to give me a lift home?"

She was tempted, more than tempted, to order him out and strand him in the parking lot, right under Donald Duck's cheerful beak. Instead, she decided to give him the ride of his life. "Sure." Johanna put the car in gear.

She drove cautiously enough through the lot. It was, after all, full of pedestrians, many of them children. Things changed when she hit the freeway. She whipped around three cars, settled in the fast lane and rammed down on the gas pedal.

Drives like she's ready to bust, too, Sam thought, but said nothing. Her speedometer might have been hovering around ninety, but her hands were competent on the wheel. And she might, he thought, burn off that temper that had fired up when he'd called her uptight.

She hated it that he was right. That was the worst of it. She knew very well that she was full of nerves and hang-ups and insecurities. Didn't she spend most of her time fighting them off or blanketing them over? It didn't do her any good to hear Sam pinpoint it so casually.

When she'd made the conscious and very calculated decision to make love with a fellow college student, he, too, had called her uptight. Sexually. "Loosen up" had been his sage advice. She hadn't been able to, not with him, who she'd been fond of, nor with any of the men she'd developed careful relationships with. So she'd stopped trying.

She wasn't a man-hater. That would be absurd. She simply didn't want to be tied to one, emotionally or sexually. Her eyes had been opened young, and she'd never forgotten how those two tools could be used. So perhaps she was uptight, though she detested the word. Better that than loose enough to tumble for a pair of wonderful blue eyes or a lazy drawl.

Mad as hell, Sam thought. That was fine. He preferred strong emotion. As a matter of fact, he preferred any emotion at all when it came from Johanna. He didn't mind her being angry with him, because if she was angry she was thinking. About him. He wanted her to do a lot of that.

God knew he'd been thinking about her. Constantly. He'd been telling her no less than the truth when he'd said he'd tried to get her out of his system. When it hadn't worked, he'd decided to stop beating his head against the wall and see where the road would lead.

It was a bumpy ride, but he was enjoying every minute of it.

He was going to have her, sooner or later. Sooner, he hoped for the sake of his sanity. But for now he'd let her drive awhile.

When he saw she was going to miss the exit, he gestured. "You want to get off here."

Johanna switched lanes, aggressively challenging traffic, and breezed onto the ramp.

"How about dinner next week?" He said it casually, as though the interlude in the parking lot had been as make-believe as the rest of the day. When she said nothing, he fought back a grin and tossed his arm over the seat. "Wednesday's good for me. I can pick you up at your office."

"I'm busy next week."

"You've got to eat. Let's make it six."

She downshifted for a turn. "You're going to have to learn to take no for an answer."

"I don't think so. Take the left fork."

"I remember," she said between her teeth, though she didn't.

She drove in silence, slowing down only slightly

when she passed through the gate of his ranch. Sam leaned over casually and tooted her horn. When she stopped in front of his house he sat there a moment, as though gathering his thoughts.

"Want to come in?"

"No."

"Want to fight?"

She would not be amused or charmed or soothed. "No."

"All right, we can fight some other time. Want to hear a theory of mine? Never mind," he said before she could answer. "Listen anyway. The way I figure it, there are three stages to a relationship. First you like somebody. Then, if things work out, you start to care for them. When the big guns hit, you fall in love with them."

She kept her hands on the wheel because they'd gone damp all at once. "That's very interesting. If only life worked that neatly."

"I've always thought it does—if you let it. Anyway, Johanna, I went past liking you last night and went straight into the second stage. A woman like you wants reasons for that kind of thing, but I haven't got a handle on them yet."

Her hands had stopped sweating and were now as cold as ice, though the heat was baking right through the windshield. "Sam, I said before I don't think this is a good idea. I still believe that."

"No, you still want to believe that." He waited patiently until she looked at him. "There's a difference, Johanna. A big one. I care for you, and I figured we'd do better if I let you know.'' He leaned over to kiss her. A very gentle threat. ''You've got until Wednesday to think about it.''

He got out of the car, then leaned in through the window. ''Drive carefully, will you? You can always kick something when you get home if you're still mad.''

Chapter 7

It had been a long day. In fact, it had been several long days. Johanna didn't mind. The pressure to solve problems and work through a few minor crises had kept her mind off her personal life.

Her lighting director had chosen Monday, taping day, to have an appendectomy. She sent flowers and wished him—not for totally altruistic reasons—a speedy recovery. John Jay, in the middle of contract negotiations, had decided to have laryngitis. Johanna had been forced to pamper and cajole—and make a few veiled threats—to work an instant and miraculous cure. Her assistant lighting man had proven to be competent and unruffled, even after three technical hitches. Still, the day had been lengthened by two hours.

Tuesday had stretched even further with meetings

to discuss the photo sessions for the ads and the final preparations for the following week's contest. Security had been strengthened to guard that set of questions. A special safe had been purchased, and only she had the combination. Only she and Bethany knew which five questions had been sealed inside. Johanna began to feel like the head of the CIA.

A meeting with her father had been draining and difficult. They'd both been professional, executive producer to producer, as they'd discussed the show's status and plans for expansion. He'd absently mentioned an engagement party and told her his secretary would be in touch.

And, of course, because she considered it part of her job, Johanna watched *Trivia* every morning. It was just a nasty trick of fate that Sam's appearance ran this week. It was difficult enough not to think of him, and impossible when she was forced to watch him every day—long shots, close-ups. By Wednesday they had already received a stack of mail from delighted viewers.

Wednesday.

He'd given her until Wednesday to think about it. To think about him. Them. She just hadn't had the time, Johanna told herself as she turned up the volume and prepared to watch the day's segment. If she'd allowed herself to think about it she would have come up with a way, a polite and reasonable way, to get out of a dinner she hadn't even accepted.

The bright, bouncy opening theme came on, the lights flashed. The two celebrity panelists walked through the arch, then paused for applause before they took their seats. Johanna struggled to look at the big picture, but she kept focusing on him.

Relaxed. He always looked so relaxed, so confident about who he was. That was something she couldn't help but admire about him. He was at ease and put his partner at ease while still maintaining that larger-than-life quality people expected from stars.

So he was good at his job, Johanna told herself as she paced back and forth during the commercial break. That didn't mean she was infatuated with him.

When the show came back on, she took her chair again, wishing she didn't need to have that very small and indirect contact with him.

It's my job, Johanna reminded herself. But she lost track of the game as she watched him. And she remembered, a bit too clearly, that after this segment had been taped she had had her first real conversation with him. She'd taken a dare, and had lost. Since that one miscalculation, nothing had been the same.

She wanted it to be the same. The quick panic surprised her, but she fought it back and tried to think logically. She did want it to be the same as it had been before, when her life had been focused on career and nudged by ambition, both heated and cooled by pride. There hadn't been any sleepless nights then. Tension and self-doubt, perhaps, but no sleepless nights.

And there hadn't been any rides down a mountain on a raft, either, her mind echoed.

She didn't need them. Sam could keep his thrills. All she required was peace of mind.

He was in the winner's circle, surrounded by lights and the audience's total support. Johanna remembered that the quick, cocky grin had been for her benefit. The minute the congratulatory applause began, she snapped off the set.

On impulse, she went to the phone. Rather than going through her secretary, Johanna dialed direct. Such minor precautions were a bit late, since her picture—with Sam—had already been in the paper, and the speculation about them as a couple had already begun. Johanna had decided there was no use adding to the gossip that was already buzzing around the office.

She was calm, she told herself even as she wound the phone cord around her fingers. She wasn't being stubborn or spiteful, but sensible.

A woman's voice answered. Hearing it gave Johanna all the justification she needed. A man like Sam would always have women around. And a man like that was precisely what she wanted to avoid.

"I'd like to speak with Mr. Weaver. This is Johanna Patterson calling."

"Sam's not in. I'd be happy to take a message." On the other end of the line, Mae was digging for the notepad she always carried in her apron pocket. "Patterson?" she repeated, then shifted the phone and grinned. "Sam's spoken about you. You're the one who does *Trivia Alert*."

Johanna frowned for a moment at the idea of Sam

talking about her to one of his women. ‘‘Yes, I am. Would you mind—’’

‘‘I never miss it,’’ Mae continued conversationally. ‘‘I always keep it on when I'm cleaning. Then I see if Joe can answer any of the questions that night at dinner. Joe's my husband. I'm Mae Block.’’

So this was Mae, the one who shoveled out the dust and grew the snapdragons. Johanna's vision of a pretty morning visitor faded and left her more than a little ashamed. ‘‘I'm glad you like the show.’’

‘‘Crazy about it,’’ Mae assured her. ‘‘As a matter of fact, I just had it on. Got a real kick out of seeing our Sam on it. Thought he did real good, too. I even put it on the VCR so Joe could see it later. We're all just crazy about Sam. He speaks real kindly of you, too. Did you like your flowers?’’

Having at last found a space in Mae's rapid-fire conversation for a word, Johanna managed to insert one. ‘‘Flowers?’’

‘‘Sam doesn't think I saw him snitch them.’’

‘‘They were lovely.’’ Despite all her resolutions, Johanna felt herself soften. ‘‘I hope you didn't mind.’’

‘‘Plenty more where they came from. I figure flowers should be enjoyed, don't you?’’

‘‘Yes. Yes, I do. Mrs. Block—’’

‘‘Mae. Just Mae, honey.’’

‘‘Mae, if you could tell Sam I called.’’ Coward, her mind said all too clearly. Johanna closed herself off from it and continued. ‘‘And that—’’

‘‘Well, you can tell him yourself, honey, 'cause he just this minute walked in. Hold on now.’’

Before Johanna could babble an excuse, she heard Mae yelling. ''Sam, that lady you've been mooning about's on the phone. And I'd like to know what you're thinking of wearing a white shirt when you're wrestling with horses. How you expect me to get out those stains is more than I can understand. Did you wipe your feet? I just washed that kitchen floor.''

''Yes, ma'am. It's an old shirt,'' he added in a half apology Johanna recognized even over the wire.

''Old or not, it's a dust rag now. A boy your age oughta know better. Don't keep your lady waiting all day. I'll make you a sandwich.''

''Thanks. Hello, Johanna.''

Mae hadn't mentioned her name. *The lady you've been mooning about.* That was something Johanna would have to think about later. ''I'm sorry to bother you in the middle of the day. You must be busy.''

''Having my wrist slapped.'' He pulled out a bandanna and wiped the line of sweat from his temple. ''I'm glad you called. I've been thinking about you.''

''Yes, well...'' Where were all the neat excuses she'd thought up? ''About tonight.''

''Yes?''

Very carefully she unwrapped the cord from around her fingers. ''We'd left things a bit unstructured, and as it turns out, I have a late meeting. I can't be sure what time I'll wrap things up, so—''

''So why don't you drive out here when you're finished?'' He recognized a lie when he heard one. ''You should know the way by now.''

"Yes, but it might run late. I don't want to mess up your evening."

"The only way you'd mess it up is not to come."

She hadn't a clue as to how to respond to that. "I never actually agreed to come." Her conscience insisted on reminding her she hadn't stuck by a refusal, either. "Why don't we make it some other time?"

"Johanna," he said, very patiently, "you don't want me to camp on your doorstep, do you?"

"I just think it would be better—"

"Safer."

Yes. "Better," she insisted.

"Whatever. If you don't show up by eight I'm coming after you. Take your choice."

Bristling wasn't nearly as effective over the phone. "I don't like ultimatums."

"That's a pity. I'll see you when you get here. Don't work too hard."

Johanna scowled at the dial tone, then dropped the phone on the hook. She wouldn't go. She would be damned if she did.

Of course, she went.

Only to prove that she wasn't a coward, Johanna assured herself. In any case, avoiding a situation didn't solve anything, it only postponed things. Loose ends were something she invariably tied up.

It was true that she enjoyed his company, so there was no reason to be out of sorts. Except for the fact that she'd been maneuvered again. No, he hadn't done the maneuvering, she corrected. She'd done that all by herself, thank you very much. If she hadn't wanted to go, she would never have called him to say she wasn't going to. Deep down she'd wanted to keep the engagement because she'd always had a need to face up to whatever could be faced.

She could certainly face Sam Weaver.

A simple dinner, she decided. Between friends. They could, cautiously, be called friends by this time. A little conversation never hurt, particularly between two people who were in the same business. Game shows or movies, it all came down to entertainment. She picked up speed a bit, and the plastic bags over this week's dry cleaning snapped and rustled on their hangers behind her.

At least this time she had her own transportation. She would leave when she was ready to leave. There was some security in that.

When she passed through the gates leading to the ranch, she promised herself that she would enjoy the evening for what it was. A simple dinner with a friend. She stopped her car in front of his house and stepped out, refusing to glance in the visor mirror. She wouldn't fuss with or freshen her makeup any more than she had fussed with her outfit. Her gray suit was stylish but certainly businesslike, as were the three hanging in the car. Her low-heeled pumps were comfortable, purchased as much for that as for fashion.

She glanced at her watch and was pleased with the time. Seven-thirty. Not so early that it would appear that she'd been cowed, nor so late that it made her look spiteful.

She looked as she had on that first day, Sam

thought. Composed, coolheaded, subtly sexy. His reaction to her now was exactly the same as it had been then. Instant fascination. Stepping out on the porch, he smiled at her.

"Hi."

"Hello." She didn't want to be unnerved, not again, not the way she seemed to be every time she saw him. She answered his smile, though cautiously, and started up the steps. His next move was so unexpected that she had no chance to block it.

He cupped a hand around the base of her neck and kissed her, not passionately, not urgently, but with a casual intimacy that shot straight through her. Welcome home, it seemed to say, and left her speechless.

"I love the way you wear a suit, Johanna."

"I didn't have time to change."

"I'm glad." He glanced beyond her at the sound of a truck. With a half smile, he shaded his eyes. "You forgot to blow your horn," he told her.

"Everything all right here, Sam?" In the cab of a pickup was a man of about fifty with shoulders like cinder blocks.

"Everything's fine." Sam slipped an arm around Johanna's waist.

The man in the truck chuckled, then spun the wheel and made a U-turn. "I can see that. Night."

"That was Joe," Sam explained as they watched the truck cruise down the hard-packed road. "He and Mae keep an eye on the place. And me."

"So I see." It was entirely too easy, standing on the porch, his arm around her, as the sun lowered.

Johanna didn't deliberately step away. The move was automatic. ''Your housekeeper told me she watches *Trivia.*''

She also said you were mooning over me. Johanna kept the fact that she'd overheard that little piece of information to herself. It was ridiculous, of course. Men like Sam Weaver didn't moon over anyone.

''Religiously,'' he murmured, studying her. She was nervous. He'd thought they'd passed that point, and he wasn't sure whether to be pleased or frustrated to discover otherwise. ''In fact, Mae considers my, ah...performance so far this week the height of my career.''

The smile came quickly. Her fingers relaxed their grip on the railing. ''Emmy material, I'm sure.''

''Is that a smirk?''

''I never smirk, and especially not about my show. I suppose I'll have to risk inflating your ego, but we've already gotten a tremendous amount of mail. 'Sam Weaver is the cutest thing on two legs,''' Johanna quoted, and was amused when he grimaced. ''That was from a seventy-five-year-old woman in Tucson.''

''Yeah.'' He took her hand and drew her inside. ''When you've finished smirking—''

''I told you, I never smirk.''

''Right, and when you're finished we'll see about dinner. I figured we'd barbecue, since I wasn't sure when you'd wind up that meeting.''

''Meeting?'' The lie had slipped away from her. Remembering, Johanna did something else she couldn't remember having done before. She blushed. Just a little, but enough. "Oh, well, it moved along faster than I'd expected."

"Lucky for both of us." He could have pinned her on it, Sam mused, but decided to let her escape. If he understood Johanna as well as he believed he was coming to understand her, she was already berating herself for the excuse, and for botching it. "I've got some swordfish. Why don't you pour yourself some wine and I'll heat up the grill?"

"All right." The bottle was already open. Johanna filled the two glasses he'd set on the kitchen counter as he breezed through the back door.

He'd known the meeting was nothing more than a weak excuse. She couldn't remember ever having been quite so transparent. Johanna sighed, sipped, then sighed again. He was letting it go so that she wouldn't be embarrassed. That only made it worse. The least she could do, she thought as she picked up his glass, was to be pleasant company for the rest of the evening.

The pool looked cool and delightfully inviting. Swimming had been a daily habit when she'd lived in her father's house. Now she couldn't seem to find time for the health club she'd conscientiously joined. She skirted around the pool to where Sam stood by the stone barbecue pit with two fish steaks on a platter, but she did glance at the water rather wistfully.

"You want to take a quick swim before dinner?" he asked.

It was tempting. Johanna found herself tempted too often when around him. "No, thanks."

"There's always after." He set the steaks on the grill, where they sizzled. Taking his glass from her, he clinked it lightly against hers, then drank. "Go ahead and sit down. These won't take long."

Instead, she wandered a short distance away, looking at his land, the tidy outbuildings, the isolation. He seemed so comfortable here, she thought, so much at home. He could be anybody, an ordinary person. But she remembered that she'd read about him just that morning.

"There's a very hot write-up in this week's *TV Guide* about *No Roses for Sarah.*"

"I saw it." He saw, too, how the sun bounced off the water of the pool and onto her skin, making her seem like an illusion. The trim gray suit didn't make him think of offices or board meetings, but of quiet evenings after the day was over.

"*Variety* was equally enthusiastic. 'Gripping, not to be missed,' and so on." She smiled a little as she turned to him again. "What was the adjective used to describe you..." She trailed off as if she couldn't quite remember, though the exact quote had engraved itself on her brain. "'Weaver executes a'— Was it 'sterling performance'?"

Sam flipped the steaks, and they hissed. Smoke rose up, hot and sultry. "'Sizzling,'" he corrected, knowing when he was being strung along.

"Yes, sizzling." She paused to touch her tongue to her upper lip. "'A sizzling performance as a down-on-his-luck drifter who seduces Sarah and the audience with equal panache.' Panache,'' she repeated. ''That one rolls around on the tongue, doesn't it?''

''I didn't realize you were such a smart aleck, Johanna.''

She laughed and crossed over to him. ''I'm also human. Nothing could drag me away from my set on Sunday night when the first part's aired.''

''And Monday?''

''That'll depend, won't it?'' She sipped her drink and sniffed appreciatively at the mesquite smoke. ''On how *sizzling* you were on Sunday.''

The grin was fast and crooked, as if he had no doubt where she would be at nine o'clock Monday night. ''Keep an eye on these, will you? I'll be right back.''

She'd keep an eye on them, but she hoped the steaks didn't do anything they weren't supposed to do until he got back. Alone, she stretched her arms and worked the muscles in her back. The late meeting had been a lie, but the long day hadn't. Wistfully she glanced at the pool again. It really was tempting.

If she were just anyone—if he were just anyone—she could share this meal with him, laugh a little over something that had happened during the day. Afterward, while the wine was still cool and the air still hot, they could slide into the water and relax together. Just two people who enjoyed each other and a quiet evening.

Later, when the moon came out, they might stay in the water, talking quietly, touching, easing gently into a more intimate form of relaxation. He would have music on again, and the candles on the table would burn down and drown in their own melted wax.

When something brushed against her legs, she jolted, sloshing wine over her hand. The fantasy had come through a bit too clearly, too compellingly, and that wasn't like her. Johanna turned away from the pool and the ideas it had had stirring inside her. With a hand to her heart, she looked down at a fat gray cat. He rubbed up against her calf again, sent her a long, shrewd look, then settled down to wash.

"Where did you come from?" Johanna wondered as she bent to scratch his ears.

"The barn," Sam told her, coming up from behind her. "Silas is one of the barn cats, and I'd guess he got a whiff of the fish and came down to see if he could charm any out of us."

She didn't look at Sam right away, concentrating on the cat instead. The daydream was still a bit too real. "I thought barn cats were fast and skinny."

Not when someone was always taking them down scraps, Sam thought ruefully as he set the bowl of pasta salad on the table and flipped the fish onto a platter. "Silas can be pretty charming," he said, and pulled out a chair for Johanna.

"Silas is pretty huge."

"You don't like cats?"

"No, actually, I do. I've even thought of getting one myself. Why Silas?"

"Marner," Sam explained easily as he served her.

"You know how he hoarded gold. Well, this Silas hoards mice."

"Oh."

He laughed at her expression and topped off her wine. "You wanted to know. I've been meaning to ask you," he said, thinking she deserved a change of subject, "when you go on nighttime."

"Two weeks." Johanna told herself she wasn't nervous, not nervous at all. "We tape in two weeks, actually, and go on in four."

"Adding more crew?"

"Some. For the most part it just means that we'll be taping two days a week instead of one. Interested in making another appearance?"

"I'm going to be a bit tied up for a while."

"The new movie." She relaxed a few more degrees. This was how her practical mind had imagined the evening. Shoptalk, nothing more. "When do you start?"

"Any day, theoretically. Realistically, in a week or two. After some preproduction and studio work here, we'll head east. They figure about three weeks on location in Maryland, in and around Baltimore."

"You must be anxious to begin."

"I always get lazy between pictures. Nothing like a few six a.m. calls to get you back in gear. How's your fish?"

"It's wonderful." And once again, she'd all but cleared her plate without realizing it. "I bought a grill a few months ago, but I burned everything I put on it."

"A low flame," he said, and something in his voice made her skin tingle. "A careful eye." He took her hand, linking their fingers. "And patience."

"I—" He brought her hand to his lips, watching her over it as he kissed her fingers. "I'll have to give it another try."

"Your skin always smells as though you've walked through the rain. Even when you're not here I can't help thinking about that."

"We should—" Stop pretending, she thought. Acquiesce. Take what we want. "Go for a walk," she managed. "I'd like to see your pond again."

"All right." Patience, Sam reminded himself. But the flame wasn't as low as it had been. "Hold on a minute." He tossed a few scraps onto the grass before gathering up the dishes. She knew she should have offered her help, but she wanted, needed—badly needed—a moment alone.

She watched the cat saunter over to the fish with an arrogance that told her he'd been certain all along he'd get what he'd come for. Sam walked like that, Johanna thought, and suddenly cold, she rubbed her hands over her arms.

She wasn't afraid of him. She reminded herself of that to boost her confidence. But it was no less than the truth. She wasn't afraid of Sam: fear of herself, however, was another matter.

She was here because she wanted to be here. Wasn't it time to face that one fact? She'd already admitted that she hadn't come because he'd maneuvered her. She'd maneuvered herself, or that part of herself that was still determined to stand apart.

There was another part of herself, a part that was slowly taking charge, that knew exactly what she wanted. Who she wanted. That was a part that had already made an enormous mistake by falling in love with Sam.

Before she had a chance to deal with the enormity of that realization, he was back, carrying a plastic bag filled with crackers.

"They'll expect to be— Are you all right?"

She was pale, and her eyes were huge. If Sam hadn't known better he would have sworn someone had come along and given her a fast, unexpected backhand.

"I'm fine." Thank God her voice was steady. She still had that much under control. "Your pets keep you under their thumb, don't they?"

Her smile didn't quite reach her eyes, but he nodded. "It looks that way." He touched her face. She didn't flinch, but he felt the muscles of her jaw tense. "You look a little dazed, Johanna."

Terrified was the word. In love with him, her mind repeated. Good Lord, when, how and, most of all, *why?* "It's probably the wine. I'll walk it off."

It had nothing to do with the wine, but he let it go. Taking her hand firmly in his, he started toward the path. "Next time you come, you're going to have to dress for this. As sensible as those shoes are, boots or sneakers are better for the hike."

Sensible. Frowning, Johanna looked down at her

trim, low-heeled Italian pumps. Damn it, they were sensible. She managed to bite off the sigh. Sensible. Like her. "I told you I didn't have time to change."

"That's okay, I can always carry you."

"That won't be necessary."

There it was again, that low, cool tone. He didn't bother to fight back the smile as he steered her along.

The sun was nearly down, so the light was soft and pearly. There were wildflowers along the path that hadn't yet bloomed the last time they'd taken this walk. He imagined Johanna could name them for him if he asked, but he preferred to let them pop out of the ground anonymously.

He could smell the water now, and could just hear its faint lap against the high grass. Every time he'd walked there in the last few weeks he'd thought of her. The birds were quiet now, settling down for the night. Those that called the night their own had yet to stir. He liked the quiet of dusk, the aloneness of it, and wondered if she felt the same. He remembered how she'd knelt in front of a bank of flowers at sundown and figured that she did.

The water of the pond was darkening, like the sky. The shadows of the trees were long and dim across it. It still made her smile to see the ducks gliding over it, preening a bit in anticipation of an audience.

"I take it Silas and his companions don't bother them."

"Too much effort to come all the way out here and get wet when they've got the barn. Here." He handed her the bag. As she had before, Johanna laughed at the ducks' antics as she tossed the crackers to them.

"I guess no one spoils them like this when you're away."

"Mae does. She wouldn't admit it, though."

"Oh, I didn't see the drake close up before." She skimmed a cracker to him. "He's beautiful. And look how the babies have grown." She scattered crumbs on the water until the bag was empty. Without thinking, she tucked it into her pocket. "It's so nice here," she murmured. "Just the water, and the grass." And you, she thought. But she didn't look at him, not until his hand was on her cheek, gently urging her to.

It was just as it had been the first time. And yet it was nothing like it. This time she knew exactly how she would feel, how she would want, when he kissed her. She knew he would touch her hair before he drew her close. She knew her mind would cloud and her pulse would quicken.

She knew, but it still stunned her.

He felt as though he'd waited forever. It hadn't been merely weeks since he'd first seen her. She'd been under his skin, inside his heart, for as long as he could remember. A dream, a half-formed wish that had only taken one look at her to click solidly into place. It was so right. Somehow it was exactly right when his mouth found hers.

She still wasn't sure. He could feel the hesitation even as he felt the passion that drummed beneath it. But he was sure enough for both of them.

It was meant to be here, here where those first

shock waves had passed through both of them. It was meant to be now, before night fell.

She tightened her grip on his shirt, holding on, holding back. In a moment, she knew, she wouldn't be able to think clearly. It would be wise to withdraw now, to leave things as they had been. But his lips coaxed her to stay. To trust.

She murmured, tensing up when she felt him slip the jacket from her shoulders. A step was being taken. Then he was soothing her, giving her time, plenty of time, but no choice at all. The buttons that ran down her back were loosened one by one in an agony of sweetness and promise. When she felt his fingers brush her skin, she shuddered at the contact and searched for the will to end it.

But his lips skimmed her throat as he peeled the blouse from her. She was helpless, but the sensation was no longer frightening.

Is this what it felt like to give in, at last, fully, completely give in to something not quite known but only sensed? Hadn't she waited for it, anticipated it, even while she'd struggled against it? Now the struggle was almost over.

He had to use every ounce of self-control not to rush her. He knew she needed time and care, even as his own needs balled like fists inside him. He'd already imagined what it would be like to touch her like this, to feel her tremble when he did. Her skirt slid down her hips. His hands followed it.

The sun had dropped away, but he could see her, her hair haloed around her face, her eyes wide and uncertain. He kissed her again, slowly, trailing his lips over her jaw as he shrugged out of his shirt. He saw her start to reach for him, then hesitate just short of contact. Taking her hand, he brought it, palm up, to his lips and felt her go limp.

He lowered her to the grass.

It was cool, soft and damp with early dew—a sensation Johanna knew she would remember always. He was over her, so she could only see his face, then only his eyes. She heard the first owl call before he bent to her. Then there was only him.

He touched. She shuddered, no longer from fear or from doubt, but from a pleasure so pure she could never have described it. He tasted. She floated, no longer helpless, but a willing partner. And when she reached for him, drew him closer, the world was shut off for both of them.

She was so soft, so generous. He wondered that he could still be surprised by how many facets there were to her. She'd opened to him now, as completely as he could have hoped.

If her touch was still shy, it was only more endearing. He wanted it to be sweet for her, memorable, and as special as he already knew it would be for him. Somewhere along the line she had stopped being a woman, however desirable, however fascinating, and had become his woman.

He took her, gently, higher.

When she moaned, desire thrummed in him, hard, demanding. He fought it back, wanting her to ride the wave as long as they could both stand it. Slowly, drawing out the process, he slipped her teddy down to her waist, then to her hips, letting the hunger build inside him.

Her fingers dug into the grass as he brushed his lips over her. She could feel her skin tremble wherever he chose to linger. Then, abruptly, the pleasure rocketed up, beyond anything she'd dreamed possible. She cried out his name, her body arching up. Pleasure doubled back, and he was with her again. Now her fingers dug into his shoulders desperately.

Stars began to wink to life above them.

The breath was dragging in and out of his lungs when he filled her. Now he was helpless, his face buried in her hair, his body more her prisoner than she had ever been his. Need expanded and became the focus of his world, and then even that shattered, leaving only her.

Chapter 8

He couldn't speak. At the moment Sam wasn't sure his mind would ever be able to direct that basic function again. He knew he should shift his weight from her but couldn't bear to break the bond.

Whatever else it had been—passion, desire, chemistry—it had forged a bond.

Overhead, the stars were still coming out. Johanna could see them now, but all she could think of was the way Sam's heart still raced against hers. She hadn't known she was capable of giving or receiving that kind of pleasure. Though the heat had eased, his body was still warm, a continuing contrast to the cool grass that waved around them. The water, pushed by the night breezes, lapped only a few feet away.

It had been a shock to realize she was capable of feeling anything this intensely, but more, she had seen his eyes, felt his body shudder, and had known for the first time in her life that she could give.

Hardly realizing she was doing so, she lifted a hand to stroke his hair. Sam was aware, even if she wasn't, that it was the first time she'd touched him without being backed into a corner. He closed his eyes and held on to that thought. What would once have been a small thing to him was now an enormous one. He'd slipped into the third phase, into love, almost painlessly.

"Johanna." When he could speak, her name was the first thing that formed. Because he wanted to see her, he found the strength to raise himself onto his elbows. Her hair was spread out on the grass that had bent under them. Her eyes were half-closed, but what he could see was still dazed with pleasure. "You're so lovely."

Her lips curved a bit, and she touched him again, her fingers on his face. "I didn't think this would happen. I didn't think it could."

"I imagined it, here, just like this." He lowered his head, just to brush his lips against hers. "But my fantasy didn't even come close to the real thing. Nothing ever has." He felt her withdraw at that, just a fraction, but enough that he felt compelled to take her face in his hand. "Nothing and no one, Johanna."

His eyes insisted that she believe him, and she wanted to, but there was still too much of a block within her to make that possible. "I've wanted you." At least she could be honest with both of them. "I can't think about what happens next."

"We're both going to have to. I've no intention of letting you go." She opened her mouth to protest, to make some excuse, and only managed to moan as she felt him harden inside her. "Not a chance," he murmured, before desire clouded his mind completely.

When she could think again, she tried to draw away. She was going to need time to put this in perspective, to work out the steps. The first was to be an adult, and not to expect.

They had shared something. Perhaps it hadn't been casual for her, but she'd always understood that every relationship had its limitations. Better to remember that now and face it from the outset. She cared, too much for her own good, but she still knew better than to cuddle up at his side and start thinking about tomorrows.

"It's late." She pulled her hands through her hair as she sat up. "I have to go."

He'd have been surprised if he could have moved again for eight hours. "Go where?"

"I have to go home." She reached for her teddy but missed by an inch when his hand braceleted her wrist.

"If you expect me to let you go anywhere tonight, you're crazy."

"I don't know what you're talking about." Her voice was amused as she tugged on her hand. "In the first place, it's not a matter of you *letting* me go anywhere." After picking up her teddy, she shook it out. "And I can hardly sleep in the grass all night."

"You're absolutely right." If she hadn't been so

relaxed, she would have realized he'd given in too easily. ''Here, put on my shirt. It'll be easier for you to dress inside.''

Because it made sense, Johanna allowed him to bundle her into it. It carried his scent. Unconsciously she rubbed her cheek against the collar as Sam pulled on his jeans.

''Let me give you a hand with those.'' Sam took her now-folded clothes and draped them over his arm. ''Better let me go first. There isn't much light tonight.''

Johanna followed him down the path, hoping she seemed as casual and at ease as he. What had happened by the pond, weeks ago and now tonight, had been beautiful. She didn't want to lose the importance of it. But she didn't want to exaggerate its importance, either.

Nothing and no one else.

No, she'd be a fool to believe it—to hope for it. He might have meant it at the moment he'd said it. She could believe that because she'd come to understand that Sam wasn't a man for lies, even pretty ones. She could believe, too, that he cared for her—again, for the moment.

Intense feelings rarely lasted, and all the hopes and promises built on those feelings eventually crumbled. So she didn't allow herself to hope and refused to make promises.

They still had a long way to go, Sam mused. She wasn't ready to take what he'd discovered he was ready to give. The trouble was, now that he was in love with her he wouldn't be able to be so patient. Johanna was just going to have to keep pace.

As they stepped onto the terrace, he set her clothes neatly on the table. A frown formed between her brows as he casually stripped off his jeans.

"What are you doing?"

He stood before her, undeniably magnificent in the light of the moon. With a smile that warned her an instant too late, he hauled her into his arms.

"It's what *we're* doing," he said simply, and jumped into the pool.

The water was several degrees warmer than the night air, but it was still a shock. Before it closed over her head, she had time for one surprised shriek. Her legs tangled with his as the plunge separated them and the shirt billowed up around her head. Then her feet touched bottom, and instinctively she pushed upward. Gasping, she surfaced, blinking water from her eyes.

"Damn it!" She drew her arm through the water, hand fisted, and shot a spray into his grinning face.

"Nothing like a midnight swim, is there, Jo-Jo?"

"Don't call me that. You must be out of your mind."

"Only about you," he told her, then sent an unloverly splash in her direction.

Johanna dodged it, barely, telling herself she wasn't amused. "What the hell would you have done if I couldn't swim?"

"Saved you." He treaded water with little effort. "I was born to be a hero."

"Jerk," she corrected. She turned, and in two

strokes had reached the side. Before she could haul herself out, Sam caught her by the waist.

"When you stop being mad, you'll admit you like it." He nuzzled the back of her neck. "Want to race?"

"What I want to do is—" She turned—another miscalculation. His hands slid up her wet skin to her breasts as he bent his lips to her throat.

"Me too," he murmured.

She lifted a hand to his shoulder where it skimmed over cool skin just beginning to heat. "Sam, I can't."

"That's okay. I can." He slid into her.

Johanna woke with a faint grumble and tried to roll over. It took her several confusing seconds to realize that Sam's arm had her pinned. Lying still, she turned her head cautiously to look at him.

He slept more on her pillow than on his own. No, they were both his pillows, Johanna reminded herself. His bed, his house. Would he think her a fool or a freak if she told him this was the first time she'd ever woken up in a man's bed? It didn't matter; she wouldn't tell him. How could she tell him he was the first man she'd cared for enough, trusted enough, to share that private vulnerability called sleep?

She still wasn't quite sure how he'd managed to nudge her into it. One minute she'd been standing, naked and dripping, by the side of the pool, and the next… They hadn't even made love there, but had simply fallen into bed much like two exhausted children.

He'd made her laugh, too, and he'd given her, all unknowing, the sweet daydream of her own making.

Now it was morning and she had to remind herself again that she was an adult. They had wanted each other, enjoyed each other. It was important not to add complications to that simple formula. There wouldn't be regret. Regret usually meant blame, and she didn't want that, either. Wisely or not, she'd made a decision. The decision had taken her into intimacy with Sam. She wouldn't use the word *affair*.

Now that it was done, she had to be realistic. This intensity, this flash of feeling, would fade, and when that happened, she'd be hurt. It couldn't be prevented, only prepared for.

Her emotions had already deepened beyond her control, but she still had her strength and her sense. No strings. He'd said it. She'd meant it.

Despite that, she lifted a fingertip to brush the hair from his forehead.

Oh, God, I'm in love with him, I'm so ridiculously in love with him, and I'm bound to make a fool of myself.

When he opened his eyes, those dark, heavy-lidded eyes, she didn't give a damn.

"Hi."

She lowered her hand, flustered because he'd caught her petting him. "Good morning."

It was there, even after their incredible night together. The trace of shyness he found so appealing. So exciting. Because he didn't want to give her time to layer it over with composure, he rolled on top of her.

"Sam—"

"It occurs to me," he began as he drew longer, lazier kisses from her, "that we never made love in bed." He ran his hand down her side, from shoulder to hip, from hip to thigh. "I'm feeling traditional this morning."

She didn't have time to analyze what she was feeling. Even as she tried to say his name again, her breath caught. This morning he wasn't so patient—or perhaps she, knowing what could be, was more sensitive.

She curled around him and let herself go.

Time had gotten away from her. Everything had gotten away from her, Johanna corrected as she stepped out of the shower and began to towel off quickly. If she threw on her clothes, let her hair air-dry on the way to work and pushed the speed limit, she might just make it.

She grabbed a few basic cosmetics out of her purse. The effort would be sketchy, but it was all she could afford. In the bedroom she ripped the plastic off the first suit Sam had brought up from her car. Yesterday's blouse would have to work with it. Cursing herself for not having planned properly, she zipped the skirt and ran down the hall carrying her shoes.

"Where's the fire?" Sam asked her as she rested a hand against the wall and struggled into her shoes.

"I'm running late."

He lifted a brow. ''Do you get demerits for being tardy?''

''I'm never late.''

''Good, then you can afford to be. Have some coffee.''

She took the cup he offered, grateful. ''Thanks. I really have to run.''

''You haven't eaten anything.''

''I never eat breakfast.''

''Today you do.'' He had her arm. To prevent the contents of the cup sloshing all over her freshly laundered suit, she kept up with him. ''Five minutes, Johanna. Catch your breath, drink your coffee. If you argue, it'll take ten.''

She swore, but downed more coffee as he pulled her into the kitchen. ''Sam, you're the one who's on vacation, not me. I've got a full day scheduled that might, if I'm lucky, end before six.''

''All the more reason you should have a decent breakfast.'' He couldn't remember ever having felt better in the morning, more alive or full of energy. Briefly he wished he was in the middle of filming so that he could pour some of that energy into a part. ''Sit. I'll fix you some eggs.''

Because her temper was beginning to fray, she drank more coffee. ''I appreciate it, really I do, but I don't have time. We're shooting ads today for the home viewers' contest, and I'm the only one who can handle John Jay.''

''A dubious talent.'' The English muffin he'd

dropped in the toaster popped up. "You can at least eat this."

Annoyed, she snatched it from him, ignored the butter and jam on the table and bit into it. "There," she said, and swallowed. "Satisfied?"

Her hair was still dripping around her face, and she'd forgotten her lipstick. Eyes still shadowed from the long night glared at him. He grinned and flicked a crumb off her chin. "I love you, Johanna."

If he'd drawn back and planted his fist on her chin she would have been no less shocked. She stared at him as the muffin slipped out of her boneless fingers onto the table. Her step back was instinctive, defensive. Sam lifted his brow at it, but that was all.

"Don't say that to me," she managed at length. "I don't need to hear that. I don't want to hear it."

She needed to hear it all right, he thought. She might not have wanted to, but she needed to. He was going to see that she did, at regular intervals, but right now she'd gone pale again. "All right," he said slowly. "It doesn't change the facts one way or the other."

"I—I have to go." She ransacked her purse almost desperately for her keys. "I'm really running late." What was she supposed to say? What was supposed to be said on the morning after the night? With her keys clutched in her hand, she looked up. "Goodbye."

"I'll walk you out." His arm went around her shoulders. She tried not to tense. She tried not to lean against him. She could feel the tug-of-war as they walked. "There's something I'd like to tell you, Johanna."

"Please, it isn't necessary. We agreed even before—before last night—that there wouldn't be any promises."

"Did we?" Damned if he remembered that, but if he had agreed, that was one agreement that would have to be broken. He pushed the front door open and stepped onto the porch before turning her to him. "We'll have to talk about that."

"All right." She would have agreed to almost anything if it had meant he'd let her go. Because she wanted to stay. More than she'd ever wanted anything, she wanted to toss her keys over her shoulder, throw herself into his arms and stay as long as he'd have her.

"In the meantime, I want you to know that I've never had another woman in that bed." He saw the flash of doubt in her eyes before she was able to mask it. And before he could stop himself, he'd hauled her up by the lapels. "Damn it, a man gets tired of having everything he says dissected in that brain of yours. I didn't say there haven't been other women, Johanna, but there's never been another woman here. Because here's special to me. It's important. And so are you." He let her go. "Chew on that for a while."

Johanna thumbed another antacid tablet from the roll. She'd told Sam no less than the truth when she'd said she was the only one who could handle John Jay. It just so happened that today she wasn't doing a good job of it. The two-hour photo session had stretched into three, and tempers were fraying. If she didn't have the crew, equipment and two cars out of the studio in another forty-five minutes she was going to have the producer of *Noon with Nina* on her back.

Resigned, Johanna chewed the antacid and prayed it did its job better than she was doing hers. She signaled for a halt and hoped the five-minute break would keep the photographer from strangling her host.

"John Jay." She knew the game. Johanna pasted a smile on her face as she crossed to him. "Can I have a minute?" Her voice was calm, her touch light and friendly, as she took his arm to guide him to a corner. "Sessions like this are so annoying, aren't they?"

He literally pounced on the sympathy. "You have no idea, Johanna. You know I want what's best for the show, darling, but that man…" He glanced over at the photographer with loathing. "He has no conception of mood or image."

"That man" was one of the tops in his business and was being paid by the incredibly expensive hour. Johanna bit off an oath in time to have it slip out as a sigh. "I know, but unfortunately we have to work with him. We're running behind schedule, and the last thing I want is to have him take shots of the cars only." She let the threat hang until she was certain it had sunk in. "After all, there are three stars here. The cars, the show itself and, of course, you. The teasers went beautifully, by the way."

"I was fresh." He fussed with the knot of his tie.

"I understand perfectly. But I have to ask you to

keep the energy up for just a few more minutes. That suit's very becoming, John Jay.''

''It is, isn't it?'' He held out an arm, turning it over to study the sleeve.

''These shots are going to make quite a statement.'' If she didn't strangle him herself first. ''All I want you to do is stand between those two cars and flash the smile America loves.''

''For you, darling.'' He squeezed her hand, ready to sacrifice himself to the masses. ''You know, you're looking a little dragged-out.''

Her smile didn't fade, only froze. ''It's lucky I'm not having my picture taken.''

''It certainly is,'' he agreed, patting Johanna's head. He already knew his producer could grow fangs if he patted her elsewhere. ''You have to try to relax more, Johanna, and take those vitamins I told you about. God knows I couldn't get through the day without them.'' He watched the photographer come back on the set. With a sniff, John Jay signaled for make up. ''Johanna, there's a rumor running rampant that you're seeing Sam Weaver.''

''Is there?'' Johanna ground her teeth as John Jay got a dusting of powder. ''It's amazing how these things get started.''

''What a town.'' Satisfied that he was perfect, John Jay strode over to do his duty.

It took only twenty minutes more. The moment she'd sent her host on his way, Johanna apologized to the photographer, offered him and his assistant lunch on her and handed out tickets to Monday night's taping.

By the time she drove from the studio in Burbank back to her offices in Century City, she was two hours behind schedule and had consumed almost half the roll of antacids in her pocket.

"You've got a half-dozen messages," Bethany told her the moment she walked in. "Only two of which require answers yesterday. I contacted Tom Bradley's agent. He's interested in doing the pilot."

"Good. Let's set it up." In her office, Johanna dropped her briefcase, accepted the cup of coffee Beth was already offering and sat on the edge of her desk. "I've thought of twenty-seven ways to successfully murder John Jay Johnson."

"Would you like me to type them up?"

"Not yet. I want to wait until I have an even thirty." Johanna sipped her coffee and wished for five minutes, five full minutes to be completely alone, so that she could take her shoes off, put her feet up and close her eyes. "Bradley has a reputation as being very professional."

"A veteran. Did his first show in '72, when he was still wet behind the ears. It ran for five years, and he slid right into the old classic *Word Bingo*. That was on the air from '77 to '85. Pretty amazing. He retired as sort of the guru of game shows, but his face is still recognizable from occasional appearances on other daytime shows and grand-marshaling parades. Luring him back to the fold would be no small accomplishment."

She stopped because Johanna was drinking coffee and staring out the window. There were shadows under her eyes, Bethany noted, and a definite look of melancholy in them. ''Johanna, you look terrible.''

Taken aback, Johanna set her coffee aside. ''So I've been told.''

''Is everything all right?''

''Everything's fine.'' Except that Sam said he was in love with her and she was so terrified she wanted to get in her car and keep driving. She drew out her roll of tablets.

Frowning, Beth eyed it. ''Was that a new roll this morning?''

''It was, before I spent most of it with John Jay.''

''Have any lunch?''

''Don't ask.''

''Johanna, why don't you take the rest of the day off, go home, take a nap, watch the soaps?''

With a small smile, Johanna rose to move behind her desk. ''I've got to answer those questions yesterday. Beth, let's see if we can set that pilot up for the week after next. Be sure to notify Patterson Productions.''

Bethany shrugged and stood. ''You're the boss,'' she said, and set the stack of messages on Johanna's desk.

Absolutely true, Johanna thought as Bethany closed the door behind her. She was the boss. Johanna rubbed at the headache behind her temple and wondered why she felt as though someone else were pulling the strings.

* * *

He didn't know what he was doing there, sitting on her front steps like a lovesick teenager. Because he was lovesick, Sam told himself as he crossed his booted ankles.

He hadn't felt this stupid about a woman since he'd fallen like a ton of bricks for Mary Alice Reeder. She'd been an older woman, sophisticated, wise and like most sixteen-year-old girls, not very interested in a fourteen-year-old pest. But he'd loved pretty little Mary Alice with a kind of worshipful devotion that had lasted nearly nine months.

Calf love, his mother had called it, not unkindly.

Since then he'd fallen into the second stage, the care-for stage, with a number of women. But he hadn't loved anyone else since Mary Alice Reeder. Until Johanna.

He almost wished he could go back to that calf love. However painful it was, it passed, and it left a man with sweet and rather filmy memories. Hearts and initials carved surreptitiously in a tree trunk, daydreams that always ended with him saving his girl from some horrendous disaster that opened her eyes to his charm and bravery.

Sam laughed at himself and looked at a spiky blue flower that was just beginning to bloom in Johanna's garden. Times changed. Mary Alice had slipped through his shaky fingers. But he wasn't fourteen anymore, and Johanna, like it or not, was going nowhere.

He wanted her. Just sitting there in front of her quiet, empty house, with a basket beside him and her flowers sleeping in the evening sun, he wanted her.

For good. It wasn't a decision he'd made with a snap of his fingers, though she might think so. It was something that had happened to him, and not entirely in a way he liked. The only plans he'd counted on, the only pressure he'd expected, had been career-oriented.

If he'd had his choice, he would have cruised along for another few months, a year. Ten years. Time didn't have a damn thing to do with it. He'd looked at her, he'd touched her, and the decision had been made for him.

Hadn't he sat right here not so long before and told her they should get to know each other better? Companions, with no strings. He'd meant it, every bit as honestly as he'd meant it when he'd told her he loved her.

She'd accepted the first—warily, but she had accepted it. The second had been met with pure panic.

What was it that made Johanna so skittish? Another man? She'd never mentioned one, never even hinted at one. Unless he was completely obtuse, the woman he'd made love with the night before had been almost frighteningly innocent. If she'd been hurt, he felt it must be buried deep in the past, and it was time for her to let it go.

Time. He didn't have much of that, he thought as he lifted the lid of the basket to check on his gift. Any day he could get the call that would send him three thousand miles away. It would be weeks before he could be with her again. He could handle that. He thought he could handle that, but only if she gave him something to take with him.

When he heard the car he set the lid carefully back in place. Lovesick, he thought as his stomach knotted and his nerves began to jangle. It was a very apt phrase.

Johanna pulled in behind his car and wondered what the hell she was going to do. She'd been so sure she would be able to come home, close herself in, maybe dive into bed and sleep for hours without thinking at all. But he was here, invading her privacy, stealing away her quiet hours. The worst of it was, she was glad, so glad to see him.

''You put in a long day.'' He rose but didn't cross to her.

''A lot of things are coming to a head at once.''

He waited until she stood in front of him. ''I know what you mean.'' He touched her then, just a light stroke down her cheek. ''You look tired.''

''So I've been informed, with annoying regularity.''

''Are you going to let me come in?''

''All right.'' He hadn't kissed her. Johanna had expected it this time, had been prepared for it. As she turned toward the house she suspected that was exactly why he hadn't done it. She spotted the wicker basket and paused as he scooped it up. ''What did you do, bring sandwiches in case I was late?''

''Not exactly.'' He followed her inside. It was precisely as it had been the last time, neat, homey, smelling faintly of potpourri and fresh flowers. They were peonies this time, fat red blooms in a dark blue jar.

Johanna started to slip out of her shoes, caught herself and set down her briefcase.

"Can I get you a drink?"

"Why don't you sit down and I'll fix you one?" He set the basket down next to the jar of flowers. "I'm the one on vacation, remember?"

"I usually just get some coffee, but—"

"Fine. I'll get it."

"But—"

"Relax, Johanna. It'll just take a minute."

He strode off as she stood where she was. As far as she could remember, no one had ever cut her off in the middle of so many sentences. Well, he'd invited himself, she decided. He could heat up the coffee as well as she. And she did want to sit down, for just a minute.

She chose the corner of the sofa and thought she might rest her eyes until she heard Sam coming back. Johanna stifled a yawn, shut her eyes and was asleep in seconds.

She awoke the same way, instantly. Somehow she'd snuggled down and had pulled an afghan up to her chin. Sitting up, Johanna dragged her hands through her hair just before she spotted Sam sitting across from her drinking coffee.

"I'm sorry." She cleared the huskiness out of her voice. "I must have dozed off."

She'd slept like a rock for half an hour. He'd tucked her up himself. "How do you feel?"

"Embarrassed."

He smiled and rose to go to the coffeepot he'd set on a warmer. "Want this now?"

"Yes, thanks."

"You didn't get much sleep last night."

"No." She took the coffee, studying the little painted cup as though it fascinated her. "Neither did you."

"I didn't put in a ten-hour day." He sat beside her. She was up like a spring.

"I'm starving," she said quickly. "There isn't much out in the kitchen, but I can put together a couple of sandwiches."

"I'll give you a hand."

Even as he rose, she was shrugging out of her jacket. "That's all right, it's no trouble." Nervous, she turned the jacket over, spilling out the contents of the pockets. Sam bent over and picked up loose change, a hairpin and what was left of the roll of antacids.

"What do you need these for?"

"Survival." Taking everything from him, she set them on the table.

"You put yourself under too much pressure. How many of these do you take?"

"For heaven's sake, Sam, they're more candy than medicine."

Her defensive tone had his eyes narrowing. Too many, he decided. "I'm entitled to worry about you." When she started to shake her head, he cupped her chin in his hand. "Yes, I am. I love you, Johanna, whether you can deal with it yet or not."

"You're pushing me too fast."

"I haven't even started to push yet."

With her face still caught in his hand, he kissed her. His lips demanded response, nothing timid, nothing cool. She could taste the trace of anger on them, the hint of frustration. Desire, kicked into high gear by other emotions, held sway. If it had been possible, she would have pulled back, ended it then and there. But it wasn't possible.

She touched a hand to his cheek, not even aware that she sought to soothe. As the kiss deepened, she slid her hand up into his hair. His name was like a sigh from her lips to his. Then she was locked close.

It was the whirlwind again, fast and furious. This time it was she who tugged at his shirt, wanting that contact, that intimate, secret feel of flesh against flesh. Her need was a springboard for his. Tangled, groping at buttons, they tumbled onto the couch.

Even last night, in that first burgeoning passion, she hadn't been like this. She trembled as she had trembled before, but now it was anticipation, even impatience, that shivered through her. To be swept away wasn't what she looked for now; to be taken wasn't enough. It had only taken one night for her to realize her own power. Now she was driven to test it again.

He struggled to keep his hands gentle as the insistence of hers had desire clawing at him. Her mouth, open and hungry, sought the taste of him, chest, shoulders, throat, while she tugged at the snap of his jeans and sent his stomach muscles dancing.

"Johanna." As much for her preservation as his

own, he tried to slow the pace. Then her mouth was back on his, silencing him, ripping the last shreds of control.

The last light of day streamed through the windows of a room scented by flowers in a house tucked almost secretly in the hills. As long as he lived he would think of her that way—in soft light, in fresh scents, alone.

She hadn't known she could be like this, so full of need, so desperate to be filled. Heedless, daring, reckless. She felt the teddy he'd slipped so carefully from her the night before tear as he yanked aside the barrier.

Then she captured him, drawing him in, arching high as pleasure arrowed into her. Fast, then faster still, she drove them both in a race for that final dazzling release.

He held on to her, even after her body went lax, after his own emptied. Her shyness had delighted him, lured him, but this Johanna, the one who could flash with white heat, could make him a slave. He wasn't certain what he'd done, he only remembered the grasping, titanic lunge into delirium.

"Did I hurt you?" he murmured.

"No." She was too stunned by her own behavior to notice any bruises. "Did I hurt you?"

He grinned against her throat. "I didn't feel a thing." He tried to shift her to a more comfortable position and spotted the remains of her teddy on the floor. "I owe you some lingerie," he murmured as he lifted it up.

Johanna studied the torn strap and rent seam. Abruptly she began to laugh. She felt like that, torn open, and God only knew what would pour through the holes. "I've never attacked a man before," she managed.

"You can practice on me anytime. Here." He picked up his shirt and slipped it over her shoulders. "I always seem to be lending you a shirt. Johanna, I want you to tell me how you feel. I need you to."

Slowly, hoping to gather up some of her scattered senses, she buttoned the shirt. "There are reasons… I can't talk about them, Sam, but there are reasons why I don't want things to get serious."

"Things already are serious."

He was right. She knew he was right even before she looked into his eyes and felt it. "How serious?"

"I think you know. But I'm willing to spell it out for you again."

She wasn't being fair. It was so important, and sometimes so impossible, to be fair. There was too much she couldn't tell him, she thought. Too much he'd never be able to understand even if she could. "I need time."

"I've got a couple of hours."

"Please."

"All right." It wasn't easy, but he promised himself he'd give her time, even though he felt it slipping away. He tugged on his jeans, then remembered the basket. "I almost forgot. I brought you a present." He plucked up the basket and set it in her lap.

He wasn't going to push. She shot him a quick look

of gratitude, then added a smile. "What, a picnic?" She flipped back the lid, but instead of cold chicken she saw a small dozing kitten. Johanna drew him out and was instantly in love. "Oh, Sam! He's adorable." The kitten mewed sleepily as she rubbed its rust-colored fur against her cheek.

"Blanche had a litter last month." He tickled the kitten's ears.

"Blanche? As in Dubois?"

"Now you're catching on. She's sort of a faded Southern belle who likes to pit the toms against each other. This one's weaned, and there's enough cat food in the basket to get you through about a week."

The kitten climbed down the front of her skirt and began to fight with one of the buttons. "Thank you." Johanna turned to him as he stroked the kitten's head. For the first time, she threw her arms around Sam's neck and hugged him.

Chapter 9

He knew he shouldn't be nervous. It was an excellent production, with a quality script, top-notch casting and a talented director. He'd already seen the rushes, as well as a preview of the press screening. He knew he'd done a good job. But still he paced and watched the clock and wished like hell it was nine.

No, he wished it was eleven and the damn thing was over.

It was worse because Johanna was engrossed in the script Max Heddison had sent him. So Sam was left to worry, nurse the brandy he had no desire for and pace her living room. Even the redheaded kitten, which Johanna had christened Lucy, was too busy to bother with him. She was involved with wrestling a ball of yarn under Johanna's feet.

Sam made himself sit, poked at the Sunday paper, then was up again.

''You could take a walk outside for a change of scenery,'' Johanna suggested from across the room.

''She speaks! Johanna, why don't we go for a ride?''

''I have to finish this. Sam, Michael's a wonderful part for you, a really wonderful part.''

He'd already decided that, but it was Luke, the character who would be exposed to millions of eyes in a matter of thirty minutes, who worried him. If he took on Michael, that would be another worry at another time. ''Yeah. Johanna, it's lousy for your eyes to hold papers that close.''

She moved them back automatically. In less than a minute she had her nose against them again. ''This is wonderful, really wonderful. You're going to take it, aren't you?''

''For a chance to work with Max Heddison, I'd take it if it was garbage.''

''Then you're lucky it shines. God, this scene here, the one on Christmas Eve, just leaves you limp.''

He stopped pacing long enough to glance at her again. She was rereading it as avidly as she'd read it the first time. And the papers were an inch from her face.

''You keep that up, you're going to need glasses.'' He saw the frown come and go and was distracted enough to smile. ''Unless you already do.''

Without bothering to glance up, she turned a page. ''Shut up, Sam, you're breaking my concentration.''

Instead, he pulled the script away and held it at a reasonable distance. ''Read me some dialogue.''

''You already know what it says.'' She made a grab for the script, but he inched it away.

''You can't, can you? Where are your glasses, Johanna?''

''I don't need glasses.''

''Then read me some dialogue.''

She squinted, but the words ran together. ''My eyes are just tired.''

''Like hell.'' He set the script down to take her hands. ''Don't tell me my sensible Johanna's too vain to wear reading glasses.''

''I'm not vain, and I don't need glasses.''

''You'd look cute in them.'' When she pulled her hands away, he made two circles out of his index fingers and thumbs and held them over her eyes. ''Studiously sexy. Dark frames—yes, that would be best. Very conservative. I'd love to take you to bed while you were wearing them.''

''I never wear them.''

''Ah, but you do have them. Where?''

She made a grab for the script, but he blocked her. ''You're just trying to distract yourself.''

''You're right. Johanna, I'm dying in here.''

She softened enough to touch his face. It was something she still did rarely. Automatically he lifted his hand to her wrist and held it there. ''The reviews couldn't have been better, Sam. America waits for nine o'clock with bated breath.''

''And America might be snoring by nine-fifteen.''

"Not a chance." Reaching over, she picked up the remote to turn on the set. "Sit down. We'll watch something else until it starts."

He eased into the chair with her, shifting her until she stretched across his lap. "I'd rather nibble on your ear until it starts."

"Then we'll miss the first scene." Content, she rested her head against his shoulder.

It had been an odd weekend, she thought. He'd stayed with her. After her first unease, they'd fallen into a simple routine that was no routine at all. Lovemaking, sleep, walks, the little chores a house required, even a trip to the market to fuss over fresh vegetables.

She hadn't felt like a producer for forty-eight hours, nor had she thought of Sam as an actor. Or a celebrity. He'd been her lover—or, as he had once put it, her companion. How lovely life would be if it could be that simple. It had been difficult, even for these short two days, to pretend it could be. It had been much less difficult to wish.

She'd changed his life. He didn't know how to explain it, or how to put it into words she might understand, but change it she had. He'd known that for certain when he'd gotten the script.

Max Heddison had been as good as his word. Sam had felt like a first-year drama student being offered the lead in a summer-stock production. It had come through Marv, of course, along with Marv's opinion about potential, the old school and the new, a million five plus percentages. Sam had taken it all in. It was never wise to forget that show business remained a business. Then he had devoured the script.

There was a part of him, a part he hoped would always be there, that could break out in a sweat at the chance to take on a new role. The character of Michael was complex, confused, desperately trying to unravel the mystery of his much-loved, much-detested father. He could already see Max Heddison in that role. Slowly, trying to see the script as a whole, as well as a vehicle, he'd read it again.

And he'd known he wanted to do it. Had to do it.

If Marv could get a million five, fine and dandy. If he could get peanuts and a keg of beer, that was all right, too. But rather than picking up the phone and calling his agent with a go-ahead, he'd bundled up the script and taken it to Johanna.

He'd needed her to read it. He'd needed her opinion, though throughout his career he'd always gone on his own gut instinct. Agent or not, the final decision had always been his. Now that had changed.

In a matter of weeks she'd become entwined with his life, his thoughts, his motives. Though he'd never thought of himself as a solitary person, he'd stopped being alone. She was there now, to share with—the big things, like the script, and the small things, like a new litter of kittens. It might have been true that she still held back from him, but in the last two days he'd seen her relax. Degree by degree, certainly, but he'd been able to see the change. That morning she'd seemed almost used to waking beside him.

He was giving her time, Sam thought as he brushed

his lips over her hair. But he was also making his moves.

"Here come the teasers," Johanna murmured, and he was jerked back to the present. His stomach clenched. He swore at himself, but it tightened anyway, as it did whenever he prepared to watch himself on-screen. He flashed on, wearing only faded jeans, a battered panama and a grin, while the voice-over promised the sultry and the shocking.

"It is a nice chest." She smiled and kissed him on the cheek.

"They spent half the time spraying it so it'd have that nice jungle-fatigue shine. Do women really pant over a sweaty chest?"

"You bet," she told him, and settled down to watch the opening credits.

She was drawn in before the first five minutes were over. Luke drifted into town with two dollars in his pocket, a reputation on his back and an eye for the ladies. She knew it was Sam, pulling bits and pieces of his art together to meld with the writer's, but it rang true. You could almost smell the sweat and boredom of the sleepy little town in Georgia.

During the first commercial he slid down to the floor to give her the chair. He didn't want to ask her now, didn't want to break the rhythm. But he rested a hand on her calf.

For two hours they said nothing. She rose once and came back with cold drinks, but they didn't exchange words. On screen she watched the man she'd slept with, the man she'd loved, seduce another woman.

She watched him talk himself out of one fight and raise his fists for another. He got drunk. He bled. He lied.

But she'd stopped thinking of him as Sam. The man she watched was Luke. She felt the slight pressure of Sam's fingers against her leg and kept her eyes on Luke.

He was irresistible. He was unforgivable.

When the segment ended, it left her hanging and Sarah's roses dying in the bowl.

Sam still said nothing. His instincts told him it was good. It was better than good. It was the best he'd ever done. Everything had fallen into place—the performances, the atmosphere, those lazy two-edged words that had first caught his imagination and his ambition. But he wanted to hear it from her.

Rising, he shifted to sit on the arm of her chair. Johanna, his Johanna, was still frowning at the screen. "How could he do that to her?" she demanded. "How could he use her that way?"

Sam waited a moment, still careful. "He's a user. It's all he knows."

"But she trusts him. She knows he's lied and cheated, but she still trusts him. And he's—"

"What?"

"He's a bastard, but— Damn, there's something compelling about him, something likable. You want to believe he could change, that she could change him." Unsettled, moved, she looked up at him. "What are you grinning at?"

"It worked." He hauled her up and kissed her. "It worked, Johanna."

She backed up enough to breathe. "I didn't tell you how good I thought you were."

"You just did." He kissed her again, then began tugging up her shirt.

"Sam—"

"I suddenly find myself with all this energy—incredible energy. Let me show you." He slid back into the chair, taking her with him.

"Wait a minute." She laughed, then moaned when his hands began to wander. "Sam, give me a minute."

"I've got hours for you. Hours and hours."

"Sam." With one laughing shove, she held him off. "I want to talk to you."

"Is it going to take long?" He tugged at the waistband of her slacks.

"No." To stop him, she framed his face with her hands. "I want to tell you how really exceptional you were. I pretended once that I didn't pay attention to your films, but I have. And you were never better than tonight."

"Thanks. It means a lot coming from you."

She took a deep breath, managing to push herself out of the chair. "You put a lot into that part."

She was leading somewhere. Though he wasn't sure he'd like the destination, he let her take the lead. "A part's not worth anything unless you do. Nothing is."

No, nothing was. "I, ah…I almost forget, when we're like this, who you are. These past few weeks, here, at the ranch, it hasn't been like being with Sam Weaver in capital letters."

Puzzled, he rose with her. "Johanna, you're not going to try to tell me you're intimidated by actors? You've been around the business all your life."

"All my life," she murmured. She didn't want to love him. She didn't want to love anyone, but most particularly not an actor, a movie star, a household name. The trouble was, she already did. "It's not a matter of being intimidated, it's just that it's been easy to forget you're not just an ordinary man who I ran into and grew fond of."

"Fond of," he repeated, drawing out the phrase. "Well, we're improving." He had her by the shoulders. That lazy drawl of a voice could fool you into forgetting how quick he was. "I don't know what the hell this is about, but we'll get to it in a minute. Right now, I want you to look at me. Really look at me, Johanna," he repeated, adding a little shake. "And tell me if you're in love with me."

"I never said—"

"No one knows better than I what you've never said." He drew her a little closer, insisting that her eyes stay on his. "I want to hear it now, and it has nothing to do with how I make my living, what the critics say or how much I'm worth at the box office. Do you love me?"

She started to shake her head but simply couldn't force it to move. How could she lie when he was looking at her, when he was touching her? She drew a deep breath to be certain her voice was calm. "Yes."

He wanted to take her then, just gather her close and hold on. But he knew that not only did he have to hear the words, she had to say them. "Yes, what?"

"Yes, I love you."

He looked at her for a long time. She was trembling a little, so he lowered his head and pressed his lips to her forehead. He didn't know why it was so difficult for her to say.

Not yet. But he was determined to find out.

"That should make things easier."

"But it doesn't," she murmured. "It doesn't change anything."

"We'll talk about it. Let's sit down."

She nodded. She didn't know what there was to say, but there had to be something. Trying to make it seem normal, she started to the front door to lock up for the night. Then she heard the quick report on the evening news.

"Sources report that Carl W. Patterson, respected producer, has suffered a heart attack this evening. Paramedics were summoned to his Beverly Hills estate, which he shares with his fiancée, Toni DuMonde. His condition at this hour remains critical."

"Johanna." Sam laid a hand on her arm. She hadn't gasped or cried out. There were no tears in her eyes. She had simply stopped in her tracks as though she'd run into a wall. "Get your purse. I'll take you to the hospital."

"What?"

"I'll drive you." He switched off the set and went to get her bag himself. "Come on."

She only nodded and let him lead her out.

No one had called her. The oddness of it struck Sam as they rode the elevator up to Cardiac Care. Her father had had a heart attack, and she hadn't been notified.

The year before, when his mother had broken her ankle in a nasty fall on the ice, he'd received three calls in a matter of hours. One from his sister, another from his father and the last from his mother, telling him that his sister and father were fussbudgets.

Nonetheless the ankle had worried him enough to have him do some quick scheduling adjustments so that he could make the trip back east. He'd only had thirty-six hours to spare, but it had been time enough to see his mother for himself, sign her cast and put his mind at rest.

And a broken ankle was a far cry from a heart attack.

Johanna was Patterson's only child, yet she'd had to hear about her father's illness on the eleven-o'clock news. Even if they weren't close, as he'd already deduced, they were family. In Sam's experience, families stuck together in times of crisis.

She'd barely said a word since they'd left the house. He'd tried to comfort her, to offer both hope and support, but she hadn't responded. It seemed to him that she was just going through the motions, pale, a little dazed, but with the automatic control that had slipped effortlessly back into place. He watched her approach the nurse's station. Her hands were steady, her voice was calm and unwavering when she spoke.

"Carl Patterson was admitted this evening. They told me downstairs he's in CCU."

The nurse—sturdy, mid-forties and used to the night shift—barely glanced up. "I'm sorry, we're not permitted to give out patient information."

"He's my father," Johanna said flatly.

The nurse looked up. Reporters and the curious used all kinds of ploys to glean information on the famous. She'd already discouraged a few of them that evening. The woman on the other side of the counter didn't look like a reporter—the nurse prided herself on having a nose for them—but she hadn't been told to expect family, either. Recognizing doubt, Johanna drew out her wallet and identification.

"I'd like to see him, if that's possible, and speak with his doctor."

The nurse felt a stirring of sympathy. Her gaze shifted and locked on Sam. She recognized him, and though seeing him face-to-face would give her something to tell her husband when they passed over the breakfast table, she wasn't overly impressed. After twenty years of nursing in Beverly Hills she was accustomed to seeing celebrities, often naked, sick and vulnerable. But she did remember reading that Sam Weaver was having a fling with Carl Patterson's daughter.

"I'll be happy to page the doctor for you, Miss

Patterson. There's a waiting room down the hall and to the left. Miss Dumonde is already there."

"Thank you." She turned and started down, refusing to think past the moment, refusing to think past the action required to get beyond that moment. She heard a bell ding quietly, almost secretively, then the soft slap of crepe-soled shoes.

The panic was gone, that first thunder of panic that had filled her head when she'd heard the news report. Replacing it was the knowledge that she had to put one foot in front of the other and do whatever needed to be done. She was used to doing such things alone.

"Sam, I have no idea how long this might take. Why don't you go home? I can take a cab back when I'm ready."

"Don't be ridiculous," was all he said.

It was enough, more than enough to cause her breath to hitch. She wanted to turn to him, to press her face against his chest. She wanted to be held, to be passive, to let him handle whatever had to be done. Instead, she turned into the waiting room.

"Sam!" Toni's eyes, already damp, spilled over. She sprang out of her chair and launched herself into his arms. "Oh, Sam, I'm so glad you're here. I've been so frightened. It's a nightmare. I'm just sick with worry, Sam. I don't know what I'll do if Carl dies."

"Pull yourself together." Sam led her back to a chair, then lit one of the cigarettes she'd spilled from a pack onto the table. He stuck it between her fingers. "What did the doctor say?"

"I don't know. He was so technical and grim

faced.'' She held out a hand to a blond man in a dinner jacket. ''I never would have survived this without Jack. He's been a wall, an absolute wall. Hello, Johanna.'' She sniffled into a lacy handkerchief.

''Sam.'' Jack Vandear nodded as he patted Toni's hand. He'd directed two of Patterson's productions and had run into Sam at least a half-dozen times on the party circuit. ''It's been a rough night.''

''So we heard. This is Patterson's daughter.''

''Oh.'' Jack rose and offered a hand.

''I'd like to know what happened.''

''It was horrible.'' Toni looked up at Johanna through an attractive veil of tears. ''Just horrible.''

Jack sent her a look that was three parts impatient, one part sympathetic. He hadn't minded comforting her, but the truth was, he'd come for Carl. It went through his mind that with Sam here, the soggy-eyed Toni could be passed along.

''We were having a small dinner party. Carl looked a bit tired, but I took it to mean he'd been working too hard, as usual. Then it seemed he couldn't get his breath. He collapsed into a chair. He complained of pain in his chest and his arm. We called the paramedics.'' He started to skim over the rest, then decided Johanna looked strong enough to handle it. ''They had to bring him back once.'' At that Toni put up a low, heartbreaking sob and was ignored. ''The doctor said it was a massive coronary. They've been working to stabilize him.''

Her legs were shaking. She could keep her hands steady and her face impassive, but she couldn't stop her legs from trembling. Massive coronary. Darlene, her father's wry and witty third wife, would have said that Carl W. Patterson never did anything halfway.

"Did they tell you his chances?"

"They haven't told us much of anything."

"We've been waiting forever." Toni dabbed at her eyes again, then drew on her cigarette. In her own way, she was fond of Carl. She wanted to marry him even though she knew that divorce would be at the end of the rainbow. Divorce was easy. Death was another matter. "The press was here five minutes after we were. I knew how much Carl would hate having them report this."

Johanna sat and for the first time looked, really looked, at her father's fiancée. Whatever she was, the woman obviously knew Carl. The heart attack was a weakness, and he would detest having it made public knowledge. "I'll handle the press," she said tonelessly. "It might be best if you, both of you," she said, including Jack, "told them as little as possible. Have you seen him?"

"Not since they took him in." Toni took another drag as she looked out into the corridor. "I hate hospitals." After crushing out the cigarette, she began to pleat the handkerchief. The silver sequins on her evening dress sparkled opulently in the dim waiting room. "We were supposed to go to Monaco next week. Carl had some business there, but for the most part it was to be a kind of prehoneymoon. He seemed so...well, so virile." The tears started again when the doctor came into the waiting room.

"Miss DuMonde."

She was up and clutching at both his hands, the picture of the distressed lover barely holding back hysteria. It surprised her to discover it was only half an act. "He's all right. Tell me Carl's all right."

"His condition's stabilized. We're running tests to determine the extent of the damage. He's a strong man, Miss DuMonde, and overall his health seems excellent."

He looked tired, Johanna thought as she studied the doctor. Unbearably tired, but she recognized the truth. She rose as he glanced her way.

"You're Mr. Patterson's daughter?"

"I'm Johanna Patterson. How serious is his condition?"

"I have to tell you it's very serious. However, he's getting the best care possible."

"I'd like to see him."

"For a few moments. Miss DuMonde?"

"He wouldn't want me to see him this way. He'd hate it."

Because Johanna could only agree, she ignored the little stab of resentment and followed the doctor out. "He's sedated," she was told. "And he's being monitored very closely. The next twenty-four hours will tell the tale, but your father's relatively young, Miss Patterson. An incident like this is often a warning, to slow down, to take a hard look at your own mortality."

It had to be said, just once out loud, though she

knew she would get no absolutes. ''Is he going to die?''

''Not if we can help it.'' The doctor pushed open a glass door.

There was her father. She'd lived in his house, eaten his food, obeyed his rules. And she barely knew him. The machines that eased his breathing and monitored his vital signs hummed. His eyes were shut, his face pasty under his tan. He looked old. It occurred to her that she'd never thought of him as old, even when she'd been a child. He'd always been handsome, ageless, virile.

She remembered Toni using that word. Virile. That was so important to Carl. He'd often been described as a man's man—salty tongued, strong shouldered, reckless with women. He'd always been impatient with weaknesses, excuses, illnesses. Perhaps that was why, when he'd reached the middle of his life, the women he'd brought into it had become younger and younger.

He was a hard man, even a cold one, but he'd always been full of life. There was a genius in him, a genius she'd admired as much as she'd feared it. He was an honest man, a man of his word, but never one to give an inch more than he chose.

She touched him once, just a hand over his. It was a gesture she would never have considered making had he been awake.

''Will it happen again?''

''He has an excellent chance of full recovery, if he throws away the cigars, watches his alcohol intake and cuts back on his schedule. There's his diet, of course," the doctor went on, but Johanna was already shaking her head.

"I can't imagine him doing any of those things."

"People often do what others can't imagine after they end up in CCU. It'll be his choice, of course, but he's not a stupid man."

"No, he's not." She removed her hand. "We'll need a press release. I can take care of that. When will he be awake?"

"You should be able to talk to him in the morning."

"I'd appreciate a call if there's any change before then. I'll leave my number at the nurse's station."

"I should be able to tell you more in the morning." The doctor pushed open the door again. "You'd do well to get some rest yourself. A recovering cardiac patient can be wearing."

"Thank you." Alone, she started back down the hall. In self-defense, she blocked out the image of her father in the hospital bed. The moment she walked back in, Toni was up and grabbing both her hands.

"How is he, Johanna? Tell me the truth, tell me everything."

"He's resting. The doctor's very optimistic."

"Thank God."

"Carl will have to make some adjustments—diet, work load, that sort of thing. You'll be able to see him tomorrow."

"Oh, I must look a wreck." The need to check was so ingrained that Toni was already reaching for her compact. "I'll have to take care of that by tomorrow.

I wouldn't want him to see me with my eyes all red and my hair a fright.''

Again, because it was true, Johanna held back her sarcasm. ''He won't wake up until tomorrow, according to the doctor. I'm going to handle the press—through a hospital spokesman, I think—and make certain his publicist has time to work up a statement. It might be a day or two before he's able to make those decisions for himself.''

She wavered there a moment, trying to imagine her father unable to make any decision. ''The important thing for you to do is to keep him calm. Go home and get some rest. They'll call if there's any change before morning.''

''How about you?'' Sam asked her when Jack had taken Toni down the corridor. ''Are you all right?''

''Yes, I'm fine.''

Wanting to judge for himself, he took her chin in his hand. There was something about the eyes, he thought. More than shock, certainly different than grief. Big secrets, he decided. Big fears. ''Talk to me, Johanna.''

''I've told you everything.''

''About your father's condition.'' Though she tried to draw away, he held on. ''I want to know about yours.''

''I'm a little tired. I'd like to go home.''

''Okay.'' Better, he thought, that they hash this, whatever it was, out at home. ''We'll go back. But I'm staying with you.''

''Sam, there's no need.''

''There's every need. Let's go home.''

Chapter 10

It was after one a.m. when they arrived at Johanna's house, but she went straight to the phone. With a pen in one hand, she began to flip through her address book. "It shouldn't take long for me to set this up," she told Sam, "but you don't have to wait up."

"I'll wait." There were things that had to be said, and he wanted them said before she had a chance to build the barricades again. Though she looked steady, perhaps too steady, he was coming to understand her. Still, he left her alone as she began to dial.

There was little enough she could do. She was certain her father would tolerate only the slightest interference from her, but he would want his people informed. Johanna fed information to his publicist, then hashed out a simple, straightforward press release.

While she was calming her father's assistant and

making sure that the daily business of Patterson Productions would run as smoothly as possible, Sam handed her a mug. Grateful, Johanna sipped, expecting coffee. Instead she tasted the soothing herbal tea she'd bought on impulse and brewed occasionally after a particularly long day.

"I'll be able to tell you more tomorrow, Whitfield. No, whatever can't be handled by you or another member of the staff will have to be canceled. That would appear to be your problem, wouldn't it?"

Across the room, Sam had no choice but to smile at her tone. As producers went, he'd never heard better.

"Where's Loman? Well, call him back." She made a quick notation on a pad. "Yes, that's right, but I'm sure he'll be giving you instructions himself in a couple of days. You'll have to check with the doctor on that, but I don't think you'll be able to discuss that or anything else with Carl for at least forty-eight hours." Her voice changed, went frigid. "That's not really the issue here, Whitfield. You'll have to consider Carl unavailable until further notice. No, I won't take the responsibility, you will. That's what you're paid for."

She hung up, incensed by the man's insensitivity. "Idiot," she muttered as she picked up her tea again. "His main concern is that Carl insisted on supervising the editing of *Fields of Fire*, and the heart attack is going to put the project behind schedule."

"Are you finished?"

Still frowning, she skimmed down her notes. "I don't think there's any more I can do."

"Come and sit down." He waited until she'd joined him on the sofa, then poured more tea into her cup from the pot he'd brewed. Sensing tension even before he touched her, Sam began to massage her shoulders. "It's hard, only being able to wait."

"Yes."

"You handle yourself well, Johanna."

She sipped tea and stared straight ahead. "I had a good teacher."

"Tell me about your father."

"I told you everything the doctor told me."

"I don't mean that." She was tensing up again, even as he massaged the muscles. "Tell me about him, about you and him."

"There's really nothing to tell. We've never been particularly close."

"Because of your mother?"

She went stiff at that. "What does my mother have to do with it?"

"I don't know. You tell me." He'd been shooting in the dark, but he wasn't surprised that he'd hit the target. "Johanna, you don't have to be a gossip buff to know that your parents divorced when you were, what—four?"

"I'd just turned five." It still hurt. No matter how often she told herself it was foolish, even unhealthy, the child's pain and confusion leaked into the woman. "That's history, Sam."

He didn't think so. Instinct told him it was as much a part of the present as he was. "She went back to

England,'' he prompted. ''And your father retained custody of you.''

''He didn't have much choice.'' The bitterness leaked out. She made a conscientious and difficult effort to bury it again. ''It really isn't relevant.''

''I'm not Whitfield, Johanna,'' he murmured. ''Humor me.''

She was silent for so long he decided to try another tactic. Then she sighed and began. ''My mother went back to England to try to pick up the stage career she felt she'd sacrificed when she'd married. I didn't have a place there.''

''You must have missed her.''

''I got over it.''

He didn't think so. ''I don't suppose divorce is ever easy on a kid, but it's got to be worse when one of the parents ends up several thousand miles away.''

''It was better that way, for everyone. They always fought terribly. Neither of them were happy with their marriage or...'' She trailed off before she could say what was in her mind. *Me. Neither of them wanted me.* ''With the situation,'' she finished.

''You'd have been pretty young to have known that.'' He'd begun to get a picture of five-year-old Johanna, dealing with the inexplicable ups and downs of a rocky marriage.

''You don't have to be very old to recognize turmoil. In any case, my mother explained it to me. She sent me a telegram from the airport.'' Her tea had gone cold, but she sipped automatically.

A telegram's just like a letter, the pretty young

maid had told Johanna. If the maid hadn't been new, the telegram would have been handed over to Carl and disposed of. But the maid had been avid to know the contents, and more than willing to help Johanna struggle over the words.

> My darling girl. I'm devastated to leave you like this, but I have no choice. My situation, my life, has become desperate. Believe me, I have tried, but I've come to understand that divorce and a complete separation from what was, is the only way I can survive. I despise myself for leaving you in your father's hands, but for now mine are too frail to hold on to you. One day you'll understand and forgive. Love. Mother.

She remembered it still, word for word, though at the time all she had understood was that her mother was leaving her because she wasn't happy.

Sam was staring at her, amazed that she could be so matter-of-fact. "She sent you a telegram?"

"Yes. I wasn't old enough to fully understand, but I caught the drift. She was miserably unhappy and desperate to find a way out."

Bitch. The word rose up in his throat, hotly, and he had to swallow it. He couldn't imagine anyone being so self-absorbed and selfish as to say goodbye to her only child by telegram. He tried to remember that Johanna had told him how her mother had taken her to feed the ducks, but he couldn't equate the two acts with the same woman.

"It must have been rough on you." He put his arm around her, as if he could find a way to protect her from what had already happened.

"Children are resilient." She rose, knowing that if he offered comfort she would break. She hadn't broken in over twenty years. "She did what she had to do, but I don't think she was ever happy. She died about ten years ago."

Suicide. He swore at himself for not remembering it before. Glenna Howard, Johanna's unhappy mother, had never quite achieved the sparkling comeback she'd sought. Disappointment had been eased by pills and alcohol until she'd taken a deliberate overdose of both.

"I'm sorry, Johanna. Losing her twice. It must have been hell for you."

"I never knew her that well." She reached for her tea again, for something to keep her hands busy. "And it was a long time ago."

He went to her, though she turned away. Patient but determined, he drew her back. "I don't think things like that ever stop hurting. Don't back off from me, Johanna."

"There's no use dredging all this up."

"I think there is." He took her shoulders, firmly enough to let her know he wasn't easing off. "I've wondered all along why you held off. I thought at first it was because you'd had a bad experience with another man. But it goes back farther than that, and deeper."

She looked at him then, her face set but her eyes

desperate. She'd said too much, more than she'd ever said before. In saying it, the memories became all too clear. "I'm not my mother."

"No." He lifted a hand to brush at her hair. "No, you're not. And you're not your father either."

"I don't even know if he *is* my father."

The moment it was said, she went white. The hands she had fisted unballed and went limp. Not once in all of her life had she said it out loud. The knowledge had been there, locked tight but never completely silent. Now she heard her words echo back to her and was afraid, terribly afraid, she'd be ill.

"Johanna, what are you talking about?"

His voice was calm and quiet, but it shot like a bullet through her shock. "Nothing, nothing. I'm upset. I'm tired. Tomorrow's going to be a difficult day, Sam. I need to sleep."

"We both know you're too wired to sleep." He could feel the violent shudders begin as he held her there. "And you will be until you get the rest of it out. Tell me about your father, Johanna. About Carl."

"Will you leave me alone?" There were tears in her voice that only frightened her more. She could feel the walls cracking, the foundation giving way, but didn't have the strength to shore it up again. "For God's sake, can't you see I've had all I can manage? I don't want to talk about my mother. I don't want to talk about him. He could be dying." The tears spilled out, and she knew she'd lost. "He could be dying, and I should feel something. But I don't. I don't even know who he is. I don't know who I am."

She fought him, pushing away as he gathered her to him, swearing at him as he held her there. Then she collapsed in a storm of weeping.

He didn't offer comforting words. He hadn't a clue which ones to choose. Instead, he lifted her into his arms. With her sobs muffled against his throat, he sat down, cradling her to him. Sam stroked her hair and let her purge herself. He hadn't known it was possible to hold that many tears inside.

She felt ill. Her throat and eyes burned, her stomach heaved. Even when the tears were over, the raw, sick feeling remained. Her strength had been sapped, as if someone had pulled a plug and let it drain away. She didn't object when Sam shifted her, nor when he rose. He was going away. It was something she accepted even as her own battered heart suffered another crack.

Then he was sitting beside her again, placing a snifter in her hands. "It might help some," he murmured. "Take it slow."

If there'd been any left, more tears would have fallen. She nodded, took a sip of brandy and let it coat the raw wounds.

"I was always in awe of him," Johanna began without looking up. "I don't know even now if I loved him as a child, but he was always the largest and most important figure in my life. After my mother left—" she paused to sip again "—after my mother left I was terrified that he'd leave, too, or send me away. I didn't understand then how important it was to him to keep his private affairs private. The public could accept and be entertained by his romances and marriages, but if he'd shipped off his only child without a blink, they'd have taken a different view. No one forgot that he'd been married to Glenna Howard and that she'd had his child. No one except him."

How could she explain how lost she had been? How confusing it had been to see her father entertain other women as though her mother had never existed.

"When he married again it was horrible. There was a big, splashy wedding, lots of photographers, microphones, strangers. They dressed me up and told me to smile. I hated it—the stares and innuendos about my mother. The whispers about her. He could ignore it. He'd always had that kind of presence, but all I could think was that my mother was being replaced with someone I didn't even know. And I had to smile."

Insensitive, selfish idiots. Even as he thought it, he tightened his arms around her. "Wasn't there anyone else…any family?"

"His parents had died years before. I remember hearing or being told somewhere along the line that he'd been raised by his grandmother. By that time she was gone, too. I'd never met her. I had what you'd call a governess, who would have literally died for my father. Women react that way to him," she said wearily. "Nothing could have stopped it—my being in the wedding was important. Impressions, photo opportunities, that kind of thing. After it was over, I didn't see him again for three months. He was spending a lot of time in Italy."

"You stayed behind."

"I was in school." She pulled a hand through her

hair, then clasped them in her lap. "It was perfectly legitimate for him to leave me behind with my tutors and instructors. In any case, his second wife had little tolerance for children. Few of his liaisons did."

Because she could feel his sympathy reaching out to her, she shook her head. "I was happier here. I spent a lot of time with the Heddisons. They were wonderful to me."

"I'm glad for that." He drew her hand into his. "Go on."

"It was after his second divorce, when he was involved with…it doesn't matter who. Anyway, I was out of school and feeling sorry for myself. I went up to his room. I don't even know why, except to be there, to see if I could solve the mystery of my father. I solved it.

"I'd always felt inadequate, awkward around him. There seemed to be something lacking in me that kept him from loving me the way that he should. He had this wonderful old desk in his room, one with all these fascinating cubbyholes and compartments. He was away again, so I didn't have to worry about him catching me poking around. I found letters. Some of them were from his women, and I was old enough to be embarrassed, so I put them away again. Then I found one from my mother. An old one, one she'd written right after she'd gone back to England. Holding it was like seeing her again. Sometimes I hadn't been able to bring the picture of her into my head, but the minute I had that letter, I saw her exactly as she'd been. God, she was beautiful, so fragile and haunted. I could even hear her voice, that trained, extraordinary voice. I'd loved her so much."

He took the snifter from her and set it on the table. "You read the letter?"

"I wish to God I hadn't." She squeezed her eyes shut for a moment, but it was now, as it had been then, too late to turn back. "I was so hungry for anything she'd touched, any part of her, that I didn't even realize at first when I was reading. She must have been furious when she wrote it. It came across, the anger, the bitterness, the need to punish. I'd known, even as a child, that their marriage hadn't been smooth. But until I'd read the letter I'd had no idea how much hate had been built up between them."

"People say things they don't mean, or at least things that shouldn't be said under those kind of circumstances."

"Well, she's gone, has been gone, and there's no way of knowing if she meant what she'd said. No way for me to know, no way for my father—for Carl to know."

Her mouth was dry, but she no longer wanted the brandy. Johanna pressed her lips together and continued. "She brought up every hurt, every broken promise, every real or imagined infidelity. Then she brought out the big guns. Leaving me with him was the biggest payback she could think of. She was saddling him with a child who wasn't even his own. Not that he could ever prove it, or that she would ever tell him who had fathered the child he'd given a name to. There was, of course, the possibility that the child was his, but… She wished him a lifetime of hell wondering. And because I read the letter, she gave me the same.''

Sam stared out the darkened window for a long time. The rage was so keen, so close to the surface, he was afraid to speak. She'd been a child, innocent, helpless. And no one had given a damn.

''Did you ever speak to him about it?''

''No, there was no reason to. He didn't change toward me. I was well tended, well educated and allowed to pursue my own interests as long as I didn't embarrass him.''

''They didn't deserve you. Either of them.''

''It doesn't matter,'' she said wearily. ''I'm not a child anymore.'' Nor had she been from the moment she'd read the letter.

''It matters to me.'' He cupped her face in his hands. ''You matter to me, Johanna.''

''I never meant to tell you, or anyone. But now that I have, you must understand why I can't let what's between us go too far.''

''No.''

''Sam—''

''What I understand is that you had a lousy childhood, and that things went on around you that no kid should ever be a part of. And I understand that there're bound to be scars.''

''Scars?'' She gave a quick, brittle laugh as she rose. ''Don't you see, my mother was ill. Oh, it was kept quiet, out of the press, but I managed to dig it up. She was in and out of sanitariums the last few years of her life. Manic depression, instability, alcohol addiction. And the drugs..." Johanna pressed her fingers to her eyes and struggled to get a grip on herself. "She didn't raise me, and I can't be sure who my father is, but she was my mother. I can't forget that, or what I may have inherited from her."

He rose slowly. His first instinct was to tread carefully, but then he realized it was the wrong one. She needed to be brought up short, and quickly. "It's not like you to be melodramatic, Johanna."

His words had exactly the effect he'd hoped for. Anger flashed into her eyes and whipped color back into her cheeks. "How dare you say that to me?"

"How dare you stand there and make up insufficient excuses why you can't commit to me?"

"They're not excuses, they're facts."

"I don't give a damn who your mother was, or your father. I'm in love with you, Johanna. Sooner or later you're going to have to swallow it and take the next step."

"I've told you all along that it couldn't lead anywhere. Now I'm telling you why. And that's only half of it. My half."

"There's more?" He hooked his thumbs in his pockets and rocked back on his heels. "Okay, give me the rest."

"You're an actor."

"Right the first time, but you're not going to set any bells ringing with that answer."

"I've been around actors all of my life," she continued, searching for patience. "I understand the strain and demands of the job, the impossibility, especially for a talented actor, of maintaining a private life that keeps anything truly private. And I know that even with the best of intentions and effort relationships suffer. If I believed in marriage—which I don't—I still wouldn't believe in marriage to an actor.''

''I see.'' It was difficult enough not to be angry with her, and it was impossible not to be furious with the people who had had the major hand in forming her beliefs. ''Then you're saying that because I'm an actor—worse yet, a good one—I'm too big a risk.''

''I'm saying that what there is between us can't go any farther.'' She stopped, wanting to be strong. ''And that if you don't want to see me again, I'll understand.''

''Will you?'' For a moment he studied her, as though he were considering it. A few steps away, Johanna prepared herself. She'd known it would hurt when it ended, but even her worst fears hadn't come close to this. When he crossed to her, she made herself look in his eyes. She could read nothing in them.

''You're an idiot, Johanna.'' He yanked her against him so hard that her breath whistled out in surprise. ''Do you think I can turn my feelings for you on and off? Damn it, you do, don't you? I can see it in your face. Well, I'm not going to step neatly out of your life, and if you think you can push me out, you're going to be disappointed.''

''I don't want you to go.'' Tears clouded her eyes,

though she'd thought she was through with them. "I just don't think—"

"Then don't think." He swept her up into his arms. "You do too much thinking."

She didn't protest when he carried her upstairs. She was through with arguing, with excuses, with reasons. Perhaps it was a weakness to want to be taken care of, but she couldn't find the strength to stand on her own tonight. She didn't want to think. He was right about that. She didn't want to think at all for whatever hours of the night were left. For once, feelings took no effort and she could let them dominate.

She needed him. If she hadn't been so drained it would have frightened her to realize it.

The bedroom was dark, but he didn't turn on the light. The fragrances from her garden were carried up and through the windows on the night air. In silence he lay her on the bed and sat beside her.

There was too much to say to speak at all just yet. He'd once thought her cool, tough and self-sufficient. That woman had attracted and intrigued him. Intrigued him enough, Sam thought, to have caused him to dig deeper. The more he knew about her, the more layers he'd discovered.

She was tough, in the best sense of the word. She'd taken the blows, the disappointments, and had worked her way through them. Some people, he knew, would have buckled under, found a crutch or given up. But Johanna, his Johanna, had carved a place for herself and had made it work.

Underneath the toughness he'd found passion. He'd

sensed and now was certain that it had gone untapped. Whether it was fate, blind luck or timing, he'd found the key that had released it. He wouldn't allow it to be locked again, or to be opened by anyone but himself.

Beneath the passion was a touching shyness. A sweetness that was a miracle in itself, considering her childhood and the disillusionments she'd faced so early in life.

Now, beneath all the rest, he'd found a core of fragility. He was determined to protect that vulnerability. And it was to the fragile Johanna that he would make love tonight.

In kindness as much as love. In compassion, as well as desire.

Softly, his touch barely a whisper, he brushed her hair away from her face. There were tears still drying on her cheeks. With his fingertips, he wiped them away. He wouldn't be able to prevent more from being shed, but he would do whatever he could to see that she didn't shed them alone.

He kissed her once, then twice, where the tears had lain. Then he kissed her again, tenderly. Night shadows shifted across her face, but he could see her eyes, half closed with fatigue but very aware, as she watched him.

"Do you want to sleep?" he asked her.

"No." She put her hand over his. "No, I don't want to sleep. And I don't want you to go."

"Then relax." He brought her hand to his lips. His

eyes, so dark and intense, seemed to absorb everything she was. "And let me love you."

It was just that easy.

She hadn't known love could be soothing. He hadn't shown her that before. Tonight, when her emotions were raw and her self-esteem at its lowest ebb, he showed her another side of desire. A desire to please, and one to nurture. A desire to have, and one to heal. He touched her as though she alone mattered.

He drew off her shirt so that the material trailed over her skin before it was discarded, but he didn't take what she would have given. With his eyes on hers, he removed his own. When she reached for him, he took her hands, pressing them both to his lips.

He undressed her slowly, carefully, as though she were asleep and he didn't want to disturb her. The tenderness of it brought its own strange ache. Though she was naked and totally open to him, he contented himself with long, lazy kisses and the feel of her hair under his hands.

Her skin looked so white against the dark spread. He ran his hand down her arm, watching the movement. The moon had waned to a thin crescent, shedding little light, but he already knew her so well. Still, he traced her face with his fingertip, outlining her features for his own pleasure.

He'd never treated her like this before. Johanna closed her eyes as she began to drift into contentment. Even through passion and hunger, he'd always shown her an unexpected sweetness. But this…this was what it meant to be cherished. This was the way promises were given when they were meant to be kept. It made her eyes swim and her heart break, just a little, at the beauty of it.

He felt stronger somehow, being gentle. He'd never wanted her more than he did at this moment, and yet he had never felt less need to rush. The passion was there, and growing, but it was filled with a need to comfort.

Time passed unnoticed, unheeded. In the darkest hours of the morning, he led her gently higher.

The rhythm of her heart beat under his lips, fast, unsteady, but not yet desperate. Her arms were around him, holding him close, but there was no urgent press of fingers. She moved with him, willing to let him set the pace, grateful that he had understood, even if she hadn't, that she needed care.

Had she ever noticed how strong he was? How the muscles of his back and shoulders flexed and rippled with his movements? She'd touched him before, held him just like this, but each time she had she'd been driven close to the edge. Now the ride was quiet and unhurried, like floating on a raft on a still lake.

Inspired by love, she sought to give him the same gentleness he showed her. Her touch was easy, her demands few. She heard in the murmur of her name that he felt as she did. They might never come together so perfectly, so unselfishly, again.

Her sigh was quiet as she opened for him. They merged without heat but with much warmth.

Later, much later, she lay beside him, sleepless as the sky began to lighten.

Chapter 11

He could have strangled her. When Sam woke, he found himself alone in bed and the house empty. In the bath, her still-damp towel hung tidily over the rail. The room carried, very faintly, the scent of her. The clothes he'd removed from her the night before had been put away. Downstairs, he saw that her briefcase was gone and the flowers freshened. Her phone machine had been cleared of messages and reset.

In crisis or in control, Johanna was always organized.

He was sure he would strangle her.

In the kitchen he found the glasses they'd used the night before conscientiously rinsed and draining. Propped against the coffeepot was a note in Johanna's neat handwriting. *I didn't want to wake you. I needed to get to the hospital early, then to the studio. The coffee's fresh.*

She'd written something else, crossed it out, then signed the note simply *Johanna.*

His mother could have written it, Sam thought as he skimmed it a second time. Only she might have added, *Leave the kitchen the way you found it.* Damn it, Johanna.

He stood in the kitchen dressed only in jeans and tossed her note onto the counter. No one would ever accuse Johanna of not having her feet firmly on the ground. But there were times when it was better, even necessary, to keep them planted beside someone else's. She still needed to accept that he was that someone else. He'd been sure he'd gotten through, but he'd forgotten how incredibly stubborn she could be.

Absently he bent down and picked up the kitten, who was doing figure eights between his legs. She wasn't hungry. Johanna had left Lucy well taken care of, with a full dish in the corner. She only wanted some affection. Most creatures did, Sam mused as he stroked her fur. Apparently that wasn't enough to make Johanna purr and settle trustingly in his arms.

It looked as if he still had a fight on his hands. Sam gave the kitten's ears a last scratch before he set her down again. He could be hardheaded, as well.

She was thinking of him. Sam would have been amazed if he had known how hard and long she'd struggled over those few brief lines she'd left him. She'd wanted to thank him for being with her and to tell him how much it had meant to her that he'd been kind and understanding when she'd been down for the count. She'd wanted to tell him that she loved him in a way she had never before and would never again love. But the words had seemed so empty and inadequate on paper.

It was hard to need someone, really need him, when you'd spent your entire life making certain you could handle anything and everything on your own. How would he have felt if he'd known how close she'd come to waking him and asking him to come with her because she'd been dreading the thought of facing this day alone? She couldn't ask, any more than she could forget that she now had no secrets from him, physically or emotionally. Dealing with this day alone was imperative if she was ever to face another without him.

The nurse on duty this morning was younger and more approachable than the one the night before. She told Johanna that her father was resting comfortably, then asked her to have a seat until Dr. Merritt could be located.

Johanna chose the waiting room because the corridors seemed so public. She'd managed to evade the reporters outside but didn't want to take any chances on having to deal with any who'd been clever enough to sneak in.

Inside, an elderly woman and a boy of about twenty sat half dozing on a sofa, hands linked. On the wall-mounted television a morning show flashed cheerfully, showing a demonstration of gourmet cooking.

Johanna moved to a table where twin pots of coffee and hot water sat on warmers. She bypassed the tea bags, ignored the little bags of powdered cream and sugar and poured a cup black. As she took the first sip, she heard the break for local news.

Carl W. Patterson was the top story. Dispassionately she listened to the newscaster recite the press release she and the publicist had written over the phone the night before. It gave a great deal more information on Carl's career than it did on his illness, and she knew Carl would have given it his nod of approval. The report ended by saying that Toni DuMonde, Patterson's housemate and fiancée, could not be reached for comment.

At least the woman wasn't a fool, Johanna thought as she chose a seat. There were some, she knew, who would have spilled their guts to the press and enjoyed the melodrama. And if Toni had, Johanna imagined, Carl would have cut whatever strings tied them together as soon as he was able.

"Miss Patterson?"

Johanna rose automatically. The moment she saw the doctor, her calm fled. The nurse had said Carl was resting comfortably, but that was hospital talk. She fought back the touch of fear and offered her hand.

"Dr. Merritt, I hope I'm not too early." Or too late.

"No, as a matter of fact your father's awake and stable. As a matter of precaution we'll keep him in CCU for another twenty-four hours. If he continues to progress, he can be moved to a private room."

"The prognosis?"

"The prognosis is good, if he cooperates. A lighter work load is essential. How much influence do you have over him?"

Her smile was almost amused. "None at all."

"Well, then, he might find himself confined to the hospital a day or two longer than he's counting on." Merritt took off his glasses to polish the lenses on the hem of his coat. "As I explained to you last night, certain adjustments will have to be made. Mr. Patterson will have to realize that, like the rest of us, he has certain limitations."

"I understand. And I wish you the best of luck explaining the same to him."

"I've already spoken to him briefly." Merritt slid the glasses back on his nose. He gave Johanna a smile that was gone almost before it formed. "At the moment, it's more important to reassure him. We'll speak about future care soon enough. He's asked to see Miss DuMonde and someone named Whitfield. It may be good for him to see his fiancée, but—"

"Don't worry about Whitfield. I'll handle it."

Merritt only nodded. He'd already decided Patterson's daughter had a good head on her shoulders. "Your father's a fortunate man. If he's sensible, there isn't any reason why he shouldn't lead a full and productive life."

"Can I see him?"

"Fifteen minutes only. He needs calm and quiet."

She was both as she walked into the small curtained-off room in CCU. Her father was as he'd been the night before, eyes closed, wired to machines. But his color was better. She stood by the bed, studying him, until his eyes flickered open.

It took him a moment to focus. It occurred to Johanna that this was certainly the longest their eyes had ever held. When she saw recognition in his, she bent to brush his cheek with hers.

"Good morning," she said, keeping her voice carefully neutral. "You gave us a scare."

"Johanna." He took her hand, surprising her. He'd never been quite so alone or quite so weak. "What have they told you?"

Why, he's frightened, she thought, and felt a stirring of sympathy. It had never occurred to her that he could be frightened. "That you're a fortunate man," she said briskly. "And that if you're sensible the world will still see quite a number of Carl W. Patterson productions."

It was exactly the right thing to say. She hadn't realized she'd known him so well. "Damned inconvenient time for my body to set booby traps for me." He glanced around the room, and the moment of closeness vanished.

"The hospital's contacting Toni," Johanna told him. "I'm sure she'll be here soon."

Satisfied, Carl looked back at his daughter. "They say they intend to keep me strapped down here another day."

"Yes. More if you make a fuss."

"I've work to do that can't be done from a hospital bed."

"Fine. I'll tell them to release you. You might be

able to edit *Fields of Fire* before you keel over again.''

His expression changed from impatience to astonishment, then to something she'd rarely seen directed at her—amusement. ''I suppose I could spare a few days. But I don't want that ham-handed Whitfield to get his hands on it.''

''I've sent for Loman.'' His expression tightened immediately, and he became the cool, disapproving man she'd lived with most of her life. ''I'm sorry if I overstepped my bounds, but when I contacted Whitfield last night and saw how things were, I thought you'd prefer Loman.''

''All right, all right.'' He waved away her apology. ''I do prefer Loman. Whitfield has his place, but God knows it's not in an editing room. What about the press?''

He'd forgotten to be frightened. Johanna thought, and bit back a sigh. It was business as usual. ''Under control. Your publicist issued a release this morning and will update it as becomes necessary.''

''Good, good. I'll meet with Loman this afternoon. Set that up for me, Johanna.''

''No.''

The effort of making plans had already sapped his strength, and that only made him more furious. ''No? What the hell do you mean, no?''

''It's out of the question.'' Her voice was calm, which pleased her. There had been a time he could have used that tone and made her quake. ''It should be all right in a day or two, once you're in a private room and stronger."

"I run my own life."

"No one's more aware of that than I."

"If you've got some idea about taking over while I'm down—"

The fury leaped into her eyes and stopped him cold. He'd never seen that look before, or the power behind it. Or, if it had been there, he'd never bothered to look. "I don't want anything from you. I did once, but I learned to live without it. Now, if you'll excuse me, I've got a show of my own to produce."

"Johanna." She started to whip the curtain aside. It was the tremor in his voice that stopped her.

"Yes?"

"I apologize."

Another first, she thought, and made herself turn back. "All right. The doctor told me not to stay long, and I've probably already overtired you."

"I almost died."

He said it like an old man, an old, frightened man. "You're going to be fine."

"I almost died," he repeated. "And though I can't say my life flashed in front of my eyes, I did screen a few clips." He closed his eyes. It infuriated him that he had to stop just to gather the strength to speak. "I remember getting in the back of the limo—on my way to the airport, I think. You were standing on the steps with that dog Max forced on me. You looked as though you wanted to call me back."

Johanna didn't remember that particular incident

because there'd been so many of them. "If I had, would you have stayed?"

"No." He sighed, not with regret but with acknowledgement. "Work has always come first. I've never been able to put a marriage together the way I could a film. Your mother—"

"I don't want to talk about my mother."

Carl opened his eyes again. "She could have loved you more if she'd hated me less."

It hurt. Even having known it all these years, it hurt to hear it said aloud. "And you?"

"Work has always come first," he repeated. He was tired, much too tired for regrets or apologies. "Will you come back?"

"Yes. I'll come back after the taping."

He was asleep before she drew the curtain aside.

Max Heddison's estate was as distinguished and well-tended as the man. Sam was ushered through the thirty-room house the actor had purchased a quarter of a century before. On the terrace were thickly padded chaises and half a dozen wicker chairs that invited company to spread out and be comfortable. An aging golden retriever was curled up in one, snoring.

In the sparkling L-shaped pool beyond the terrace, Max Heddison was doing laps. Across the sloping lawn, partially hidden by squared-off hedges, were tennis courts. To the east, identifiable only by a distant flag, was a putting green.

A houseboy in a spotless white jacket offered Sam his choice of chairs. Sun or shade. Sam chose the sun.

As he watched, Sam counted ten laps, cleanly stroked and paced, and wondered idly how many Max had done before he'd arrived. The official bio said Max was seventy. It could have taken off fifteen years and still have been believable.

He accepted coffee and waited while Max hauled himself out of the pool.

"Good to see you again." Max dragged a towel over his hair before he shrugged into a robe.

"I appreciate you letting me drop by this way." Sam had risen automatically.

"Sit down, boy, you make me feel like a king about to be deposed. Had breakfast?"

"Yes, thanks."

The moment Max sat, the houseboy was back with a tray of fresh fruit and dry toast. "Thank you, Jose. Bring Mr. Weaver some juice. Straight from our own oranges," he told Sam. "I figure it only costs me about three dollars a glass." With a grin, he dug into his breakfast. "My wife's the health nut. No additives, no preservatives. Enough to drive a man to drink. She's at her morning class, which means I'll have time to sneak a cigarette before she gets back."

Sam's juice was served in cut crystal. He sipped, letting Max fall into a conversation about pruning and organic sprays.

"Well, I don't suppose you came here to discuss fertilizers." Max pushed his tray aside and reached in his pocket for a pack of unfiltered cigarettes. "What did you think of the script?"

"Who do I have to kill to get the part?"

Max chuckled and drew in smoke with great pleasure. "I'll hold that in reserve. You know, I don't care too much for today's moviemakers—money-makers, I should say. In the old days, men like Mayer might have been despots, but they knew how to make films. Today they're a bunch of damn accountants running around with ledgers and red pencils—more interested in profit than entertainment. But my gut tells me we might be able to give them both with this one."

"It made my palms sweat," Sam said simply.

"I know the feeling." Max settled back, regretting only that his cigarette was nearly done. "I've been making movies since before you were born. Over eighty of them, and only a handful ever made me feel that way."

"I want to thank you for thinking of me."

"No need for that. Ten pages into the script and your name popped into my head. It was still there when I finished." He crushed out his cigarette, sighing. "And, of course, I went straight to my consultant with it—my wife." He grinned, drank more coffee and thought it a pity his wife had ordered decaf. "I've relied on her opinion for over forty years."

It made Sam remember how important it had been for him to hear Johanna's.

"She finished it, handed it back to me and said if I didn't do it I was crazy. Then she told me to get young Sam Weaver to play Michael. By the way, she admires your...build," Max said. "My sainted wife's an earthy woman."

The grin came quickly and lingered. ''I'd love to meet her.''

''We'll arrange it. Did I mention that Kincaid's been signed to direct?''

''No.'' Sam's interest was piqued again. ''You don't get much better.''

''Thought the same myself.'' Max watched Sam thoughtfully from under his bushy white brows. ''Patterson's producing.'' He saw Sam's eyes sharpen and reached casually for more coffee. ''Problem?''

''There might be.'' He wanted the part, more than he could remember wanting any other. But not at the cost of his still-too-tenuous relationship with Johanna.

''If you're concerned about Jo-Jo, I don't think it's necessary. The complete professional, our Jo-Jo. And she respects her father's work.'' He saw the dull anger in Sam's eyes and nodded. ''So, it's gotten that far, has it? I wasn't sure Johanna would ever let anyone get that close.''

''It wasn't so much a matter of choice as circumstance.'' He hadn't come just to talk about the script. When Sam had called to make the appointment, he'd already decided to dig for whatever Max might have buried. ''I take it you haven't heard that Patterson had a heart attack last night.''

''No.'' The concern came automatically. The friendship went back a quarter of a century. ''I haven't so much as flicked the news on today. I go for days at a time without it. How bad?''

''Bad enough. As far as I know, he's stable. Johanna went back to the hospital this morning.''

"He lives hard," Max mused. "Carl never seemed to be able to settle down long enough to enjoy what he was working for. I hope he still gets the chance." Max tipped back in his chair and looked out over the pool, the grounds. "You know, I have three children of my own. Five grandchildren now, and the first great-grandchild on the way. There were times I wasn't there for them, and I'll always regret it. Holding a family and a career together in this business is like juggling eggs. There's always some breakage."

"Some people juggle better than others."

"True enough. It takes a lot of effort and more than a few concessions to make it work."

"It seems to me that in Johanna's case she made all the concessions."

Max said nothing for a moment. He considered having another cigarette but decided his wife's sensitive nose would find him out. "I hate old men who poke into young people's business. Ought to be out playing checkers or feeding pigeons. But…just how serious are you about Jo-Jo?"

"We're going to get married," Sam heard himself say, to his own astonishment. "As soon as I talk her into it."

"Good luck. And that comes from the heart. I've always had a soft spot for that girl." Max poured another cup of coffee and knew he was a long way from ready to feed pigeons. "How much did she tell you?"

"Enough to make me understand I've got an uphill battle."

"And how much do you love her?"

"Enough to keep climbing."

Max decided to risk a second cigarette. If his wife came sniffing around, he could always blame it on Sam. He lit it slowly, savoring the taste. "I'm going to tell you things she wouldn't appreciate me saying. Whether it'll give you an edge or not I can't say. I can tell you I hope it does."

"I appreciate it."

With the smoke trailing lazily from between his fingers, Max looked back. A long way. "I knew her mother well. A beautiful woman. A glorious face. Bone structure always makes the difference. Johanna favors her physically, but it ends there. I can say I've never known anyone more completely her own woman than Johanna."

"Neither have I," Sam murmured. "It doesn't always make it easy."

"You're too young to want things easy," Max told him from the comfortable perspective of seven decades. "When something comes easy, you usually let it go the same way. That's my philosophy for the day. Now, Glenna was selfish, driven by her own demons. She married Carl after a brief and very torrid affair. Affairs were just as torrid thirty years ago, only a bit more discreet."

He drew in smoke and remembered a few of his own. Though he'd let them go without regret upon his marriage, he could still be grateful for the experience.

"They were a golden couple, the photographers' darlings. Carl was dark, ruggedly handsome, broad shouldered. Glenna was almost waiflike, pale, fragile. They threw incredible parties and incredible tantrums. To be honest, I quite enjoyed both. You may have heard I was a hellion in my youth.''

''I heard you were a hellion,'' Sam agreed. ''But I didn't hear it was something in the past.''

''We'll work well together,'' Max declared. He took one last drag before crushing the second cigarette out. ''When Glenna was pregnant, she spent thousands decorating the nursery. Then she started to lose her figure and went on a rampage. She could sit for a photographer like a Madonna, then toss back a Scotch and curse like a sailor. Glenna had no middle ground.''

''Johanna told me she was ill, a manic-depressive.''

''Perhaps. I don't pretend to understand psychiatry. I will say she was weak—not weak-minded, but weak-spirited—and tormented by the fact that she was never as successful as she needed to be. There was talent in her, real talent, but she didn't have the drive or the grit to stay on top. It became easy for her to blame Carl for that, and the marriage. Then it became easier to blame the child. After Johanna was born, Glenna went through phases of being a devoted, loving mother. Then she'd be almost obscenely neglectful. The marriage was crumbling. Carl had affairs, she had affairs, and neither of them ever considered putting the child first. Not in their nature, Sam,'' he added when he saw the fury flare. ''That's not an excuse, of course, but it is a reason. Carl wouldn't have cared if Glenna had had one child or thirty. He'd had no more than a passing interest. When the break finally came, Glenna used the child as a weapon. I don't mean to make Carl a hero, but at least he never used Johanna. Unfortunately, she was never that important to him."

"How could two people like that ever have someone like Johanna?"

"Another question for the ages."

"Is Patterson her father?"

Max lifted both brows. "Why do you ask?"

It was a confidence he felt he had to break. Not for himself. Sam had already decided her parentage meant less than nothing to him, but the truth would be important to Johanna.

"Because when she was still a child, Johanna found a letter her mother had written to Patterson right after she'd gone back to England. She told him she'd never been sure if he was Johanna's father."

"Good God." Max ran a hand over his face. "I had no idea about that. It's a wonder it didn't destroy Johanna."

"No, she wasn't destroyed, but it did plenty of damage."

"Poor little Jo-Jo," Max murmured. "She was always such a lonely little girl. Spent more time with the gardener than anyone else. It might not have mattered if Carl had been different. I wish she'd come to me with this."

"I don't think she's told anyone about it until last night."

"You'd better not let her down."

"I don't intend to."

Max fell silent for a time, thinking. Johanna's parents had been his friends. He'd been able to accept them for what they were and for what they weren't, all the while regretting it for the child's sake.

"For what it's worth, I'd say the letter was pure spite and total nonsense. If another man had fathered Johanna, Glenna would have blurted it out long before the separation. She could never keep a secret for more than two hours. Make that two minutes if you added a drink. Carl knew that." His face clouded as he hunched over the table. "I'm sorry to say that if Carl had suspected Johanna wasn't his flesh and blood he never would have kept her under his roof. He'd have put her on a plane to her mother without a backward glance."

"That doesn't make him a saint."

"No, but it does make him Johanna's father."

"We have something special for our home audience," John Jay began, giving the camera a brilliant smile. "If you've been listening this week, you know that our Drive American contest is already underway. We at *Trivia Alert* are very excited about having the chance to show all of you at home how much we appreciate you. To win, all you have to do is watch and answer. Every day this week, sometime during the show, I'll be asking questions. Today it's time to tell you at home what you have a chance to win."

He paused, giving the announcer the time to describe the cars and eligibility requirements. As requested, the studio audience applauded and cheered.

"The week of Fourth of July," John Jay continued on cue, "one of you at home will win not one but both luxury cars. All you have to do is answer five questions in order. Send your answers to Trivia Alert, Drive American, Post Office Box 1776, Burbank, California 91501. Now for today's question."

There was a dramatic pause as he drew the sealed envelope from the slot. "Question number three. What is the name of Captain America's alter ego? Write down your answer and be sure to tune in tomorrow for the fourth question. All complete sets of correct answers will be part of a random drawing. Now, back to our game."

Johanna checked her watch and wondered how she could get through two more segments. They were already behind schedule due to a delay caused by an overenthusiastic member of the studio audience who had called out answers during the speed round. They'd had to stop, reset, calm the contestant and begin again with a new batch of questions. Usually she took that sort of thing in stride, but somewhere along the way her stride had broken. For the past few hours, Johanna had been struggling to find her pace again.

When the segment ended, she nearly groaned with relief. She had fifteen minutes before they would begin again. "Beth, I have to make a call. I'll be in the office if a crisis comes up."

Without waiting for a response, she hurried off the set. At the end of the corridor a small room was set up with the essentials. A phone, a desk and a chair. Making use of all three, Johanna called the hospital. She still had ten minutes left when she learned that Carl had been downgraded from critical to serious condition. She was rubbing her eyes and thinking about another cup of coffee when the door opened.

"Beth, if it isn't a matter of life and death, put it on hold."

"It might be."

She straightened immediately at the sound of Sam's voice. "Oh, hello. I didn't expect you."

"You don't expect me nearly often enough." He closed the door behind him. "How are you doing?"

"Not bad."

"Your father?"

"Better. They think he can be moved out of CCU tomorrow."

"That's good." He came over to the desk and sat on the edge before giving her a long, critical study. "You're dead on your feet, Johanna. Let me take you home."

"We haven't finished, and I promised to stop by the hospital after the taping."

"Okay, I'll go with you."

"No, please. It's not necessary, and I'd be lousy company tonight."

He looked down at her hands. They were linked together tightly. Deliberately he took them in his own and separated them. "Are you trying to pull back, Johanna?"

"No. I don't know." She took a long breath, and

her hands relaxed in his. "Sam, I appreciate what you did for me last night more than I can ever tell you—the way you listened and didn't judge. You were there when I needed you, and I'll never forget it."

"Sounds like a kiss-off," he murmured.

"No, of course it isn't. But you should understand now why I feel so strongly about being involved with you. Why it won't work."

"I must be pretty stupid, because I don't. I do understand why you're scared. Johanna, we have to talk."

"I have to get back. There's only a few more minutes."

"Sit down," he told her as she started to rise. She might have ignored the order, but the look in his eyes had her sitting again. "I'll try to make it quick. Time's either a blessing or a curse now, anyway. I've got to fly East the day after tomorrow to start filming."

"Oh." She dug deep for a smile. "Well, that's good. I know you've been anxious to start."

"I'll be gone three weeks, probably more. It isn't possible for me to put this off."

"Of course not. I hope—well, I hope you let me know how it's going."

"Johanna, I want you to come with me."

"What?"

"I said I want you to come with me."

"I—I can't. How could I? I have my job, and—"

"I'm not asking you to make a choice between your job and us. Any more than I'd expect you to ask me to make one between mine and the way I feel about you.''

''No, of course I wouldn't.''

''I'd like to think you meant that.'' He paused a moment, searching her face. ''The script that Max sent me—I want to do it.''

''You should do it. It's perfect for you.''

''Maybe, but I want to know if it's perfect for you. Your father's producing it, Johanna.''

''Oh.'' She looked down at her hands a moment, hands that were still caught in his. ''Well, then, you've got the best.''

''I want to know how you feel about it, Johanna. How you really feel.''

''It's more a matter of how you feel.''

''Not this time. Don't make me use pliers.''

''Sam, your professional choices have to be yours, but I'd say you'd be a fool not to grab a chance to work with Max and Patterson Productions. That script might have been written for you, and I'd be disappointed if I didn't see you in it.''

''Always sensible.''

''I hope so.''

''Then be sensible about this. Take a few days off and come east with me.'' Before she could protest again, he was continuing. ''You've got a tight crew, Johanna. I've seen them work firsthand. You know they could run things for a couple of weeks.''

''I suppose, but not without any notice. Then there's my father…'' She let her words trail off. There must have been dozens of reasons, but they seemed to slide away before she could get a grip on them.

"All right. Take a week to make sure your crew is on top of things and that your father's recovering. Then fly out and meet me."

"Why?"

"I wondered when you'd ask." He reached in his pocket to pull out a box. Through his life he'd done a great many things on impulse. This wasn't one of them. He'd thought it through carefully, and had kept coming up with one answer. He needed her. "Things like this usually speak for themselves." After opening the lid, he took her hand and set the box in her palm. "I want you to marry me."

She stared at the single flawless diamond. It was square-cut, very classic and simple. The kind of ring, Johanna thought, girls dreamed about when they thought of white chargers and castles in the sky.

"I can't."

"Can't what?"

"I can't marry you. You know I can't. I had no idea you'd started thinking like this."

"Neither had I, until today. When Marv called I knew I had two choices. I could go East and stew about it or I could take the step and let you stew about it." He touched her hair, just the tips. "I'm sure, Johanna."

"I'm sorry." She offered the box back to him. When he didn't take it, she set it on the desk. "I don't want to hurt you, you know I don't. That's why I can't."

"It's about time you unloaded some of the baggage you've been carrying around, Johanna." Rising, he drew her up with him. "We both know what we've got doesn't come along every day. You might think you're doing me a favor by turning me down, but you're wrong. Dead wrong."

His fingers tangled in her hair as he kissed her. Unable to deny him—or herself—she curled her arms up his back until she gripped his shoulders. She held on to him even while her mind whirled with dozens of questions.

"Do you believe me when I tell you I love you?" he demanded.

"Yes." She held him tighter, burying her face against his shoulder to absorb his scent. "Sam, I don't want you to go. I know you have to, and I know how much I'll miss you, but I can't give you what you want. If I could...if I could you're the only one I'd give it to."

He hadn't expected to hear even that much. Another man might have been discouraged, but he'd run into too many walls in his life to be put off by one more. Particularly since he had every intention of tearing this one down, brick by brick.

He pressed a kiss to her temple. "I already know what I need and what I want." He drew her away until their eyes met. "You'd better start thinking about yourself, Johanna. About what you want, what you need. Just you. I figure you're smart enough to come up with an answer before too long." He kissed her again until she was breathless. "Keep in touch."

She didn't have the strength to do anything but sink into the chair when he left her. The show was starting, but she continued to sit, staring at the ring he'd left behind.

Chapter 12

The man was playing games. Johanna knew it, and though she tried not to nibble at the bait, she was already being reeled in. He'd been gone two weeks, and she hadn't gotten a single phone call.

But there had been flowers.

They'd arrived every evening. Black-eyed Susans one day, white orchids another. She couldn't walk into any room of her house without thinking of him. After the first week they'd begun to arrive at her office—a small clutch of violets, a huge bouquet of tea roses. She couldn't even escape from him there.

The man was definitely playing, and he wasn't playing fair.

Of course, she wasn't going to marry him. That was absurd. She didn't believe people could love, honor and cherish for a lifetime. She'd told him so, and she'd been sorry, but she had no intention of changing her mind.

She might carry the ring with her—for safekeeping, that is—but she hadn't taken it out of its box. At least not more than two or three times.

She was grateful that her work load had intensified so that she was unceasingly busy. It didn't leave much time to mope around missing him. Unless you counted the long, solitary nights when she kept listening for the phone.

He'd told her to keep in touch, but he hadn't told her where he'd be staying. If she'd wanted to, she could have found out easily enough. It did happen that a few discreet inquiries had put the name and address of his hotel in her hands, but that didn't mean she would call him. If she called, he'd know she'd gone to some trouble—damn it, a great deal of trouble—to find out where he was.

Then he would know she'd not only nibbled at the bait but swallowed it whole.

By the end of the second week, she was furious with him. He'd pushed her into a corner where she didn't want to be, wedged her in and then strolled off, leaving her trapped. A man didn't ask a woman to marry him, drop a ring in her hand, then waltz off.

Once she'd considered putting the ring in the mail and shipping it off to him. That had been at three o'clock in the morning on the fifteenth day. Johanna had rolled over, slammed the pillow a few satisfactory times and vowed to do just that the minute the post office opened in the morning.

She would have, too, if she hadn't been running a few minutes late. Then she'd been tied up at lunchtime and unable to get five free minutes until after six. She decided against mailing it, thinking it would be more civil and courteous to throw it in his face when he got back into town.

It was just her bad luck he'd chosen to send forget-me-nots that day. They happened to be one of her particular favorites.

As the third week approached, she was a wreck. Johanna knew she deserved the wary glances of her staff. She pushed through Monday's taping, growling at every interruption. Her excuse was that she'd agreed to take duplicates to her father that evening.

He wasn't particularly interested in the show, she knew, but his recuperation wasn't sitting well with him. He wanted to live badly enough to follow his doctor's orders, but that didn't mean he couldn't review everything Patterson Productions had a part in. Johanna waited impatiently for the copies, pacing the set and toying with the ring box in her pocket.

"Here you go." Bethany put on an exaggerated smile. "Try not to gnaw on them on the way home."

Johanna dumped them in her bag. "I'll need you here by nine. We can work until it's time to set up for taping."

"Whatever you say."

Johanna narrowed her eyes at the overbright tone. "Have you got a problem?"

"Me?" All innocence, Bethany opened her eyes wide. "No, not me. Well, there is my back."

''Your back? What's wrong with it?''

''It's nothing really. It always aches a bit when I've been flogged.''

Johanna opened her mouth, then shut it again on a puff of air. ''I'm sorry. I guess I've been a little edgy.''

''Just a tad. Funny, if someone had been sending me flowers every day for weeks I'd be a bit more cheerful.''

''He thinks that's all it takes to twist me around his finger.''

''There are worse positions to be in. Forget I said it,'' Bethany said immediately, holding up a hand. ''There's nothing more diabolical than sending a basket of tiger lilies. The man's obviously slime.''

For the first time in days, Johanna smiled. ''He's wonderful.''

The smile confirmed what Johanna's scowls had already told her. ''You miss him?''

''Yes, I miss him. Just like he knew I would.''

Bethany looked at romance in the most straightforward of terms. If you cared, you showed it, then put all your energy into making it work. Her solution for Johanna was just as simple. ''You know, Johanna, it's the same distance from the West to the East Coast as it is from East to West.''

She'd already thought of going. Not that she'd *considered* it, but she had thought of it. ''No, I can't.'' She fingered the box in her pocket. ''It wouldn't be fair to him.''

''Because?''

"Because I won't...can't..." On impulse she pulled the box out and opened it. "Because of this."

"Oh, my." Bethany couldn't help the long-drawn-out sigh. "My, oh, my," she managed, already smelling orange blossoms. "Congratulations, best wishes and bon voyage. Where's a bottle of champagne when you need it?"

"No, I didn't accept it. I'm not going to. I told him no."

"Then why do you still have it?"

Because the question was so reasonable, Johanna could only frown and stare at the diamond while it winked at her. "He just dropped it in my hand and walked off."

"Romantic devil, isn't he?"

"Well, it wasn't exactly— That's close enough," she decided. "It was more of an ultimatum than a proposal, but either way, I told him no."

It sounded wonderfully romantic to Bethany. She stuck her tongue in her cheek. "So you just decided to walk around with it in your pocket for a few days."

"No, I..." There had to be a reasonable excuse. "I wanted to have it handy so I could give it back to him."

Bethany thought that over, then tilted her head. "I think that's the first lie I've ever heard you tell."

"I don't know why I've still got it." Johanna closed the box with a snap, then pushed it into her pocket. "It's not important."

"No, I've never thought proposals of marriage or gorgeous engagement rings were anything to get excited about." She put a hand on Johanna's shoulder. "What you need is some fresh air."

"I don't believe in marriage."

"That's like not believing in Santa Claus." At Johanna's lifted brow, Bethany shook her head. "Johanna, don't tell me you don't believe in him, either? He might be something of a fantasy, but he's been around a while, and he's going to stay around."

It was hard to argue with that kind of logic. Johanna decided she was too tired to try. "We'll talk about the logic of that some other time. I have to drop off these tapes." With Bethany beside her, she started out. "I'd like you to keep this to yourself."

"It goes with me to the grave."

"You're good for me," Johanna said with a laugh. "I'm going to be sorry to lose you."

"Am I fired?"

"Sooner or later you're going to fire me. You won't be content to be anyone's assistant for long." Outside, Johanna took a deep breath. So much had changed since she'd walked with Bethany from the studio weeks before. "Leaving Santa Claus out of it, do you believe in marriage, Beth?"

"I'm just an old-fashioned girl with strong feminist underpinnings. Yeah, I believe in marriage as long as two people are willing to give it their best shot."

"You know what the odds are of a marriage making it in this town?"

"Lousy. But strikeout or home run, you've got to step up to bat. See you tomorrow."

"Good night, Beth."

She did a great deal of thinking as she drove to Beverly Hills. Not all of it was clear, but every thought circled back to Sam. Johanna was coming to realize that her thoughts would, whether she was with or without him.

The gates were locked, as they always were. Reaching out, she pressed the button on the intercom and waited for her father's housekeeper to ask her name. In moments the gates opened soundlessly.

The drive toward the house didn't stir any childish memories. She saw the estate as an adult. Perhaps she always had. It was stunning—the white columns, the terraces and balconies. The exterior had changed little from her earliest recollections.

Inside, it had gone through major overhauls, depending on its mistress. Her mother had preferred the feminine and delicate look of *Louis Quinze.* Darlene had chosen art nouveau, right down to the light fixtures. Its last mistress had gone for the opulently elegant. Johanna didn't think it would take Toni long to put her stamp on it.

The door was opened for her by the gray-uniformed maid before she'd reached the top of the wide, curved steps.

"Good evening, Miss Patterson."

"Good evening. Is Mr. Patterson expecting me?"

"He and Miss DuMonde are in the sitting room."

"Thank you."

Johanna crossed the glossy tiles, skirting the fish pond her father's last wife had installed. She found her father looking well, and impatient, in a dark blue smoking jacket. Toni sprawled lazily on the sofa across from him, sipping wine and flipping through a magazine. Johanna nearly smiled when she saw that it was one on home fashion and decoration.

"I expected you an hour ago," Carl said without preamble.

"We ran late." She took the tapes from her bag to set them on the table beside him. "You're looking well."

"There's nothing wrong with me."

"Carl's a bit bored." Toni stretched herself into a sitting position. She wore silk lounging pajamas the color of ripe peaches. The pout she wore went with them beautifully. "Perhaps you can entertain him better than I." Rising, she stalked gracefully out of the room.

Johanna lifted a brow. "Have I come at a bad time?"

"No." Carl pushed himself up and headed for the bar. Johanna bit back a protest and was relieved when he poured club soda. "Do you want anything?"

"No, thank you. I can't stay."

Carl halfheartedly added a twist of lime. "I assumed you'd stay until I'd previewed the tapes."

"You don't need me for that." He wanted company, she realized. Because she remembered how old and alone he'd looked in the hospital, she relented. "I could put them in for you, answer whatever questions you might have about the first segment or two."

"I've seen the show before, Johanna. I doubt I'd have any questions about my own show."

"No." She picked up the bag she'd just set down. "Then I'll leave you to it."

"Johanna." He cleared his throat and he turned back, then took his seat again. "You've done a good job with it."

This time both brows rose. "Thank you." She set her bag down again and checked her watch.

"If you've got some damn appointment, go on, then."

"No, actually, I was just marking the time. Since it's the first time in my life you've ever complimented me on anything, I want to remember when it happened."

"There's no need to be sarcastic."

"Maybe not." She crossed the room to sit but stayed on the edge of her chair. She'd never been comfortable in this house. "I'm glad you're doing so well. If you're interested, I can see that you get dupes of tomorrow's taping for the evening shows. We're giving away a trip for two to Puerto Vallarta during the speed round."

He only grunted at that. Johanna folded her hands and continued. "If a contestant reaches the winner's circle and can answer all of the questions himself, without deferring to his partner, he'll win a car. We're using a sedan this week. Four-door."

"I'm not interested in the prizes."

"I thought not, but you might prefer a different angle or see a flaw when you preview. I'm sure you know that you can accomplish as much here as most men can in an office."

"I won't be sitting here forever."

"There's no question of that." No, he would be back, full steam, very soon. Maybe this was the time, the only time. "Before I go, I'd like to ask you something."

"If it has to do with the new pilot, I've already seen it and approved it."

"No, it's personal."

He sat, cradling his glass. He didn't mind giving up liquor half so much as doing without his cigars. Rather than answer, he simply nodded for her to go on.

"Why do you want to marry Toni DuMonde?"

As far as Carl was concerned, the question had come out of left field. No one questioned his motives or his reasons. "I'd say that was between Toni and myself. If you're uncomfortable with the age difference—"

"It would hardly matter to me if there was twice as much difference as there already is," Johanna said. "I'm just curious."

"I'm marrying her because I want to."

Johanna sat for a minute, studying him. Maybe it was just that simple with Carl. I want, I do. I covet, I take. "Do you plan to stay married to her?"

"As long as it suits both of us."

She smiled a little and nodded. That, at least, was the unvarnished truth. "Why did you marry my mother?"

If her first question had surprised him, this one left him speechless. Staring at Johanna, he saw the resemblance he'd always ignored. But there was more character in this face. More courage. "Why are you bringing this up now? You never asked about her before."

"Maybe I should have. We began to talk about her when you were in the hospital, but I suppose I wasn't ready. Now I have a decision of my own to make, and I can't do it until I understand a little better. Did you love her?"

"Of course. She was beautiful, fascinating. We were both building our careers. There wasn't a man who met Glenna in those days who didn't love her."

She didn't find reasons for love and fidelity in those answers. "But you're the only one who married her. And the only one who divorced her."

"The marriage was a mistake," he said, abruptly uncomfortable. "We both realized it before the first year was out. Not that we weren't attracted to each other. As I said, she was beautiful, very delicate. You favor her." His glass paused halfway to his lips when he saw her expression. Perhaps he'd never been a loving father, but he'd always been an astute man. "If you're concerned about her health, don't be. Glenna was always erratic. Drinking made her more so, but I've never seen any part of that in you. Believe me, I've watched for it."

"Have you?" Johanna murmured.

"You've never been one for extremes," he went on. "Apparently you inherited enough from me to offset the rest."

"Did I?" This time her voice was firm and her eyes

level. "I've always wondered what, if anything, I inherited from you."

His look was so blank that she couldn't believe he feigned it. "You're a producer, aren't you? And a good one. That should say something. The Pattersons have always been strong, practical people. Ambitious. I'd say, now that I think of it, that you take after my grandmother. She was strong minded, never one to sit around and let the world go by. Got the hair from her, too," he decided, looking thoroughly at his daughter for the first time in years.

A little dazed, Johanna reached up to touch her hair. "*Your* grandmother?"

"Didn't get it from your mother," he said with a sour laugh. "Got hers from her hairdresser. That was one of her most prized secrets. Hers was brown, mousy brown. God knows you didn't get your drive from her. That's the Patterson in you." He didn't say it with pride, just stated it as fact.

So this was her father after all. Johanna sat, waiting for a flood of feeling. When none came, she sighed. Nothing had really changed. Then her lips curved. Then again, maybe everything had.

"I'd like to hear about her sometime. Your grandmother." She rose, taking a look at her watch in earnest. "I really have to go. I'm going to be out of town. Everything should run smoothly enough without me for a few days."

"Out of town? When?"

"Tonight."

* * *

Johanna caught the last plane out. She'd had just enough time before final boarding to call Bethany and give her quick and not completely coherent instructions about the next day's business and the care and feeding of her cat. Bethany had been awakened out of a sound sleep, but she could be depended on.

Strapped in, Johanna watched L.A., and the resolutions she'd lived with all of her life, slip away. She'd taken a step, the largest one of her life, without even being sure she would land on solid ground.

Somewhere over Nevada she dozed, then woke over New Mexico in a kind of blind panic. What in God's name was she doing, traveling thousands of miles without so much as a toothbrush? It wasn't like her not to plan or make lists. They were taping the next day. Who would handle the details, check the staff? Who would deal with John Jay?

Someone else, she told herself. For once it would just have to be someone else.

She traveled from one coast to the other, sleeping in fits and starts and wondering if she'd lost her mind. In Houston she nearly lost her nerve, as well. But she changed planes and strapped in a second time, determined to see it through.

Perhaps she wasn't being smart or responsible, but everyone was entitled to do something on impulse once. Even if they lived to regret it.

Almost certain she would, she arrived in Baltimore just after dawn. The terminal was deserted except for a few napping passengers waiting for connections. The air was cool in Maryland, and she was grateful for her suit jacket. The same jacket, Johanna remembered, that she'd put on that morning when she'd still been sane. The sky, full of pewter clouds, promised rain as she climbed into a cab and gave the driver the name of Sam's hotel.

This was it, she told herself. It helped a little to close her eyes and ignore the unfamiliar landscape. If she didn't watch it, she wouldn't think too much about being on the other side of the country. In L.A. people were rolling over in bed, snuggling into pillows with morning still hours away. Here they were waking up, preparing to face the day.

So was she.

She paid off the driver and tried not to think. The rain began as she walked into the lobby.

Suite 621. At least she knew the number, so she'd be spared the embarrassment of going to the desk and convincing the clerk she wasn't a fan. Clutching the strap of her bag, she rode to the sixth floor. It was easy enough to step from the elevator. She even managed to walk down the hall to his door.

Then she stared at it.

What if he didn't want her there? What if he wasn't alone? After all, she had no claim on him, had made no promises. She'd refused to accept, even to listen to, his promises. He was free to…to do whatever he wanted, with whomever he wanted.

Certain she couldn't go through with it, she turned away and took two steps back from the door.

It was absurd, she told herself. She'd just spent

hours in a plane, traveled thousands of miles, and now she couldn't even get up the nerve to knock on a door.

With her shoulders straight and her chin up, she knocked. When her stomach rolled, she reached in her pocket automatically for her antacids. Her fingers closed over the small velvet box. She drummed up her courage and knocked again.

He woke swearing. They'd worked until after two, and he'd barely had the energy to strip before tumbling into bed. Now the damn assistant director was banging on the door. Any idiot knew they couldn't film any of the scheduled outside shots in the rain.

Groggy and full of the desire for vengeance, Sam dragged the top sheet from the bed and wrapped it around him. He tripped over the hem, cursed again, then yanked open the door.

"Goddamn it—" His mouth dried up. He had to be dreaming. Johanna was a continent away, snuggled under the covers. Then he saw her lips curve before she began to stumble out an apology.

"I'm sorry I woke you. I should have…waited. Called." *Stayed away,* she thought desperately.

Then she didn't think at all, because he was dragging her inside. The door slammed and she was pressed back against it, her mouth captive.

"Don't say a word," he ordered when she sucked in her breath. "Not a word. Not yet."

It would have been impossible to speak. Even as he pulled her through the sitting room, he was peeling off her jacket, fighting the buttons on her blouse. With a throaty laugh, she tugged at the sheet. It was left behind in a stream of white as they worked their way to the bedroom.

Her skirt slid down to her hips, and he lifted her out of it. While his hands played over her, she stepped out of one shoe. They were nearly at the bedroom door before she managed to rid herself of the other.

He wasn't even awake. Sam clung to the drowsy fingers of sleep as they fell onto the bed.

She was here. Dream or reality, she was here. Her skin was just as soft under his hands, just as fragrant. Her lips as they parted for his had the same unique flavor he'd craved since he'd tasted them last. At her sigh, as her arms locked around him, he heard everything he needed to hear.

Delighted with each other, they rolled over the already rumpled bed as the rain grew heavy and streaked the windows.

She'd been right to come. Whatever had happened before, whatever happened after, she'd been right to take this moment. And to give this time to him. There would be no questions, no need for explanations or excuses, just gladness that was racing harder and faster toward dazzling pleasure.

In tune, body and mind, they came together, taking that pleasure to its pinnacle.

The thunder started as he gathered her against him again. Or perhaps it had been there all along but they hadn't heard it. Now, as the storm rattled over the city, they were together and alone and in love. Sometimes that really was all that mattered.

She kept her hand on his heart and her head on his

shoulder as they floated down to solid ground. The gloom kept the room dim, but for Johanna there had never been a more beautiful morning.

"Were you just passing through?" Sam murmured.

She spread her fingers over his chest, watching the movement. "I had urgent and unexpected business on the East Coast."

"I see." He hoped he did, but he could afford to wait. "You on a contestant search?"

"Not exactly." The nerves began leaking back. "I take it you don't have an early call today."

"If the rain keeps up, please God, I won't have one at all." Slowly, like a man who had all the time in the world, he stretched. "We were scheduled to shoot down at the Inner Harbor. Terrific place. Best crab I've ever eaten." He was already imagining showing it to her himself. "Once that's wrapped, we'll be finished here."

A pout, something she never allowed herself, formed on her lips. "You've run a little over your three weeks."

He certainly hoped it was annoyance he detected in her voice. "A little."

"I guess you've been too busy to call and let me know how things were going."

"No."

"No?" She propped herself on her elbow to frown at him.

"No, I haven't been too busy to call. I didn't call."

"Oh, I see." She started to push herself up and

found herself flat on her back again with Sam leaning over her.

"I hope you don't think you're getting out of this room."

"I told you I have business."

"So you did. Is it a coincidence that you have business in Baltimore and just happen to be staying at the same hotel—apparently in my room?"

"I'm not staying."

"Guess again." He nipped her gently on the jaw. "Why did you come, Johanna?"

"I'd rather not discuss it. I'd like my clothes," she said stiffly.

"Sure. Let me get them for you." He strolled out, leaving Johanna with the dubious cover of a pillow. She started to rise when he came back in with her suit bundled in his arms. Then she could only gape, open-mouthed, as he opened the window and tossed them out.

"What in the hell are you doing?" She forgot the pillow as she leaped up and ran to the window. "You threw out my clothes." Dumbfounded, she could only stare at him. "You threw them out the window."

"Sure looks that way."

"Are you out of your mind? I flew out here with the shirt on my back, and now it's six floors down and soaked. I don't have anything to wear out of here but my shoes."

"I was counting on that. Seemed like the best way to guarantee your staying put."

"You *are* out of your mind." She started to crane

out of the window, remembered she was naked, then dropped on the bed. ''What am I supposed to do now?''

''Borrow another of my shirts, I guess. Help yourself.'' He gestured toward the closet. ''You might toss me a pair of jeans while you're at it. It's hard for me to talk to you reasonably when we're not wearing anything but smiles.''

''I'm not smiling,'' she told him between her teeth as she heaved jeans in his direction. ''That was one of my best suits, and I—'' Her fingers froze on the buttons of the shirt she'd pulled on. ''Oh, God. Oh, my God, in the jacket. I had it in the jacket.'' With the shirt still half buttoned she jumped for the door. Sam was just quick enough to slam it closed before she ran out.

''I don't think you're dressed for a stroll, Johanna. Not that you don't look terrific. In fact, you look so terrific I think I'd like you to give me my shirt back.''

''Will you stop being an idiot?'' She tried to shove him aside but met with solid resistance. ''You threw it out the window. I can't believe what a complete fool you are. You threw my ring out the window.''

''Whose ring?''

''My ring, the one you gave me. Oh, for God's sake.'' She ducked under his arm to run to the window again. ''Someone's going to take it.''

''Your suit?''

''No, I don't care about the suit. The hell with the suit. I want my ring.''

''All right. Here.'' Sam drew it off his pinky and

offered it. "The box must have dropped out of your pocket when—when I said hello." Johanna had given a cry of relief and grabbed for it before she realized she'd been taken.

"Damn it, Sam, you had it all the time and you let me think it was gone."

"It was nice to know it was important to you." He held it between them. "Are you going to let me put it on you?"

"You can take it and—"

"I'm open to suggestions." Then he smiled at her in a way she found completely unfair. Even her temper failed her.

"I'd like to sit down a minute." She did, sinking into the bed. The relief was gone, and the anger. She'd come for a purpose. and it was time to see it through. "I came to see you."

"No? Really?"

"Don't make fun of me."

"All right." He sat beside her, draping an arm over her shoulders. "Then I guess I can tell you that if you hadn't come, or called within the next twenty-four hours, I was heading back, movie or no movie."

"You didn't call me."

"No, I didn't, because I think we both knew you had to make the next move. And I hope you suffered as much as I did." He pressed his lips to her hair. "So what's it going to be?"

"I want to tell you that I spoke with my father last night." She tilted her head so that she could look at him. "He is my father."

Gently he brushed her hair back from her face. "Is everything all right?"

"It's not like a story where everything turns out beautifully at the end, but it's all right. I don't suppose we'll ever be close, and I can accept that now. I'm not like him, nor like my mother, either. It's taken me all this time to figure out that that's okay. I'm okay."

He kissed her hair again, enjoying the fragrance as much as the familiarity. "I could have told you that, if you'd listened."

"I can listen now, now that I've told myself." With a long breath, she took his hands in hers. "I need to ask you something, Sam. You could almost say it was the championship question."

"I work best under pressure."

But her eyes didn't smile. "Why do you want to marry me?"

"That's it?" His brows rose, and then he was laughing and holding her close. "I thought you were going to ask me a tough one. I want to marry you because I love you and I need you in my life. It changed when you walked into it."

"And tomorrow?"

"A two-part question," he murmured. "I could promise you anything." He drew her away to kiss her cheek, then her brow, then her lips. "I wish there were guarantees, but there aren't. I can only tell you that when I think about tomorrow, when I think about ten years from tomorrow, I think about you. I think about us."

He couldn't have said it better, she thought as she

touched his face. No, there weren't any guarantees, but they had a chance. A good one.

"Can I ask you one more thing?"

"As long as I'm going to get an answer eventually."

"Do you believe in Santa Claus?"

What made it perfect, even more than perfect, was that he didn't even hesitate. "Sure. Doesn't everyone?"

Now she smiled, completely. "I love you, Sam."

"That's the answer I wanted."

"Looks like you win." She held out her hand so that he could slip the ring on her finger. It felt as though it belonged, and so did she. "Looks like we both do."

* * * * *